PRAI ...ONS

Please return or renew this item before the latest date shown below

Renewals can be made

by internet   www.fifedirect.org.uk/libraries

in person   at any library in Fife

by phone   08451 55 00 66

Fife COUNCIL

Thank you for using your library

PRAISE FOR *NIGHTS OF VILLJAMUR*

'I was reminded of Jack Vance or Gene Wolfe ... this is a promising start to a series worth pursuing'   *The Times*

'Genre labels just don't apply here. With *Nights of Villjamur* Mark has managed to incorporate so many wonderfully varied ideas and themes into a decent blend of excitement and interest that the marketing department is going to have to invent a whole new section just for him'   Peter F. Hamilton

'A dark epic which shows its debt to *Gormenghast*: death stalks the shadows and scheming, idiosyncratic characters have their own agendas. This is fantasy with vast scope and ambition'
Guardian

'While the sun over Villjamur is dying, Mark Charan Newton's star as a writer is burning with a fierce talent'
Stephen Hunt, author of *The Court of the Air*

'*Nights of Villjamur* is a terrific debut, it starts with a bang and keeps on going, building action upon action with terrific pace and plenty of surprises before relenting and letting you catch your breath before it starts up again ... refreshingly deft story-telling from an author who clearly knows how to write and I look forward to the next in the series'   *Sci-Fi-London.com*

THE BOOK OF TRANSFORMATIONS

Mark Charan Newton was born in 1981, and holds a degree in Environmental Science. After working in bookselling, he moved into editorial positions at imprints covering film and media tie-in fiction and, later, science fiction and fantasy. He currently lives and works in Nottingham. *The Book of Transformations* is the third book in the Legends of the Red Sun series, following on from *City of Ruin*.

For more information and updates, visit his website
www.markcnewton.com

THE BOOK *of* TRANSFORMATIONS

Legends of the Red Sun
Book Three

MARK CHARAN NEWTON

Visit www.panmacmillan.com to read more about all our books
and to buy them. You will also find features, author interviews and
news of any author events, and you can sign up for e-newsletters
so that you're always first to hear about our new releases.

TOR

First published in the UK 2011 by Tor

This edition published 2012 by Tor
an imprint of Pan Macmillan, a division of Macmillan Publishers Limited
Pan Macmillan, 20 New Wharf Road, London N1 9RR
Basingstoke and Oxford
Associated companies throughout the world
www.panmacmillan.com

ISBN 978-0-330-52167-3

Copyright © Mark Charan Newton 2011

Map artwork by Hemesh Alles

The right of Mark Charan Newton to be identified as the
author of this work has been asserted by him in accordance
with the Copyright, Designs and Patents Act 1988.

1 3 5 7 9 8 6 4 2

A CIP catalogue record for this book is available from
the British Library.

Typeset by SetSystems Ltd, Saffron Walden, Essex
Printed and bound by CPI Group (UK) Ltd, Croydon, CR0 4YY

For Rachel,
who puts up with it all ...

ACKNOWLEDGEMENTS

As ever, writing a novel is rarely a solitary effort. I would first and foremost like to thank Cheryl Morgan for her help and advice with research for one character in particular, though any insensitiveness and miscalculations remain very much my own. A shout-out also to James (formerly of Speculative Horizons, now an editor in his own right) for suggestions on an early draft, and to Liviu of Fantasy Book Critic and Stephen Aryan for comments on a later one.

Thanks, of course, to my editor Julie Crisp for slapping this manuscript into shape, and to Chloe and the rest of the team at Tor UK, who work phenomenally hard behind the scenes in allowing me to get away with writing more books.

And again thanks to the many online bloggers and reviewers who send a link my way or argue with me on my website – it really is appreciated, and they make the whole scene a lot more fun than it would be otherwise.

'When deeds speak, words are nothing.'

Pierre-Joseph Proudhon

KULLRÚN

TINEAG'L

VILIREN

Y'IREN

JOKULL

VILHOKR

E'TOAWOR

FOLKE

DALÚK
POINT

FOLKE   FOLKE SMÁR
MIKILL

BLORTATH

GISH

NAYK

VILLJAMUR

WRAITHROCK
STRAITS

SOUTHFJORDS

T   N

YSLA

The Cultist
Isle

WESTERN END
of
the BOREAL
ARCHIPELAGO

ONE

This was no time to be a hero. Under the multicoloured banners of the sanctuary city of Villjamur, under the reign of a new emperor, and amidst a bitter northerly wind reaching far through the knotted streets, something was about to start.

Seven human teenagers sauntered back and forth in front of a gate that permitted access to one of the highest levels of the city.

Sleet was whipping by in the channels between these old stone walls – buildings three or four storeys high, with fat timber frames and decorated with hanging baskets inhabited by little more than limp tundra flowers.

From his horse, Investigator Fulcrom could glean only so much about the movement of the youths: their first walk-by was purely to check out the guard situation, maybe gauge the soldiers' temperament. A little tease. Those kids had done well to get this far, given the current political climate. In their baggy breeches and hooded wax coats, they moved with long, easy strides right past the military installation. They possessed every intention of creating a scene. At least, that was what the guards were meant to think.

But Investigator Fulcrom, a brown-skinned rumel in his younger years, knew better. He'd seen this kind of thing before, from his casual dealings with the underworld – an advantage that these simple guardsmen did not possess. No, these youths were decoys – they didn't have the guts to challenge the guards outright. Sure, they laughed and whistled and threw around tentative insults and crude hand-slang gestures; but this wasn't the real deal, not by a long shot.

So if they're not looking for a fight, what're they up to?

About a dozen armed men and women sporting the crimson and grey colours of the city guard peered on glumly from behind the bars of the massive rust-caked gate. Fulcrom suspected they were probably annoyed to be out in this weather as much as being faced with these young piss-takers.

Another group of kids loitered by the massive, arched door belonging to a disused tavern. *Are these connected with the main display?* In the shadows they chattered and pointed at a piece of parchment nailed to the wood. Fulcrom knew they were looking at the artwork of MythMaker, an unknown figure who would occasionally leave his hand-drawn stories about the city. It was rare to see one of the sketches here – rare, in fact, to see them much at all these days. The parchments were usually left by schools, or in places where children would loiter, and Fulcrom wondered for a brief moment if it may or may not have anything to do with the events about to transpire.

Back to the main show: a second taunting walk-by from the youths still yielded no response from the soldiers.

Cobbled streets weren't as dangerous to traverse these days, not with the cultist water technique imported all the way from Villiren to keep the ice at bay, so the kids strolled safely in a line, right before the assembled military.

A shadow flickered, followed by a sharp ripple of wind: a garuda skimmed the air overhead, making its presence known. Fulcrom tracked the garuda as it flew between the spires that defined Villjamur. A few of the older structures here were latticed with ladders and scaffolding, bearing workmen and cultists as they continued the Emperor's massive programme of regeneration. Either side of Fulcrom, the streets weren't at all packed – merely a few of the usual well-to-do citizens that you found about the fifth level of the city, trudging from store to store. Faded shop facades indicated tools or gemstones or bistros, and not for the first time Fulcrom noticed a couple of those new private soldiers of the Shelby Corporation stationed as guards. Beyond, cobbled lanes arced upwards, winding and twisting like slick-stone veins into the heart of Balmacara, the dark fortress that was the Imperial residence. Suddenly the bird sentry banked upwards, drifting into the haze, then scrambled to a standstill on one of the overhead bridges, where it stared down ominously across the scene.

Fulcrom inched his horse forwards, closing the distance. He should have been at the office by now. He had dozens of high-profile burglaries to be investigating, but he wanted to see how this played out, and his tail swished with anticipation. He was fifty years old – remarkably young by Inquisition standards – but he could tell a ruse when he saw one. *Pity the guards can't . . . How useless can they get?*

He would have intervened, but it would be bad etiquette. In the moment's pause he absent-mindedly wiped the excess mud from his boots, then rearranged his crimson robe.

A greater density of people now began to mill about around him, drifting forwards, curious about the show. Women in drab shawls, men hunched in furs and wax raincoats, the dozens soon became a hundred: here was the promise of something to break the monotony of everyday life in Villjamur. Citizens were currently experiencing lockdown conditions – the Council was in its regular session, and virtually no one was allowed near the upper levels, the forbidden zone lying beyond the guarded gate.

The third walk-by now, and all laughter had faded as the youths began aggressively throwing rocks at the guards. The stones pinged off the bars, or slapped against the wall to one side.

'Get the fuck away, brats,' a veteran guard growled. Stubbled and heavily built, he looked like he knew his way around a fight. The man unsheathed his sword with a zing.

One of the youths strutted forwards, took a wide-legged stance and beckoned the guard forward, much to the entertainment of his mates.

There followed a *clank clank clank* of a mechanism; the gate started to lift and the youths inched away, peering at each other, then around the streets.

Fulcrom followed their gazes, but could see nothing out of the ordinary. They were just looking for escape routes.

So where is it? When's it coming?

The guard grabbed the youth who was beckoning him by his collar, slammed him into the ground and pointed the tip of his blade at the kid's throat. In all the commotion, Fulcrom couldn't hear what was being said, just continued to followed the anxious glances of the others. A woman from the crowd screamed for the guard to leave the kid alone.

Suddenly, from two streets away, four figures garbed in dark clothing and riding black horses burst through the bad weather and, with immense speed, approached the gate. The one at the front swung his sword and decapitated the veteran guard – blood spurted across the cobbles, his head flopped uselessly to one side, the kid in his grasp shrieked in disgust. The other youths made their escape.

The four riders, their faces obscured by black scarves, collided with three guards, knocking them aside, then spilled through the gate. Another soldier was trampled, another was driven back into the wall with a scream, and then the others were hurled aside by a violent purple light that burnt at their flesh.

The crowd were in hysterics.

Cultists? Fulcrom pulled up his crossbow, loaded it, and nudged his white mare in an arc across the wide street, trying to make his way through the fleeing masses.

He spotted a gap – and moved in pursuit of the riders, with two city guards moving in to flank him. The winter winds whipped across his face.

*

Like hammers on anvils, hooves pounded on the cobbles.

A trail of seven horses curved upwards through the high-walled streets and galloped through a thronging iren. Screaming people lurched aside while traders cursed as their cheap wares were scattered across the ground. Bones of the unfortunate were crunched into stone, but Fulcrom ignored this and focused on plunging through the horse-made gaps in the crowd, his heart racing. These invaders were quick and skilled and working those horses with purpose. *They know where they're going*, Fulcrom thought. *This has been well planned.*

As the skies above cleared, the sun cast its amber haze across the buildings. The pursuit moved ever upwards, carving through the higher levels of Villjamur, away from the iren, through narrow side streets, under flamboyant balcony gardens, and past lichen-blighted statues. More military riders drifted in alongside Fulcrom, and warning bells resonated in the distance. Fulcrom shouted directions in the hope that the military would follow, but they didn't – they were young and unskilled riders, almost injuring their horses as they pushed them around dangerously tight corners.

Up ahead, one of the insurgents suddenly turned around and, from some handheld device, launched back two purple bolts of energy. Fulcrom yanked his mare out of the way. The soldier to Fulcrom's left had his arm burned; another's horse crumpled under him when her leg was shredded by the light. Fulcrom pushed aside his fear: whoever they were, they needed stopping.

Across another plaza, the chase continued: wealthy women shrieked, and their husbands stood blinking dumbly in the light as their perfect morning was upset by the hubbub.

'Out the fucking way!' Fulcrom yelled, using his tail for

balance now. Leaving the military riders behind, he nearly slipped off his saddle when his horse lurched to the left to avoid colliding with two basket-carrying women. For a moment he thought he had lost the four marauders, until he glimpsed them up ahead. They were moving now at a much slower pace, heading across a thin bridge.

He headed after them holding his breath; this wasn't a pathway meant for horses. It was narrow and crumbling and stretched from one platform to another like some rickety plank. The cityscape spread open below him, the glorious spires and slick slate roofs, the baroque architecture, the massive structures of legend.

If he fell from his horse he would die.

His horse tentatively plodded along to the other side before he nudged it into a gallop again, on to precarious terrain where the cultist water treatments had begun to wear off. By now Fulcrom had worked out where the riders were heading: the Jorsalir Bell Spire. Where the Council was said to be in session.

The criminal gang had dismounted by a row of expensive terraced cottages, which were used for retired military leaders, great whitewashed structures with winter hanging baskets and thatched roofing. Another road sloped up and down along a high viewing platform that overlooked the tundra beyond.

Fulcrom slid off his mare and approached. The figures were hooded, garbed in similar featureless dark outfits.

Fulcrom drew his sword. 'Strangers, state your business.' His voice seemed lost in the city's haze.

'I'd stay away from here if I were you, brother.' Fulcrom couldn't discern who spoke due to the scarves protecting their faces. The accent was bass but curious – definitely affected by some distant island.

The speaker seemed to be at the centre of this group; he didn't turn around.

'What've you got there?' Fulcrom approached closer and pointed to the sack in which the man who had spoken was rummaging.

The figure turned around and commanded, 'Brother, I have warned you – keep back.'

A thought struck Fulcrom: they had not yet killed him, or tried to, and he knew there was little he could do alone against so many if they tried. *These people want someone to witness this.*

'On behalf of the Inquisition, I demand you halt and show your faces,' Fulcrom ordered. He withdrew his gold, crucible-stamped medallion from beneath his robe.

'And how exactly are you going to stop us?' The figure reached into his pocket and flicked an item that landed at Fulcrom's feet, some coin perhaps, but it disappeared instantly. Fulcrom instinctively leapt back, but nothing happened.

As he walked forward he collided with something ... invisible. He spread his hands, testing the unseen force between him and the stranger, who was now laughing behind the scarf.

All Fulcrom could do was watch. Infuriated, he slammed the heel of his fist against the force, but again nothing happened.

'Your name?' Fulcrom demanded. He tried using his sword to strike the shield around him – the physical absence – but it merely bounced off the nothing that was between him and his target.

A moment later and he watched the group run across the bridge in a neat line with sacks tied back over their shoulders, their heads held low. They sauntered across the wide road between the crenellated walls towards the Bell Spire, which looked so high it threatened to puncture the clouds. Guards, stationed there today, approached them, but Fulcrom saw the assailants use the same trick they had on him, a disc to the guards' feet, and then they, too, were caged by an impassable force.

So they weren't killed either – what does this group want everyone else to see?

The group moved towards a huddle of Jorsalir priests, who tottered sheepishly away, and the gang then began to climb one of the walls with frightening agility, probably using relics to aid them. Two garudas flapped in to intercept them, but flashes of purple light punctuated their wings so badly that they plummeted out of the sky.

All Fulcrom could do was watch. He couldn't be certain, but it appeared as if the would-be terrorists were leaving devices all around the base of the thick, conical spire. Frustrated, Fulcrom walked along the edge of his barrier, still prodding it to test for weakness in that direction, but he could only go backwards, and there was no other route to the Bell Spire that way. He rested his hands on the invisible barricade and gazed helplessly across to the brigands, his breath clouding before his eyes.

The figures climbed down from the spire, leaping near the base – and almost floating back to the cobbles. They stepped up on the edge of the crenellations, spread some rigid-looking rain capes and leapt down to drift across the sleet-filled cityscape with the grace of garudas.

A moment later and the base of the Bell Spire exploded; bricks scattered like startled birds, slamming into the surrounding structures and rattling onto roads. A thunderous crack like the wrath of Bohr split the bridge first, sending it buckling in on itself and crumbling down onto the level below. The spire leaned to one side, groaning, and eventually it twisted in upon itself, as masonry dust clouded up around.

The ruins collapsed down across Villjamur. Block and brick slid into this fresh abyss, and people screamed from every direction as dozens of bodies fell from the site of the Jorsalir monastery, and Fulcrom lost sight of them a hundred feet below. For a good minute he stared helplessly, refusing to believe that all he could do was watch. People swarmed down below, in hysterics. He wondered how many councillors had been in that building.

Fulcrom turned to head back the way he came, and the only way he could go, to try to reach the crisis down below, but he noticed many of the nearby banners had been some-how replaced whilst he was facing the devastation. There were no crests here any more, no flowers, no depictions of great creatures, no displays of wealth.

Only black rags rippled in this chilling wind.

Two

A firework exploded and the sound sent the animals cowering in their cages and rattling the bars in a feral chorus. Lan strolled along the drearily lit dust-track underneath the arena, to check that the hybrids were not too distressed. It was freezing, and the sounds from the half-empty arena seemed hollow in a way that reminded her once again of the near-pointlessness of her life in the show.

To one side, a two-headed cat growled at her meekly. Lan paused and put both her hands between the bars to rub each skull, calming the striped beast. It scratched one nose against her hand in utter contentment. She glanced aside at the rows of bars that glinted dully in the light of several cressets. How did these poor creatures feel – trapped, barely witnessing sunlight, and with hardly any food?

That goes for both of us. Rations decreased every now and then; a cost-saving, Astli explained, against the dwindling revenues. Lan's grey breeches and thick black shirt appeared rather loose on her these days. Not only because of the lack of good sustenance for the performers, but because she didn't like to eat under the suspicious gaze of the others. How long could she keep this up for?

Her life was reaching an important crossroads: what was the point of the circus, now that it couldn't travel? With the icy weather, people didn't want to move far from their homes, let alone travel to the suburbs of Villtreeb, a town the fraction the size of Villjamur. Astli had chosen this spot to settle because it was the transport centre of the island of Jokull, a shanty town that had spawned where muddied roads met and parted. Traders and travellers still depended upon Villtreeb even in the Freeze. Astli had recently 'released' half the entourage, and the trickle of visitors these days was barely enough to keep them in business. A few girls had even been sold into prostitution, or 'servitude' as he liked to call it. Whether or not Astli knew after all these years who Lan really was, she couldn't be sure – but she was thankful to be able to scrape through without having to debase herself in this way. *Everyone suffers. Just deal with it.*

Astli incessantly declared that, even in the ice, people would need entertaining, perhaps even more so as it was something to take their minds off the difficult times. Perhaps, Lan thought disgustedly, that was why he brought in dancing girls. 'Astli's Aces' had been present for several weeks now, to provide a fetish-performance to boost crowd numbers and provide some improvement in the accounts. Grubby men slumped in the front rows, drooling at the dancers' contortions. *Was this what women were reducing themselves to?* Lan thought. *Is this what it's really like to succeed as a female on Jokull, an enlightened Empire island? At least tribeswomen seem to have respect from their men.*

Drums rumbled in the distance, a crash of symbols, a muffled cheer: Astli's Aces were on stage right now, prancing around in fever-inducing attire. The girls were certainly beautiful, sashaying around the arena with such vigour, and ignoring the whistles and cat-calls. Something primitive inside made Lan almost envious of the appreciative attention, despite knowing what she'd be in for if they discovered her true nature.

An echo of voices preceded a group of visitors who shuffled towards her. There were backstage tours these days, anything for quick coin. Ringleader Astli, with his ridiculous silk cape and a gaping smile, was leading them through.

Families came to ogle at the much talked-about hybrids. Children of all ages pointing and laughing at the exotics: chimera and chronos and the thousand-eyed kujata; there were creatures down here said to have existed only in mythologies. To Astli they were the freak-show, easy money, but Lan, pitying their mutations, felt too much kinship for them.

It wasn't their fault they were different.

It wasn't anyone's *fault* to be different.

Lan glowered at the tourists as they were awed by the caged hybrids. Astli glared at her with narrowed eyes then shoved her to one side. 'You sow, you should be preparing for your next act, not dawdling with these freaks.'

Lan sank back and whispered, 'I'm sorry.'

'I don't pay you to be *sorry*,' the scrawny man hissed. 'I'll rent you out as a whore if you don't listen. Get to your room and get changed.'

Lan said nothing, just tried to avoid his manic gaze, those wild, wide eyes, that long dominating nose, and his age-blighted skin. He could be so cruel to the women – physically and mentally – it was one of the things that constantly surprised her, that women could be so consistently maltreated by some men, that their voices ceased to be heard, and they never fought back.

Astli turned his attention back to the gathered audience. 'Ladies and gentlemen: regard the Satyr! Note its lower half is that of a goat, its top half that of a human. Look at the horns! It is said to be rather fond of wine . . .'

Lan strode away, down a set of stone stairs and through the labyrinthine corridors underneath the arena, where the crowd's calls were muted. Only a few of the other performers were milling about down here. The knife thrower, Jak, slender and aloof, who always had time for her, though unsuccessfully tried to touch up any of the women when he was drunk. Two of the gladiators, Prett and Daloin, were strong-armed, oiled and clutching small swords. These men would mock fight some of the hybrids towards the end of the evening, and they seemed to have worked their way through half of Astli's Aces in the darker hours, after showtime. It seemed all the entertainers did was drink and fuck, and Lan would only ever commit to one of those acts, fearing for her life should she engage in the other.

Lan marched past them to the dressing room, closed the door and allowed a moment of peace to embrace her. Performing in front of people tired her, as did spending so much time with others. It was only here, in solitude where she could be herself, that she could build up her reserves of mental strength, and regain her composure.

Clothes were strewn about the room. Aged dressers were speckled with crude drawings and trinkets and costume jewellery. Coloured lanterns shimmered in the reflections of several mirrors, making the room seem deep and endless. Snake-like scarves in multiple colours writhed over the top of an opaque dressing screen, alongside discarded lingerie, high-heeled boots and beakers of alcohol. A perfume cloud still lingered.

Lan shared this room with a couple of the stage girls – it wasn't ideal and there were ... difficulties, but while she was still being treated as a female, she considered herself lucky. It wasn't easy, having to hide herself from the other girls every night, waiting for most of the others to rest or to be outside before she changed into her costumes. How she'd managed to avoid being outed for so long was a mystery to her. Girls stared at her, made a mockery of her height. They even commented whenever it seemed too long since her period, so much so that she had mentally partnered up her cycles with one of the other girls so she didn't slip. The performers here were always judging each other, often unkindly, which contrasted sharply to the sense of community she had assumed there would be. Maybe it was her paranoia, but she swore they talked about her behind her back.

A thrilling cheer boomed from the arena. It wasn't long until her act now, maybe thirty minutes at the most. She hurriedly changed into her costume, a simple, full-body, tight-fitting, dark-blue outfit that offered warmth and flexibility. Tonight it was the tightrope first, finished off by a couple of minutes on the trapeze.

Realizing the time, she hurtled out the door, around the corner, taking the stairs two at a time – and suddenly had to stop herself from colliding with a stranger, whose attention was fixed on the caged hybrids.

He wore layers of cream-coloured robes, and his hood was pulled up so she could only see his stubbled face.

'Are you lost?' Lan asked.

'These are, quite simply, shit,' the stranger announced, gesturing towards the animals with a flick of his hand. 'They're genetic freaks, that is all. Mechanisms of the natural world. These are *not* real hybrids.'

'I'm sorry?' Lan asked.

'I said your fucking freak-show does not impress me much.' There was something vaguely accented about his voice, despite his angry words, and come to think of it, the way he moved his hands seemed forced and exaggerated.

'If you need a refund,' Lan said, 'I don't think Astli—'

'Money means nothing to me,' he interrupted. 'I came here only to research hybrids – to see how flesh and bone have been spliced and grafted with skill. Your freak-show is ter-rible, and I've seen better things in the wild. I could *make* more exotic things with my own hands.'

Lan was curious now. 'You make them yourself, do you?'

'My name is Cayce and I'm from the Order of Chirurgiens,' Cayce declared with some pride, still regarding the animals with disdain.

A cultist, Lan thought. 'And is your specialization ... medical? It sounded like you said surgeon.'

'Chirurgiens. I alter anatomy. I manufacture transformations. I can change, within theory, almost anything about an animal. Like I say I've made better—'

'Can you change *humans*?' she asked cautiously. There wasn't a day that went by where she didn't think about it.

Cayce moved away from the cages and faced her clearly. There was something remarkably noble about his long face, an elegance, a healthy, almost false sheen to his skin. He was delicate in his appearance and mannerisms, his full lips, his limpid blue eyes. Beneath his hood she could see his hair was blond and spiked. 'Ah, you're one of *those* people, then,' he declared dismissively, and turned away.

'One of what?' Lan asked. 'Hey, don't just say that and look away.'

Cayce didn't look back, merely shook his head knowingly. 'You want to be made to look prettier, right? Vanity, just vanity, much like you find all over these islands. I blame your culture entirely. You are, it seems, all the same.' He seemed to have formed his opinion of her in a heartbeat.

'No,' Lan replied desperately, tugging the sleeve of his cloak. His sharp glare forced her to let go. 'Look, I'm interested in what can be done – I know I'm not the prettiest girl in the world, and I don't much care about that. You say you can change humans, and I want to know more about that, really.'

'Externally, why, I can change anything.' He jabbed a finger against his skull and offered a smile. 'The insides, though, they are often still a mess.'

'Are you really a cultist?' Lan asked.

'How else, young lady, do you think it happens? Say a prayer in a Jorsalir church?' He chuckled softly.

A thunder of applause erupted from the distance, a reminder that time was passing, that she'd soon need to be on stage. One more act before her own, and she didn't have long . . . She might never see this man again.

'Look, I really need to know something,' she said. 'You say you can change humans, but . . .'

Cayce gave her his full attention once again.

'It's not easy to say this . . .' she stuttered. It never was, because it took her out of her mindset – to think of herself objectively, which she did not like to do, because it hurt, and it stopped her from coping with everyday life. Her heart clattered along and she dared to ask the question.

'Can you keep a secret?'

*

Cayce went away, but told Lan to wait. Several torturous days drifted by without a reply. Her show went on. *The show must always go on.* Her concentration lapsed, and more than once that week she nearly stumbled off the high-wire. Astli very nearly struck her after that, warning her that if there were any slip-ups, if the accompanying fall didn't kill her then he would.

For the first time in her life, though, none of this seemed to matter. Year after year she had thought herself unable to be true to what she felt, but now a miracle was being offered to her.

Messengers finally brought her letters. Furtively she would rip them open under the envious gazes of the other entertainers.

'Care to show that to us, *honey*?'

'Got yourself a lover out of town? Tell him I'll take your place, honey – you know I'm much prettier than you.'

'He can even bring a friend, I don't care.'

Lan ignored them and read and re-read Cayce's missives. First he had scribbled a resigned declaration that what she asked for simply couldn't be done. Her heart broke, but then a day later she received another note declaring that he had changed his mind, that he had considered some new techniques and that the possibility of failure wasn't a reason for them *not* to try. A few days after this, Lan received another letter telling her to travel to a tavern to the other side of

Villtreeb, in a district cluttered with run-down taverns and dreary granite hotels. Slipping away after one performance, she took one of the workhorses, and braved the snow and ice. Only when she came out here, into the open plazas and past the decrepit shop facades, did she realize just how lucky her own life was. Irens here were void of much business, street corners became centres for illicit transactions, priests gave sermons alongside barrel-fires, dealing out nuggets of wisdom to a handful of onlookers. Lan climbed the slippery streets and passed under a hefty Jorsalir cathedral.

When she arrived at the rendezvous she found the tavern virtually empty. It was the usual kind of dive found all across the islands in which traders came to talk business and shake hands over nefarious deals. One secluded corner of the bar, beneath row upon row of antique agricultural implements, would become a meeting point between herself and the cultists over the next few nights.

Old networks had been dug up, they told her, and information was relaying back and forth across the island of Jokull, across the Empire. Her main contact smoked a roll-up, and every time he took a drag it seemed as if he might never complete a sentence, a habit that made the conversation agonizingly slow. Still, she had waited long enough. Cayce's order of cultists was interested in her. It was suggested that they could be of help.

The second meeting, in their hooded cloaks, and with sharp shadows fallen across their faces, the cultists from the Order of the Chirurgiens – and Cayce himself – interrogated her. They searched her memories, dredged her soul. She told them everything.

'I've always been a woman,' Lan told them matter-of-factly. She'd repeated this to herself so many times in her head it was now like reciting a mantra. 'It's not a question of choice, I always knew I was a girl. That is my true gender. I'd played

17

with dolls, with other young girls instead of boys, wanted to dress as them, and none of this ever seemed wrong. I guess some of us are simply born in the wrong body.'

They never released their gaze from her own; never gave her any indication of their opinion.

'Throughout my childhood,' she continued, 'my father would incessantly plead with me to act "normal". He'd hit me, at times viciously, trying to make a man of me. I was lucky enough to be schooled well, though bullied massively. I was beaten up more times than I care to remember. My father and teachers didn't stop any of this, they said it would do me good. When I showed no signs of changing, I was taken to medical cultists, given erratic and eccentric treatments to make me more masculine. I was kicked out of school and whilst at home would try on my mother's pretty dresses. After I was caught doing this my parents locked me in a room for days, whilst Jorsalir priests attempted to exorcize the demons within me. Apparently in our blessed church you are either male or female, and your gender matches your anatomy which matches your soul, and there's no changing it. The world is black and white through Jorsalir eyes.'

'I wouldn't put too much trust in the words of priests,' one of the cultists muttered, possibly a woman – it was hard to tell with any of them, which was strangely comforting. 'The Jorsalir church has never been a fan of . . . development. That they are so entwined with the structures of the Empire remains saddening. They loathe people like us.'

Yeah, well I'm sure you didn't have one abuse you at length, she thought, repressing that bitterness. 'Anyway. I've conditioned myself to not let any of it affect me. I assume that they just feared what they didn't understand.'

'One of the many reasons that we cultists must keep to ourselves,' Cayce observed dryly.

'So eventually I fled from home and spent a couple of years

in various rough spots of the city, even a short while in the caves of Villjamur. I found happiness with a friend for a while, but I can't remember much of those days.'

They said nothing, merely listened.

'Do you need any money, for all of this?' Lan offered. She had some money tucked away, not much – her late father had grown fat off the ore industry and had dealings in Villiren. Because of their rift she hadn't spoken to him in five years, so it had come as a gut-wrenching surprise when she inherited what little was left of the family money. Cancer had eaten up her mother a year ago, and Lan being the only blood relation left, and because of a quirk of Villjamur law – she was legally a man – the property deeds became hers without much question.

'It may surprise people like you, but we are not at all interested in money,' Cayce replied. 'You see, where we come from, it is not of much use.'

'Ysla.' They breathed the name of their home island as if it was some nostalgic memory. She thought about the strange things that might go on there. An island populated *only* by cultists. She dreamed of magic.

'We will be in touch,' Cayce said, 'so, if you please, do not go anywhere for a while.'

As if.

The cultists filed out one by one and Lan returned across the cold streets in deep thought. It had seemed like this questioning was all a formality, that Cayce already understood her needs, but she didn't want to get her hopes up.

*

Another long wait followed, whilst she moved through the same routine: performance after performance, in front of diminishing crowds. How long would she have left before Astli reduced his staff again?

Night after night, while the other performers retreated to

19

the dormitory, she waited alone by the moulded entrance to the amphitheatre in case another letter arrived.

*

Another freezing evening and another show, but this time there was a knock at the dressing-room door and a bald man kitted out against the cold asked her to travel with him to an outpost on Jokull. 'Bring whatever you need for a short trip, and most of all prepare for cold weather. Snow's deepened along the east of the island. Roads are shitting precarious at best.'

This is it then.

Lan was out of there. Her pulse was uncontrollable and she wanted to cry with joy, but she held herself together. She threw a few items into a bag whilst the others stared on impassively. One of the girls blurted out, 'Where the hell d'you think you're going?'

Lan thought she heard someone mutter 'Dyke.'

'I need to go out for a while.'

'Show's about to start. Think you can just walk out now?' Marre, a thickset girl in a shimmering silver outfit, made for the door as if to try to block Lan's path. She fingered her dark locks and pouted her lips.

'Don't tell Astli, please,' Lan whispered, pausing from her packing, emotion bubbling in her eyes.

'This once,' Marre grunted, exposing a rare glimpse of humanity, and lumbered back to her chair.

*

Lan's hands around her escort's waist, they rode for days across Jokull in the biting cold, deep into raw wilderness. Much of the island was layered in snow and ice, the landscape so similar no matter where they rode, a dull and bitter place to live. Animal life here was sparse, and how anything could salvage an existence here was beyond her. Tiny hamlets persisted, names she had never before come across – Thengir, Valtur – and people managed to make a living on simple

20

rations, fresh fish, berries and seabirds. It was a humbling journey.

Her companion maintained an almost complete silence, grunting his replies to her. His face was permanently screwed up in concentration. She wondered if he had been born with such a scowl.

The cultist must have known what she was, and maybe that was the reason he treated her with virtual hostility – he was not the first. He was indifferent to her every need, as if he resented having to accompany her to the destination. Bringing up her concerns wasn't something she was prepared to do – as she always had, she would silently plod on without initiating *that* conversation.

Isolating and imposing, the wilderness continued to unsettle her, with the ice wind blustering into her. She could have been on another world entirely. For so long, all she had known was the chaotic clamour from the auditorium, screams of the crowd, girls cackling at her in the changing rooms, the animals screeching . . . And now the only sound was that of the horse doing her best to plough across the long-forgotten roads of Jokull, and when they rested all she could hear was her own breath. She didn't have any idea of where they were or where they were going. And she didn't care. Soon she would be free.

*

On the second night they rode through thick bushes right into the heart of a dying forest that her escort declared portentously as Vilewood. Little could calm her nervousness at entering the darkness. The pungency of the sodden vegetation was intense, and occasionally a bird would dart past, startling her.

Eventually, she could see pairs of white lights bordering a path towards a clearing, and their horse headed instinctively in that direction. On closer inspection the lights were shaped like candles, but the flames were like none she'd ever seen, tiny spheres balanced on the tips of sticks – cultists were indeed the proprietors of bizarre objects. The trail of lights cut through the forest, and her vision was soon limited to no further than their radiance.

'We now dismount,' the cultist declared.

They arrived at what she thought was a small shack of a church, but it wasn't the male and female gods, Bohr or Astrid, who were worshipped here, but that mysterious technology over which the cultists had a monopoly. Any Jorsalir carvings had been destroyed – instead, diagrams of bizarre instruments and etchings of numbers and symbols were scrawled across the walls.

Lan was ushered through the arch and down a spiral staircase, her bag of clothing in her hands, and guided onto a small plinth in the dark where she sat with her legs dangling over the edge, waiting, shivering and listening to an increasing hum.

It was all so quick.

Bright lights and disjointed thoughts, and her eyes closed as if by force—

*

Eyes wide open.

White stone carvings and columns and friezes filled her vision. A massive daedal mural covered the ceiling, a picture of metallic landscapes and curious, box-like creatures. For a moment she stared dumbly, and then the contents of her stomach began to churn.

Men and women in pale-coloured garb glanced over her as she shakily pushed herself up. Their presence was a blur. Instantly Lan made to vomit and a woman darted in to throw a bucket under her head. She threw up into it, collapsed to her knees, clutching the container and, when she'd finished spluttering, looked around embarrassed, cautiously wiping her mouth on the cloth handed to her.

'Welcome, sister.'

Lan pushed herself upright and breathed heavily. 'Sorry about . . . doing that. I couldn't help it.' *What an entrance, Lan.*

The faces of those gathered were pleasant, full of cheer, and she could sense that they meant her no harm.

'It's all right, sister,' a voice chimed.

'Such methods of travel have side effects,' another explained. 'These things often happen when your body is snatched from one place and relocated thus.'

They seemed like a chorus narrating her progress in a play.

'Where am I?' she said.

Sensual incense and warm lighting drifted from strange sources; this room appeared acutely modern. Seeing Cayce's face, and it being the only vaguely familiar sight, she floundered towards him.

'Ysla,' he said. 'Welcome to Ysla.' She remembered his voice, his particular tones. Cayce stood aside and watched as the gathered people began to analyse her and sketch her. A hubbub fluttered around the room as more people came in to observe this newcomer, this outsider.

'Ye-yes. Of course,' Lan stuttered, and then her reason for being there struck her in force. As she became utterly self-conscious of being a freakish experiment, the muscles in her legs gave way and she almost collapsed.

Cayce swept in, took her arm and, with one hand under her shoulder, eased her back onto her feet. He hauled her hessian bag across his shoulder and the crowd parted to let them through.

Her legs wobbled again as they went up a set of stairs up to the exit. Then suddenly, there at the top, in this world beset by ice, she experienced such warmth, such brightness . . .

There was not a single cloud in the sky.

THREE

Days later, and she was on a brilliant white beach stained pink by the rising red sun.

Pebbles. Wisps of seaweed. A sword half-buried in the sand, the hilt jutting up without function. Further along the beach were bizarre metal lattices towering up into the skies. They bled into the distance, several of them, elegant, rusting and redundant behemoths.

These were the first images Lan saw, as the mental fog was dispersed by the tidal roar and the pungency of the coast that assaulted her. The sea breeze was cool against her skin: the thought prompted her to glance across herself. Bare feet, khaki breeches, her long-sleeved white shirt – she had no recollection of these items at first, they weren't hers, *they weren't her*, but soon enough the images flashed back.

It's all happening so quickly . . .

Her new body thronged with pain. Muscles seemed to spasm whenever she moved, and even though there weren't bruises where she expected them, it didn't diminish the pulses of agony. Cayce had warned her, of course, and she knew exactly what to expect – but the theory and the reality were quite separate. These were the effects of sorcery, even if Cayce would have hated her using the term. She was living a fantasy, a dream, and she couldn't quite believe it. Cayce had explained that it was something she must grow used to, and from now on she must to learn to lose the years of

24

layered frustrations, drop her self-consciousness around others.

Because she had undergone a major transformation.

Lan shaded her eyes from the intensity of the light and pushed herself up, sand clumping to her arms. She still hadn't become used to this temperature, this balmy, sultry warmth. There were a lot of things she wasn't used to.

Further down the shore, two of the indigenous Cephs were handling a boat, steering it onto the shore. Their *handling* was awkward. Pale-skinned and hairless, the creatures were humanoid save for their arms, which were thick purple and pink tentacles several feet in length. They curled to and fro, each with pulsing suction cups.

The Cephs hauled nets bulbous with fish, and lugged them up the beach, through sedges and reeds and onto land. Aside from their shaggy breeches, they were utterly bare-skinned, and she still could not quite discern where the human body ended and these marine appendages began, so gradual was their change in morphology. Contrary to what she had first thought – that these were creations of the cultists – Cayce had informed her that they were part of the natural tribes of the Boreal Archipelago. Over the tens of thousands of years of human and rumel military dominance, they had taken sanctuary off and on the coast of Ysla, where they remained living peaceful, simple lives.

Lan breathed in deeply this clean air, content with watching the Cephs go about their business, their tentacles unfurling majestically around bundles of fish, or massive planks of wood in order to repair their huts.

The sky was vacant except for the flight antics of pterodettes, and their reptilian squawks echoed across the bay. Out to sea, a few tiny boats were navigating the treacherous channels, gullies and tiny whirlpools around the reefs. The surf folded over itself, endlessly – and the repetitions were intoxicating. The landscape served to calm her mind and, if ever there was a place in which to recover from such painful surgical procedures, then this was it. If she could bring herself to believe in the Jorsalir tales, then this would be what she hoped the heavenly realms would be like.

Am I dead?

She stood upright, stretched tentatively, then more snaps of pain savaged her nerves. She grinned. *No, most definitely alive.* Lan bent her arms this way and that, trying to work out the pain.

She turned back to face the city in the deep distance, a construct of wood and stone and metal. It blended in with the texture of the vegetation, yet towered above, dominating the panorama.

Villarbor, the forest city.

Cayce called it a treetop metropolis in which cultist magic flickered in and out of existence, but to her eyes Villarbor was a city of violent sorcery. She had been barely conscious when she entered the place, but there was plenty of the weird to alarm her. Nothing there seemed to make sense; it was a phenomenally different way of life. Magic charged through the skein of streets. Buildings were constructed from, and within, the trunks of titanic trees that seemed settlements in themselves.

Each lightning-pulse of magic that now boomed in the distance sent a quiver through her body.

With that in mind, she sauntered along the sand, a slow arc around the beachhead. *Such beautiful heat*, she thought. *I don't ever want to go back to Jokull, that freezing island.*

Further up the shore she spotted a lone figure. Cayce was sitting on a rock smoking a roll-up. He was wearing a cream-coloured outfit. She could smell his heady weed from a distance. As she approached, sand squelched between her toes.

He looked her up and down, brushing his stubbled chin. He analysed her anatomy, and she knew by now that there was nothing sexual in his examination. This was merely one of his inspections.

'So you are enjoying the beaches, I see,' Cayce said.

'Something like that. The Cephs – they're bizarre people, aren't they? We don't have anything like that where I'm from.'

Cayce frowned, scanning the Cephs in the distance, but he didn't acknowledge her words. Rubbing his arms, he said, 'You look really good, Lan, and I mean that. You were already in impressive physical shape – there are a good many unhealthy people, with all that ice.' Despite his slightly unusual accent, he spoke with utter confidence, as if he was always declaring something profound, and whether or not he knew it, his words were helping to rebuild her in places his science couldn't quite reach.

'When will I have to leave?' she asked. 'I'd love to hang around a little longer.'

'We are all done, as far as I'm concerned,' he replied. 'Ysla, for its own sake, does not permit visitors. So, I'm afraid you will have to leave soon. You simply cannot stay – and it is not just for our good, but yours, too.'

Lan thought as much. 'In the morning?'

'Indeed.' Cayce jumped down from the rock, his cream cloak flailing around him in the breeze. Marram grass rippled along the edge of the dunes whilst a flock of gulls suddenly filled the sky before drifting in circles along the shore.

'There are some festivities tonight – cultural celebrations for one of the orders. You may as well enjoy the night before you head back – just, if you please, try not to talk to too many of the others.'

'For my own good?' Lan asked.

'You have, it seems, caught on well.' Cayce turned and Lan moved to follow him across the sand.

*

27

The approach to Villarbor was contoured with surges of trees and plants that seemed alien to the Archipelago. Spiked structures and fat-leafed things and explosions of gaudy colours. Heavy, almost monstrous insects droned in and out of the foliage, snapping back branches with their clumsy flight. Other creatures drilled holes through bark, filling their venous sacs with sap.

The stone track was well-kept, tidied regularly by small teams of men and women. They cleared paths of vegetation with strange relics shaped like a crossbow, with minimal effort, and it was not at all obvious how the devices worked.

Lan never understood why, on an island without money, anyone would want to do such jobs, yet they did. *Surely you should be paid for having to do chores like this?* They stopped their tasks to gather around and talk to her, and she had to strain to follow their accents. She forced a smile in her effort to cease being self-conscious. Their clothing was garish, and woven with little patches in the style of harlequins. Not one of them dressed identically, and both genders sported equally unique variants of style, and wore bright flowers in their hair – which made her frown since back on Jokull flowers were generally worn only by women.

Cayce humoured them all for a moment, but then steered her onwards towards Villarbor. She waved her goodbyes over her shoulder.

Further up the road she asked, 'Are we in a hurry for a reason?'

'They will spend all day talking to an outsider,' Cayce replied. 'We do not get many of your kind here – a layperson from the Empire, I mean.'

'Why is that anyway?' Lan asked.

'It is just easier that way,' Cayce said.

'You said that last time, too.'

'I probably did,' was his non-committal response. 'We are

simply taught that outsiders have a tendency to corrupt – I wish our society to remain harmonious, is all.'

'One more question,' Lan said.

'Just one?'

She paused and chuckled. 'I know, I'm sorry. It's just exciting for people like me, that's all.'

'Your question?'

'How come you were allowed off the island? Seems as if everyone else is curious about me – but does no one ever leave?'

'Few people *want* to leave. They are free to do so, of course, but they hear of the many tragedies of the Archipelago, and want nothing whatsoever to do with it.'

'And you . . . How come you travel?'

'My experiences and feelings are not entirely like the others,' he replied, and marched on before she could press him any further.

*

Fields rolled back in all directions. Various colours denoted what must have been dozens of different crops covering small plots of land, unlike the vast, intensive efforts on Jokull. Clusters of huts and thickly wooded copses were dotted everywhere, surrounded by strange climbing fruits.

The sun was sliding from the sky, the heat still unbelievably prominent. Cayce said that the cultists managed the weather in Ysla. Whilst around the Archipelago winds and clouds heaped ice and snow, here there was little but clear skies and intoxicating warmth. It was no wonder the cultists kept this island to themselves.

She had seen the process of manipulation and been mystified. Figures perched on a hill, tilting some device towards the sky and, on the next hill along, another working in tandem. Purple shafts of light had buried deep into any clouds that persisted, disintegrating them slowly or ploughing through into the heavens. Whatever they were doing, these acts were certainly keeping the weather favourable.

Lan didn't spot where the city actually began. As they approached the urban fringes of the settlement, they passed through smaller hub communities – and Cayce explained that this was the real principle behind Villarbor; not one central-ized district but lots of them, all small interconnected zones. Between each stretched small grassland meadows, which were punctuated by mats of purple or white flowers, then second-ary growth forest and coppiced trees – and then majestic woodland. Now and then they became something more for-mal, gardens that frothed over into one another, coloured plants blending into the distance.

The smells, the pungency, the colours, the textures, were like nothing she'd ever known.

'The gardens are remarkably pretty,' she commented, still on Cayce's heels.

He strode on and said, 'They are not meant for aesthetic purposes – we use everything in this particular district for medicinal value. Each plot is divided up by the ailment they treat. Districts specialize, most for food, but others for pur-poses like this.'

They passed a single-storey house surrounded by one such garden, and three women standing in casual conversation.

'Good afternoon, sisters,' Cayce called out.

One of them, a dark-haired girl, seemed to act coyly towards him, waving but turning away quickly, her white skirt trailing her in an arc.

'Guessing you're a heartbreaker here,' Lan observed, hop-ing that the casual conversation might open him up.

'I have no idea what you mean,' he replied.

'You know. Girl saves herself for you, thinks of you a lot, tells all her friends how charming you are.'

Cayce shrugged and laughed. 'I would, indeed, hate to be in such a position of power over another person.'

Power – there it was again, a word that seemed electrically charged on this island, one spoken of with great disdain.

Into the forest proper and, after stepping between two giant buttress roots, they entered a zone that was clearly central to Villarbor.

Woodland towered before her, a million shades of green and brown that ultimately blended to become a dark haze in the distance. Thick, red-brown trunks extended upwards, losing themselves within a densely packed canopy. Alongside the trees, metallic structures extended like scaffolding. On others, vast ornate staircases wound themselves anticlockwise around the timber. Tracks had been cut between trees, in numerous directions, through an undergrowth of ferns.

'What species are these?' Lan asked.

'Oh, we have various *Tsuga*, *Taxodium*, *Sequoia* . . . We have some rarer varieties further in.'

'Why such interesting names?' Lan stared up at the amazing textures to the bark.

'These are, to our knowledge, the names given to the species when the seeds were stored, several millennia ago. Civilizations rise and fall, and after one particular fall, possibly due to some apocalyptic event, the landscape became devoid of forests. The forests of the world have since been re-grown. It is a sadness that we no longer know their original names.'

Clustered huts formed tree-crown dwellings. Walkways traversed the canopy and, above, unbelievably, people were wandering back and forth as if on the streets of a city. Food-filled baskets were constantly lowered and raised from the ground. Tiny lights cascaded down from branches, illuminating the more atramentous corners of the treescape – and Lan wondered how magical it would look at night. Within the gaps in the canopy, brown balloon-like crafts were gracefully lowering themselves towards respective platforms. People disembarked in their droves, mainly humans, but rumels, and the occasional Ceph too – from this distance, they all looked like insects.

Everything here seemed superbly crafted, and unique. The details carved into every structure were massively ornate, intricate geometric designs, or baroque and sprawling, as if the trees themselves had grown in that mesmerizing manner.

Lan turned to Cayce. 'So what's your house like?'

'Nothing here is mine,' Cayce laughed.

'Well, where do you live?' she asked.

'Villarbor.' He gestured to the forest.

'You own the entire city?'

'No one *owns* any of it.' Cayce wore his usual serene expression. 'There are no rulers to order us about. We share communal hab units grafted into sections of the forest. We choose where to live and, quite unlike Villjamur, no one has to pay a fortune to be in the most fashionable areas. We self-organize and choose everything about our way of life ourselves. Should any of us wish to live elsewhere, we can move and build other places, fashion them out of the forest providing others are not against this wish. One can make each place with as much craft and care as one desires.' Cayce paused to contemplate his words. 'When the first cultists came here,' he explained, 'around about the time Villjamur was established, they adopted the ways of the local tribes – the newcomers did not want to interfere with the natural way of the land, and that philosophy of self-organizing has evolved into what we have now.'

'I understand, I think . . .' Lan lied. 'It just makes no sense without money and a governing body.'

'We have found governments and traders do not have the majority's interest at heart,' Cayce replied. 'We cope well – we organize, distribute, work mutually with other autonomous hubs and districts across the island . . . I know what you are thinking – this all seems impossible without money and without rulers. But, it helps that we are cultists, so we can do anything we want, because money does not dictate or place values. I had to run the decision bringing you here past assemblies of the community – because there is a reason we generally keep outsiders away, a reason we don't like their influence or their ideas – and why I'm reluctant for you to converse with us too much: what we have here *works* well. The Empire is a hegemony, attempting to impose its dominance on the rest of the Archipelago, crippling island after island in order to sell the fineries you see in Villjamur, and you would do well to understand that. But out here, in Villarbor, it just would not be sustainable. On an island like this our systems would implode. Here, we take only what we need. We will have some food tonight and you may sample some of the delights the forest offers, and then you can return to Villjamur as one of the sacred few to have witnessed this place.'

*

Cayce led her into a humid tree grove. Fat roots had formed an organic archway, and citizens of the forest stepped out from between them, drifting along wide paths through the vegetation. The pace of life here was leisurely. People were standing idly chatting, gripping baskets of metal, hunks of bars and piping and cogs. Children played games among the foliage, whilst a handful of smaller ones sat down on the grass listening to a man for what must have been a lesson.

'Presumably without money, these children don't have to pay to be schooled?'

'Certainly not!' Cayce replied. 'They have access to everything – it is extremely important that every child can learn to read and write.'

Lan was surprised, recalling the guilt of her own expensive education, despite the abuse she suffered. 'What are they being taught?'

'They're being taught how to think.'

The treetops flared with purple lighting, which stretched

under-canopy in flat pulses, and Lan's heart raced at this electrical activity. No one else took notice of it.

They passed through an area that might have been an iren in Villjamur. Here it was something entirely ... relaxed – a few rows of people openly weaving fabric or cooking food, stopping occasionally to talk to passers-by. Lan marvelled at the quality of decorative crafts on display, and the variety of fruit and vegetables. The choice.

Lan noticed that some of the wooden habs flickered inside, as if a smith was working steel – but she suspected it was magic being worked, rather than metal.

'Is everyone here a cultist?' she asked.

'By your definitions, probably,' Cayce remarked. 'With one exception, I should add. On Ysla, we are *all of us* equal. On Imperial soil cultists use relic technology for their own gains, occasionally bartering their skills for positions of power, even to fight against others in order to further their agendas. One will find none of that occurs on this island – we do not express power over people in our communities, or even the local tribes.'

*

In the evening, Lan joined Cayce's table at a large outdoor banquet, and basked in the balmy air. *Such a mild evening ... It's something I'd almost forgotten.*

Coloured lights and strips of bright material littered the forest clearing like a star-field. Children mingled with adults at a vast table shaped like a broken letter O, with people sitting both inside and out, mainly humans, but also a few rumels, and even one Ceph further down, who Cayce glanced to more than once. In the centre, a group of musicians played lute-like instruments, and drums and violins beat out loud melodies based on local folk songs. The forest vibrated with an energy that reminded her of the shows. There must have been a few hundred people there, each of them drinking and eating exotic foods – ones that could only really grow so far south, with such an altered climate. Succulent fruits and mellow-tasting mead, and thick stews and soft bread. The tables were overflowing.

And this was the first time she'd been amongst so many people, able to feel quite *safe*. Yes, she could think about herself now with great relief. There was no deep-rooted fear that she would be victimized. When people talked to her there still remained an echo of her former self-consciousness, and that would perhaps linger for some time, but for now she could cover it up with her interest in this other culture.

As incessant as midges, the locals attempted to quiz her about the outside world. Cayce kept suggesting that people leave her be, to allow her to recover in peace, and she softly smiled her apologies to them.

The discussion surrounding her was wide-ranging, though often concerning matters of organization: transportation, how many people would man the bridges the next week, assemblies to be held, union guilds, schooling, districts, skills. For the most part it seemed all these people did was plan what needed to be done, but there was a good deal of talk of spiritual practices and liberal arts. There was a lot of talk of the finer points of sorcery, too, but most went over her head. Conversations at some parts of the table flared into altercations and semi-rows, though elders stood up and softly waved for calm. *They all seem a lively bunch on Ysla.*

A name was suddenly whispered across the table, and the expressions on faces soured considerably and conversations quietened.

Lan leaned towards Cayce. 'Who's Shalev?'

As he struck alight a roll-up, Cayce observed the reactions of others along the table. Eventually, still looking their way, he answered Lan. 'She is someone who was ... of an unpleasant nature. She did bad things.'

'A criminal?' Lan asked.

'We have no criminals here.'

'What—?'

'Keep your voice down,' Cayce muttered calmly, and took a drag. 'I said we have no criminals. We have no prisons. We do not punish in the same ways as the Empire.'

'How do you stop people from stealing things?'

'If no one owns anything, how can someone steal? If someone can have anything they want by asking, work, relic, or by doing it themselves, then there exists no need to steal. Most crimes are against property – and here, that is a non-existent term.'

'Who decides these rules?'

'We all do,' Cayce replied. 'We all have a democratic say in our own affairs, and this includes making the rules by which we live.'

'I take it there's no Inquisition here, so who the hell polices all of this?'

'No, there's no Inquisition. We have our own community body who see to it that everything is fair, and democratically assign a punishment according to the offence that is committed, and to ensure the victim is suitably compensated.'

'What about murder?'

Something flickered behind Cayce's eyes then.

Lan pressed him further. 'Is that what this Shalev person did, kill someone?'

Cayce glanced at the others who were now listening in to the conversation. 'No. Not just some *one*. Shalev was thought to have killed several people through her erratic practices. She was an unstable person, who did not fit in with our ways despite being brought up here, for the most part. Shalev is not an indigenous cultist. She came from a neighbouring island. She was difficult for many here to understand, and she was never popular because of that. Then her experiments became more reckless, and civilians were killed due to some of her relics. She failed to accept responsibility for her actions, and was exiled from all the communities across the island.'

'Where do you think she's gone now?' Lan asked.

Cayce glanced down at the table. This was the first time she had seen him lose his cool demeanour. 'Shalev always talked about hurting the Empire – in fact, this was a contributing factor to her being exiled. Shalev wanted to impose our own systems elsewhere – as there has been much talk amongst our own people over the centuries of doing the same. But Shalev wanted to use violence to achieve this, which contradicts our way of life. So, in answer to your question, I fear she has headed to Imperial soil.'

*

Cayce walked her back to a hab, both of them harmlessly giddy on the local alcohol. It was still humid despite being deep into the evening, and as they stepped across the firm decking, Lan quizzed Cayce relentlessly. 'Why help me, Cayce? I want to know. I'm just a nobody, so why? Please, be honest.'

'You are quite the solipsistic lady.'

'No, it's not that. I want to know who the person was who helped me. Who you really were, before I walk back to that cold island on the other side of the Archipelago possibly never to see you again.'

Cayce gazed at her for some time and gestured for her to enter the hab. Hesitantly she shuffled inside. The darkness abated as he lit a lantern, and the soft glow warmed his anxious face.

Everything inside looked carved from the forest, from the floors to the furniture. Pinned up against the walls were detailed diagrams of the human body, in one corner a stack of books leaned over precariously, whilst thick bundles of paper were scattered haphazardly across the floor. A window faced out across the dark forest crown.

He drew curtains across the window to block out the night, and bolted the door shut – suddenly Lan grew fearful.

'Sit,' he instructed, and she quickly collapsed into a wooden chair by the desk.

He stood before her, sliding off his white robe. Then he commenced unbuttoning his undershirt.

She froze, said nothing. *Is he going to hurt me?*

Very slowly he peeled back his shirt and dropped it to the floor in a pool of his clothes.

Lan's jaw dropped.

Scar tissue blossomed around his deltoid muscles, and between there and his pectorals she could see severe blistering – no, the faint bubbles of suction cups, some even protruding, pushing up through human skin. He had been very grotesquely altered. The colour of his arms was noticeably lighter than around his abdomen – they did not look to be his own.

He watched her watching him and she began to apologize pathetically for her stunned reaction. From *her* of all people.

'Now you have seen,' Cayce whispered dolefully. 'I . . . I was once a Ceph. I once swam underwater with them. I understand, to some extent, how you yourself feel. I longed to be human – deep within me I felt such a distance from the sea. I hated the cold depths. I craved light and knowledge, the land and human culture. I left my people, and am shunned by them now, for they do not appreciate the ways of this island. They are brutal and simple people. At a very young age I was made human by the cultists here, and given all the accoutrements of a human being. I became one of them, I learned their languages and their ways and practised until no one could tell me apart from any other. I grew to be who I am now, and it was not easy, but among this society I was welcomed, and that . . . that open-mindedness and generosity is something I wish to show others.'

He held out wide the arms that were once not his own.

'So, Lan, I understand your desire for transformation. That is why I helped you.'

*

There was so much more Lan wanted to know, but it was time to leave Ysla.

Morning sunlight filtered into the hab and she listened as Cayce talked to her from the other side of his desk. He was informing Lan of the details of her transformation, how it would affect her, and she readily drank in his words, trusting him instinctively after he had revealed his own secrets to her. She had no doubt that this man understood her, though it did not make what he said any easier to absorb.

'We've been able to give you as much of a functioning female anatomy as we thought we could,' Cayce said. 'And of course, we have . . . smoothed away masculine contours from your form, especially on your face, and in other ways – with hair and voice. These were simple enough. So firstly, you should be able to experience intercourse as a full woman, but I cannot say how much pleasure you will receive from it.'

'I never got much anyway,' she replied, grinning. Besides, for years she had never gone *that* far because she ran the risk of being discovered.

Cayce ignored her dry humour, stalling over his next sentence. 'You'll also still . . . You will be unable to have children, and . . . there's no way we can encourage natural menstruation.'

Lan suspected as much, though always retained that vague hope of having the option, but now that hope had ultimately died, a small light in her heart went out for ever.

'Aside from that,' he continued, 'and given that gender is a fluid notion – we are not Neanderthals who deal in binary on Ysla – I think you have many good reasons to be happy,' Cayce concluded. 'And are you happy with your physical state?'

'I always felt like a woman anyway, but, you know, it's so

39

much more meaningful now? This isn't just about how I look.' She allowed a contemplative pause, and it was only in this silence that she realized how much more softer her voice had really become. 'How much of this will remain a secret?' Lan asked. 'I wouldn't want any of this getting out, is all. How many people know of what you've done to me?'

'I understand.' Cayce peered up. 'A small network of cultists will be aware, but that is it. Besides, with all that ice around to worry about, who else will care?'

'*I'll* care.'

Cayce folded his arms, hands under his armpits. He gave her a look of deep empathy. 'Of course.'

'I'm sorry,' Lan said. His words were all very pleasant, but wasn't she still some experiment to them? This was a mutual arrangement, after all. 'There's just so much to cope with.'

'I told you there would be. People come looking for physical changes all the time, but they don't understand just how connected the body and mind can be.'

'I understand,' she replied.

'You may always have ghosts,' Cayce warned. 'Do not think they vanish overnight.'

Before Lan departed she didn't quite know what to say. Cayce merely stood there, alongside a doorway at the top of the stairwell leading down to where she'd be transported back to the freezing ice-wastes of Jokull. Others from the island had gathered in their multicoloured clothing – faces with which she was distantly familiar. The sun was intense, as it always was here. She gazed behind into the distance to see Villarbor, and its hundreds of hub communities stretching across the many shades of green that comprised the landscape. *What a view* ... She would certainly miss this island, but was honoured to have at least witnessed such exoticism.

Cayce guided her to the steps. 'The local tribes like to point out to us that for rebirth, first you must choose the path of death. I would recommend that it is an opportunity to let go of the person you were.'

'I will,' she replied. 'I'll go to Villjamur – I have just a little money saved, but yeah. No more life at the circus for me.'

'Very wise,' Cayce replied.

'Cayce, I don't know what to say . . .' She was welling up, and thinking her emotional outburst absurd, but how could she thank this man who had given her a new life, the life which she naturally felt for all these years, which was both ever-distant and as close as a dream?

'The pleasure is, indeed, all mine, sister,' Cayce said gently. 'I have explored new science here, and my order are thrilled with the work we have done together.'

She suddenly embraced him, unable to hide her gratitude, and then she turned down the stairs, under the gazes of others, back towards the musky darkness.

To a new life.

Four

There was some kind of military operation under way – she could at least be certain of that. Thousands of red-skinned rumels were massing on the snow before her, all garbed in alien clothing, carrying banners with bizarre insignia, and ranked in eerily precise rows. Orders were being issued in that base, guttural language of theirs, and then the sound of marching muted by the snow.

But in the distance she could see thousands of those ... *things.*

Verain shuddered. She cringed at their ragged movements, at their monstrous insectile appearance. *Those shells and claws.* Though some distance away, they still put the fear of Bohr or indeed any other god into her. Each of them seemed to loom above their nearest rumel counterpart, yet despite the physical dominance, they were somehow subordinate to the red-skins.

Verain and the other cultists – what few of them that were left by now – stood dumbly examining this movements of a civilization across the landscape, through the Realm Gates. This was the tail end of an invasion force and she knew, without knowing how, that they were making war on the cities on the next island south. From what she had seen of their work already, she felt remorse for whoever would have to oppose them.

Dartun's words were mumbled sentences at first, until the wind died down. He urged them on, his strong voice calling out for them to hasten their progress. Dogs barked and tugged on their reins, their four sleds skidding forwards, the brightness of the light now like some vision of a heavenly realm, but no sooner had they moved through the thick flakes of snow when they came to a halt.

She could feel her pulse in her throat. *I just want to get out of here, please...*

A few of the red-skin rumels approached them on horseback and for some reason she could not get used to the fact that this variation of the race could exist in another dimension. Three sentries examined Dartun in the blinding light of the Realm Gates. She observed the matrix of tiny purple lines within a much brighter glow – that was where home would be. That was where she longed to return.

There came orders from behind, and in harsh tongues, there appeared to be an exchange between silhouettes in the Realm Gates' light, and the rumels before them.

Presently the cultists were all ushered forward, free to go now, *finally*, with nothing but sleds and dogs. The cultists of the Order of the Equinox set out across the snow and back into their home-world.

*

Later, much later.

And from the sanctuary of her hood, Verain peered back over her shoulder, but thankfully could no longer see the gates. Snow stormed around their small group, vicious spirals of whiteness that obscured both the horizon and the foreground. Moments of calm revealed rolling hills or ice sheets, blackened trees that clawed the grey skies. Everything here seemed identical to the moment they left, the same vistas, the same terrain, the same forests and villages.

And the ceaseless snow...

They paused, their sleds sliding to a stop. Strands of her coal-black hair wafted before her eyes and she tucked them behind her ears. She appeared to be, and felt like, a mess. She was slender before she had come all the way out here, but now she felt dangerously malnourished.

There were ten of them. Ten, from the dozens who had journeyed out beyond the Realm Gates, trailing Dartun and his lust for answers and the knowledge to extend his life. Now garbed in thick clothing and furs, they had little sense of where they were headed. A couple of dogs barked, a bizarre tinny edge to their cacophony. They, too, had been altered – she knew it, though her mind wasn't clear as to how or why.

Her mind was not clear at all.

Dartun Súr stepped out alongside her. There was a silvery sheen to his face, and patches of some substance could be seen beneath where his skin had been ripped along his neck. If she stared hard enough she could see that his eyes were glowing red, his movements fluid – yet it was still him, the leader of their order, the man who had dominated the culture of the cultists in Villjamur. A man who pushed for progress and had great visions for the future.

A man she loved.

Only now he bore the marks of having been . . . *there*.

His cloak was now frayed along the edges, his clothing worn in places. His musculature had been enhanced. He now possessed the posture of a hardened soldier, not hunched from studying ancient relics well into the night. He seemed ragged yet powerful. Dartun Súr had led them to another world in search of eternal life, and he looked like he had found it.

Images flooded back to Verain – impressions of that *other* place, beyond the Realm Gates.

Memories slammed into her mind:

A world enveloped by night. Dust-storms and eternal thunder. A landscape littered with the remnants of cultures, of shattered cities and of bonescapes. War raged in pockets of wasteland, creatures she had never imagined, or those that she thought originated from prehistoric cultures, clashed with ferocity.

44

Verain attempted to piece together what had happened. She realized she had no sense of time – *Bohr*, her mind was a mess. How long had it been since they'd first entered the gates? How much time had passed exactly? In her mind, it seemed months had gone. It seemed important to make sense of her presence here. The Order of the Equinox had followed Dartun in his quest and they had found that their relics, their pieces of ancient technology, were quite useless against this highly evolved culture. And they had been captured, imprisoned and tortured. Yet why was she here, relatively unscathed from these events?

She shuddered and erased the thoughts from her mind, and hoped the scars would leave her memory. What was important now was that she survived; because she would not have escaped merely to perish so uselessly. *I will not let myself die out here.*

FIVE

Ulryk's Journal

I woke with the first rays of our dying red sun, and used its light to guide me to the ancient city, that throng of spires & bridges, that place of legend.

Villjamur.

By horse I rode across snow-smothered fields, through villages littered with little broken shacks. Botanic specimens poked up through ridges of snow, dead or naked and no longer able to offer anything to the world, no culinary or medicinal benefit. How my old brethren would have abhorred such a sight. Bones of animals lay strewn about without dignity along dirt tracks, stripped of all the value they had been deemed to possess. Abandoned.

I could not ascertain the age of any buildings out here. They were perhaps hundreds, maybe thousands of years old, or perchance they had crumbled very recently from small-scale conflicts or were disabled by the weather. They were snow-tipped and crippled and devoid of life. This dying earth showed no remorse.

Villages and towns were settlements directly from hell. There existed – though barely – some very desperate people. Forgotten men and women scraped together a way of life from this noble land; and they came to me in groups, hoping I could help. For the most part all I had were guiding words, ones crafted from the very form of Bohr Himself (if I still believed in them), and I prayed that such utterances could offer solace.

In one village I was able, with caution, to utilize the book I carried and disaggregated the ice from a local lake. They intended to fish there, though I was not confident they would find much, but I left them with the hope — because without hope they would most certainly perish quickly.

Many of the people in rural areas seemed vacant inside — I saw it in their eyes, though they were different from the dead who, kept mobile by some fake cultist trickery, drifted between shadows; a presence that tormented the locals.

But some have sunk to terrible depths. On one dark night, through a village I do not wish to name, I witnessed people feasting on the flesh of other humans. I could barely meet the whites of their eyes, focusing instead on the morbid morsels within their fingers and the kin-blood that dripped onto the frozen ground. It did not take second sight to know these moral turpitudes were not few and far between. Skeletons were hanging from trees, bones rattled against bark in the wind — my instincts suggested some kind of local law was in operation out here, away from Imperial soldiers which, I noted, were in short supply, and I knew better than to question the presence of these execrable totems.

Of true humanity, I noted very little present.

*

I progressed further, as the echoes of the past came to my mind yet again.

Nightmares.

I saw the burning buildings and heard the screams, which still ricocheted around my skull. Those things really happened. I saw the hired militias hauling supporters and protectors into the street and their heads being severed before their families. Women being taken to one side as payment, and raped repeatedly. Those things really happened.

And my secret shame was that all I could do was watch; watch as civilization began to crumble on a far-off island. I watched lives disappear or be ruined. And their sins? Simply protecting me, protecting the truth, protecting my path to Villjamur. Because of what I knew, because I was betrayed, because I put my faith in those close to me.

Those things really happened.

In the distance I could see it, finally, the capital of this Empire. The oldest city we had on these islands, though it did not always go by this name. In written history — for what that was worth — Vilhallan was how she was born, eleven thousand years ago, before the so-called Treaty of Science, where the cultists allied themselves with a society crafted by King Hallan Hynur. An ice age destroyed much of that, though I suspect that was a natural phenomenon. Not like this . . . How few people knew these facts of the city in which they lived?

I saw the giant walls and the dark mass of people banking up against them, and leading in that direction was the smeared, well-trodden mud-road that pulled the landscape open like a wound. There were plumes of smoke drifting above like devil-wraiths. The city needed spiritual attention. Garudas circled the city, weaving between those bridges which span almost from cloud to cloud — paths one could believe the gods may tread. The spires went ever upwards, beyond comprehension, and from many of those buildings were banners rippling in the onshore breeze.

It was exactly how I remembered, and it had been so for millennia. It was the home of many of our ancestors, of heritage and culture, and being so it was my last hope. Perhaps it was to be the hope of every one of us left alive.

Villjamur.

If only you knew of the magic you were hiding . . .

SIX

The cut-throat razor lay in the bucket of hot water. He plunged in his hand to retrieve it, and began to shave: gentle scrapes, always two strokes down before moving along, two strokes then move along, carving away thick lines of foam. Rumels' skin was tough and leather-like, and he had only to shave once a week because of the slow rate of hair-growth, but his was still a routine of perfection. When he had finished he rinsed the razor before placing it to one side.

Wearing only a pair of breeches, Investigator Fulcrom faced himself in the mirror, his damp brown skin shimmering in the lantern light. He had a slender face and body for a rumel, who were normally broad and relatively squat creatures, and he had wide black eyes that, so the ladies told him, were adorable. Making postures at his reflection, he noted that his intensified workout regime had really worked. All those sit-ups and push-ups each night were clearly taking effect. Absent-mindedly, he brushed a finger down his ribs over an old knife wound.

He investigated his well-defined face for any missed areas and, after dabbing his skin with a towel, he slicked his mop of silver hair across to the left – always to the left.

For a rumel he was still young, but had recently felt deeply unsatisfied with his life. Well, with his work at least. He had been a full investigator for a decade now, but when he'd worked with old Investigator Jeryd on one of his darkest

49

cases, things had changed dramatically for him. Villjamur had been – still was – plagued by refugees, and there had been a plot to dispose of them in the tunnels under the city, in what amounted to genocide. Urtica was at the core of it, but he had blamed it on the then-Empress Rika. Only Jeryd and Fulcrom knew of these events, but couldn't prove anything, couldn't tell a single person. All they could do was rescue the refugees from execution, only to release them back outside, beyond the walls of the city, into the hostile ice. Time dragged by, and one by one, the refugees probably perished of hypothermia or disease or starvation. Meanwhile, no one in Villjamur knew what had happened to Jamur Rika since she fled the city with her sister just before she was due to be executed. There had been no reports on her progress, and he was wary of enquiring through any official channels, just in case anything untoward should happen to him. *There are some questions you just don't ask...*

Ever since then, Fulcrom had found it difficult to believe there was much justice to be found in Villjamur. It certainly wasn't like the stories that inspired him as a kid, or like the notions that MythMaker peddled in those sketches. Back then he'd loved those tales of slick and smooth investigators stalking the evening in search of villains.

Fulcrom put on a clean undershirt, a formal shirt then an over-cloak. His top-floor apartment on the fifth level of the city was not too close to the raucous bars, but near enough to where things went on in the city.

A pterodette gave a reptilian squawk outside his window, and he took a glance out to regard the cityscape beyond, as the green creature flapped its scaly wings and darted up into the cloud-base. The view from his window was impressive: turrets and spires and bridges, thousands of years of architecture, and low sunlight that forced half of Villjamur into shadow. The octagonal structure of the Astronomer's Glass

Tower glittered from above the roofs of the opposite buildings.

A final look in the mirror, a quick adjustment of his collar and, picking up his Inquisition medallion, he set off for work.

*

Villjamur was still dripping after the previous night's snow – not as much as usual, which led Fulcrom to question if the ice age was just an empty threat of the politicians. For years people had talked of the coming of the ice, what the causes might have been, and what it now meant. Imperial astronomers had given their predictions and, staying true to them, temperatures had plummeted, but just recently, there seemed to be a recovery. No matter how cold it was, people always ventured outside, every day, as if in bloody-minded defiance.

Like some ancient beast, Villjamur woke from its slumber. Little streams of smoke drifted up from chimney tops. Granite blended into patches of time-eroded limestone.

Citizens milled around backstreets and main avenues, a blur of furs, cloth and boots. Traders, some of whom were draped in cheap gold, strode half asleep to the irens at Gata du Oak, hauling handcarts or, if they were lucky, leading horses loaded up with wares. All along Matr Gata, pots were simmering with oysters, dumplings, breads stuffed with offal, the vendors regarding the street with bored glances and calling out prices. From the back of a converted caravan a member of the Aes tribe was giving an illegal shell reading. Only one religion was permitted in the Empire, the Jorsalir tradition – a pact that bound the church and state together – and as soon as Fulcrom approached him, the tribesman, who was wearing furs and a number of teeth around his neck, packed up his accoutrements and smiled his apologies before backing off down an alleyway.

A jingle of chains and something was launched up to a high open window to the side of the massive ornate facade of the Hotel Villjamur. A pretty grey-skinned rumel girl stepped down its faded gold-edged steps, wearing a blue cloak and matching head-scarf, and she smiled at Fulcrom as he walked past. Kids scampered by, and one of them arced a snowball that splattered against a window pane of the Dryad's Saddle inn, narrowly missing Fulcrom as he slipped and slid his way to one of the bridge staircases.

The bridges themselves began to vibrate under the strain of activity. Any ice that had formed overnight peeled itself away from the city's high places to plummet towards the ground. Much of it ricocheted off slate roofing, stalling its descent, but some thick chunks clattered into the cobbles, narrowly missing people. Every day someone would be killed or seriously injured. It was also starting to cause massive structural damage, accelerating the ageing of the stone, pushing cracks in masonry further apart. The ice was bringing the city to its knees.

Fulcrom's relationship with Villjamur was uneasy. Born and raised in the city, he had a strong affinity for the place, and the beauty was here to see every morning; but he knew there were other sides to it. Out here, on the levels of the city before Balmacara, people were well-to-do, healthy, stayed on the right side of the law, and had something of a decent existence. The buildings were beautiful – thin, three- or four-storey constructions, painted in a variety of weather-worn shades.

But there was also Caveside, a larger section of the city, one hidden from view. Hundreds of thousands of people lived in Villjamur, but the majority of them suffered in relative darkness. Fulcrom had heard tell that most of the residents had descended from the cave dwellers who had lived there before the city was founded eleven thousand years ago. It was the oldest part of the city and very few people ventured from one sector to the other. If the rumours were to believed, it was like hell on earth.

*

Fulcrom criss-crossed alleyways to navigate the wet, labyrinthine backstreets of the city, towards the headquarters of the Villjamur Inquisition. The entrance was a large yet discreet black double door that stood at the top of wide, crumbling steps. There was nothing ornate here, no fancy brickwork, merely two cressets set behind glass. Only the two brutish-looking guards indicated that something went on inside this building. They nodded to Fulcrom as he flashed his Inquisition medallion at them.

'Sele of Urtica, sir,' one grunted, opening the door for him.

Fulcrom entered and passed Ghale, the human administrative assistant, who was dressed as smartly as always in a frilly white shirt, green shawl and long black skirt. Her blonde hair was pinned up in one of those new styles.

'Sele of Urtica, investigator,' she announced. 'Can I get you anything?'

'Good morning, Ghale. No, I'm fine, thank you.' He made to move on.

'A drink, perhaps?' She held her hands out in front of her.

'No. Thank you anyway.' Smiling awkwardly, Fulcrom headed immediately into his office.

It was a drab affair, like many of the rooms within the arterial layout of the Inquisition headquarters. Musty old rumels lingering in their chambers for hours, working by lantern-light, poring over administration, missives or fine-tuning the legal framework of the city. Such an existence was not Fulcrom's preferred way of helping the city – being left to rot behind a desk would be a nightmarish future.

One side of Fulcrom's vast office was lined with shelves rammed with leather-bound age-ruined books. He had them arranged neatly, ordered by subject and year. Two angular diamond-shaped insets allowed in light through coloured glass, and a painting of an evening city scene, a retro original, was hung above the door.

After he placed his outer-cloak over the back of his chair

meticulously, he set about starting a fire, rummaging through the accoutrements to one side. He was nearly out of kindling.

Presently, after a few moments, the flames spat into life and, as Fulcrom warmed his hands, one of the most senior officers, Investigator Warkur, an old black-skinned rumel, barged into the room without knocking.

'Fulcrom,' he grunted stridently. 'You got a moment?'

'Of course,' Fulcrom replied. 'Take a seat.' He indicated the leather chair behind his stately mahogany desk. After clearing a couple of the papers, he struck a match and lit a candle within a small glass lantern. 'Apologies about the mess.'

'Don't be a jerk, Fulcrom – damn place is immaculate.' Warkur reclined into the chair with a thunderous groan. He was a bulky rumel with a scar along his lantern jaw, allegedly from a garuda fight forty years ago. He had a broader nose than most rumels, and his black eyes were set unnaturally deep, so Fulcrom was never quite sure if he was looking at him or somewhere in the distance. Warkur was one of the old-school investigators, the kind they didn't make any more, and with nearly two hundred years on the service, the man didn't care much for modern ways. He had outlived a handful of emperors, as he constantly liked to remind people, which meant that he had little tolerance for changes in procedures. Too jaded to ever make the position of Arch Investigator, he now spent his days mentoring the younger investigators, which suited Fulcrom fine.

'What's the problem?' Fulcrom asked.

'How long you got?' Warkur sneered. Then, 'Nah, I'm grouchy this morning. One of our three Inquisition printing presses is defunct, and no one knows what to do about it – expensive bits of kit, too. And, I slept in my office again – Stel's going to roast my behind if I do another night here, I swear.'

'Surely she understands the commitment, sir?' Fulcrom asked. 'If you need a hand with anything . . .'

Warkur waved a fat hand. 'I know you've been handed some pretty dire cases lately, Fulcrom.'

'It's not a problem, sir.'

Warkur glanced to the floor, rubbing his face with his palms to bring himself to a more alert state. 'We've got an issue that goes right to the top – Balmacara. Now, it's not a case or anything, it's more of a ... project.' He leaned forward. 'I don't have to remind you that sometimes these matters go beyond mere secrecy.'

Fulcrom stole a quick glance to check the door was closed properly.

'Now the Emperor's worried, Fulcrom. He's convinced Villjamur is very quickly falling to the underworld and that damn Shalev character is causing him a massive headache.'

'I can well understand,' Fulcrom agreed.

'Urtica claims that the woman is behind most of the current crime, especially the acts of terrorism plaguing every military station and every shop on these outer levels, including the attack on the Jorsalir Bell Spire. City patrols are in a snit. Morale is shot to shit.'

'And he has a plan?' Fulcrom suggested.

Warkur regarded him with a glare that said *shut up*. 'Yeah. Emperor Urtica has a plan all right. There's this special project he won't talk about, and he needs staff from the Inquisition to help. I can't spare all that many men. In fact, I can only spare one.'

'And that's me?'

'And that's you.'

'What do you need me to do?'

'Good question.' Warkur leaned back in the chair with a sigh. 'I'm not entirely sure what the role will be, but it needs someone efficient and alert, apparently. Something to do with new technologies, so no doubt you'll have some of those cultist bastards hanging around. You're young, you've got a good brain, and you're about as thorough as we get in

55

this business. Just look at this damn office of yours for a start.'

'Thank you, sir.'

'Don't thank me yet. I've not got a clue what you'll be doing – could be hell for all I know. Thing is, Urtica trusts *you specifically* – when your name came up he remembered you from when you discovered who was behind the raid on the Treasury a few years back.'

'He remembers that?'

'Politicians have a long memory when it suits them.'

'When would you like me to start?' Fulcrom asked.

'Later today. You'll need to go up to Balmacara after noon. It's a special kind of project, and since this kind of work might be new to the Inquisition, I'm putting you in charge of all *special* projects – your own department. Given that you're working with the Emperor and might not be completely able to follow our routines, then it might as well be you.'

'Might I ask how many are in this department, sir?' Fulcrom asked.

'Just you.'

*

After processing some administration of overnight detainees, Fulcrom took one of the Inquisition horses from the rear stables and rode up the levels of the city. Drizzly mist had drifted in from the coast, tainting the air with its chill, and many of the tall buildings dissolved into its mass.

Villjamur was layered like a cake, seven tiers in all. Fulcrom liked to boast he could run a circuit of the second level in two hours. The vast, house-rammed platforms were built in enormous arcs. The layers backed onto the caves at one end and, at the front, onto the city's walls, which prevented any invading army from penetrating. The higher people lived was a general indication of the more money they had, and the formidable dark structure of Balmacara, the Imperial residence, dominated the city's skyline, and could just about be spotted from every level.

Surrounding him were whitewashed or pebble-dashed structures, or faded thin limestone houses three or four floors high that leaned precariously into each other. Timbers seemed about to buckle around their midriff, but still these old buildings held themselves with a fading dignity. Traders moved back and forth from the many irens throughout the city, or to the shops higher up, whilst citizens, layered up in furs or rain capes, rooted around the wares, or headed to a tavern or bistro.

Fulcrom's mare sauntered gingerly along the cobbled streets, and he made a point to greet as many people as he could. Citizens were worried – sure, there was significantly more crime these days, but people's fear of it was far greater than the reality. The way some people spoke, it was as if the city had crumbled and Caveside gangs were in control. The reality was far from that; though Fulcrom had had his work cut out in dealing with burglaries and violent assaults and muggings, at least he wasn't investigating murders.

So what could the Emperor want with him? And what exactly was he going to be doing? Fulcrom explored the depths of his mind, but aside from the connection that Warkur had mentioned there was nothing he could think of. Perhaps it was something to do with the case he and Jeryd had worked on, when they helped the refugees . . .

No, you're just being paranoid. It was only Jeryd who was known to be involved, no one else.

More likely it was that Fulcrom had been selected because it was well known that he had no life outside of the Inquisition – a sobering thought. He had no partner to attend to now, and his only family in the city were very distant relations. *Yes, I'm a loner in this world, but I'm happy enough.*

At each level he accessed, even after showing his medallion

bearing the angular symbol of the Inquisition's crucible, guards searched Fulcrom thoroughly. Soldiers had garrisoned themselves in small stations on each level and, with the recent attacks, it was procedure for random stop-and-searches of civilians. He knew better than to make a fuss. He would rather set an example that if it was all right for the Inquisition to put up with this, then citizens could too. At least he was permitted up here – most of the citizens had to possess specific written documentation in order to head upwards.

Ever since the incident at the Bell Spire, the anarchist movement which originated and operated deep within the caves, Urtica had ruled with an iron fist. Fulcrom was especially surprised – not too long ago, the anarchists were a joke collective of angry and bitter individuals who knew little of politics. But ever since Shalev had arrived, only days after the legendary Night Guard soldiers had left for the north, the anarchists had suddenly become something to worry about.

*

'No, the Council were not in the Bell Spire,' declared Emperor Urtica, commander of the Urtican Empire, ruler of seven islands of the Boreal Archipelago and, Fulcrom had to confess, a man with a bit of a temper on him, 'because I'm not that fucking stupid.'

Fulcrom should have known better than to ask the obvious question, even a few weeks after the event, but he didn't expect the Emperor to be so ... *sharp* in his response.

An aura of fear purveyed the golden halls of Balmacara. Gossip rippled through the administrative staff and servants, and filtered out to the rest of the city. All the stories he had heard filtered back into his mind.

Urtica was in his late forties, tall, and with short, dark hair showing a lot of grey. His grey tunic showed just under a purple robe – which differed from the green of the other councillors, but similar enough to suggest he wanted to be seen as a man of the people. There was definitely a charm about him, some innate handsomeness in his symmetrical features and broad chin, but any pretensions to glamour were cast aside the instant he opened his mouth.

'My apologies, my Emperor, the Inquisition only gets few briefings on these matters,' Fulcrom muttered humbly. 'And I knew, of course, that you all survived – however, I merely spoke rhetorically, in appreciation of your tactical awareness.'

'Yes, well . . . all right then,' Urtica said. 'Just try not to use honeyed words too much. That's all everyone else does around here.'

The room was ornate, with huge mirrors and portraits and a fireplace so big a bull could stand in it. Light from the numerous windows lit the room with a dream-like haze. Urtica was seated behind a vast marble desk, edged with garish gold-leaf trim. Resting neatly upon it was what appeared to be a draft of the *People's Observer*, Urtica's new Imperial newspamphlet after he had closed down the others in the city. Copies of this journal were issued free, both on the outer levels as well as Caveside. Some were even being shipped to the Empire's outposts, so that the various por-treeves, commissioners and commanders might dictate Imperial information to their subordinates. Pencil marks were scattered about its surface – corrections, Fulcrom assumed. He had only seen one copy of *People's Observer*, and knew by now that it would never deal with events worth debating. For the most part, it seemed to discuss the dealings of various lords and ladies and socialites, with the occasional terse update on the war that was about to start in Villiren, where the legendary Night Guard had been despatched.

Urtica went on to explain how he had escaped being blown up at the Bell Spire. He'd made sure that he leaked a false location of the Council, as he did every time, and then changed the real venue at the last moment. Ever since the Atrium had been set alight by terrorists shortly after the former Empress Rika escaped, he knew better than to trust people in Balmacara. Twenty days had passed since that room had gone up in smoke, twenty days of total lockdown across Villjamur, and still, despite the amplification of military personnel, some ... some bloody *terrorists* had managed to get through their security and wreck an iconic structure of the city.

'*Bastards!*' Urtica slammed his metal cup against the desk, and it rattled to a halt – utterly dented from his venom.

'Indeed,' Fulcrom echoed.

'I understand you were one of the only riders who managed to get near the bastards?' Urtica sprawled back in his massively ornate wooden chair and placed his boots on the desk, a perfect posture of contemplation.

'That's right. They are, or were, working with cultists, according to your Imperial briefings.' And Fulcrom described what he witnessed on that day.

'Cultists are a very powerful lot ...' With a sudden calm, Urtica began to guide the conversation somewhere else. These were all things the Emperor must have been told long after the incident – he was therefore now testing Fulcrom.

Fulcrom was getting nervous. He potentially had a long career ahead of him, and right now that seemed to be in a vulnerable position.

Urtica continued. 'The incident at the Bell Spire was just one of many, but it is getting too close for comfort. I have no idea how this crime wave has flourished, but flourish it has. They say they are anarchists, and that they are claiming the city for the people. Roughly translated, at the moment that means they are undermining authority – *my* authority.

'Their politics have begun to have a new texture entirely – even when there was that minor riot months ago, they were a laughable lot. Not now. They're organized. Their leaflets have made their way about the city. There are intelligence reports of city intellectuals joining their schemes, educated men and women becoming bloody turncoats. They talk about things like wage slavery and self-organization. They recite extracts from what they claim are Council documents, and want to show the city how the functions of the Council and the Inquisition do not work for the good of the populace.'

Fulcrom shook his head. 'Appalling, my Emperor.' Though he was quietly disgusted with how little information made its way into the Inquisition channels. Much of this was news to him.

'Lies spread like a disease, Fulcrom. Meetings are being held in the dark, in undisclosed corners of the city, and whenever the military arrive they find only empty rooms. There is talk that money has become *redundant* in some Caveside zones, that goods are being provided for free amongst certain groups. It is said that the Cavesiders think Shalev is some kind of saviour, but you and I know better. She is a violent terror-maker.'

'I was reading a report only this morning, my Emperor,' Fulcrom replied. 'Shops are being targeted for robberies. Military personnel are being beaten up on the streets. Those on the higher levels of the city live in constant fear.'

'And that's something I will not allow. I don't need to tell you how much work this is causing us, being in the Inquisition.'

A dignified smile from Fulcrom's lips. 'We're certainly stretched.'

Urtica acknowledged his words. 'You people work hard. I myself have agents who have infiltrated all of this nonsense only so far, but these people are highly organized, and I don't like it one bit. I cannot allow for miscreants to dominate the affairs of the Empire.'

Fulcrom loathed the sycophantic language he was using. After all, this man before him was responsible for trying to murder the refugees outside the city gates. 'You sound like you have a plan, my Emperor.'

'That's right.' Urtica lowered his feet and leant forward across the desk, his gaze holding Fulcrom's own, analysing him. 'Now, so far the city guard have proven useless and, for all I know, those ruffians are mixed up in it all. But you, Fulcrom – as a member of the Inquisition, who I believe I can trust – are going to be part of my plans.'

'I'm absolutely honoured,' Fulcrom lied.

*

Urtica had made a pact with cultists. That was, at first, all he would say.

The two of them strode towards a meeting chamber in a distant corner of Balmacara, one tucked inside the rock which the residence backed onto. Servants and administrative staff fluttered around the Emperor like moths to a light, and Fulcrom noticed how their expressions were keen, stressed and frantic with worry that they might commit a gaucherie before him.

The corridors were, at first, ostentatious – decadent cream tiles, statues and busts and paintings, the light of a thousand lanterns and candles flickering in the gold trim. Then a mere carpet, yesteryear's decorations, busts of lesser-respected figures. And as Fulcrom descended into Caveside itself, a change to raw stone and crude cressets that emitted a dreary light, a corridor devoid of life save the two bodyguards Urtica had enlisted to follow from a distance.

Two doors on the right, one made of iron, and Urtica wrenched down the handle, heaved it open. The guard the other side moved hesitantly then snapped to attention.

'And I suppose you call this security?' Urtica sneered at the massive hulk of protection. 'I could have been absolutely anyone. I could have killed you.'

'Apologies, my Emperor. Won't 'appen again, sir.'

'Make sure it doesn't.' Urtica plunged past the man and into the chamber, while Fulcrom calmly followed.

Around a vast circular oak table, three people were seated, all wearing the cloaked and hooded garb typical of cultists. There was nothing on the walls here, no ornamentation, nothing grand – and, in fact, the stone had been carved from the caves themselves, a rippled and textured effect that made bold shadows from the light of the wall lanterns. It seemed the important thing about this room was that it was kept away from prying eyes.

Those around the table all stood as Urtica settled himself, then motioned for them to all be seated again. 'Please,' he said, and indicated a vacant chair to Fulcrom.

Urtica made the introductions. Two men and the woman to one side were cultists from various sects that – as far as Fulcrom could tell – had been offered wealth and security to work on behalf of the Empire.

'You three know the background,' Urtica continued. 'Investigator Fulcrom here doesn't.' He turned to face Fulcrom. 'They have been assisting me with a rather special project. Despite our best efforts to close down movement throughout the city, to pour military personnel into the streets, the violence from the caves keeps escalating.'

Fulcrom regarded him coolly. 'It's understandable you wish for this to end, as do we in the Inquisition.'

'And this is where our cultist friends come in,' Urtica smiled. 'They're in the final stages of developing their technologies to a level where they can blend with flesh and bone. You have heard of the famed resistances given to the members of the elite Night Guard, now assembled in Villiren. Well this is slightly different. These cultists can transform a human and rumel. They can *enhance* one to the point of endowing special powers.' In a posture of pride, Urtica leaned back, his arms folded.

'You don't want me...' Fulcrom tried his best not to sound too apprehensive. He loosened his collar.

'No of course not,' Urtica laughed. 'We already have three individuals in mind for the job.'

'Who are they?' Fulcrom asked. 'And how do you see me fitting into this scheme?'

'Obviously we need three individuals we can not only trust,

but tolerant to the process – we'll be endowing them with supreme powers, and I'm afraid we've lost some early volunteers throughout the process, since not everyone is up to the task. So we will require people who we have some ... leverage over, as a way of securing trust.'

'Blackmail?' the investigator added.

'It is merely a security, you understand. They will be the owners of amazing anatomies. Essentially we will be creating a new form of individual to help protect the city, a hero to the people – no, more than that. A superhero if you will, more than someone who can front an army. We need these new-style crime-fighters in order to tackle these anarchists and all the terror plaguing my city.'

Fulcrom remained wide-eyed. The cultists simply slumped back in their chairs with hubris.

Urtica continued. 'And you, Investigator Fulcrom, are to be their liaison with the law. In fact, we will want you to work closely with them so that they have access to all levels of information in the Inquisition, and – according to your superior officers – you have a very deft touch with people. These individuals will require managing, in order to produce steady performances. You are to brief them on troubling cases, and all the necessary leads.'

'Superhero,' Fulcrom echoed, too scared to question the decision.

The cultists then explained the projects in a manner riddled with meaningless jargon. They spoke of complex surgeries and talked of specimens. Each of them took it in turns to lecture on various aspects of the process – meta-anatomy, metallic enhancement, organ replacement, rewiring.

Urtica knew all he needed to, and even Fulcrom could see that he also did not comprehend what was being discussed here.

'So, investigator. Can we guarantee your assistance in the matter?'

'You can indeed. Can I ask who it is that you've selected to form this new trio?'

'Of course,' Urtica declared. 'We've already got one of them incarcerated and we want you to be there tonight to see the next being . . . *initiated*. This one shouldn't be too difficult to persuade. In fact, you know him already.'

SEVEN

The best parties are the ones you don't plan, Fulcrom thought to himself as he meandered about the penthouse apartment situated on the fifth level of the city. That was probably why he could never organize a decent one himself: he was a ruthless planner, so any gatherings he conducted – rare though they were – were too precise, too stale and awkward for anyone to really enjoy themselves.

But this, Fulcrom thought, was a thoroughly ostentatious affair. Say what you want about the man, but Aide Tane knew something about putting people in a room and creating a good atmosphere. Daughters of landowners were dancing with investigators and sons of councillors and those with connections throughout the city.

Tane, in his short time spent with the Inquisition, was already a legend for hosting these events – his parties were whispered about long before and long after each night had ended. In his high-ceilinged, modern apartment, with those new-style paintings, white-tiled floors, ornate cressets, and the coloured sculptures made by the hands of Villjamur's famous glassmakers, men and girls – rumel and human – would convene to forget about the rising levels of crime and the ice age and the far-off war in Villiren.

They tipped wine down their throats. They brushed their lips casually across those of a stranger. Fulcrom was only too aware that they did this because they wanted to forget. On some nights, in the wealthy quarters, you might have several parties going on simultaneously, and each would contain a board with the evening's scheduled dances, so couples and groups could plan their entertainment well in advance.

Little of this appealed to Fulcrom; he could not rid himself of the thought of the refugees outside who were probably perishing in the plummeting temperatures.

In one corner, two young men around the same age as Tane, in their late twenties, were busy showing off the hilts on their new swords, and testing the steel. Behind them a girl was on her toes whilst she said something discreetly into another man's ears. The musicians – lutists, drummers and singers fresh from the underground scene – carved amazing melodies and rhythms into the night. All the latest fashions were on parade – high collars, thick, low-cut dresses, and above-the-knee boots. Someone opened a window to rid the room of the humidity of so many bodies – a miraculous gesture considering the freezing conditions outside – and a cool wind brought in the scent of the pine forests.

One of the rumel investigators sauntered up to Fulcrom and, with toxic breath, muttered, 'Say, that Tane, he makesh ... makesh a terrible inveshtigator's aide, but throwsh one helluva night, ah'll give him that.'

Idiot, Fulcrom thought. But then again, perhaps he was right. Would Tane ever make a good aide? The man had been attempting to pass major exams for four years now. If it wasn't for all his questionably large trust funds, which he so helpfully donated to supplying the Inquisition ... *Don't be so hard on the lad*, Fulcrom told himself. *Not tonight.*

Girls kept sauntering up to Fulcrom in dresses which weren't fit for an ice age. Pretty young things with wide-eyed looks that promised the world, and when they spoke to him they licked their lips. 'Why, I just *love* handsome rumels like yourself.' 'You're so fine looking, and people speak so well of your deeds.' 'How come you don't settle down with someone?'

Maybe Fulcrom was too polite, too diffident to really enjoy being a part of this lifestyle. He cringed at their suggestive words and kindly declined their offers. All the time, Ghale, the Inquisition receptionist, was dancing with some other rumel, constantly glancing towards Fulcrom to see if he was looking her way.

Fulcrom sighed. Would he ever be ready to love again? *Maybe some things I won't ever get over*, he thought. *How many years has she been gone now? It's a good thing you're a workaholic.*

A conversation behind him caught his attention: 'I don't know why he bothers. Everyone knows he's bloody incompetent.'

They were senior administrative staff from the Inquisition, black-skins who he'd met only in passing, the kind who hid behind their books rather than step outside to do a day's graft on the streets.

'Indubitably,' one continued, 'but he's minted, so they say. Arch Investigator knew his family, allegedly.'

'How did they get so rich anyhow?' said the other, garbed in a red tunic. 'And why's he even bothering to work if he possesses such . . . ?'

Fulcrom peered across to Tane, who was suddenly standing before them: tall, blond, blue-eyed, and dressed immaculately in a purple tunic with gold detailing and buttons. Good-looking, the kind of man who bled charm, and even though he had witnessed this insulting conversation, Tane maintained a smile – his final barrier against what was being said.

He sighed and leant down to address the two who were bad-mouthing him. The slender human seemed to let the rage come then go with his breath. 'Because, my dear fellows, some of us actually want to do some good in the world. Have you perhaps considered that, chaps?'

'Tane, look . . . Sorry, we just didn't realize you were there.'

'Which, of course, makes it quite all right?' They stood and backed off, smiling tentatively. Tane's height bestowed on him the advantage of looking down upon their exit, as they squirmed through the mass of drunken bodies.

The slender human sighed, closed his eyes as the sound of the music washed over him, and Fulcrom had to feel sorry for him. He stepped over to place a hand on Tane's shoulder – *tonight, poor Tane, you will find you have purpose in life.*

'I wouldn't worry about them, Tane,' Fulcrom said. 'Your time will come – sooner than you think.'

*

However, Fulcrom didn't expect Urtica's agents, some of his new secret guard, to claim Tane so late in the evening. The idea was to strike while the party was in full flow, to frighten Tane in front of so many people – to batter his ego into submission. Fulcrom had his doubts about this method, would have preferred something more cooperative, but the Emperor had initially wanted to use even more force. This was to be a more diplomatic solution.

The partygoers looked ready to push on through till dawn. It was late, way past thirteen, when the door burst open and four figures in tight grey clothing, wide-brimmed hats and with scarves around their mouths, marched arrogantly into the room.

Everything happened in the candlelight.

Matching Tane for height, they hauled the man up from his seat to meet him eye to eye. The few conscious people in the room turned to regard the scene, and Fulcrom waved for the grey coats to stay calm. 'It's fine, guys.' He knew they needed to put fear into the man, but they looked ready to pulverize him.

So these were the Emperor's special agents, the ones he was getting to do his dirty work behind closed doors, a more sinister replacement for the Night Guard. They gave him the creeps, but that was all right – the fear, he knew, was important.

69

'What . . . what have I done?' Tane spluttered, his mannered cool suddenly nowhere at hand. He glanced at each of the grey coats in turn, a look of startled exasperation on his face.

'We're going to *sort you out*, Tane,' one of them sneered, Fulcrom couldn't discern which.

'You're not wanted in the Inquisition, so we hear,' another hissed, grabbing Tane by his collar. 'Some say you're a spoilt little fuck.'

'Who claims such nonsense?' Tane asked anxiously, struggling to pull his head back.

'Just a rumour – the same rumour that says you're a good man,' Fulcrom intervened; the grey coats were enjoying their act a little too much for his liking.

The one holding him paused to look at Fulcrom, then released Tane, who brushed himself down. He now stared at Fulcrom with renewed awe.

'Maybe I am, but I don't see what business it is of anyone here.' Tane made sure he addressed all the grey coats. 'And just who the devil are you anyway?'

'You mean well, sure, but you're an incompetent fool,' another man in grey hissed, his eyes flaring with venom. 'This is common knowledge.'

'Look, I'm afraid you just can't come in here . . .' Tane tried to push through them but the group hauled him back, thrust him into the chair and slapped his face – Fulcrom thought it was probably a good thing he was still drowsy from all the drink. A few of the partygoers rubbernecked from their slumped positions, and a couple were still kissing on a chair in the far corner, oblivious to the scene.

'Shut up and listen, *fuckwit*. You're keen, but you've got problems, we know this. We also know how your parents got their money, and we know why you're so keen to help the Inquisition.'

Tane's eyes widened. *That's right*, Fulcrom thought, *this is*

what really frightens the good man Tane. It frightens him to have
his secrets paraded in front of so many people.

'We know why you're throwing all these parties,' a grey
coat whispered, 'buying friendships, making people happy,
and you think your feeble attempts at playing investigator
aide will rid you of some of the guilt—'

'All right, all right!' Tane shouted. 'You've proved your
point. Gentlemen, you have earned my attention. Now, please
– what on earth do you want with me?'

'You'd do well to listen to these fellows, Tane,' Fulcrom
interrupted. 'Don't mess around or they'll make life damn
awkward for you.'

'Are you *with* them?'

'Look, the city has need of someone like you, Tane. Someone who's honest and keen. Someone who we know will
serve us without running off. Someone with whom we have
an understanding – one that says you will be . . . *compliant.*'

'Blackmail, I suppose,' Tane observed.

'Hey, he's not as stupid as everyone makes him out to be,'
one of the others said, and Fulcrom glared at him.

They didn't need to humiliate the man. Tane would come
all right, all they needed to do was make him feel threatened
in the right way – publicly. A grey coat grabbed Tane's mop
of hair and pulled his head back, though to Tane's credit, he
didn't let the pain show.

'Compliance is what impresses us the most,' the agent said.

'So I'm compliant,' Tane replied. 'Just let me go.'

The grey coat turned to him and nodded; Fulcrom was
surprised that the man actually responded to his signal by
releasing his grip. Tane lunged backwards, and took a casual
stance. How much authority did Fulcrom possess exactly?

'He's yours – you can handle it from here,' said one of the
agents. To Tane he said, 'If you fuck up at all, and Fulcrom
gives us the nod, we will not hesitate to hunt you down

wherever you're hiding and kill you in a slow and painful manner.'

'Fine,' Tane whispered. 'But, look, I don't even know what you want with me.'

With a surprising calm, they all slipped out of the room one by one, leaving the door ajar.

A little breathless now, Tane dusted himself down and composed himself, then turned to Fulcrom. 'I knew you kept yourself to yourself, but this is a bit of a surprise.'

'Not only to you,' Fulcrom replied.

'What do you need me to do?'

'We're taking you deep into Balmacara. But first, take a look around, remember these faces, these people you're trying to impress. You want everyone to love you . . .' Fulcrom leant in closer to breathe, 'Think how popular you'll be if they knew where you got your money from?'

The expression on Tane's face, one of utter resignation, confirmed to Fulcrom that they had him on board, that he would cooperate.

'Exactly. They'll probably want to lynch you themselves. You have been *chosen*, Tane. Don't let me down.'

'OK. At least let me clean up this mess before we go.'

The next one wouldn't be so easy, Fulcrom realized. The next one wouldn't respond to intimidation.

*

There was a riotous noise outside his window. A drunken youth out in the ice decided that so-and-so was sleeping with his girlfriend, and now was the time to pick a fight in order to resolve the issue. Vuldon heard the way the kid's sword was unsheathed, with great strain or hesitation. The guy was either emotionally unstable – and would get himself killed; or he was too cold to fight properly – and would still get himself killed. These weren't the conditions in which to start pointless fights.

Villjamur isn't a nice place any more. Barely was in the first place ... His old life flashed back briefly: knife fights in the dark; brutal combat on bridges; arriving too late and discovering blood-covered floors and severed heads ... *No, perhaps those days were bad enough.*

Vuldon closed the shutters behind the thin glass to keep in the warmth, poured himself a glass of cheap Black Heart Rum, lit an arum weed roll-up, slumped in a battered leather chair and, as he did every night, dredged his memories for something to cling to.

As he brooded in his isolated terrace apartment, alone in the darkness, he couldn't quite make the memories become continuous. They came piecemeal, these images of his life, brief and distorted. Nearly every night he'd review a particular moment with distant melancholy.

Those days are long gone, Vuldon, so let it be.

But he failed to abide by his own mantra. Every muscle that ached, every bone that didn't sit quite right, he could assign the probable cause, or guess at things that may or may not have been the root of his pain: a broken-up knife fight or a clifftop scramble or slipping from a bridge whilst trying to save someone.

Thirty years ago, almost to the day.

Thirty years and now they were coming for him again, the Emperor's men. Agents who worked behind the layers of the city, men that not even the Night Guard knew about. Vuldon knew them all right – he'd worked with their likes before, in whatever guise each city ruler decided to cast them.

Vuldon wasn't stupid. He'd been waiting. He'd tracked their movements two hours before: their trademark loitering, the way they'd check street corners and grace rooftops. They were there if you knew where to look. They were heading for his home on the second level of Villjamur, a dreary third-floor hole above a closed-down tavern; about as far from his former glamour as he could possibly be.

They kicked open his door whilst he slouched on a chair in

the dark, the bottle of Black Heart Rum on the floor beside him, a roll-up between two of his fingers, its embers glowing in the half-light.

In their long grey coats and wide-brimmed hats they stood around him, scarves across their mouths, mere shadows against the dusk spilling through his open doorway, five of them in all, tall and slender. They were lingering like wraiths, with their hands in pockets, cool and aloof. Same as always, they didn't like to get too close to people like him who knew their way around a fight – didn't want him to see who they were.

Fuckers.

'What took you so long?' Vuldon muttered. Arum smoke circled around his reclined form. 'You lot are more cautious than ever. Least you're not as clumsy as the city guard.'

'Gotta be these days, Vuldon,' one of them said, a harsh and wispy voice. 'There's a lot going on in Villjamur – most of it underground.'

'Yeah? I don't pay attention to any of that any more.' A drag on the roll-up. 'So what do you want?'

'You, Vuldon. We've come for *you.*'

'The hell do you want me for? You think you can use violence on me?' He laughed, though the noise seemed more hollow than he would have liked.

'No violence here, we know it won't work – you're too stubborn anyway.' This voice was different – firm and polite, probably the leader. He spotted a tail wafting behind them – that meant a rumel, and that reeked of the Inquisition.

'You got that right,' he replied.

'You're a legend, Vuldon,' the voice continued. 'In fact you're *the* Legend.'

'Legends don't live above a grotty tavern.' Vuldon dismissed them with heavy hand gestures, palming them away, *leave me alone.* 'I'm too old,' he repeated in his dreary room, unable to see much but their silhouettes. 'You only know me from the stories. Isn't how it was. I'm getting on for sixty now.'

'We have cultists who can sort that out,' the rumel said.

'We have new techniques,' another chimed, one of the agents.

Vuldon couldn't see their faces, not that it mattered. They gave him the creeps, the way they'd come in and invade people's evenings like this. 'Leave me to die in peace. I can't do anyone any harm that way.'

'Emperor Urtica has made a request for you to return.'

'Urtica?' Vuldon enquired. 'What happened to the Jamur girls?'

'Don't you read the news? They've long gone, tried to kill all the refugees. Urtica took over, arranged to have them executed but they managed to escape. Urtica's in charge of the Empire and Villjamur.'

Vuldon didn't seem too bothered that the Jamur lineage had cleared out of the city. Jamur blood sent a rage burning in his heart.

Thirty years ago ... 'So what does *Urtica* want of me exactly?' Vuldon demanded. 'Have you taken a good look at this place?' He struck a match and fumbled around to light a lantern.

Vuldon gestured at himself: he was standing there wearing a gown and loose, ragged breeches. Everything in his house was as crippled as he was: strips of curtains, stained carpets, dishes he hadn't washed in ages, piles of paper in one corner. Grey hairs on his once-muscular chest seemed to stand out as a sign of his age, so he covered himself up, suddenly aware of what he had been – a long time ago.

'You stink,' one of the agents said. 'This whole fucking place stinks.'

'Not exactly made much of myself these days. Told you, this isn't like the stories. You were probably kids when you were hearing those for the first time.'

'You could be *someone* again, Vuldon,' the rumel said, a

brown-skin, with more than a hint of optimism in his voice. 'If you come with us, we'll see to it that you're treated well.'

'Why me?' Whatever answer they gave wouldn't satisfy him: it wasn't how these people worked. These agents would tell you only what could influence you – truth and lies, well, they never came into the picture.

'Because you were the first one and the best, Vuldon,' the rumel declared. 'You were the Legend. You know how it all works, you know how to play this game. You understand criminals better than anyone else – hell, we've all heard tales, even in the Inquisition.'

'That's the problem – plenty of tales, not enough fact.'

'You've got your old job waiting for you, in a new guise. We're offering a chance to reinvent the Legend – all you need to do is come with us.'

As they spoke he glanced to the floor, walking his mind back in time. 'I don't care for that name any more. I've not thought about him in decades – just leave me alone.'

'You're lying,' the rumel said. 'I can hear it in your voice. Think on – *Legend*. We'll be back tomorrow evening.'

Vuldon eventually looked up but they'd gone and left the door open. The family next door were starting to surface, their kids screaming the place down. A cat trotted by in the corridor, looking in tentatively, nosing the air, then moved on, thinking better of it. Vuldon peered around his room at his meagre possessions: decrepit furniture, a few old books, a stack of blank parchment, empty bottles of alcohol and ink, unwashed plates.

Brushing his thick stubble, Vuldon chuckled. *Not even an animal will venture in here.*

He felt too jaded to close the door, but eventually he forced himself to do so.

With a groan he took the lantern and shuffled slowly to his bedroom, but pausing by a cupboard. A minute passed, maybe two, as he contemplated what was beyond.

When he finally nudged it open a bar of light fell across some of his old clothes – the ones from way back. Dust motes filled the air. His fingers walked across some of those items, across some of his memories. There it was, his old uniform, the one he wore when he was someone else, but he didn't want to get it out just yet.

No, he wasn't ready for any of that, and shut the door, and headed to his bedroom.

As he lay in bed that night, his own history came back to provoke his dreams.

EIGHT

Lan awoke in a cell, her body thronging in agony. The brick walls around her drifted in and out of focus. More than once she was forced to lie sideways on the mattress to relieve the pain, her hands bound behind her, rope around her torso, only to stare at the ceiling, her head aching as if she was on the bad end of a riotously good night's drinking.

Everything since her return from Ysla had merged into a sequence of disconnected images. Had the cultists done something to her head and messed with her memories?

No, they had not, and the realization came back to her like an echo.

*

The cultists had taken care to provide her with forged documents to allow her back into Villjamur, as a woman, and without any attention being drawn to her history.

As she rode up to the main gates of Villjamur, guided only so far by the cultist associate on horseback, she had been mortified to witness the tent-city outside, where refugees had massed. A humanitarian disaster spread for half a mile along the main road into Villjamur, a settlement of tin shacks and canvas houses and small pit fires that leaked paltry trails of smoke. Grubby and layered in rags, people bore expressionless faces, yet eyed her closely as she rode through their mass. Now and then she spotted people clothed in fine Jorsalir robes, handing out flatbreads. It was a haunting trek up to the gates.

After passing through the high levels of security at the gates of the city, a task made effortless due to the fine faked documents produced by Cayce, there was a small administrative matter to attend to, where she had to collect her key from one of the sub-Council posts annexed to the Villjamur Inquisition, which merely required a number to be recited and money would be handed over.

Is it really that easy to be reborn in Villjamur?

She eventually strode back to her family's old home, a large two-up, two-down on the fourth level of the city.

Nostalgia washed over her as the lanes and crumpled granite facades ignited her memories. When she stood inside for the first time, smelling the musk of her dead parents, she immediately began the process of shredding all traces of her former existence – letters and deeds and heirlooms. The Caine family name was assiduously eradicated from Villjamur. Despite the fact that she had been left the property, despite clear evidence that her parents must still have possessed some love for her, for her own sanity she needed to purge the past. Like herself, she would have the house transformed. She had suspected that many of the rooms would hold bad memories for her, but she was relieved to discover that she had blocked much of her childhood from her mind. Memories were unreliable at the best of time, but over the years she had accepted what her parents felt towards her, accepted their hatred of who and what she was. As she let them go for the last time, she felt relief. Lan repeated to herself that people only ever feared and loathed anything that was different. Her transformation was nearing completion.

*

Lan had been in Villjamur for twenty days since her operation on Ysla, and her body still hadn't fully recovered from the procedures. Bruises had formed in surprising places, and she discovered internal aches in previously unknown regions. Just underneath her ribs, a small, knife-thin wound was noticeable, but aside from that there was very little in the way of actual scarring. She felt moments of acute weakness and dizzy spells and occasional nausea but, over time, they too diminished. By the twentieth day of her return, she was feeling well again.

Ever so slowly, she was learning what it was like to be a woman in Villjamur. It was years since she had lived in the city, and there was a lot to get used to.

Lan was now fully – anatomically – a woman. She possessed the same rights as a woman, and she would be treated by others like a woman. But the city, it seemed, was not constructed for the benefit of womankind. Doors were opened, quite literally, and that was rather lovely at first, but she became ultra-sensitive to further gestures from men. She did not feel especially pretty, but could feel their gazes. Looks from others were penetrating and loaded with new psychology, and other women seemed to judge her out-of-touch fashions. Whenever she spoke up in the iren, the traders would patronize her. She sought employment – she had enough money for the short term, but wanted to be out doing something, engaging with the world, and with enough wealth to live well. She wandered from street to street, up and down the levels for several days, exploring what work was available.

The few job offers available were positions such as waitressing or making clothing. Guilds seemed to bar many female members, and she could hardly pursue a 'career' as housewife. If she really wanted she could have joined the military, who accepted women, but a life enduring extreme conditions at the fringes of the Empire wasn't quite what she had in mind. Still, she had time on her hands, which meant she possessed something greater than most women in the city: the luxury of choice.

During her routine search for employment a bizarre sense of paranoia followed her. Whether it was acclimatizing to her new body, or something sinister, she didn't know, but she couldn't help feel that she was being actively *monitored*. Were the cultists observing her in some perverse reality experiment? Cayce did suggest he might try to locate her at some point to check on her adaptation to the magic – no, *technology*, that was what he called it, and he corrected her every time she used the 'm' word.

Maybe they were watching her. Maybe they were keeping her safe.

*

One morning, with sleet in the air and a distant tang of frying food, Lan was browsing stalls, searching for spices to cook her evening meal. The iren was packed with soldiers, their swords unsheathed and exposed to the crowds.

Lan wondered why such an innocent location required so many soldiers from a Regiment of Foot, in their intimidating mud-brown uniforms and cheap armour. The iren was busy nonetheless, with row upon intricate row of commercial activity. Fish traders had all sorts of specimens lined up under coloured awnings, whilst smiths were out hawking their wares – new blades or shields crafted from stronger metal. Cheap gemstones were being promenaded in handcarts that clattered across the cobbles, whilst trails of young women fawned over them. Everywhere were shouts of orders and prices as vendors grilled spiced seafood over hot coals.

'Lan!'

Was that someone calling her name?

'Lan!'

No one in the city could have known her, especially not as she was now. Foolishly, she turned around to see who it was—

Slam. Screams rippled across the plaza.

One of the last images she remembered was of a group of soldiers rushing forward – then retreating under newer orders.

Two punches to her stomach and a strike around her head and she blacked out.

*

Later, when her groggy head cleared, figures garbed in long grey coats with scarves around their mouths came into her cell and bombarded her with questions. Lan was hunched sideways on a mattress, rope around her chest, handcuffs binding her wrists, digging into her skin. Beneath her restraints, she was wearing a thick grey tunic over black breeches, but inexplicably she felt it somehow wasn't enough.

Lan could soon see that the cell was actually more like a bedroom, which was not what she imagined a prison unit to be, and it suggested that she wasn't in immediate trouble. People came into the room. The figures jutted lanterns towards her face with severe motions. Relentlessly they asked her questions, demanding her to confirm details they seemed to already know.

She was forced to confirm she had been taken to Ysla to visit the cultists.

She felt their interrogation to be deeply abusive. Soon she wanted to cry but she wouldn't let herself, not in front of them. It was carefully explained to her that her body had already proven extremely adaptive to ancient technologies. If they knew that, why did they ask questions?

What was it Cayce had said? *Not everyone is as pliable as you.* And the words were repeated back to her at least twice.

At first she told them little – paranoid and deeply afraid that she would lose a sense of her new self, as much as anything else.

Thankfully, after a few hours they untied the rope around her abdomen, and left the room to contemplate her answers. Lan immediately began busying herself by investigating the cuffs around her wrists. Escape artistry wasn't foreign to her: she understood the quirks, the tricks, the insider knowledge. She knew that most handcuffs could be mastered with a pick or even applied pressure, though it would have helped if she had seen the mechanisms beforehand. By touch she guessed these were nothing unusual, and that she could open them with a blow on the right spot. Looking around, she noted a metal ridge on the bed frame. It was an awkward manoeuvre but she managed to twist herself around and, with her hands held behind her, she repeatedly hammered the handcuffs down, close to the hinge. It took eight blows until they sprung open, then she enjoyed letting the pain in her arms subside.

Seems they do not use expensive restraints in Villjamur, she thought, rubbing her wrists.

Her kidnappers returned and didn't quite know what to make of the open cuffs she'd cast down the foot of the mattress, but to her surprise they didn't beat her – instead, they gave her water and good food, flatbreads and spiced curries. Such luxuries confirmed to her that they weren't going to immediately kill her. It was, perhaps, some consolation.

*

A clank of iron woke her. Those grey-coated figures returned, hovering in the doorway. But someone else stepped inside her cell: a tall brown-skin rumel sporting the crimson colours of the Inquisition. His words came with an unusual tenderness.

'Hello, Lan, I'm Investigator Fulcrom. Are you feeling all right? Please, come with us. I'm sorry you've had to go through all of this. They were ... wrong to be so harsh.' Tense glances were exchanged between the investigator and the grey coats. 'We'll explain what we require in a moment.'

Lan pushed herself up from the mattress, spun her legs over the side and brushed back her hair. The rumel took her hand and lifted her to her feet.

'There you are,' he said.

Lan rubbed her eyes and shuffled after them.

Soon they passed through a more civilized location –

smooth walls and floors, cressets giving light and warmth, brass trimmings and skylights. It was daytime at least, but she could see only pale grey clouds. In this rare moment of normal vision, she glanced at the faces of those escorting her, but they were hidden still by the scarves across their faces. With rimmed hats or hoods, only their eyes were exposed – they were all human, all pale, all weirdly androgynous-looking. Aside from the rumel, of course, who now and then turned back to give her reassuring glances.

It took two of them to open the massive oak doors, and she was led through them. The next room was certainly imposing – the movement of air and the echo of boots against stone indicated it was vast. In the dim light she could make out very little, save for the glittering metallic instruments at the far end of the room, like bookshelves, but with wires and vials of fluids. A light shone on them – from them – and they seemed to spark alive.

In the centre of the room were three leather chairs, two were already occupied. Whilst the figures in grey fanned out in a circle around them, she was propelled into the final chair. She peered at the other two present: one was a broad and stocky man who must have been in his fifties. With a square, stubbled jaw, an arm as wide as her thigh, he appeared to be every bit a thug, but there was something immensely sad about his posture: he was slumping – had spent years slumping – and his gaze was directed mainly at the ground. When he did look at her, his vision passed over so casually she might as well have been an item of furniture. He wore black breeches, and a dark red sweater that was too tight for him – he was once heavily muscled, probably still was under a few years of bad living.

The other man was in his late twenties, tall and slender, with blond hair and dazzling blue eyes. He sat back with one shin resting on his other knee, his hands folded casually in his lap as if he was waiting to be served a meal in a bistro. He gave Lan a polite smile, but she was in no mood to return it.

Who were these two? Only the three of them were illuminated by tall lanterns in the centre of the table; the circle of grey coats stood back, in the shadows. Suddenly, the circle parted at one end, and there were others who joined them. Someone whispered the Sele of Urtica, and then she heard that name repeated. Urtica.

It can't be him, she thought. *What would he want with me?*

'I am Emperor Urtica,' the man declared. He was much better-looking than she imagined. The atmosphere in the room changed with his mere presence – it was now soaked with fear. 'This to my right is Investigator Fulcrom.' The brown-skinned rumel, in his crimson robes, moved forward, and gave a warm greeting to them all, before stepping aside for the Emperor to continue.

'You three,' Urtica announced, 'have each been chosen for a reason. All of you are bound, in some way, by your pasts, and I will make it abundantly clear that we will not hesitate to use these pasts against you as a secure bond against the gifts that will shortly be bestowed upon you.'

'Think I give a shit about that?' grunted the broad-shouldered man. His mood was utterly despondent. 'I've no reason to do what you say.'

'I have heard much about you, Vuldon, and admittedly your case is not the same as these two,' Urtica muttered. 'I understand your bitterness. You have other motivations – as do you, Tane. I knew your family well.'

The skinny man sat up and leaned forwards, taking time to compose himself. 'What *exactly* are you insinuating?'

'I will forgive you your rudeness this once,' Urtica replied calmly. 'Investigator, please continue the briefing.' Urtica motioned for the rumel to speak.

'Thank you, my Emperor,' Fulcrom replied, with a small

bow of the head. He turned his attention to the others. 'Tane, you have an unrelenting – if a little unfocused – will to do good. You have a moral code, and this is good. You're also not wanted in the Inquisition, and so your name has been put forward especially for this mission. You should just shut up for once and pay attention – you'll do well out of this . . . if you're *pliable.*'

Tane sat back, disgruntled, possibly weighing up whether or not to make a witticism.

'Vuldon – you used to be a legendary hero of this city. Unlike the others, no one has forced you to be here. Emperor Johynn and his lineage are long gone, so you can put your faith in Urtica, and in what is being offered to you. It's a chance to regain what you once had. *We* can make that happen.'

Vuldon's expression seemed to be hiding years of pain.

'And you, Lan,' Fulcrom turned to her, 'are a fraction more than a coincidence. You have proven remarkably adaptable to cultist technology, according to our notes, and we have had some minor failures with adaptation in earlier experiments. You are resilient and your past career in the circus has given you a useful athleticism, so you seem rather perfect for the forthcoming role. I'm aware of what's gone on and it seems there is a gap in our legal framework when it comes to understanding your transformation. We're therefore going to gloss over such changes in order for one *further* transformation.'

She was totally disarmed by his directness, and also by the way he did not abuse the power of secret knowledge: he was privy to her history, and yet he spoke to her without disrespect.

'And what is our role supposed to be?' Lan enquired.

'You are,' Urtica interrupted, 'to become the Villjamur Knights, protectors of the city. It is a prestigious role.'

So why treat me like shit . . . ?

'You are', he continued, 'to see that the citizens of this ancient city are well protected, but your precise roles in all of this will shortly become a reality. Now that your introductions are over, you should familiarize yourself with each other. You three, and Fulcrom here, are going to be spending a lot of time together.'

'And, pardon me for asking, but why should we do any of this?' Lan asked, feeling no fear of the Emperor, not after all she'd been through. 'It's clear that you need us – or rather, we mean something to you.'

All eyes turned to Urtica as if expecting his rage to be on display. Instead he leant forward onto the table. 'Would you wish to be placed in stocks, and for a crier to announce to the city who you used to be?' The Emperor moved behind her now, and whispered into her left ear, 'Indeed, the cultists did a very good job on you, but it doesn't take much for a crowd in this city to become fearful – hysterical enough to pull you apart with their bare hands. Of course, I would not like to see such an act.'

As Lan let the paranoia sink in, Urtica stood to regard the room. 'Are there any more questions?'

'It's Shalev that's causing you much trouble, isn't it?' Vuldon said, but the Emperor remained silent.

'I thought you didn't pay attention to things these days?' Fulcrom replied.

Vuldon looked away, while Tane cleared his throat and announced, 'I would just like to add that I'm definitely in. I think it's an absolutely super idea.'

'Stop sucking up to him, kid, you don't know what it involves,' Vuldon grunted, glancing up for the first time. 'What're our obligations in all of this? If we agree, what the fuck will you have us doing? Bet we ain't going to be standing on display.'

'I'll leave the particulars for Fulcrom to explain, but we will begin with your transformations this very evening. After that, you will develop into a force used to tackle the great unrest that has been plaguing our city. There will be further training, accommodation and support. As you made perfectly clear, Vuldon, you in particular have no reason to do what I say. Fulcrom will explain the details of what our offer will involve, but now I've Council business to attend to. It has been a pleasure to meet you all, and I hope to see each of you turn in for duty.'

Urtica spun on his heels and, with a nod to Fulcrom, marched from the room. A small body of guards emerged like ghosts from the darkness to escort him out.

In this ensuing silence, Lan, Tane and Vuldon all observed each other with uncertainty.

Fulcrom leaned forward into the light. 'Well, I suppose you're wondering what happens next?'

NINE

Fulcrom was making it up as he went along. The Emperor seemed concerned only with results, the cultists with science, and he alone was charged with organizing three individuals into a crime-fighting unit worthy enough to use the city's name. What's more, due to the nature of his duties he was relieved of some of his general work with the Inquisition and now had been given the broad but spurious command of 'Special Investigations', whatever that meant. Still, this was a challenge. Something new. Something to get his teeth into.

Fulcrom guided them down to cells deep beneath Balmacara, where the cultists had rigged up a palace of technological trinkets. As the group descended a spiral staircase into the cultists' workspace, they watched agape at what was presented. Under arched brickwork stood huge conical devices that hummed with energy. Purple light sparked across the surface of orbs the size of small houses. Shelves were buckling under the weight of coloured jars and blades of all shapes and sizes. The air itself seemed like a living thing – there was an atmosphere of intense anticipation. People expected things, events and history to be generated within these walls.

Nearly a dozen cultists, in their esoteric black outfits, worked diligently by lantern light at tables overflowing with wires and vials and mould-ravaged books. Those who approached treated Lan, Tane and Vuldon with an eerie level of respect, as if they'd already been invested with their supposed powers. A few councillors had drifted down in order to witness their pre-transformation state. Hands were shaken, pleasantries exchanged, and Fulcrom was treated like royalty. But he knew these politicians feared anything the cultists would generate, and their presence was merely a meek declaration of political backing.

Tane was by far the keenest of the group. With much to lose, and few career options, he seemed to make the mental switch to his new life remarkably quickly, and had nothing but bright eyes and quick jokes for the cultists and officials. *His reluctance to take anything seriously is probably why he made an awful investigator's aide.* Vuldon was about as happy as a storm cloud. Fulcrom had made it clear to the man that he could opt out at any point, but Vuldon continued to grumble, 'There's nothing else left for me, that's why I'm here. If you can call it a choice, so be it, but this is the least shit option in life right now.' So Fulcrom steered him away from those with hope-filled eyes, or who expected something more pithy and profound from him.

Lan was an enigmatic woman. Fulcrom watched her the most, since he wasn't convinced of her engagement with the project. If she didn't commit fully, she wouldn't be much use. She was here under pressure, because of her secret – and *what* a secret it was. Marvelling at the talents of cultists, he found it hard to believe she had ever been a man, but forced himself to purge any prejudices from his mind.

Each of the three were taken to a room little bigger than a gaol cell, but within was a comfortable bed, surgical instruments, a changing screen, and lanterns that hung from the curved ceiling. Now they awaited the event that would change their lives.

*

Vuldon was first. His was the simplest procedure of the three, low-risk, merely a modification of the processes used to enhance the legendary Night Guard soldiers. His development was going to be a vastly enhanced musculature, fibres rebuilt, signs of ageing peeled away, giving him unmatched strength. A reconstruction of his sense of dignity, of the quality that made him the legend of the past – and what a legend it had been.

The files the Inquisition had kept on Vuldon had been studied by Fulcrom. It was estimated that, in his few years duration as the city's hero, he had saved three hundred and twenty-three citizens from death or violence; foiled seven attacks by vicious tribes to scale the city walls; saved the then-Emperor twice; prevented a fire from ravaging Balmacara; and saved a small school from a mad-axe murderer. His value was impossible to deny.

Fulcrom asked this figure of dormant pugnacity many gentle, searching questions, seeking to bypass his reluctance to talk. Eventually, hunched on the bed in his rather effeminate white gown, his already powerful shoulders providing an intimidating bulk, Vuldon began to open up. For the first time he gave more than a handful of bitter grunts.

He spoke of the old days. He spoke about the Inquisition in particular. 'Shouldn't like a man who wears those colours.'

'Few citizens do,' Fulcrom replied. 'I know about your past—'

'What you *know*,' Vuldon interrupted, 'is probably the wrong side of the story. Some cleverly spun tale written down in spurious histories. A few edited documents.'

'They were different times, back then,' Fulcrom pleaded. 'A different emperor, a different regime.'

'You think this one's any different? They've only ever got their own interests at heart.'

Vuldon went on to talk about his wife, a glamour girl who ended her life after things went badly for them. 'She drank herself into her coffin after choking on her own vomit,' Vuldon said. 'You know what that's like, investigator? To find the woman you love not able to cope with the fuck-ups you've made – or rather, the fuck-ups blamed on you?'

'I . . . honestly, Vuldon. I'd love to give you some nice line here, but I can't; but if it helps, I understand – I lost a partner, too.'

'You responsible for her death, rumel?'

Fulcrom shook his head. 'What I will say is that it sounds like you hold yourself responsible, which I don't think is fair on yourself. Time can do strange things to one's memories . . .'

Vuldon gave him a brooding glance, and Fulcrom respectfully lowered his eyes. Somewhere, under that hunched and rather wrecked mass, was a skilled and determined human, and Fulcrom would damn well coax it out of him.

'So this new transformation,' Fulcrom said, 'do you think you're ready to go ahead and be part of the Knights? We so desperately need your experience, Vuldon. You were the first of your kind, and you know how these things work. Here's a chance to reclaim your former glories, to make it clear to people that the past was wrong, that the city can trust you again.'

'There's not a lot I can't handle after what I've been through,' Vuldon muttered, lifting his legs up onto the bed, lying down with a deep groan. The hanging lantern made a lot more of the angles of his face, and he appeared truly brutal even in this relaxed pose. 'I'll do what it takes. I've nothing else, though if we're going to undergo such transformations, I'd prefer, where possible, to be renewed – lose the name. The Legend is exactly that, a legend, a myth. Let's keep him that way.'

*

Fulcrom left the room, passing a stream of cultists and surgeons carrying vials and cases, in order to visit the next of the Knights.

He found Tane in repose on his bed, one arm propping up

his head, a half-eaten platter of food by his chest, like some artist's vision of an emperor. 'Fulcrom, old boy, the food here's quite superb. I've just eaten a boatload of fruit which I've never even heard of before, let alone seen.'

Fulcrom had to laugh. 'I hope you're going to take this job seriously.'

'Absolutely.' Tane continued his way through the platter with a wide smile at Fulcrom. He offered some to Fulcrom.

'You don't seem to be taking it seriously,' Fulcrom observed, politely waving away the offer.

'I've spent all my life trying to pass those exams for the Inquisition and I've got nowhere. Now I have been offered a rather lovely route right to the top, avoiding all that street duty nonsense and all those horrid legal texts. Do you honestly think I've no reason to be anything but delighted? I've always wanted to help people, and I can make a real difference being one of the Knights.'

'OK, but don't think you're going to have it all easy. You're going to be transformed, Tane – altered. *Changed*. You'll undergo ailuranthosurgery. Do you know what that means?'

'I was informed that it was something to do with feline-like abilities . . .'

'Werecat, Tane. You'll be merging into a semi-form of a wild animal.'

'Tigers, someone said, yes, yes, yes. They don't sound all that wild, if you ask me. Rather regal from the stories I've heard. Which of course suits me down to the ground.'

Fulcrom felt his frustrations flaring. How could the man be so casual about this? 'But the point remains, Tane, that you're going to be forever different. It will bring with it a whole load of new psychologies.'

'One must allow for risks in life, Fulcrom, in order to progress. Obviously I'm a little nervous—'

A male scream echoed outside along with the sound of roaring static.

Fulcrom tilted his head. 'That's coming your way, I hope you know.'

Tane gaped at him. 'Is it . . . going to hurt?'

'Of course it is, you idiot. You're probably going to ache for days afterwards, and you're . . .' Fulcrom allowed his emotions to simmer. 'Look, just don't make any jokes, don't try to sweet-talk any female cultists, and for Bohr's sake do what they tell you to do. It's for your own good.'

*

Lan was the last of the Knights Fulcrom visited: Her transformation was the most complicated of all, and he prayed to . . . *Well, the god Bohr seems pretty out of touch with all of these procedures, doesn't he?* Fulcrom hoped to whatever powers were involved in all of this that her body could withstand these further changes.

When he reached her, Lan was perched on the edge of her bed, staring deep into a fire burning in the grate, her arms rigid by her side.

'I'm sorry for putting you through such things again,' Fulcrom began.

Lan simply shrugged.

'So you're the only one in the group who doesn't really want to be here?'

Lan glanced up at him, and he could see then that she was a slender lady, with such tight musculature. There was something vaguely familiar about her appearance – she looked very much like someone he once knew . . .

No. Don't think of her now. Lan's hair was long and dark, her fringe bold, and he noticed her nails were well bitten. Her brown eyes displayed a distance that he wondered if she'd put there herself, to cope.

'Well, I've been thinking about it,' she replied. 'The only thing that repulses me is that there is knowledge being used against me – the fact that knowledge is being used to keep me here. The rest, I'm OK with – I maintain that there were nicer ways of asking though.'

'We've got knowledge on the others too, though it doesn't make it any better, I know. It's just a security bond, something to guarantee you'll not abuse your powers – and I want to stress that they aren't my orders, this isn't my style, but I understand that there is a requirement that you yield to the Emperor's will.'

There was a world of thought in her expression, and Fulcrom could tell his words were being analysed. He liked that.

'I did have *some* money,' Lan said, 'but I knew I'd have to get employment eventually, which I knew was going to be limiting, being a woman.'

She stared hard at him then, as if testing him for a response.

'And this . . .' Lan sat up to gesture around the room with one hand. 'This doesn't seem so bad. It's all a little too high profile for my liking, but still. You know, really, they could have just asked me nicely, rather than assaulting me.'

'They need to use fear to get what they want. If it's any help, I've learned from working in the Inquisition that more often than not, you just need to treat people with respect, no matter who they are, and they're more likely to respond positively that way. That's how I would've done it.'

'I like you, Investigator Fulcrom,' Lan said boldly. 'You're probably the first person I've met on Jokull who's treated me as an equal.'

That was a relief.

'Though,' she went on, 'I believe it's freakish that any-one in your position can keep your shoes so remarkably clean.'

He glanced down to his immaculate boots, then ignored her comment. 'Lan, in a few minutes those cultists will treat you . . . just like they're doing with Tane and Vuldon. I'm sorry, but it won't exactly be comfortable.'

'Cultists,' Lan repeated, 'I've noticed that they have a tendency to look at everyone like they're an experiment, which, I guess, is a form of equality.'

'It's a good opportunity, these new transformations,' Fulcrom pressed. 'Especially yours.'

'Gravitational forces,' she breathed. 'That's what they said, isn't it?'

'Yes. You'll more or less receive metallic plates and a whole bunch of stuff I don't quite understand, and they'll enhance your mobility and you'll be able to alter your interactions with gravity. Which will be interesting to see, given your already useful skills from the circus.' Pausing on that word, he realized he wanted to know a good deal more about her former life. She seemed so gentle; it disturbed him knowing the pain she would go through. 'So can we trust you to work for us, Lan? I need to know you want to do this, rather than just being forced to do so.'

'Answer me this,' Lan demanded. 'Are the three of us experiments? Has this been tried before on others? I've worked with cultists, as you know, but they seemed very thorough and detailed. These ones are wandering about behind the scenes and don't let on much.'

'The process has been refined somewhat, in secrecy, though I believe the Emperor has only known about the available tools in recent weeks, and he's immediately seen their potential.'

'What happened to the others?'

'Others?'

'The others – who this has been tried on?'

Fulcrom wanted to move things on. 'The science has been refined now, and that's all you need to know, Lan – the rest, I'm afraid, is confidential.'

As he turned to leave she said, 'Shalev – that's who you're looking for, isn't it? Vuldon mentioned her name earlier.'

Fulcrom froze and turned to assess her words. 'That's true, yes. We think she's behind much of the surge in crimes recently. Do you *know* something about her?'

'When I was on Ysla – with the cultists – they mentioned the name Shalev. It's a woman, by the way.'

'Why did you take so long to say anything?' Fulcrom enquired, attempting to remain calm at this information.

'Well . . . no one asked what *I* thought until now.'

'What do you know about . . . her, about Shalev?'

Lan said, 'I didn't hear much, only of her escape – it was when I was . . . you know.'

Fulcrom acknowledged her words.

'She murdered people, on Ysla, apparently. They've pretty strange ways over there – a bizarre culture – but she wasn't welcome there. She'd been sent to a part of the island in whatever exile those people can permit with their strange lack of law. Then she vanished. She wasn't like the rest of them I think. She had a bad history with the Empire regarding her homeland. That's all I know – I swear.'

'Thanks, Lan. That's the most we've heard in a long while.'

*

Later that night, sprawled in a vast chair in an antechamber adjacent to the main operation theatre, Fulcrom was sipping a mug of spiced tea whilst staring into the light of the only lantern in the room. An open notebook lay to one side and, in it, he had been pencilling in plans and strategies to ensure the Knights could reduce the crime-wave that had washed over Villjamur. He'd also made notes about Shalev, exploring what Lan had told him, that the woman might have some personal vendetta against the Empire, and was targeting symbols of the city.

Fulcrom waited as the screams of the Knights ebbed and

flowed through varying stages of their transformations. He closed his eyes hoping that these pains were not going to scar them for life. Distantly he thought of what it was about Lan's appearance that provoked him, or at least his memory. *Adena ... of course, how could you be so stupid*. The acknowledgement and memory of her disarmed him.

Emperor Urtica fresh from his Council business suddenly marched into the room.

Fulcrom raised to greet him, with a bow. 'Sele of Urtica, my Emperor.'

'Less of that, investigator,' Urtica instructed, and gestured for him to sit back down.

Urtica paraded around the room ending up behind Fulcrom's chair, and suddenly slapped down his Imperial hands on Fulcrom's shoulders. Fulcrom noticed the man's hands were shaking slightly. *Is he nervous?*

'They were right about you,' Urtica declared.

'What's been said, my Emperor?' Fulcrom enquired.

The Emperor moved in front of him, a darkness momentarily blocking the light of the lantern on the table. 'That you possess remarkable skills with people. You've managed these misfits rather well already. They'd never listen to someone as ... well. Let's just say that I do not have the patience to put up with errors and slowness in individuals.' Urtica paused for a moment, as if considering his next statement. 'I need to trust you will have the people of this city enthralled by your achievements, investigator. I . . . I don't trust that many people in Balmacara. People there seem to always want things from me, or seek my favour.'

Is this some sort of mind-game? 'I don't ask for faith in me,' Fulcrom said. 'We'll work hard. You'll see results.'

'Results – yes.' Urtica perked up suddenly, like a different man. 'I need to see results – the city needs to see results, and the fears of our citizens need to be abated. You are responsible for this, and your management and crime-solving abilities come recommended very highly, so do not let me down.'

'My Emperor,' Fulcrom replied, 'I'm simply honoured to serve you and the city.'

'Splendid,' Urtica said. 'Because if you fail I will have you killed in a heartbeat.'

With that, the Emperor departed the room, leaving Fulcrom alone with his pulse racing. There was little Fulcrom could do about his new role and knew all too well what would happen if he opted out. Still, at least it seemed a good opportunity for putting something positive into the city.

It wasn't every day that happened in Villjamur.

Ten

Councillor Mewún shuffled from his temporary office and moved further into the heart of the Imperial residence of Balmacara. Dressed in official state colours of a green tunic and grey cloak, he strolled down the endless, shining corridors, considering the ornaments, portraits and marble decor. As far as temporary workspaces went, this wasn't too bad.

He smiled politely at the administrative staff who rushed past with armfuls of papers, and he stopped only to reflect upon his greying, balding head and expanding waistline in one of the gold-gilded mirrors. With the excitement and energy of Urtica's new political regime, the last few months had simply flown by. A slender young woman passed him in the corridor, one he recognized as a being a former servant to Councillor Boll, who was murdered some time ago. She was full of saccharine smiles, yet with her soft young skin and red curls, she was a startlingly tender and humane contrast to his paperwork.

She made the mistake of asking him a question: 'Have you had a good morning, councillor?'

Mewún took this as an opportunity to rid himself of his anxiety about city affairs. 'Not so far, no,' he told her.

'Oh?' she asked, taken aback on realizing she must actually engage in a conversation whether she liked it or not.

Tough, he thought. 'Oh indeed. Refugees are collapsing dead, heaping up on the doorstep to our city, and nothing can be done about it. They can't come in, of course, what with resources being so precious. No, the lucky corpses lay on pyres, those worse off rot in the snow, bringing further disease to their neighbours. We fight a brave war on our northern front, which depletes our resources further. And this endless winter ... well, it certainly makes logistical decisions and planning more challenging, I suppose.'

'The fact that smart people such as yourself are helping Villjamur is very much noted, councillor,' the girl droned.

'Ah, to be so uninvolved with the affairs of this world. To be so naive! I envy you.'

She gazed right past him, choosing to remain silent. It was a good thing. He was fully prepared to spurt his anger at the fact that forces in Balmacara could organize a military campaign, but not, it seemed, know when to take his laundry.

Mewún made to leave, hearing the scuffed footsteps of the girl's escape.

Amidst another flurry of activity from servants carrying trays of food, Mewún eventually progressed from Balmacara's depths and slipped out of one of the side entrances – which was Urtica's suggestion. Mewún was fine with all of these procedures, of course, though he couldn't help but think the Emperor was being a little too ... paranoid.

Outside, the weather was arse-bitingly cold. Even around the back of Balmacara, in the shadow of the chunky basalt walls where one of the majestic, arch-shaped new Council carriages awaited. A brown mare stood glumly with her face lost in a cloud of her own steam; the winter had found a way to stretch its icy tendrils even to her.

'Morning, councillor.' The stout old man standing before him was his driver, and he opened the door of the carriage, which was a huge dark-wood affair outfitted with luxurious ruby red trim. Mewún popped up, ducking his head, and plunged inside with a groan.

'Thank you, Edsan,' Mewún called out, once he was safely within the opulence of the carriage.

'Where's it to today, sir?' his driver enquired.

'The indoor iren project, if you please.'

'That open now, sir?'

'Not yet, no, but very soon – I'm giving a site visit to make sure we're all set for the grand opening.'

'Very good, councillor.' Edsan slammed the door and, through a little hatch, Mewún watched him trudge around the front of the carriage. A few minor rumbles later, a few terse words, with the undergear cranking as the mighty wheels turned, they rocked forwards.

Mewún shifted into the corner, rummaged around in his pockets, and drew up a roll-up and a box of matches. A few moments later, he promptly lit up and eased back, allowing the sounds of the city to wash over him, the calls of traders, the sharp orders of the military, the crunch of wheels and the horse's hooves on stone. Outside, the sun peered beyond the clouds, giving the city a rich, red veneer. Snow seeped from roofs round chimney breasts, dripping onto the streets incessantly, whilst children hurled snowballs at each other. They must have been entering an open plaza, as the scents of fried food from vendors filled his nostrils—

Something brown flashed by the hatch. *What was that?* Something rattled underneath.

Mewún scrambled to the opening to see a hooded figure in brown clothing sprinting down the street in the opposite direction.

As he frowned, he heard something fizz, and could smell burning, followed by an enormously bright flash and loud ripping and fire streaming upwards and *oh shit oh shit* his skin was burning . . .

*

'Fulcrom, get over here.'

Fulcrom strode cautiously through the chunks of charred

wood to Warkur's side. The rumel superior's face seemed distinctly unimpressed by the carnage, and who could blame him? Debris littered a zone nearly a hundred feet wide: flesh was scattered amidst the remnants of a carriage and, a few feet away, the burned and mutilated corpse of a horse lay gruesomely on its side. Even Fulcrom, who had seen his fair share of dire things on the streets of Villjamur, was forced to cringe. At the moment it wasn't snowing, but he wished it would, just enough to cover this mess.

The iren had been forcibly closed, the traders ushered on, the citizens steered away. It was possible there were some civilian casualties amidst the wreckage, but it wasn't easy to tell. Other Inquisition aides had been sent to recover the bodies and any evidence, and they sifted through the scene with sketchpads or assiduously made notes.

'What're you doing here – aren't you supposed to be looking after the Knights?' Warkur snapped.

'I heard about the incident and rushed here as soon as I could. Looks like we'll need military assistance on this.'

'If my hunch is right, we'll need whatever help we can get. You know who I'm thinking did this?'

'Did you see the flag too?'

'What flag?'

'On the wall over there.' Fulcrom pointed to an old red-brick structure between two whitewashed shops. Tied to a windowsill was a black flag: similar to ones that had been found at the site of every major anarchist crime to date.

'You and your powers of observation,' Warkur muttered. 'I'm not as young as I used to be – I'm missing even obvious things now.'

One of the human aides, a red-haired man, lunged onto the scene out of breath: 'Sir, we've got some information on the event.'

The carriage was one of the new models – strips of wood bore fresh Imperial logos, but there was no glory to be found in this mess, only the remains of a politician. A councillor had been in the carriage. The aide provided the name of Mewún, who had left Balmacara earlier.

Fulcrom knew the name, though couldn't put a face to it – but the title was enough. Sure, councillors were murdered from time to time, and there had been public incidents in recent months, but generally such matters were kept low-key and away from prying eyes.

'This is some damn public spectacle,' Warkur said.

'It was obviously intended that way,' Fulcrom added. 'We know these *anarchists* like to make a show of things. They must have known a councillor was using this route, or they followed him from Balmacara.'

Warkur shook his head in disgust: 'How've they become so damn effective all of a sudden?'

'Do you want me to pursue this case, sir?' Fulcrom asked.

'Though I don't fully trust orders from the top, and we could do with someone like you checking the day-to-day investigations, you've got enough on with the Knights,' Warkur said, waving him away.

'Well, we all have plenty to be getting on with, sir,' Fulcrom replied.

'It's possible all investigators are going to have to work together from now on. Means we'll have to pass over full control of monitoring the refugees outside to the military.'

And I know just what the military would do to them under Urtica's control, Fulcrom thought grimly.

'So', Warkur continued, 'you just look after those precious Knights and make sure they're ready to prevent shit like this from happening again. If our Emperor's beloved news rag is anything to go by, they'll have some pressure coming their way. They'll be famous. Everyone out here knows their names and faces. With all that damn fuss, they'll find it difficult to get close to the enemy. In the meantime, I'll start drawing the investigations together. See if we can spot patterns or find new leads. Fuck, at this rate I might as well get some tribal priests in for shell readings – maybe they can help us find out who the hell these anarchists are.'

Warkur kicked a piece of wood, and it skittered across the street and into the wall. A few passers-by had snuck into the scene, and there were several more leaning out of windows despite the cold, voyeuristically curious. Two human aides were now surveying the debris and lifting pieces of flesh into large metal containers. It would take a while to clean it all up.

'These Knights of yours – they'd better be good,' Warkur bellowed, before skulking off into the distance.

What difference can three humans possibly make in a world like this? Fulcrom thought.

ELEVEN

After a few days' travelling, and with the sun about to dip over the horizon, Dartun called a halt. He seemed suddenly attentive to their surroundings.

'We're being pursued,' Dartun announced, his breath clouding in the air. He held his hand to his eyes and scanned the horizon.

'What should we do?' Verain called out.

'Confront it.' His voice seemed to lack his usual vibrancy. For a man who had been given new life, he certainly seemed to lack it.

'Why?' Verain asked.

'Because I can sense it needs to be removed from our paths,' he replied.

Sense? How has he ever been able to sense *things before? Surely he can't mean intuition – that kind of talk goes against his whole logical philosophy.*

'Who's following us?' Verain persisted. 'Where *are* they?'

'Due south, and based in a small piece of woodland.'

How can he know such things? she thought, trying to follow his gaze and seeing only the empty landscape.

'They are from this world.'

That offered some consolation. They wouldn't, at least, be facing the horrors that they'd just left behind them. Dartun seemed to sniff the air. His mannerisms startled her, but his sudden smile was vicious. 'They were sent to track us, possibly to even kill us. I would like to see them try.' Dartun waved them on again, the dogs hauled forward, ropes snapping tight, their paws kicking up puffs of snow as they slowly dragged the sleds on. Verain continued to worry about the changes to Dartun: since returning he had not so much as held a relic in his hand, had not once harnessed the technological wizardry of ancient races.

Come to think of it, where are the relics? When she expressed her concern to Dartun, he barely acknowledged she had spoken. This was a far cry from the man who had plucked her from her life as an orphan, who had chosen her for her skills with relics, who had taken her into his great Order of the Equinox, his inner sanctum, then his heart, and shown her great tenderness. Now, he was as cold to her as the wind that whipped across her face.

The landscape was punctuated only by a cluster of shattered shacks, broken villages and torn-down church spires. The weather was brutal. Bitterly cold, the ice was blinding, and the wind felt raw upon Verain's skin. Occasionally, when her hood blew back, she had to close her eyes and hunch double to shelter from the pain of the elements.

It wasn't long before Verain's legs buckled and she tumbled face-first out of the sled into the snow . . .

*

The world seemed a blur – a haze of images, nothing more. She came to her senses to find Dartun crouching over her pouring hot fluid into her mouth.

Minutes passed and all she could do was stare up at him. They had paused to make camp near where she had fallen. Canvas wind-blocks provided shelter and a fire was burning.

Dartun regarded her, and she felt like an object of his investigations under his gaze. 'Your strength should return soon,' he said – more a statement of fact than words of encouragement. 'I was foolish to push us so hard. I suspect one thing I have learned is that where I walk, others will suffer.'

'W-what d-does that mean?' she replied.

'Only that when we were there – through the gate – what was done to me has enabled me to survive much, whereas the rest of you ... Well, of course, you remain unchanged.' He seemed almost delighted at that last statement.

'I wouldn't say we remain unchanged,' one of the other cultists muttered – Tuung, a bald man whose attitude was dour even before they went through the gates. 'I'm now cold, probably suffering from frostbite, and starving. And I'm mightily pissed off. I wasn't like that before, I can tell you.'

Dartun laughed at them like they were charming, naive children.

'Still,' Tuung continued, peering down into the flames. 'Least we're alive.' The look he gave Verain said: *Remember how the others died, right? Remember what they suffered, the hideous brutality they faced?*

'Why were we set free, Dartun?' Verain asked, shivering.

All that could be heard was the wind groaning as it drifted across this landscape.

'Because', Dartun said, 'we have work to do on their behalf. Temporarily, we are working for them.'

And now she remembered. The patches of memory were starting to slot together to form a narrative in her mind.

Like visual echoes:

Images of the genocide across Tineag'l, before the cultists stepped through the Realm Gates the first time. Villages with blood-trails through the snow, the corpse in the bath, dead bodies of the very old and very young left strewn behind buildings like waste outside a tavern. Then she had thought it just brutal warfare – that they had been the innocent victims of an invasion. Now she knew why people had been taken by the creatures made from blackened shell, now she understood why the island had been cleansed. And she wished she didn't.

Humans were considered to be a finite but necessary resource in the other world. For one of the indigenous cultures there humans were organic, living ore; nothing more, nothing less. They were subjected to death factories, to diabolical bone merchants, a utility to be used and discarded as necessary for furtherance of a war that wasn't their own.

So it begged the question, if humans were so valuable a resource – why had their small group been set free?

*

The next morning the cultists from the Order of the Equinox continued on their journey south. The horizon was unperceivable. The sun broke through the cloud to tint pink the surrounding. Shadows presented themselves, giving away the location of unknown objects across the snowscape.

And unknown people.

Dartun pulled the reins and the dogs slowly slipped to a halt. In the distance, he pointed out a cluster of figures moving slowly northwards and, as Verain squinted, Dartun stepped off the sled and knelt by one of the dogs.

A cream-coloured beast with a dash of grey across its face, it didn't yip excitedly like the others, and there was something almost mechanical about its movements. Dartun held his head against the animal's and whispered something and suddenly the dog became startlingly active. It sprinted towards the figures in the distance, claws turning up little plumes of powder across the ice.

Dartun stood casually, shading his eyes with one hand, watching its progress.

*

This much was obvious:

Papus was going to kill him. And here she was, weeks away from comfort, weeks across the Archipelago, and still no closer to her victim. Papus cursed the weather, cursed the island of Tineag'l, and cursed the Empire. Most of all, she cursed herself. Why had she not ignored her determination to get one over on Dartun? Why had her competitive drive overwhelmed her sensibilities, and landed her all the way out here?

No, I'm doing a good thing, she reminded herself.

Dartun had made corpses walk across the island of Jokull, and his band of cultists had constantly threatened her own group, the Order of the Dawnir, the most ancient and largest sect of cultists, of which she was Gydja, the most senior member. Dartun needed to be stopped, but sometimes she thought maybe . . . maybe he *couldn't* be stopped.

She had brought thirty of her own order across the seas to Tineag'l, and they had come prepared. Longships had been anchored four days' travel to the west, on loan from the Empire – Imperial authorities wanted him stopped as much as she did. Well, maybe not *as* much. But there was no doubt: this was a big mission, to bring Dartun Súr to justice, dead or alive. It was her determination and competitiveness that kept her going.

They had passed through decimated villages. Front doors had been kicked in, central monuments had been demolished, windows were smashed in, and taverns wrecked. They were scenes of horrors. Blood still remained from whatever massacre had occurred.

Now, after weeks of following Dartun's trail, with only relics for warmth, she felt they were getting closer. Cloud broke, leaving sunlight bleeding across the snowy wastes. She peered from beneath her dark furs at the horizon, and pulled out her *Finna* relic. It was a brass compass to the casual observer, but this was not an instrument to find *directions*. Once activated, minute lightning bolts flickered across its surface – and the device could locate any relic activity, point in the direction of anyone harnessing the power of the ancients, within vast areas. And the ancient power of the Dawnir left echoes, indicated by the intensity of light on the dial. There had been a moment a week ago which panicked her greatly –

when there had been little activity at all, as if Dartun and his cultists had simply ... vanished. Then two nights ago, the *Alf* flared up again, purple webs aggregating with ferocity, and her worries over its effectiveness abated.

Seven sleds carried them north by north-west, the dogs tearing up the ice, driving into the constant glare of the sunlight. About two hours into their day's travel, the sled up ahead halted, and she brought her own to a stop.

One of her group, Minof, a bearded giant of a cultist and someone she was glad to have close by, peered through a telescope in one direction.

'Gydja!' he bellowed.

Papus climbed out of her sled and trudged around the yipping dogs to his side. 'What can you see?' she asked.

'I think it's them.' He offered her the telescope, shaking the flakes of snow from his beard and fur hood.

Through the device she could see only whiteness at first, then the occasional streak of a change in the landscape's texture, or a knuckle of rock jutting out of the snow like the hull of a sinking ship. She scanned across the landscape in the rough direction that Minof had been looking, then felt the force of his hand guiding the end of the telescope until she could see what he had seen.

They were very hazy, and very small, but there was indeed a huddle of figures in the deep distance – probably no more than ten people in all – with sleds of their own. At first Papus felt a jolt: this was the first sign of life they had seen out here for some time. Then, a pang of nerves hit her: if this was Dartun, she would soon have to inform him that he was wanted by the powers of Villjamur – a statement that would almost certainly initiate conflict.

'Do you think it's them?' Minof grunted.

'They're too distant to tell,' Papus replied, lowering the telescope.

There was hubbub within her own group, as several men

and women clustered to see what the issue was and why they had stopped. Loudly, she explained Minof's sighting, and gauged expressions for signs of a reaction. Most of them appeared to be simply relieved that their time out here might be at an end, and she very much sympathized.

After some debate, Papus ordered that they assemble any necessary relics and approach the group. It took them ten minutes of organizing themselves before they pushed on. A moment later, as she saw something approaching she gave the word to halt again.

A dog was trotting towards them. It was a gentle-looking thing, white with flashes of grey around its face. It padded quickly across the snow, paused to look at them, then sat about forty feet away.

Minof grunted and started forward to meet the dog.

'Be careful,' Papus warned.

Minof called to the animal, which sat up and shuffled towards him. Wind built up now, but otherwise there was only silence from her group. Flecks of snow – not from the sky, but gusted up from the land – drifted now and then across her vision.

Papus pulled her hood tighter and held up the telescope to watch the interaction. On closer inspection, the dog's movements weren't quite right: there was something almost mechanical about the way it moved, and it possessed none of the flowing grace found in her own animals. And on further examination the dog's eyes . . . they were red, like two burning embers had been set within its skull, and its teeth glinted in the sun like daggers.

'Minof!' she shouted, as the man moved in to rub the canine affectionately, 'I think you should step b—'

The dog exploded.

A huge plume of snow and blood banked into the air, and bass vibrations rocked the ground. Someone screamed, her own dogs howled, the cultists in her order began to panic. Moments later, the remnants of flesh and bone, and shattered plates of metal, fell across the surrounding snow with gentle thuds. Pink snow littered the detonation zone.

There was very little left of Minof or the dog.

'Fuck,' someone behind her breathed. Someone else was in hysterics.

Poor Minof ... she thought, her mind a sudden tangle of fear and guilt. Most of the group just stared dumbly, but a few jogged forward cautiously evaluating what had occurred.

*

'What was that?' Verain demanded.

'You can recognize an explosion, surely?' Dartun replied flatly. They had watched the dog trot into the distance and, just now, seen the red eruption, felt it through the earth, observed the eerie calm of the aftermath. *What the hell was that all about?* She regarded some of the other dogs now and, out of curiosity, walked among them to see if they seemed suspicious. Each of them seemed eager to see her, one even licked her hand – nothing about these dogs suggested they were anything but animals.

A couple of the other cultists sidled up to her, and their expressions equalled her own. Any conversation was rushed and kept quiet. What was going on? Why had Dartun despatched a dog to explode?

As she turned, she could see Dartun gazing out into the distance, his fuligin cloak flapping in the wind like a banner of war. His profile was noble, his posture almost too perfect. Was there anything really left of the man she had been in love with?

They lingered in the breeze for some time. He was still standing motionless, watching the group in the distance. No one dared say anything to him.

Tuung stepped up alongside Verain and folded his arms,

tucking his gloved hands under his armpits for warmth. Sunlight brightened his reddened face and he squinted at her. 'Can't you have a word with him?'

'What about? He barely listened to me before we set out for this wasteland. Do you honestly think after all we've been through he'll suddenly want to open his heart?'

Tuung grunted. 'We don't even know what we're doing now, or where we're headed.'

'We're going home to Villjamur,' Verain replied.

'What, just like that? We fuck off into these Realm Gates, get the shit kicked out of us, have most of our order slaughtered before our eyes in the most scarring manner imaginable, and we *just fuck off* back home again?'

His reminders of the horrors they experienced were not welcome. 'Expeditions fail all the time. Explorers get lost and turn back. Ships catch the wrong winds, get dragged off course – these things happen, it's life. We tried, we failed. We're still alive.'

Tuung grunted again: 'That may be true. But most explorers know where they're going, know what they're getting into – have a choice. Do we? Do we have any idea what Dartun is up to?'

Verain looked to where Dartun was still staring at the group in the distance.

'They're coming now,' he announced.

Verain approached Dartun and hesitantly placed a hand on his arm. If he felt her gesture, he didn't show any acknowledgement. 'Who are they?' she asked.

'The Order of the Dawnir. Papus. Her cultists are coming to confront us.'

She didn't ask how he knew. She didn't want to know.

She's come, at last ... Verain felt a pang of relief. The last time she had seen this woman, Verain had revealed many of Dartun's nefarious activities, including the intention to explore the Realm Gates. She had not betrayed her lover –

she merely feared for everyone's safety, her own included. He had become obsessed with becoming immortal once again, and he didn't seem to be thinking right. Now she had come to take them back to Villjamur and Verain hoped their encounter would be peaceful.

'She must have been trying to stop us seeing the other-world,' Dartun said, 'or maybe she wants a resolution to our years of feuding. Perhaps she caught wind of my experiments on the dead, who knows. A little late for either, I suspect. It all seems so . . . petty.'

Tuung traipsed forward, rubbing the back of his head. 'Uh, we've not got any relics that work, Dartun. They were made redundant on the other side of the gates. I'm not sure what you want us to do exactly, but we're not in a great state to engage in combat.'

'He's right,' Verain said. 'We shouldn't fight them.'

'We won't need relics,' Dartun declared. 'I can handle this miserable woman on my own.'

Verain opened her mouth to say something, but nothing came out. Dartun began walking forward on his own. No one followed him. The weather settled: clouds had dissipated from the immediate area, leaving a beautiful and unusual lilac glaze to the scene, and wind licked up tiny wisps of snow. Dartun marched about fifty or so paces into isolation, down into a very slight gully, but his torso still clearly visible.

And waited.

The figures in the distance vacated sleds, then slowly huddled into formation, before moving to meet him.

Verain watched, her heart thumping, her nerves getting the better of her. 'Surely we should do something?' she pleaded with Tuung.

'You heard the man,' Tuung replied bitterly. 'Sod all, is what we can do. Besides, the relics aren't working, are they? Most of the weaponry has been deactivated, so unless you fancy using something as primitive as a sword . . . Way I see it is like this: if he lives, great, we stick with him and go home. If he gets killed, we still head home in some way, only as prisoners.'

One of the others grunted a laugh, but the rest stared at the ground or deep into the distance – anything to face the reality of what was happening. Her attention moved back to Dartun, who was still in the same pose, still standing defiantly, his cloak wafting in the breeze while further along the slope the Order of the Dawnir were slowly closing the distance.

*

They must have appeared like a local tribe the way they were wrapped in dark furs and waxed capes. Papus made her cultists pull in closer, tighter, cautious of any relics Dartun might activate.

The arrogance of the man! Papus thought. Through the telescope she could just see him standing there, waiting for her, almost without a care in the world.

Is he smiling?

She put away the telescope and gripped the new relic in her pocket, a *Skammr*, something she had worked with for some time, though not been able to use until now. The device was constructed so that she could disable all other relics within the immediate vicinity, completely muting the power of the ancients for just a short period. Though untested in the field, she knew it would work, though it could only be used sparingly, and given that Dartun had presented himself as a vulnerable target, she didn't even think she would need it more than once.

What if he was surrendering? she thought. *Would he willingly seek to hand himself in – could he be tired of being out here?* Others from his order seemed to be loitering by the sleds up the hill, so this didn't appear to be an aggressive manoeuvre. And where were the rest of them, for that matter? The Order of the Equinox ought to have been much larger than what was gathered here.

Every step closer presented to her a confirmation it was indeed Dartun. When they were about fifty paces away, she held an arm out to halt her entourage. 'I think it's best if I initiate contact alone,' she said.

'Please, Gydja,' someone said – Bael, one of the younger women in her order. 'Not after what happened to Minof. This man is deeply untrustworthy.'

Papus considered the point and observed Dartun, who stood waiting for her, nonchalantly. 'All right, we go on as a group.'

Defiantly, and as much in unison as they could manage, the cultists marched as one, as the Order of the Dawnir, to police this rogue cultist.

Forty paces away, Dartun called over to her: 'You must truly love me, to come so far.' She heard his hollow laugh echoing across the ice.

Arrogant swine, she thought. Dartun had found a flat section of thick ice within a gully, which looked like the snow had settled on a small lake with a few cold-crippled trees poking up from their white smothering. His shadow was bold across the ice.

She commenced her well-rehearsed statement. 'Dartun Súr, Godhi of the Order of the Equinox, you are—'

'You *do* love stating the obvious, Papus,' Dartun interrupted. 'Why have you come out here?'

'We're here to bring you to justice, Dartun, as simple as that. In the name of this Empire, we request that you return with us to Villjamur in order to face charges for your crimes.'

'And what crimes would they be?' Dartun replied, glancing up and down their row of cultists, a smirk on his face.

'Animation of the dead, for one thing,' Papus sneered. 'You have abused your position as a cultist and breached our ethical boundaries.'

'Sod you,' Dartun spat, 'and your ethical boundaries.'

How dare *he talk to me like this.* Papus wanted to get this man back to Villjamur immediately. She peered to her left, shading her eyes from the glare. One of her order stepped forward: it was Telov, a chunky blond man with a weather-beaten face. He withdrew from his furs a set of chains that began to glow and splutter with a fierce purple light.

'I would strongly advise against using that,' Dartun growled.

'Why? You've no relics,' Papus observed. Dartun merely stood there, his hands by his sides, and only then did she think it strange he was not wearing as many layers one might expect for such freezing conditions. His dark cloak barely clung to his somewhat tattered frame. Admittedly he did not look his best – his clothes were torn, and she could see exposed skin in places, and in others ... was that metal showing through?

Telov held the neutral ends of the chains out cautiously in front, and it was clear from his movements that his nerves were getting the better of him. She had wanted to capture Dartun for so long and now this seemed an anticlimax. Was this legendary cultist simply going to let himself be taken back to Villjamur?

Dartun suddenly lowered his head and closed his eyes. She heard a faint drone coming from him. Without looking up, Dartun reached out to grab the chains in Telov's hands, chains that at this frequency of energy should have given him such a shock as to send him unconscious.

There came an electrical snap: energy was being forced back through the chains into the neutral handles – and Telov's hands began to burn. He screamed, couldn't let go, fell to his knees still gripping the heated handles, crying while smoke streamed from his palms.

Papus quickly activated the *Skammr* and the chains were jammed and deactivated, and ancient energy, in the form of purple light, dissipated. Telov collapsed to his side and buried his hands into the snow.

She was stunned: how, without any relics, was Dartun able to do that?

Dartun spread his stance and, with his arms either side, his glance calm, took in the situation. Once again he faced Papus and smiled. 'Sure you can handle me?'

'How did you do that?' she demanded. 'You aren't carrying any relics.'

'I'm not who I used to be,' Dartun replied.

The *Skammr* should have worn off by now. She gave the signal and four of her cultists ran forwards with relics: an electrical net spurted slickly into the air, and with a liquid grace fell onto Dartun – but he simply ripped through it with his bare hands.

How is that possible?

Two others tried to use weapons to beat him, one a sword, another a crossbow: miraculously, with a quick gesture of his right hand he managed to bend the metal of the sword so that it had become inert, and the crossbow bolt he caught with his left hand; doubly impressive because he wasn't even looking in that direction.

Dartun flipped back his cloak and peeled away the skin on his arm: where she expected blood to surge and tendons to be exposed, a strange, almost white ceramic arm was in place, and it glittered with tiny webs of light.

More of her order charged, relics in hand.

The arm was a revolution in technology. It stuttered into life, vibrating minutely, one minute quite inflexible, the next very fluid. His face was set in a savage sneer as one by one he ripped into her order. She watched the violence in awe.

He jumped and bent back and forth with impossible flexibility. There was so much blood and ice spraying, and he moved so quickly, it was hard to discern the action, but she saw him cleave one of her members in two, sever another's head sending it skittering across the frozen lake.

She was agog. Mortified.

Soon she was the only member of her order left standing, and Papus was stunned at the carnage around her. Tears filled her eyes as she regarded her whole cult wiped out with so much ease. Dartun was hardly tired by the spectacle, panting lightly, his breath clouding the air.

He stood to regard her, basking in the aftermath. His arm shimmered as the sun broke through, washing the scene with a pink light.

'You're ... you're not even human,' Papus managed to say. She felt her stomach churning.

Oddly, her words seemed to knock him back, and he shook his head as if in a half-daze. He suddenly stared at her like he didn't know what he'd been doing.

Papus took this moment of respite to survey the wreckage of her order, her life. Blood covered the narrow region of the lake. Body segments were scattered and heaped where two or more had fallen on each other under Dartun's swift blows.

She would not let herself die in the same way. She would, at least, honour her order. As Dartun scanned the scene seemingly as confused by his work as she was, Papus primed all the relics beneath her furs, shivering with shock. She produced an *Aldartal*, triggered it—

Time froze rigid: nothing moved at the periphery of the scene, everything stopped. Except for Dartun, who sluggishly pulled himself free of the relic's energy, slowly – as if covered in some abstract treacle – and stuttered into a state of normal time.

'How ... ? How did you do that?' Papus asked. Her fears were assuaged by her all-consuming desire to understand what he was.

'You'll have to try harder than that,' he muttered. There was an air of insouciance about the manner in which he moved, as if he had all the time in the world to kill her. She deactivated the *Aldartal* and—

—the wind groaned once again, her hair spiralled before her face, and they were back in normal time.

'Enough of this.' Dartun lifted his surreal arm.

She turned to flee. He marched after her, and she sprinted across the ice to escape him. Frantically, in her pocket she activated a *Deyja* for a cloak of invisibility. A purple flash – like sheet lightning – and she was gone.

They paused for a moment, uncertain of how to proceed. Dartun tipped his head this way and that, as if trying to listen.

Even if, despite his new-found powers, he couldn't see her, out here it was pointless – he would easily be able to observe her indentations in the snow, her frantic scrabbling across the white surface, the scuff-marks on the ice.

And as soon as she shifted even slightly, he clocked her.

Dartun continued his pursuit, his arm a gleaming white stammer of vibrations.

Something *Brenna*-based next, two small solid aluminium balls that she plucked from her pockets, activated, then rolled back towards Dartun. They skittered across the ice into his path and, as he stepped around one, they both exploded, aggressively spurting up fire and tiny, razor-sharp chunks of metal.

A short scream: *At least he's vaguely human*, she thought.

Dartun stopped and flinched, as the fire ravaged his clothing. The shrapnel had shredded the skin across his face, and now, blood-streaked, he collapsed to his knees – *finally!* She heaved a sigh and, crawling on all fours and still invisible, she sagged tentative relief. Now to finish this off.

Papus slipped out a dagger from her boot and stood up. She walked over to him and prepared to stab his kneeling form in the back of the neck. Suddenly he lunged up at her, his face a snarling bloodied mess. He grabbed her by the throat with his human hand. She tried to slice at it, but the other arm punched her stomach—

And punctured it.

Stunned, a burning pain surged through Papus's body – and she could see her own blood flowing like wine along Dartun's arm, down into the little nooks and crannies in the surface. Dartun was elbow-deep inside her abdomen.

She stared into his eyes and saw something mechanical behind his glare, like a subtle functioning of relics. Then he must have clutched something inside her – *oh, fuck* could she feel it – and he tugged hard. Her own innards were yanked out before her eyes, flecks of her blood peppering the air.

Papus collapsed, her head striking the ice.

*

Verain experienced a state of being both relieved and appalled as Dartun returned covered in blood. What horrors she had witnessed she had observed from a distance, and the details were unclear. She knew there had been a slaughter, however – that much was obvious.

After the butchering of the final cultist, Dartun had remained there for several minutes, patrolling up and down the devastation, and she wondered what he must have been thinking. The remains were gruesome, like the despicable culling of seals that many of the tribes across the Archipelago performed each year. She could not take her eyes off the scene, even as Dartun made his way back through the thick snow, to reach the remnants of the Order of the Equinox.

'I have dealt with the matter accordingly,' Dartun announced.

'You don't say,' Tuung blurted out from behind her.

'Your face . . .' Verain began. His skin was gently pock-marked, like a volcanic rock.

Dartun reached up his hand to sense the details, and seemed unmoved. 'It'll be back to normal soon enough – a side effect against one of her relics.'

'Are they all dead?' she asked.

'They are indeed,' Dartun beamed.

'So what now, eh?' Tuung said. His tone was frail, that of a man on the edge. 'We're shattered and hungry.'

Dartun's expression was distant, withdrawn. Something wasn't right, but she didn't know what. 'I understand your concern,' he droned. 'I will ensure that you are well cared for.' Verain fell under his gaze, and she didn't know what to think. Was that affection?

'It is essential we *all* survive and return to Villjamur, and I must confess I have neglected your welfare.' Dartun still didn't seem to be particularly bothered that he was drenched in blood. She could barely look at him in this state. 'We will get off this island and seek a town and some accommodation and some nutrition.'

'Thank fuck for that.' Tuung headed back to the dogs.

TWELVE

On one of the central sections of Villjamur, beneath the disused aqueduct, a short walk from the corner of the long street called Gata Sentimental with its narrow, five-storey buildings, and under the subtle night shadows caused by a bold stone bridge, two men in hooded tunics and thick overcoats were navigating their way across the vast, empty iren, avoiding the patches of moonlight. A pterodette lunged down, inches from the cobbles, hunting bats, before it scaled one of the numerous, crenellated towers of the city at a high velocity. A sharp air pervaded the scene, and a fog was beginning to roll in from the sea, bringing with it a deadly evening chill.

'There's a foul air tonight,' one of the men muttered.

'Quit your fairy talk, Liel,' sighed Brude, a barrel of man. Stubble smothered his face, and his small, beady eyes examined the distance for signs of life. Satisfied, he regarded his companion. 'You've been spurting all sorts of shit since the banshees stopped their keening, and tonight's no different from any other. Or have you been hanging around with kids and reading too much MythMaker, eh?'

'No,' Liel replied. 'But them banshees going all silent just ain't natural, I can tell you that much. Word is, someone's got their tongues.'

'It's easier, idiot, because who's now here to scream for the dead? No one, that's who. There's less fear when you're murdering someone, so it makes life easier. Now, stop being so pathetic. You should be more like your mate, Caley – he's not chicken shit and he's years younger than you.'

Liel squirmed a nod.

Brude couldn't stand the scrawny man being so paranoid. He was eighteen, slow for his age, and his incessant paranoia was infectious. Brude turned his furtive attention to the edge of this iren, one of the largest in the city, where a few glass shopfronts were glittering like starlight.

Among them he searched for a name . . .

Granby's Gemstones.

There it was, a decorative and faded green facade, its square sign creaking gently in the wind. In the daytime, people of the city would mill about outside this shop and goggle at the metallic trinkets and precious stones beyond the glass.

Shalev's instructions were, as always, to the letter. Forty days had passed now since she'd been working with them – the anarchists. Forty days of furtive undertakings, though strictly speaking, they wouldn't ever call it work; they wanted to refer to it always as a *collective*. Work was still a form of wage slavery, they claimed. Work was getting grimmer and grimier, poor conditions forced upon people by propagating the fear of how bad the ice would become. Other folk felt they wanted *secure* jobs in such conditions, despite the poor pay and treatment. They wanted to remain in their front-room cloth manufacturers, labouring under restrictive conditions by the underground docks, but Brude wasn't into such self-abuse. Rumour had it that the Freeze was destined to keep the ice here for decades, so he was fucked if he was having any of that.

Shalev had given them hope . . .

Caveside was a different place now and it had all happened quite suddenly. Two months ago the enormous but over-looked sector of the city was practically a slum, an enclosed shanty suburb that housed the majority of the population. There was resentment against topsiders, deep unrest and petty crime had flourished.

But now? Now Shalev was manufacturing miracles.

First came her remarkable cultist-engineered seeds. Barren zones of land, on which nothing could ever grow, were suddenly able to support tight patches of crops. Tolerant plants could now thrive with little light or water, and what were back gardens only in name became allotments. Food bloomed in the darkness.

Poorer smiths began to manufacture things for Shalev in exchange for food, and weapons: clubs, daggers and maces spread amongst the Caveside dwellers. But whereas once these would have been used on one another, now Shalev brought them together as a group. Connections were made externally and, somehow, surreal though it seemed, crops were being exported *out* from under the city to rural collectives, in exchange for their support. A barter economy, one without money, grew quickly – out of nothing – and Brude didn't quite know what to make of it all. But what he did know was this: Granby's Gemstones was on Shalev's hit list. That such a place could continue to exist was a symbol of the extravagance of the upper city, which flaunted such wealth at a time when thousands of refugees were dying right on Villjamur's doorstep. It was a shocking, garish display of crass commercialism, Shalev had said. Or rather, that's what people reported that Shalev had said, because the level of secrecy was immense for newcomers to their circles. Given the brutal determination of the military in this city to hunt her down, that was certainly understandable.

And all of this was why Brude and Liel were going to filch its jewels.

A couple of muscled lads were a whistle-call away, waiting with blades in case any of the city guard strolled by, but the added security didn't fully reassure him. Brude and Liel flitted into the shadows as a priestess tottered across the ice to a nearby Jorsalir church, her skirts hitched up so the hem wouldn't get wet. Once she had passed, the two men scurried along the perimeter of the open square, to the small alleyway alongside the jewellers.

Liel stood languidly, a blade clutched in his tiny fist. Brude searched in his own overcoat for the device passed along to him from Shalev.

Where is the damn thing, I hope I haven't left the bugger in the caves. A-ha!

He whipped the object out with a conjuror's flourish. It was a small tool that utilized some form of magic to cut through glass. Brude was adroit in urban techniques, having spent years educating himself in the ways of the thief, but this was something entirely new to his repertoire. He tilted the device, a long rectangular strip of brass, this way and that in the moonlight, discerning the correct side, then pressed it against the grainy glass for several seconds. He moved it along, held it for several seconds, moved it along, and so on, until he had drawn a barely visible circle about an arm-span across on the surface of the glass. Once the ends of the lines connected, he waited. The line suddenly glowed purple, flared brightly and, with a snap, the circled patch of glass fell in one piece into the darkness of the shop, whereupon it shattered. Liel and Brude quickly scanned the area in case anyone heard.

Liel tugged at Brude's sleeve, and the thuggish man turned to follow his gaze.

'Brude! Up there, Brude. Top of those walls, I swear I saw something.'

'There ain't a thing there, runt,' Brude grunted. 'Now come on.' He heaved his boot up onto the windowsill, cleared the broken glass, then peered inside. In the near-darkness, he could see the glimmer of gemstones in their cabinets.

The wealth here is ... staggering. Oh my ... emeralds and rubies ... Praise Bohr, it's a fucking miracle all right. And a few were his for the taking, as payment, so long as he distributed the rest to the collective.

'Brude,' Liel whimpered, 'you really should look at this. I ain't kidding.'

'Fucksake, what is it?' Brude demanded, turning back.

Liel wafted his arm. 'Up there, on them roofs. Few hundred yards away, a fraction left of the Astronomer's Glass Tower.'

From out of the sea of fog and above the crenellated sector walls, a figure could be seen gliding from rooftop to rooftop, tiptoeing across the moonlit tiles – then, seemingly, it ran through the air over a gap of at least twenty yards, its arms and legs flailing, only to push itself off another set of roof tiles with the daintiest of touches.

Fluidly, it manoeuvred itself towards them.

'Hmm . . .' Brude placed his finger and thumb in his mouth and, very loudly, gave two sharp whistles. A moment later, boots were clattering on the cobbles: the back-up was arriving. 'Tell them what's going on, I'll get some gems, then we fuck off quickly. Right?'

Liel nodded tentatively, his eyes still fixed on the approach of this rooftop newcomer.

Brude glanced at their comrades, three blond thugs standing furtively next to Liel, both kitted out in tight military-style clothing and both brandishing swords. Brude nodded to them, and they whispered back, 'Evening, brothers.'

As Liel opened his mouth to explain the situation, and Brude poked his head back into the shop, a voice called out from across the street:

'I wouldn't do that if I were you, chaps.' He was well-spoken, whoever he was, silhouetted against the moonlit glare on the wet cobbles, with his hands on his hips. A tail swished back and forth, and for a moment Brude assumed it was an Inquisition rumel. Brude pulled his attention away from the jewellers and, standing alongside his comrades, peered through the fog that had now made itself present at street level.

'The fuck are you, telling us what to do?' Brude called back. 'You Inquisition or something?'

All he could see at first was that the silhouette started walking towards them. Was this the same one as the figure previously spotted on the rooftops? He couldn't have dropped here that quickly. He must have approached from a different part of the city.

'I'm one of the Villjamur Knights,' the stranger replied.

'What does that mean?' Brude replied.

'It means' – another voice now, bass and firm – 'that we're here to stop you from clearing out this shop.' A figure came from the side street to Granby's, a hulking mass of an individual.

Bloody hell, Brude thought, *what muscles . . .*

Brude realized that their exits were cut off on two sides and they would be required to fight their way out. Then a third figure came from over the nearest rooftop, gliding to the ground like a garuda – but there were no wings here, the figure merely moved through air as if able to bend it to its will.

And a moment later, noting the long hair and feminine grace, Brude realized this figure was a woman. *What the hell is a woman doing here?* he thought.

The smaller of the approaching men moved into a solid patch of moonlight and Liel gasped. Brude cuffed the younger man's ear for showing fear. 'Idiot,' he whispered, but the runt had a point in being afraid. The stranger was . . . *animalistic*, though not unlike a rumel. His nose was flared and broad and black, and his face showed signs of . . . fur. There was something remarkably feline about him. From his fingers extended thick claws. He stood tall, and walked with an alien grace. And he seemed to stand there, bathing in their shock.

'You think you three freaks can handle the four of us?' Brude heckled, drawing a large dagger.

Two of the thugs sprinted with their swords brandished, heading towards the hulk in the alleyway, and they vanished into the street-level fog. Waiting in the darkness, Brude heard their shuddering screams, the sounds of blood pooling slickly on stone, their swords clattering to the ground.

The remaining thug gawked at Brude, who signalled for him to move. The man dashed ahead towards the cat-like figure, who side-stepped him, raking his claws down his back. The man moved back with a scream, clutching his ribs with his free hand. He turned, striking his blade this way and that, slicing nothing but air as the figure repeatedly moved out of range with acrobatic speed. The blond thug lunged to and fro, tiring quickly, then the cat thing struck him: he swiped his clawed hands across the man's face and throat, and in an instant the thug collapsed pathetically, clutching at his wounds.

The final figure – the woman – moved towards Liel and Brude. With her dark hair tied back, and relaxed pose, this plain and willowy girl appeared fairly harmless. Brude decided he would act, and he moved towards her, brandishing his dagger. As he made the first swipe she seemed to move backwards, stepping up onto the air itself, and pulling away from him at a curious angle. She stepped across him – in mid air – and he found himself chasing her legs, trying to slice at her heels.

With her arms extended, she kicked him in the face and he spun backwards, slipping on a patch of ice to collapse on the ground. Pain shot through his entire body, and his jaw thronged from the impact. The woman lowered herself to the ground and effortlessly kicked away his blade.

Brude lay there dazed, wondering if he was going insane. The other man – the cat thing – was present, standing along-side the woman, both now looking down on him. Brude could clearly see the cat thing's short, grey-striped fur, and the bizarre vertical pupils, which were set in an otherwise slender human face. Each of them wore a thick, fitted black suit, with some sort of symbol in the centre of the chest – an upright silver cross, set within a circle, dividing it into quarters.

'This fellow absolutely stinks,' the cat thing muttered.

'Really?' the woman replied, looking down on Brude. 'I can't smell a thing.'

'Yes, well, it seems there are a few disadvantages to these so-called powers that no one told me about. You could do with putting on a little less perfume yourself.'

'Why thanks. I'll keep your precious nose in mind when I'm getting ready.'

The big man spoke: 'You would've thought he can smell the shit that comes out of his mouth.'

Liel was shoved forward onto his knees alongside Brude. The snivelling man was absolutely petrified, with tears in his eyes, but was otherwise unharmed – he had probably surrendered at the earliest opportunity. His hands were held behind him by the brutish man, who spoke. 'We take this one and drop him with Investigator Fulcrom for questioning. This other fucker, we let go.'

'Why would you let him go?' the cat-man asked. 'We've just caught him.'

'Because, you fool, we want people to know what we're capable of doing.' The brute snapped back Liel's arms with a crack and a scream, and the runt began to cry again. The muscled man pulled out some rope from a thick belt, and bound his broken arms together.

He knelt down, bringing his broad stubbled chin, wide nose and dark eyes ever closer. He clutched Brude's throat in one fist.

'I'm called Vuldon, and we three represent a new entity. We're called the Villjamur Knights. You might want to make it perfectly clear to your comrades, or whatever the fuck you call yourselves, that we are going to hunt you down one by one until the city up here is safer. You *will* comply with the Emperor's laws.'

Brude squirmed a nod, desperately, and meekly pawed at Vuldon's fist.

'All right, that's enough, Vuldon,' the woman said.

He didn't let go.

'Vuldon,' the woman urged, 'don't kill him. Come on, let's go.'

Vuldon eventually released his grasp. Air rushed in. Brude spluttered and heaved, turning on his sides to grip at the wet cobbles.

A moment later, once he had composed himself, he realized that the so-called Villjamur Knights had gone, taking Liel with them.

Brude was left wounded, in the company of corpses.

*

Vuldon shoved the man into a cell, which was more like a cage, and the scrawny fellow curled himself up into a ball, hugging his knees, shivering. The room was constructed from a dreary red brick, the ceiling curved and dripping with moisture from somewhere. There was a bucket in the corner.

'Go easy on him,' Lan cautioned, but such requests seemed to be futile. As she lit a coloured lantern to one side, she met Tane's gaze, but he was coy about confronting their concern over Vuldon's potential. Vuldon seemed to have rediscovered old ways.

Vuldon stepped inside the cell and stood for a moment with his legs apart, his fists clenching and unclenching repeatedly. With the side of his boot, he gave a gentle kick to the skinny figure, who turned onto his back, groaning.

'What's your name?' Vuldon demanded.

'Liel . . .' the thief spluttered. 'Please don't hurt me. I never wanted to be there.'

'What was your purpose tonight – simple theft?'

'We was just going to take a few jewels, yeah, nothin' else, I swear.'

'Who for?'

'Just us, just to buy a bit of bread, nothing else.'

'Liar,' Vuldon said, and threw a lightning-quick punch to Liel's stomach, forcing a gasping scream from the man's mouth.

Lan flinched. Tane couldn't even watch.

'Now, who were you working for?' Vuldon demanded.

Liel was writhing back into a ball again, so Vuldon kicked his back. Liel cried out.

'Who're you working for?' Vuldon raged.

'Sh ... Shalev.'

Vuldon smiled grimly at Lan. 'You see? A little persuasion gets you a lot. You can't pussyfoot around in this job.' He hauled Liel up by his neck and lugged him forwards against the wall.

'Vuldon!' Lan snapped, stepping into the cell. Vuldon seemed to be a structure made entirely of muscle and anger. She did not and would not reveal her fear. She'd been through worse in life, was living through several mind-fucks, and this lump of masculinity *would not* upset her further.

'You think you can get answers by being nice?' Vuldon grunted, stepping aside. 'Be my guest.'

Lan brushed past him and crouched by Liel, whose face was creased in agony. He was crying, and had been for a long time now. She placed a hand on his arm and he flinched – she was alarmed that could elicit such a reaction.

'Liel,' she said soothingly. 'No harm will come to you if you can help us. We just need to find Shalev and, if you can help, we'll free you. It's as simple as that.'

'No one knows w-w-where to find S-Shalev,' Liel mumbled through his sobs. 'That's the p-p-point. It's a secret to us in Caveside. All we knows is things is happening down there, and we can all help out if we want.'

Lan rested her hand on his shoulder, and this time he didn't flinch. He stared through tear-filled eyes at the wall. 'What details can you give us?'

Vuldon lumbered in the cell again. 'This is useless.'

'Keep him away!' Liel said in a panic, and Lan, surprised at her own assertiveness, held out a hand, a line which Vuldon did not pass.

'I'll fucking kill you if you don't tell us anything,' Vuldon taunted.

'No,' Lan said, 'he won't.'

Liel didn't know where to look, so he drew his knees up and buried his head in folded arms. 'We're not allowed to know, none of us is. Nearest any of us can get is the Central Anarchist Council – bunch of people who used to be some-bodies, then nobodies, then somebodies again once Shalev came along. They ask for certain jobs to be done out in the main city, and we help them in exchange for some food and weapons. No money involved, like, it's all helping each other out.'

'What about the Bell Spire – do you know who was involved with that?'

'N-nothin'. There's a core group of fighters maybe, but it's usually just Shalev doing that – and as I said, we don't know nothing about her.'

'Can you tell us anything about this Central Council?'

'It's temporary, they say. Only until things is more equal between the caves and the upper city.'

Lan asked, 'What else is going on down there?'

Liel gawked up and for the first time this evening had composed himself. 'Plans. Big plans. I've only heard tell, like, but nothing in stone. But it's gonna be big and a lot of people are getting excited.'

'Tell us the rumours, idiot,' Vuldon grunted from the shadows.

'That the upper city ain't gonna be no more,' Liel said.

'They're gonna take it down, and everyone with it. I told you, big plans.' Liel began to chuckle, and Vuldon rushed in with a punch across his jaw and the man collapsed unconscious in the corner of the cell.

Lan glared at Vuldon, trying to control her rage at this brute.

'What?' Vuldon merely shrugged and turned away.

'I think we should let the Inquisition conduct interrogations in future,' she muttered.

THIRTEEN

Ulryk dismounted from his black mare with a soft grunt and gently rubbed her long face. She particularly liked attention to her nose, and he made sure to reward her with some fuss from time to time. He needed to feed her very soon – it had been a long journey.

The guards at the third gate of Villjamur stepped out from their station, a baroque little structure constructed from dark granite, and stood gawking at the two of them. All three military men wore the same crimson uniforms, with subtle grey stitching, tight armour and heavy swords. The mud outside the doorway to their station was not as trampled as outside the first gate, which indicated that visitors did not usually get this far.

In the biting cold, with flecks of snow spiralling around them, Ulryk showed the guards his papers, as he had done at each of the first two gates, but more importantly he displayed the medallion that hung around his neck. He was wearing several layers of simple brown clothing and had to root some way through it before it could be produced.

It was a gold eight-pointed star, a triangle set inside, and within that an eye.

The three guards gathered around to scrutinize it, though their faces registered their ignorance of such items. Ulryk despaired. He had hoped that such a senior Jorsalir symbol would at least be noted in this great city, as they were in other parts of the Empire.

'I recognize the eye,' one of the guards said, 'and know what that means, but what do the other parts represent?'

'Such symbols,' Ulryk declared, 'are everywhere, and in anything, if you wish to see more meaning. But I would not worry about comprehending such matters – my order forbids such discussions anyway – but suffice to say it's worn only by the most senior members of the Jorsalir community.'

The senior guard leant back, a stern-looking man with a face full of frown-lines and weather-beaten skin. 'Well, this Jorsalir trinket of yours would've been enough to get you in, and those papers of yours suggest you got some important stuff to be doing.'

'That is most perceptive of you,' Ulryk offered, doubting the men would have been able to discern the ornate script. 'I do indeed.'

'Political goings on, eh?'

Ulryk shook his head. 'A mission for Bohr's eyes only, I hope you understand.' He smiled.

'Aye, fair enough. On yer way. Sele of Urtica.' The guard gave a curt nod and one of the others ran behind their station post to activate the gate. A moment later, mechanisms were being cranked, and a massive cast-iron door groaned open.

'Sele of . . . Urtica.' *Of course. The new Emperor.*

*

It's been a successful start, Investigator Fulcrom thought, back in his office in the Inquisition headquarters. Before he started this morning, he'd received a full briefing from the Knights, and was most impressed at how well they were working. Vuldon's knowledge of urban matters seemed invaluable, and they had already captured one Cavesider who had been associated with Shalev, albeit distantly. But it was enough for him to include it in his reports to the Emperor, and that was what mattered.

Fulcrom stoked the fire and sat back in his chair, watching the flames rip into the wood. He felt the pressure from the Emperor, but knew he could rise to such a challenge. It certainly made a difference from his day-to-day routines, and overseeing the vague assignments under the banner 'Special Investigations' was growing on him. He liked the challenge of the new, something with which he could really make his mark on the city, make a difference.

A knock on the door disturbed his thoughts.

'Come in,' he called.

'Investigator Fulcrom?' It was one of the male administrative staff. 'Do you have a moment to talk to a visitor? I've been told this is one for your, uh, department.'

'Yes, of course. Show them in.'

The figure headed back outside and there was a shuffling of feet in the doorway.

His visitor entered the room and Fulcrom raised an eyebrow. The man was no taller than five feet, garbed in the brown robes of a Jorsalir priest, with close-cropped grey hair and a trim beard. The lines in his broad face were deep, suggesting he'd probably seen much of the world, and not all of it good. The man placed his numerous hessian bags to one side. There was a pungent, earthy aroma about him, indicating many days spent on the road.

'Sele of Urtica.' The figure handed Fulcrom the documentation which he would have used to enter the city. Fulcrom took a look over it, and noted all the iconography and decoration of the Jorsalir church, and though he knew forged documents existed to get into Villjamur, these high-level authentication papers seemed official enough. Fulcrom was instantly intrigued.

'Sele of Urtica, friend. Please, take a seat.' Fulcrom handed the papers back and indicated the chair. Hastily, he lit two blue paper lanterns and placed them at opposite ends of his dark wooden desk.

The traveller seated himself with a gentle sigh, and placed his hands on the tabletop. 'It is indeed reassuring to see one so efficient in his day-to-day business,' he began, looking around at the inordinately neat office. 'It brings to mind my own quarters.' His rasping voice carried a thick accent, one which accentuated each word – particularly the ends – with clarity.

Fulcrom never really noticed the neatly stacked piles of paper, the symmetrically organized writing implements and notebooks. 'I just can't seem to work any other way. So, stranger – how can I help?'

'My name is Ulryk.'

'I'm Investigator Fulcrom. You're no longer at your monastery I see?'

'How did you . . . ?' The priest paused. 'The seals on the documents. Of course.'

Fulcrom acknowledged the comment. 'I'm intrigued – how did you end up in Villjamur?'

'I was a chief librarian of a Jorsalir monastery based further along the Archipelago, and I have spent many months making my way through the snow to here.'

'It looks like you have spent a lot of time writing, judging by the black ink staining your nails,' Fulcrom observed. 'Your fingers, too, seem to show signs of being a scribe.' He sat opposite and waited for the man to speak.

The priest gave a beatific smile. 'I see why you are an investigator. Yes, I have spent . . . decades hunched with a stylus.'

'What did you write about?'

'I translate books,' Ulryk replied. 'Religious texts of major significance. Very few people can read the languages with which I am familiar. I sought to make the – ' he paused briefly ' – *sacred* teachings of the Jorsalir church better known.'

'And is that why you have come to Villjamur, to further your translation work?'

Another smile, this one more distant. 'You could say such things. Tell me, investigator. How well do you know your city?'

'I've seen much of it, if that's what you mean. I know most districts, most streets.' Fulcrom chuckled. 'Why, do you require a guide?'

'I very much doubt a guide could show me where I need to go, precisely. No, I need an inquisitive mind most of all, and someone to permit me access to some of the labyrinthine depths of this city.'

'I'm familiar, to some extent, with the ancient passage-ways.'

'This city is older than you think, investigator.'

'I'm not sure I follow you entirely. Why do you need to go under the city?'

'What if I were to tell you that all you know of the history of this world was a lie?'

'I'd say you were mad.'

Ulryk laughed a surprisingly hearty laugh, all the time shaking his head. He rubbed his eyes – here was a tired man indeed, Fulcrom thought.

'Many say that I am, investigator,' Ulryk muttered. 'May I check with you, how the laws are between the church and the Inquisition? Is the Villjamur Inquisition bound to the church? It does not happen in other cities but I must be certain.'

'There are no connections, so I'm afraid backhand deals or special favours are out of the question, if that's what you mean,' Fulcrom replied, which seemed to satisfy the priest. 'Look, I can't really help you without knowing a little more information.'

'I would not ask for such deals, but I am a man in need of help, investigator, and I have few other places to go. I need your assistance in granting me access to certain quarters of the city, and I can see that from my experiences getting into the city, these are times of high security.'

'You could say that,' Fulcrom replied. *A man who comes to the Inquisition for help often feels powerless, though rarely a criminal. What is he after exactly?*

Ulryk's gentle gaze betrayed nothing. 'I have travelled from Blortath, one of the non-Empire islands.'

'It surprises me that the Jorsalir church are represented outside the Empire.'

'They like to keep it quiet in case Imperial rulers think they are up to mischief. The largest Jorsalir monastery of them all, Regin Abbey, is unknown to few save ecclesiastics. It contains the largest library of texts in the Boreal Archipelago, and my work was maintaining these works. We have millions of books, investigator.' Ulryk reclined into his chair. 'Volumes of leather made from the hides of animals long extinct from our lands, and languages long forgotten. They were written by the great civilizations of Azimuth and Máthema, and before then, in the legendary Rumel Wars.'

'Books exist for that long?'

'If they are well looked after. Admittedly, some are translations of earlier sources, and thus not as reliable. Some are too precious to even open, which makes one wonder if it can even be called a text any longer, more an artefact.'

'So this is what you do then, as librarian?' Fulcrom enquired. 'You translate books and look after their storage. Hardly seems the cause for such a journey, though I must admit it sounds a rather pleasant existence.'

'For years it used to be so – that is, until I learned that much we know about the world is *inaccurate*.'

'A bold claim.' Fulcrom was endeared by the priest. There was something about his manner that intrigued him, a deep sense of calm, of peace, even though the lanterns exaggerated the angles of his face, making him look older.

Ulryk leaned forward across the desk with a sudden urgency. He paused to gaze around, then whispered, 'My discoveries have caused a schism within the church. They *will* come for me.'

Fulcrom wondered just how much trouble a librarian could get into.

*

They took tea and talked. Fulcrom lit a yellow lantern. Given that he had no business with the Knights for another few hours yet, he allowed Ulryk to continue his story.

'Why bother telling me all these things?' Fulcrom asked.

After a moment's reflection, Ulryk said, 'Because I am an honest man.'

'You'd be surprised how many criminals have told me just the same.'

A warm smile from the priest. 'They might still be honest men, investigator, even if they caused harm. But I feel the need to unburden myself and share this knowledge – it is no good just in my head and you are the first secular official I have spoken to for . . . years.' Ulryk chuckled. 'My, it has been a long time. It feels a relief to finally tell these things to someone who would not punish me for the act.'

'You mentioned a schism in the church,' Fulcrom said. 'What's the split over?'

'The gods,' Ulryk sighed, suddenly on edge. He slid the chair back and shuffled slowly to the tiny window alongside the bookshelves. There he gazed out across the street, his face creased with anxiety. 'Are we . . . quite safe, here?'

'This is the Inquisition,' Fulcrom declared. 'As a free man, you're in no safer place.'

'Good,' Ulryk continued. 'Yes, the split is over gods, but investigator, what do *you* know of the gods of this world?'

'I'm not much of a religious man, I'm afraid,' Fulcrom offered apologetically.

Ulryk waved for him to go on. 'Tell me their tales, as you have heard it. Please, indulge me this once.'

'Well, uh, all I know is that the creator gods, Bohr and Astrid, were part of the legendary Dawnir race in the heavens that came to this plane of existence. The two moons of this world were named after them. They had great powers and could channel the world's energies. Then one of the races they created – the Pithicus? – formed a rival clan, and the War of Gods followed. That was, uh, a few hundred thousand years ago?' Fulcrom laughed. 'It sounds ridiculous, but it's all I know I'm afraid – I neglect to go to church these days. I guess I have too much work to do.'

'No, you did well,' Ulryk enthused, approaching, and Fulcrom only then noticed that his eyes were an intense shade of green. 'That's an accurate description of our history as told in *every* Jorsalir church throughout the Empire. And this is where the schism begins, right at the very start of things. What I discovered through my translation work was a *different* version of this history. Over the last few years I have checked and rechecked my sources, but a certain batch of ancient tomes seem to contradict this history, with vivid accounts of a very different beginning – some even with sketches, diagrams and art.'

'I can see why that could cause an upset,' Fulcrom agreed.

Ulryk came to sit again at the desk and gave Fulcrom a look of despair.

Fulcrom would often be confronted with the insane, those seeking attention, those on the fringe of society, those in need of a care he couldn't give them – it was all part of working in the Inquisition. But there was something about the raw honesty of Ulryk that suggested this was totally genuine.

'Could the documents have been forgeries?' Fulcrom asked.

'Unlikely. In fact, I have evidence that some of the official histories were forged. Subtleties in the vellum, the inks used, the languages, matched ductus and the likes . . .'

'What were these new histories?' Fulcrom asked. 'What was it about the gods specifically that has caused a so-called schism?'

Ulryk's temper – if it could be called that – flared. 'I will first address the matter that this schism is very real, investigator. Thousands of lives have been lost already, and the communities built around the church were decimated once I leaked this information. I am a fugitive of the church. A year ago men and women were butchered simply for protecting me and allowing my passage to the Empire – where the church has greater connections, I might add. I have seen children hung from trees and the blame placed upon me – all because of the information I possess.'

'I don't think this is the whole story,' Fulcrom said. 'The church would have no reason to burn villages in your name, for what could be considered the simple blasphemy of a madman.'

A silence, then Ulryk muttered, 'It was not all, admittedly. For several years up until that point, I had translated sacred Jorsalir texts into local languages, and had given them away for the people to practise their spiritual paths without the power of the church interfering. I felt that it was unfair to monopolize the words of Bohr and Astrid. Then, nearly two years into testing the fake histories which I had discovered, I began to cease helping the communities around the abbey. How could I believe in the lies I was spreading? One member of my former community came to the doors of our main church and revealed my actions. I was betrayed at a most critical time. I went on the road, and I hid for several months, refining my theories and processes, whilst schooling others in these new theories. There were many friends in the towns and villages who sheltered me, up until the church's military wing went into action. I was the subject of a witch-hunt and almost everyone who has known me is dead.'

'And you faked your papers to get into the city, didn't you?' Fulcrom suddenly realized. 'You used your skills with script to trick the city guards – and myself. There's no way you would have been let in otherwise. The church would have seen to it.'

Ulryk closed his eyes.

For some reason, that act of forgery seemed to confirm Ulryk's desperation – here was a man of intelligence, and Fulcrom could trust in the fact that at least Ulryk believed himself.

'These histories . . .' Fulcrom asked. 'How do they differ?'

Ulryk's gaze was intense. 'According to the new histories I discovered, the Dawnir were created by the hands of one man – as a matter of fact, he created many creatures. His name was Frater Mercury, and he was skilled with technologies that could create, from nothing, elaborate and detailed mythological beings, as well as many creations of his own muse. He was a powerful man – too powerful, in fact, for his time. As far as I can gather, a collection of religions united under the Jorsalir banner raising a rebellion against the use of such technology, which was perceived as highly dangerous. This eventually spilled over into combat – the land was ripped apart in a great war – and Frater Mercury was forced to leave this plane of existence. Using his aptitude with technology, he stepped into another dimension, taking his creatures with him. And, what was left of history was rewritten by the Jorsalir collective church – featuring your charming recollections of Bohr and Astrid. These stories and widespread violence suppressed Frater Mercury's technology, though of course the cultists have salvaged much. The secrets of that society still exist – the church has kept vaults of ancient texts hidden, many of which are manuals left by Frater Mercury – few people can decipher them today, perhaps only myself. I believe a key text lies somewhere in this city. It is here, investigator, though so old it might be in no fit condition to decipher – though try, I must. And I can offer proof of these texts being somewhat ... magical, I suppose. Come with me – I need to show you something. Will you indulge me further, investigator?'

Ulryk stood, preparing to leave the office.

I have been doing so for the past hour ... Fulcrom reached for his over-cloak. 'I think I need some air to blow some sense into me.'

*

Under a violet sky streaked with grey clouds, Fulcrom marched across the streets of Villjamur with Ulryk. Together they were doing their best to avoid the many horse-drawn carriages, carts and clusters of civilians who were sifting through the city. A dark-haired woman in glorious gold and royal blue clothing was handing out copies of *People's Observer* to passers-by keen to read the latest sanitized news from Balmacara. Two garudas sailed overhead on patrol, bound on a gentle landing arc towards a nearby wall, the downdraught ruffling Fulcrom's white hair, which he immediately smoothed back down.

Fulcrom noticed how Ulryk was constantly gazing about himself with the wonder of a child, and twice Fulcrom had to guide him out of the path of others. One man drew a sword on the priest when they collided, but Fulcrom flashed the Inquisition medallion, and the assailant backed away.

They went past excited children, who were grouped around one of the city's noticeboards, and instead of some official declaration, a parchment had been nailed there by the Myth-Maker.

Ulryk asked Fulcrom what the drawings concerned.

'It's a *story*,' sighed a red-haired kid in scruffy breeches who'd overheard him. His tone seemed incredulous that the priest did not already know who or what the MythMaker was.

Fulcrom scanned the parchment, the edges of which rippled in the breeze. On the paper were a few rectangular frames and, within them, characters had been drawn in various poses. There were two figures in this series, each wearing cloaks, and in the first box they were standing on the top of a tower. Lines of text had been scrawled underneath to indicate their speech. Fulcrom had to admit the artwork, though crude, was impressive.

'Whose story is it?'

'The MythMaker,' three of the kids said at once insistently.

'And what is the story about?' Ulryk asked the redhead, who was on tiptoes, glancing between the eager heads.

'Saving the city,' the kid snapped despairingly. 'Legends, and that kind of shit. You know, like creatures from the past and all that. The hero is saving Villjamur from the evil monsters out in the country.'

Ulryk beamed at Fulcrom, his eyes creasing in delight. 'Such joy in these innocent young minds.'

'Indeed,' Fulcrom said, and contemplated hauling down the artwork because it blocked an official noticeboard. But he noticed an older child explaining the story to a younger one who clearly could not read, so decided it was perhaps doing no harm.

Eventually, Fulcrom and Ulryk ended up standing by the rear of a bakery. Warmth from an oven was melting the previous night's snow from the roof, and water dripped down in a gentle trickle, into a gutter, then down a drain.

Fulcrom stood with his hands in his pockets as Ulryk withdrew a heavy book from his satchel. It was more than a little battered, crafted from brown leather, and the pages inside seemed blighted by mould and damp.

'Watch the water,' Ulryk cautioned, 'and place your fingers in your ears.'

Fulcrom did as he was told, chuckling to himself at the absurdity of his situation. *Well, at least with Special Investigations, or 'weird shit' as the other investigators whisper, I'm no longer staring at corpses.*

Ulryk began to intone from the book, as if preaching. His mouth became contorted, shaping word forms that were clearly not of Jamur origin. Fulcrom regarded the dripping stream of water, and waited patiently.

Slowly – remarkably – the water began to alter its course ... yes, it reversed itself, sloshing up from the drain and back up into the gutter, then spouting up onto the roof.

Ulryk guided Fulcrom's hands towards the water. 'Go on,' he encouraged, 'it's quite all right to touch it.'

The water struck his hand, which interrupted the upward flow, and he could feel the force of it against his palm. Fulcrom was staggered, withdrawing his hand to dry it, whilst watching the flow continue once again. 'How did you do this?' he asked.

Ulryk held up the book. 'It is the power of words, investigator. I had to show you something incredible, so that you might have faith in me. Do you believe some of what I say now?'

'What is that?' Fulcrom indicated the book.

'This is merely one of many powerful texts that I have recovered – perhaps the most powerful of all.'

Fulcrom simply watched the water flowing in reverse, against the forces of nature, in thick upward slops. He had considered the story in great depth, and now added this new variable into his thoughts. *If he's a man of magic, he could have harmed me. His story seems strange, but he's not asking for much* ... 'You could have a relic up your sleeve.'

'Do you see any? You may search me if you wish.' He placed the book in his satchel and held his arms open. 'Though later, when I have found my way around the city, I can show you more magic. Consider this a deposit of sorts.'

'A search won't be necessary. OK, I can help you out where I can, though I'm not sure what I can do. If you need special passes or protection, I can see to that. I'm afraid I'm a little stretched for time these days.'

'I simply need one man of influence to help me on my way about the city!' The priest suddenly leapt up and down, a vision of joy upon his face, and Fulcrom wondered what he was getting himself into.

FOURTEEN

Ulryk's Journal

I arrived in the great Sanctuary City, the city of legends, Villjamur, and it is most claustrophobic. People drifted about with their heads down low among shit-sodden streets. They navigated islands of ice. There was little joy to be found in the old, winding lanes, and once one saw past the veneer there beat a heart of darkness.

After speaking to Fulcrom, I took lodgings in an innocuous hotel at the base of the city. There were no other guests to my knowledge, and my small, sparsely furnished quarters seem perfectly located – the back of the building, with no other windows looking on mine. From here, one could see the street below and for some considerable distance any lines of approach to the building.

Finally I once again commenced the evening rituals after so long a gap.

I locked the door of my room. A rapid pulse revealing my nerves, sweat trickling down my neck, I set several candles around the fire, with certain powders arranged in neat, spaced and intricate piles, as the Book denotes. I unwrapped it, laid before me on the floor my copy of The Book of Transformations, and lined up the pages of woodcuts and made the appropriate offerings.

I bathed in warm, yellow light, I read aloud the script that only I can discern.

*

I am his protégé and apostle. I am the only one who has solved His questions thus far. He said He had found me, altered the elements of the world so that I would find the first book, buried at the heart of Regin Abbey. A man who could read the scripts of old was required to be worthy enough for blessings from the real God, the real Creator and I am that man. I am His chosen one. He came to me, almost two years to the day, in that distant corner of Regin Abbey, in that hidden room, where I was the first to walk in thousands of years . . . Oh how his presence warmed my bones and rekindled my spirit.

He came to me first as a dream, then a ghost, then something more. After I was translating one particular ancient text, something seemed to happen to me: whether or not something existed within the lines of that book to cause a momentary trance, I will never know, but it felt as if I had lost a day in my mind. I thought I was going mad. Then I felt an urge to explore further books within the library. My dreams guided me, and then He made himself known to me. His words, which were present directly within my head rather than through my ears, were like nectar. I felt instincts and urges to head to barren regions in the library in Regin Abbey, through storerooms and secret rooms until I stumbled into a room I later discovered was for banned texts. There The Book of Transformations was to be located. I studied it for days. I was not born for such a destiny, He told me, I earned it through my assiduous nature.

At the time I was not aware of the power of the Book. It was mysterious and frustrating, though I could fathom few of its secrets. I discovered more and eventually found that with this book I could communicate with Frater Mercury. He then guided me to discover the secret history of the Boreal Archipelago, the many thousands of years of lies.

If I was to be His tool for greater things then so be it. I would find His other book and remake Him here, as He wished.

*

With The Book of Transformations in my hands earlier today, I spoke to Frater Mercury.

It had been weeks since I was able to open the channels of communication and He seemed most annoyed at first, because I used methods that were not fully approved, but I managed to calm Him, and reassure Him. I asked Him — or His hazy, smoky form — of His requirements, if He could offer any further guidance, and what the situation was now like in His own world.

He said terrible things would happen, were happening, and would be made worse if I didn't help Him. The situation was clear. The other race, Pithicus (our corruption of the word Akhaioí) are stationed outside His city, and sent someone back into our world. The enemy had done things to this figure, transformed him beyond recognition, and sent him on a path here — to Villjamur. The Pithicus had become a devastating force: they had caused more deaths than he could count; more than He can regenerate. His civilization of the Dawnir — those we once thought to be our gods — had to resettle in the Boreal Archipelago, the land in which many of their ancestors were born, as soon as was possible.

There seemed very little left for them in their world.

Frater Mercury asked for me to continue with the plan of recovery. He wants to return to the land from which he was exiled, so he may open the way for the Dawnir. He wants to renew his science, to begin again and to bring His creations with Him.

I still needed to know where the other book is to be found, but His knowledge of the city is vastly outdated, and I must rely upon Fulcrom's advice. What was here in His time was a different city, one now demolished and scattered to the winds, built again, then again, until Vilhallan and then Villjamur swelled up from the remains.

His maps are meaningless now. It is up to me to find the book, in a city of which I have no knowledge, where a church figure may or may not be hunting me, preventing me from returning him—

*

A disturbance. I knew they were coming, and it was more than just my paranoia.

Below my window was one of their abominations, a nephilim. It was a smaller one designed so as to cause no stir in the city, and for all I know it could well have been one from the very tombs under Regin Abbey. The creature loitered there, in the sleet, hunched in its wax coat, while all around it people carried lanterns that forced harsh shadows across the street. The demon must have been able to sense me, having hunted me across the Archipelago, so I used a text from the Book to create an aura of invisibility around my window, and I saw it looking up at me, with skin so old the thing appeared as if it was almost made of bone. The dark holes of its eye sockets then regarded something else along the street, and then it lumbered away. Though I know I could avoid its clutches, the very sight of this abomination sent a deep fear into my heart.

The church will stop at nothing until I am dead. I have to hurry and locate the mirror copy of The Book of Transformations, and only then can I bring Frater Mercury into this world, for it is clear He is the real Creator. He has to return. He has to put right the histories that were overwritten with a false mishmash of tribal gibberish.

Oh, my faith has been shaken to the core. Much of the Jorsalir teachings were not based on histories but on real practice, and those exercises – meditations and the likes – were still valuable to me. But right then, I didn't believe I could ever be at peace. I found it insurmountable to describe to anyone what it was like to have one's beliefs gradually evaporate before one's eyes. All those years of learning, of routine, of praying . . . and it was misguided – not wrong, but channelled in the wrong way. Given all that I'd learnt, how could I preach when no one will believe me?

Only Frater Mercury can put the world right again. I need Him to provide real truth. The world deserves to know the truth.

My search for the book continues.

FIFTEEN

Clothed in black, the Knights lingered on a bridge adjacent to the Astronomer's Glass Tower. The monument towered upwards, glinting as if it was a gargantuan sword puncturing the low clouds. Lan did not know the material it was crafted from, this alien structure in a city full of eclectic architecture, but it stood out from most buildings she had seen, with several sides and its tip like a multi-faceted crystal used by tribal healers.

Within, it was said that astronomers could monitor the orbit of the moons, or calculate how long the ice age would last. Vuldon made wild claims: he had seen within, many years ago, where astrologers, not *astronomers*, divined the night sky for guidance for the Emperor on various Imperial policies. This would have been blasphemous to Jorsalir ears.

Dozens of buildings were being patched up or fully rebuilt. Spires and bridges were being repaired after a millennia of neglect and decay. Those on the verge of crumbling were being ripped down in controlled cultist-guided explosions, and new architecture built. During the day metal, skeletal frames were loaded, crosshatching much of the stonework, with masons crawling across them like ants. Work had already commenced on the enormous job of repairing the Jorsalir Bell Spire. The Knights had passed the site on the way here, and various tundra flowers, messages and strange totems adorned the boards blocking off the wreckage. Luckily, since much of the structure tumbled into an area being redeveloped, the death toll had not been great – forty, when it could have been in the hundreds.

Lan had seen the Emperor's plans for the city. Villjamur was to be reconstructed in the shape of the great cultures of the past, and the Knights were here to protect that dream. Which meant clearing the streets of crime.

'It's awfully cold up here.' Tane slapped a black-gloved hand on the rail of the bridge and peered between the buildings either side. Then he turned his focus to the city beyond. 'I can smell what's being cooked in bistros even from up here. A few herbs and spices.'

'I can smell more bullshit,' Vuldon replied.

'No, it's true.'

This was the seventh night in a row they had waited on the bridges, scrutinizing the city for any signs of trouble. It seemed an odd brief, to fight crime in such a random way, and to be so visible to the citizens. But they understood that they were there for morale, a visible presence, as much as a deterrent. At least it was a gentle way to get used to her powers. Though they had received days and days of training before being released into the city, she still couldn't quite master her sense of balance and spatial awareness. She had twisted her ankle on a rooftop or narrowly missed knocking herself out on a bridge a few times.

'So this is what my life has become,' Vuldon grunted. 'Waiting to see what a cat-man can find for me to hit.' He shifted his weight from foot to foot, rubbing his arms to stay warm.

'I prefer werecat,' Tane replied tartly.

'And what exactly was your life before this point, Vuldon?' Lan asked. 'Sitting alone in the dark feeling sorry for yourself? Face it, you love doing this again.'

'Fair enough, lady,' Vuldon replied with a sharp grin. Occasionally he seemed so soft and strange for such a brutish-looking man. 'So, Tane, the werecat, what can you hear? Now a councillor's been blown up, we need to haul in some fuckwits so it looks like we're doing our jobs effectively. I know how the authorities work – they don't deal in subtleties. They want numbers to recite at each other in meetings.'

Lan had felt the burden of expectation on them ever since Fulcrom had reported the assassination of Councillor Mewún at the hands of the anarchists. He had asked the Knights to step up their patrols, to question the public, to make themselves seen, and to bring in anyone they suspected of misdemeanours or being connected to the terror group. Moments like this, hanging around and waiting for more intelligence, seemed to exaggerate that pressure.

'Give me a moment. I think I've got something.' Tane leant forward and tilted his head this way and that, his face-fur clear in the moonlight. Whether or not it was her imagination, every day he seemed less like a human. 'I'm hearing raised voices – there is an incident ... somewhere around Gata du Quercus. Yes, I am most definitely getting something, someone just screamed.'

'Any idea what it is?' Lan asked.

'I think,' Tane said, leaping up onto the side of the bridge with surprising agility, 'that we've a bit of a brawl on our hands, chaps. It could be a gang of some sort, I'm not sure. I can't quite perceive exact sounds from this distance. Maybe it's the anarchists?'

'Fucking crowd control, then,' Vuldon said. 'Gata du Quercus it is. I'll try to be quicker this time.' He turned to sprint down the bridge, whilst Tane leapt down onto the roof below and sprinted along the tiles on all fours.

Lan inhaled and tapped in to whatever it was she could control, connecting with the new forces inside her and tuning them with the gravity that pulled her to the earth. She pushed herself up onto the side of the bridge, steadying herself for balance. *Find it ...*

One foot out . . . She still hadn't grown used to her powers, but within a minute she had glided down. A rush of chill wind, the tiles moving towards her vision, then – *look up!* – she nearly hit her head on a piece of guttering. The city seemed constructed purely to annoy her. She pushed off with one foot, skimmed down slanted roofing, then hovered gently upwards, upwards, and started running through the air . . .

Such freedom!

*

Lan glided down to land behind Tane, who was crouching by a street corner, gripping the brick edge of a building, claws bared, his head tilted to listen into the distance.

Vuldon turned up a few moments later, slightly breathless. 'I might be strong, but I sure as hell can't get around the city like I used to.'

'That's because you're old,' Tane whispered.

'Shut it, *kitten*,' Vuldon said.

'Guys, please,' Lan interrupted. 'Tane, are we near the situation?'

'It's right ahead, my dear.'

Towards the end of the street, two rival factions were in a stand-off. Rumel versus human, a conflict possibly born out of racial tension. Tane glanced back. 'They're saying something about rumels causing the genocide on another island. Does that mean anything to you?'

Lan and Vuldon shrugged.

She said, 'Well we can't let this flare up any more – we're here to keep order.'

'Where are the city guard right now?' Vuldon demanded. 'They should be looking after little skirmishes like this.'

'I suspect that there is your answer, old boy.' Tane pointed a clawed finger at the few armoured men lined up alongside the humans. 'It appears that the fear has infected them, too.'

Lan thought suddenly of Investigator Fulcrom, a rumel.

'We can't just stand here and allow it to inflame. Let's go.' She pushed past Tane, and towards the fray, surprised at her own assertiveness.

There were maybe twenty rumels and twice that for the human line. All wore work gear, dark breeches, dirtied jumpers and cloaks. Broken bottles, swords and torches were being brandished, and chanting and screaming increased in intensity as she came nearer. She saw there were a couple of men with the rumel, standing between the sides, hands held out and demanding peace. At the centre of the ruckus was a rumel woman and a blond male human, him protecting her. A human leapt forward from the opposing ranks to strike the other man, drawing blood from his head. Vuldon burst from behind, and into the group, the sheer force of his mass ploughing several men to the ground in an instant.

He dragged one of the human offenders nearer and kicked him in the stomach. Another two attacked him with swords but he grabbed their wrists, broke their arms. He stood to regard the simmering masses. No one dared to go near him.

Vuldon did nothing but breathe heavily and stare at the offender at his feet. Tane joined them, and together the Knights stood between the two opposing lines.

A silence of sorts fell across the scene.

'What's going on here?' Lan demanded to the group.

'Why should we tell you, bitch?' came a reply.

'Shouldn't you be in the kitchen, sweetheart?' laughed another. 'Why're you dressed like a bloke?'

Lan blanked their comments. 'I'll repeat my question: what is going on here?'

'Fuck this.' Vuldon grabbed the man on the ground by the scruff of his neck, then yanked him upright, clutching his throat in one immense fist. 'Someone will give the lady an answer, or I squeeze. And don't even try to call my bluff. This runt means nothing to me, and the older I get, the more impatient I become, so you better hurry up.'

'He's not lying,' Tane chimed in, grinning.

'It's them.' A stout human gestured to the interspecies couple. 'Shouldn't be allowed, not with them rumel invading Tineag'l like that. How can we trust rumel scum now?'

Lan marched up to the man and woman in question. The fear was clear to see in the black-skinned girl's eyes. She was pretty, delicate and well-dressed, and this scene was no place for her. Lan placed an hand on her shoulder, then told the couple to run – which they did in an instant, the blond man mouthing, 'Thank you.' Their steps echoed down the street, between the crumbling stone walls, fading into the distance.

'Why've you let the fuckers get away? Slut!'

Vuldon heaved his victim into the air, and tossed him wailing into the mass of bodies. Tane and Vuldon moved forwards, full of violent promises. Some of the gang challenged them, foolishly, and the boys set to work.

They threw stomach-blows, kicking legs away from under people, slamming them into walls. A couple ran down a side street, some drew the injured bodies to one side, the rest saw sense and backed off, surrendering themselves.

'What're you meant to bloody well be then?' someone called out. 'On yer way to a fuckin' party?'

A ripple of awkward laughter, and Lan became aware of the Knights' matching black costumes.

'We are the Villjamur Knights,' Tane declared. 'And as citizens of this city, as subjects of the Emperor, you must respect *order*.'

Tane's anger surprised even Lan: he sprang up and then into the group to grab the man – a skinny fellow with bad teeth and no hair – and slit a line across his face. He collapsed to the floor screaming, and Tane held out his claws. 'Does anyone else have a problem with our attire?'

This act made Lan feel uneasy – she did not like the way the two of them would use their powers so casually. She would have to mention this to Fulcrom later.

'So,' Vuldon said, 'which of you are in league with the anarchists?'

'None of us,' a man called out. 'But we've nothing against them. They're changing things, so why don't you just leave them be.'

'They're criminals,' Vuldon replied. 'Anyone caught associating with them will be imprisoned.'

'What, and now you want us to admit we're one of them? Fuck off, mate.'

Vuldon cringed at his own stupidity. 'Go. And if there's more trouble, we *will* hunt you down.'

Grumbling, the group dispersed. Somewhere out of sight a bottle broke, a sword scraped on stone.

Lan turned to the rest of the Knights. 'So no one's willing to reveal who the anarchists are. How can they be so good at hiding?'

Tane padded a circle on the cobbles, peering around the street corners, or through grubby street-level windows. Two dead bodies lying on the ground he regarded with absolute indifference.

Vuldon picked up the discarded weaponry, drew out some material and wrapped them up for the Inquisition. 'We're gonna have to stay out each night and catch the anarchists in the act. That's the only way.'

Lan didn't think much of that. 'We're charged with an impossible task: to find the most efficient criminal operation in a city that's getting out of control. It seems so hopeless. We'll never do it.'

'And I thought old Vuldon was the one who liked a good mope.'

Tane raised one eyebrow in her direction.

SIXTEEN

Covered in sweat, and wearing loose-fitting pale clothing, Lan marched from the training area, through the catacombs, with the warm light from cressets lighting the way back to her room. Today more techniques had been gleaned from ex-military combat specialists, where she had been forced through routines and manoeuvres that were brutal and efficient.

Lan came to the realization that her new role was in fact growing on her. Though she understood her anonymity was constantly in the balance, this existence was one she'd never been able to enjoy previously.

She had respect. She had a challenge. She had a future.

And being one of the Knights meant helping society, and that helped her feel good about herself, too – not that she'd actually helped too many people so far . . .

Lan pushed open the door to the plush, marble-tiled bathroom, and saw that her bath had been filled for her. The scent of lavender wafted through the air, and there were several small lanterns placed about the room. Without any further hesitation, she removed her clothing and plunged into the warm water, feeling the heat begin to penetrate her aching muscles.

Well, perhaps it is nice to think of my own needs from time to time . . .

*

An hour after her luxurious bath, Lan stood on the safe side of a thick pane of glass staring out at the snow, whilst Tane and Vuldon slouched on the plush sofas behind her contemplating some of the Inquisition reports, studying the recommendations and suggestions of those with a better knowledge of the anarchists' movements.

'Still no developments in finding Mewún's killers, apparently,' Vuldon announced. 'And the councillors are becoming increasingly worried about travelling through the city on their own.'

'Never mind that, old boy,' Tane added, holding up a parchment. 'It states here – albeit with appalling punctuation – that crime has gone up massively in the last fifty days. There have been more reports of burglary and vandalism than in recent memory. Shops are being destroyed, bistros burned down. Says there are two hundred thousand people on this side of the city, and most of them are worried about walking through the streets alone. That isn't right. I think we have some work to do.'

'It would be nice to have some strategies in place for us,' Lan said, 'rather than just being let loose aimlessly.'

'We can think of things ourselves,' Tane declared excitedly.

'The city's so big,' Lan added. 'There's such a huge area to cover. We need Fulcrom's help, too. I trust him – he seems a good sort.'

'I've never yet met an investigator I can trust,' Vuldon drawled.

Lan forgot her worries by staring at the sea. Nearby, hamlets cluttered up the shoreline, little white cottages were dotted into the distance, and Lan imagined they had to be brave people, whoever lived there, facing those bleak wintry seas.

Today, the submarine giant was passing again. The top of the creature's grey crown breached the surface, and all around him the water banked and swirled, whilst seabirds arced in the skies, following his painfully slow progress through the tides. As he came nearer, into the shallower waters, torrents skimmed down his thick, green hide. He took one, longing glance into their clifftop retreat, then one to the land beyond as if he knew he could never survive there long enough to enjoy it – before he moved further along the shore, spraying seawater across the villages.

The Knights had been given use of this clifftop dwelling. It was safer for them here, Fulcrom had told Lan. Such sanctuary allowed them to develop their skills according to the designs of cultists without distraction. These headquarters were less than half a mile from the centre of Villjamur, where the city buried its back end into a range of hills, and under which the underground docks opened out and met the sea. Although built into a cave network, there had been a lot of structural and design work. The walls had been smoothed and covered in plaster then white paint. Ornate cressets burned from walls, coloured lanterns stood in corners, cushions and throws and thick-pile rugs were scattered tastefully about the place. Fires burned in the corners and thick windows faced outwards that were so clear they assumed cultists had interfered with the production.

At the sound of the door opening, Lan turned to face the room.

Feror, the cultist-cum-attendant who saw to their every need, tottered in with his notebook. He was nice enough, a tough, wiry old fellow, with lank brown hair and a soft smile. He wasn't a servant – cultists didn't seem to stoop that low. Now and then he'd plug in some relic to 'monitor' them. Cultists. The people in black lingered like swamp midges. They pottered from adjacent rooms, or catacombs deep in the cave system, carrying relics, pieces of technology she'd never understand, before disappearing with patronizing smiles. There were orders here who had been operating in secrecy for years, now on projects that the new Emperor had tapped into.

'Good morning, dear Knights,' Feror called out. 'How are we today?'

Tane and Vuldon barely grunted their acknowledgement, and Lan felt guilty on their behalf. 'We're fine,' she said, 'feeling well. Not much for your little notebook I'm afraid.'

'Oh, it all counts,' he replied, enunciating crisply, in his rather charming way. He began to prod them with a few questions, and they gave brief answers. Yes, they felt fine. No, there were no side effects yet. No, their muscles did not ache. No, they had not fainted, or had spells of dizziness or nausea.

Beleaguered by such endless repetition, Lan distracted him with a query about his family, and he responded with vigour, telling of his second daughter's first day at school, how his wife was developing a range of relic-based techniques of heating liquids quickly. Lan was fascinated by people's lives: perhaps it was because she hadn't experienced an easy life herself.

Feror, ever the patient and passive man, eventually went away clutching his notebook to his chest, humming to himself as he went, and Lan pondered just what secrets that notebook held. 'I'm bored with this research,' Tane declared, and flounced around the room with as much energy as some of the dancing girls in the circus. Ever since his transition, he possessed an over-the-top and hyperactive edge. 'Bored, bored, bored.' He stood before Vuldon, whose broadness dwarfed the slender werecat. 'If we're not actually getting outside fighting crime, surely we could be, I don't know, having people round. Drinks and dancing, parties, that sort of thing. I can throw quite the event . . .'

'We're supposed to keep a low profile when not at work, idiot,' Vuldon grumbled. 'Emperor's orders. Out there you can be as attention-seeking as you want. When you're not beating someone up, be quiet.'

Tane sighed theatrically, and collapsed onto a plush green settee alongside Vuldon. Lan was entertained at first by their repetitive bickering – Tane's optimism repeatedly corrected by Vuldon's pessimism – but now it was becoming annoying. While most of the time they got on, occasionally the conversation would deteriorate into childish banter as the two of them prodded each other, testing how far the other would go in response.

Tane suddenly held a hand out for silence. 'Fulcrom's here,' he announced.

There were only three of them in the room and a moment later the door at the far end opened. Investigator Fulcrom strolled in, and greeted them amiably.

'Spot on again!' Tane said. 'I could smell you a mile off.'

Fulcrom chuckled, and stood with his hands on his hips, his Inquisition robes parting around his tunic. 'I hope my current scent works well for you, Tane.'

'What've you got for us this time, investigator?' Vuldon stood up and folded his thick arms. Lan knew that Vuldon didn't much like the Inquisition, but surely he could trust Fulcrom?

Fulcrom motioned for them to be seated and then lowered himself onto the floor by the settee, a gesture of respect, Lan thought, that spoke volumes. The hazy light from the window spilled across him and the surf droned against the base of the cliff, resonating even up here.

Drawing his knee up, Fulcrom leant back casually and said, 'The Emperor wants to open a new indoor iren in a few days. Its construction has been kept from public eye, mostly because of the anarchists, and generally because he doesn't quite know who to trust.'

'Indoors?' Lan asked.

'It is,' Fulcrom said. 'A hundred or so trader units under one roof, more or less. It's to encourage more people to part with cash during the Freeze, in a safe and sheltered environment. Some of the city's top smiths and artisans are ready to move their wares there. He's hoping such moves will give people hope.'

'While refugees die in the ice outside the city's walls, the Emperor wants to build a palace in which the wealthy can entertain themselves?' Lan asked. She stopped herself from going further, fearing what would happen if she did.

'It isn't our concern,' Fulcrom said, with an understanding glance at her. 'We all have to do our jobs without ever being able to sway Imperial policy. It's the way of the world, unfortunately – but you should be grateful for what has been done.'

'Are we not allowed to help *them* at least?' Lan snapped.

Fulcrom drew a deep breath, but he didn't put her in her place; he didn't react the way she expected.

'I've done many things for this city without thanks,' Fulcrom said. 'I've saved lives only for the very same people to die later. I regularly tell families that their loved ones have been killed, sometimes in the most brutal way. I do such things without your smart outfits, a glamorous abode, or enhanced abilities. I do it because I care for people.'

Lan closed her eyes and wished she hadn't been so blunt. 'I'm sorry,' she breathed.

'Touching,' Vuldon grunted. 'What do we have to do for this fancy iren? Pose for artists?'

Tane chuckled at that, as he padded around behind Vuldon. 'You *do* have a sense of humour after all.'

'No,' Fulcrom said. 'There's going to be an opening ceremony, and Urtica is concerned that it will be a prime target for the anarchists. Security is going to be tight but you three are to make sure nothing happens on the day. It also means, as well as fighting crime on the streets at night, we're to assemble a more thorough investigation and head out into Caveside in order to seek out the offenders.'

'A little unsubtle, don't you think?' Vuldon asked.

'Perhaps,' Fulcrom replied. 'But the Emperor has suggested it's time you became better known. He's already made sure the city criers are spreading the good word, and there will be more write-ups in *People's Observer* in addition to that introductory article a few days ago. It takes time for people to find out about these things. People keep hassling the Inquisition, worried about who you are – because not everyone knows yet, so we must help that along. But that's all something we can do behind the scenes.'

'I'd rather not be up in front of people,' Lan said. 'Not everyone is like Tane, and wants attention drawn to themselves.'

'Such scandalous accusations!' Tane mocked outrage, arms wide.

'I think it might be good for the city,' Fulcrom said. 'Heroes don't just exist – people create heroes in their own minds. In the Freeze they want to believe in something, and with the current crime situation, having *manufactured* heroes could be good for them. You'll most likely raise morale. I'm not quite sure you realize how much you might mean to the city.'

'What, even Misery over there?' Tane gestured to Vuldon, who remained unperturbed.

Fulcrom was looking serious now. His gaze was optimistic, full of a visionary hope. He was immensely persuasive. 'None of you chose to be who you are, and none of us can control what the Emperor requests – but you have to do what is requested of you, for your own good, and that of the city's. That's no bad thing, all right.'

'I'm in,' Tane said. 'And so is Vuldon.'

All eyes turned Lan's way, but how could she explain just how different her situation was from their own? She loathed the attention.

'Fine,' Lan sighed, and stood to walk to the window again. 'Let's just do this, then stop the anarchists so we can all have a quiet life.'

'Sounds like a plan to me,' Tane declared, and padded off to his chamber. Vuldon followed him a moment later.

Fulcrom joined her to gaze out across the sea, watching the white tips of surf break across each other.

'What's wrong?' Fulcrom asked. 'Is it the focused attention?'

'A little, if I'm honest,' Lan said eventually. 'But it's not just that – I'm worried about the boys. They sometimes use their powers so unnecessarily. They can be too harsh. We've brought a couple of people in, but they could be innocents, and treating innocent civilians so brutally seems . . . Well, I'm just not comfortable around it.'

'They're just getting used to their new powers – mentally, that is. It was one of the things we expected – especially from Vuldon, who, according to plan, is the strongest individual in the Empire. But you – how are you coping? Tane says you seem a little . . . reluctant.' Fulcrom placed a hand on her arm and she suddenly froze. She both wanted it there and . . . no one had touched her like that: gently, softly. Not in this form. Not for years.

'I'm sorry,' he said, withdrawing. 'You've been brought into this position against your will, but there's nothing I can do about that. I'd like to help you get over that – that's my job.'

'Is that why you're being so nice?' she asked. 'Because it's your job?'

'It may well be my job, but there's no reason to treat you all like shit is there? You're hardly going to trust me if you hate me.' Then, 'Besides, we're in this together. If we don't catch Shalev and the anarchists, the Emperor will have me killed.'

Lan was shocked, and her expression must have showed it. Fulcrom continued. 'He's said as much. I'm to manage the operation to help purge the anarchists, and I'm to keep an eye on you lot. If you fail, I fail.'

'You spend more time with me than Tane or Vuldon, is all.'

Fulcrom and her had shared several hours of conversation, debate about life and the city, yet at no point had either of them revealed much about themselves. Fulcrom didn't seem to have a life beyond upholding the law.

'They have their moments too.' Fulcrom smiled.

They remained there, in companionable silence, watching the return of the submarine giant as he moved out to sea, and on the horizon, dark, low clouds began to mass.

Later, they could see lightning.

SEVENTEEN

Despite the comfortable wooden benches along the edge of the room, the Knights found themselves pacing. There was an open fire, and the floor was a beautiful mosaic of tiny red, black and green tiles. They were in a low-ceilinged, red-brick chamber, situated directly behind a platform overlooking one of the largest open plazas on the third level of the city.

In a ceremony just for them, the Knights were going to be presented to the people of Villjamur, and Lan truly couldn't be bothered with it all. Why all this showboating? She had just begun to channel any annoyances with her situation into fighting criminals, and she felt good about doing good. Now they were set to become celebrities.

Fulcrom *must* have encouraged this situation. He was a thorough planner, his actions were seldom without purpose, and he worked to a level of efficiency that was beginning to annoy her.

OK, so he interests me. So what? Nothing was going to happen – nothing really could. She hadn't been involved with anyone for years, but she couldn't open herself up to another person, even if he was from a different species. She knew she couldn't have children, so that got rid of the classic human–rumel issue, but what about him? *Stop it, woman. You're thinking like you're shacked up with him already.* She shook herself out of her thoughts. *That way will only lead to pain . . .*

Tane paced the room, seemingly delighted, and the man couldn't stop smiling.

'I remember having to do shit like this back in my day,' Vuldon groaned. 'You get used to it.' His arms were folded, as always. He paused to stare at a religious mural on the wall, but he might as well have been staring into space. *It must be tough for him*, Lan thought, *to have to dredge up his past.*

According to Fulcrom, Emperor Urtica himself had requested this rally to promote awareness of the Knights. The noise of the crowd outside was intense. Impressive, she thought, that so many people wanted to see what the fuss was about. On the way here she had seen large boards erected, each bearing an artist's depiction of the Knights standing side by side before the city. Placards displaying 'Fight Crime' and 'Meet the Heroes', and 'Save Villjamur From Terrorists' were being handed out by the city guard for people to carry in the crowds. Helping to embellish the reputation of the Knights before people even saw them were bards and poets singing songs on the major routes to the iren.

Suddenly she saw Tane looking towards the door, his senses flaring, then it opened – and Investigator Fulcrom, clothed in his finest Inquisition robe, entered bringing echoes of the hubbub from outside in. Smiling and full of encouragement, he said, 'Right, you're on.'

Lan glanced to Vuldon, who sighed, 'Let's get this charade over with.'

Fulcrom led them outside to a section of the vast balcony concealed by heavy and lurid purple banners, providing a relative sanctuary. From in front of the material divide, they could hear the Emperor speaking: '. . . crime has become so troublesome and overburdening to the city guard and Inquisition that we must have new figures to aid the city – and what figures they are. Already they have put twenty criminals into gaol, and saved thirty lives . . .'

Lan nudged Fulcrom and whispered. 'When did we do that? That's not true, is it?'

'No,' Fulcrom admitted with a wry smile, 'but he likes to get people excited.'

'Hmm.'

'. . . and', the Emperor continued, 'they represent a new move for this developing city. Citizens . . .' He let the word hang in the air.

'Here you go,' Fulcrom whispered.

'. . . I present to you the Villjamur Knights.'

Lan, Tane and Vuldon all walked forward from behind the vast banners. The sun was out, bright and blinding and shining off a thousand wet rooftops. Below them, immense crowds were applauding and whistling and cheering, peering out from behind crenellations, or perched on windowsills. Exposed to such an intense noise, Lan felt hesitant. Tane and Vuldon seemed perfectly at ease.

The Emperor himself was standing to one side in his finery, clapping and gesturing them forward so the crowd could get a better look.

Tane and Vuldon marched to the edge of the balcony, receiving gasps from those nearest and, reluctantly, she followed. The citizens of the city, in their dreary layers of waterproofed cloth, extended as far as she could see. The mob was endless. Some started chanting for them to do something, tricks, fly, whatever.

'Lan, why don't you hover for them?' Fulcrom called, and motioned her forward.

Begrudgingly she stepped up onto the rail of the balcony then jumped upwards and backwards – slowly and with a flourish, her hands either side for balance – and there were screams and whistles of awe as she landed softly a few moments later.

She immediately turned to Fulcrom. 'It's like being in the circus all over again.'

'They need to see it,' Fulcrom said beaming.

When she turned back, Tane was crouching on all fours, traipsing up and down the rails with perfect balance, and Vuldon was picking up huge hunks of masonry and throwing them in the air to catch in his other hand.

But will they be comforted by this performance? she thought.

*

That evening things returned to normal: the crowds had dispersed, people were tucked up in their homes, and Lan was on her own.

The Knights split up and spread themselves across the city as individuals, confident in their own skills, and wishing to extend their watch across a wider area.

It was early evening, and whilst the irens were busy packing up, wares being shoved into crates, vendors watering down their fires, two young men burst through the throng to attack a middle-aged lady who was hunched under a thick fur coat and fat emeralds. They grabbed her bag and jewels and ran zigzags through the departing crowds.

Lan leapt up along the side of a building and sprinted underneath the guttering, around thirty feet up from the streets, safely out of the reach of snow and ice. People pointed and gasped at her progress, cheering in some quarters, but she tried to ignore the attention, and scooted after the delinquents. The weight of the world yanked her muscles down to one side, causing her body to ache, but whenever she concentrated, she found herself able to override the natural forces in order to maintain her upright position in this new plane. She leapt over open windows, across alley-ways. Horses and carts rumbled by underneath to her left. The light of the day was vanishing fast – but she was gaining on the thieves.

She could see them now, aiming for the more concealed passageways, so she pushed herself away from the wall and back upright, gliding down to the ground. She ran through the air, towards them and, with one foot extended, kicked the neck of the nearest – who was no more than a boy. He lurched sideways, collapsing to the ground, dropping his bag.

Jewels spilled across the icy flagstones.

As Lan landed she thrust her heel in his stomach, winding him, then she peered up from her crouch to see the other vanishing down a dark passageway. With a crowd gathering round her, applauding her, Lan pulled some rope from her side-pack and tied the youth's hands behind his back.

She marched him back to the Inquisition headquarters.

*

With a pocket half-full of jewels, Caley skidded into Caveside, through a wide opening in the rock that looked like the maw of a gargantuan beast. Resting his hands on his thighs, he heaved breath into his lungs, confident that that bloody Knight woman was no longer following him. Standing, he straightened his woollen hat and unbuttoned the collar of his shirt a little more, allowing himself to cool.

That was close, he thought. *Can't believe she caught Rend. The twat was always the careful one and now look at him.*

He marched into the caves proper, his nose twitching at the stench of wood fires and something more unsavoury. The texture of the streets changed: lanes became thinner, and the buildings were taller, almost leaning on each other for support, with thick wooden beams and thousands of tiny coloured stones pressed into their surfaces. Many houses had once been whitewashed but were now all shades of grime caused by smoke from chimneys. Some of the houses betrayed an older history, having been carved out of the rock, and were rounded with crude circular windows. Warm light glowed from their insides, and when looking across the rest of the underground city, these windows were like starlight. It went some way to make up for the absence of stars and moons up above.

Not every Cavesider was poor. There were signs of wealth

down here, from those who leeched a living off the outer city, some who dealt in illicit gemstones or middlemen who supplied cheap labour throughout Villjamur and surrounding farms; those people occupied the houses higher up, nearer the outer city, away from the decrepit sewers and poorly supplied shops.

The cobbles hadn't been maintained, and more than once Caley caught his toe on a hunk of stone jutting out. Rotting vegetables and dead rats littered the side of the street, in places piling up against walls. A woman – one he knew to be a prostitute – was strutting into an alleyway, holding the hand of a client, something that was happening less and less these days. A tavern at the end of this stretch of road opened its doors to turf out two brawlers, who carried on their fight on the side of the street, whilst around them cats padded explorative paths into the darkness.

It wasn't all bad, here – being sheltered by the caves, it was warmer than the outer city. And things were starting to change. People had more food these days, and money didn't matter with the exchange irens operating without coin. Caley marvelled at how he could simply trade things without scraping around to find the money. People were in better spirits.

That was because of Shalev.

But he needed to let Shalev know of what had happened to Rend – they all stuck together, they were all one community. If someone was caught, they would have to deal with the issue. Shalev had made a family of these Caveside dwellers.

He sauntered half a mile deeper into the caves, across the border of what the Emperor was now labelling as Underground East and Underground South, in an effort to map out the urban sprawl. He headed through what was locally known as Blacksmith Plaza, Sahem Road, Mudtown and Carp Alley. There were passageways and routes here that few knew about, and through which even fewer had travelled, dirt tracks and alleys with hundred-year-old graffiti. A couple of old guys were playing a complicated board game on an upturned cask of beer, whilst somewhere inside an old pipe was whining out a folk tune. A dog trotted up alongside him briefly, then vanished into one of the alleyways.

He palmed hand-slang with a few of the kids he knew. The citizens he passed all knew him in one way or another, and that was good – because otherwise they might have killed a stranger, such was the level of secrecy around here. He saw more than one person instinctively reach for a weapon, these underground soldiers, these comrades without uniform.

Two of his brethren stood guard with fat sabres beneath their cloaks in front of a recent excavation into the cliff face. He nodded to them and entered. It was a magic-blasted route, a damp-smelling, claustrophobic passage, and, standing tall, he continued with one palm gliding against the smooth rock, focusing on the single spot of light in the distance.

Just as he reached it, a hand grabbed him by his shirt and he was yanked forward into the chamber beyond and sent sprawling across the floor.

'Hey,' he spluttered, rubbing his chin, 'it's me, retards, Caley.'

A row of swords were pointed towards him, glinting in the candlelight. Seven men and three women were staring down, and Caley squirmed under their glare.

'Let him through,' a female voice commanded.

As they stepped aside, Caley stood and brushed himself down, nodding to them all.

The room was spectacularly decorated in mosaics, echoing patterns Caley thought came from far-out islands – not that he'd been to any. There were bookshelves and workbenches and row upon row of relics and a fire in the grate. And there, perched on the end of a desk, was a woman with no hair, and bright-blue eyes. He was unable to guess her age, but placed her in her forties. She had a round face, not unpleasant, and her nose appeared slightly squashed, as if some invisible force pressed lightly on it. Wafts of incense floated around the room, and whether it was that, or the way she controlled the mood in the room, he felt utterly at ease.

'What is it, brother?' she asked.

'I needed to see you, Shalev. Rend was taken when we was out nicking stuff from this rich woman. We got a good haul, look . . .' He thrust his hands into his pockets, then offered Shalev a scoop of gems and necklaces.

Shalev smiled crookedly. 'A good haul indeed, Caley.'

He loved hearing her talk – her tone was rich and rounded, her accent heavy and exotic. She invited him to dream of a world far from his own existence.

The others in the room began to stir, moving towards Caley's hands, but Shalev asked a question out loud.

'Do you think', she declared, 'it is right to be tempted by such trinkets? These are the things that separate them out there from you down here. The trinkets are obtained by forcefully removing their materials from other islands, often by slaves who have been forced to submit to the labour. And they are now used to keep you out of the newer houses, out of real daylight. Just you remember that. These are what repress you.'

Caley got a better look at the folk gathered here, most from the old unions, the smiths, or some who made a career scavenging the old mining deposits for remnant ore, and who somehow scraped a living. There were a couple of scholarly types, too, who went around as intellectuals, filling the back rooms of taverns with their theory. Still, they were good sorts. And all could not take their eyes off the contents of Caley's hands, so he placed them on the desk behind Shalev to rid himself of the burden.

'Good, Caley. You're learning well. So, tell me – what happened to Rend?'

'Give you one fuckin' guess,' Caley retorted.

'Don't speak to her like that,' someone behind him said.

Shalev waved the comment away. 'I'm not your superior,' she reminded them.

''Xactly,' Caley muttered. 'You ain't no real Council.'

'They are our temporary Central Anarchist Council though,' Shalev corrected, 'and they have a role to play in regenerating this underground society before we can spread out power evenly. Once we have established ourselves in the city and created a more equal society then we shall dissipate naturally. So we should treat each other with great respect, Caley.' She regarded him with such a powerful gaze he thought he might turn to ice. 'I am going to hazard a guess that it was the Villjamur Knights who took Rend?'

'Yeah, the female one. She ran across the damn walls of the buildings to get to us!'

'The Villjamur Knights,' Shalev breathed, more to herself than anyone else. 'They are becoming annoying, are they not?'

'It ain't safe out there any more. We can't just go around nicking shit without one of 'em waiting in the shadows.'

'Absolutely.' Shalev pushed herself off the desk and towards the grate, whereupon she studied the flames. For a while no one said anything, and Caley shuffled his feet waiting for something to happen.

Suddenly Shalev had an answer: 'The creation of the Knights is simple: to promote fear in those who challenge the Empire. A popular strategy. So if they are after such a campaign, we will use the same technique, too. It would be a good idea to target more obvious symbols like them. We will target the military, perhaps, the city guard who patrol the streets and we will kill them publicly – moreover, fewer guard will make it easier to take back more purses or more items from shops, which feeds into our greater purpose. And the aim of our more vicious attacks is simple: to remove the structures of power and authority. It is power over another that prevents there ever being a fair society, and the Emperor will not have a clue that our aim is a complete deconstruction of Villjamur.'

She turned and ruffled Caley's hair and examined the gathered body of men. 'Are we agreed, brethren?'

A chorus of ayes.

'But I moot that we do not kill *all* of those in authority,' she continued. 'First, we bleed them of information, since we need more knowledge about the Knights – these may present a severe problem for our movement.' Shalev picked up a copy of the *People's Observer* and gestured to the front page. 'This vicious filth and hate-spreading propaganda suggests they are invincible, but we know better than to believe what we read, don't we? They must have weaknesses, and we will find them. These walking weapons *must* somehow be disabled.'

*

Mid-evening, no later than nine, Lan returned to the streets and teamed up with Vuldon on a small bridge over a hefty drop. One of the distant spires, towards the front of the city, was churning out thick smoke. Skies had cleared, presenting the smoke cloud as some horrible shadow-creature, leering over the first and second levels of Villjamur.

'Should we investigate?' Lan asked.

'Could be a house fire or could be a more serious attack,' Vuldon replied. 'We'll not find out by staying here.'

She kept pace with him, skipping slowly across the rooftops, while he traversed the bridges, spiral stairwells and discreet alleyways framed by high stone walls. She could hear his breathing and boot-scuffs constantly as he thundered beneath her along the streets like a bullish military horse.

The spire, when they reached it, was set on the second level of the city; a huge, curved building, probably no more than a hundred years old, crafted out of coarse granite blocks. From the ground the thing seemed immense. Starlight defined its edges, which led to impossible heights and up there somewhere tiny flames began to lick their way out, flaring into the night sky.

Vuldon said to Lan, 'You should get up the side of the building if you can and crack open some windows on the way. If I remember jobs like this, you might get a lot of people at the windows trying to jump in order to get the fuck out of there. Can you carry a human or rumel? You might have to.'

'I'll do my best,' she replied. 'I'm not as strong as you, but my inner forces should be enough. I think by now I can do some tricks with gravity.'

'If you're not sure—'

'I'll be fine,' she snapped.

'Good. I'll clear the way from the ground up, and smash my way through any closed doors.'

Lan crouched then pushed herself upwards and onto the side of the building, sprinting up the stonework. Out of the corner of her eye she saw Vuldon slam-kick the front double doors and barge his way inside.

The wind grew stronger as she climbed higher. As she reached a level parallel to bridges, people began to shout at her, but she couldn't hear what they were saying. With her heel she smashed in the first window, but the fire hadn't reached that far down. When she withdrew her foot she nearly slipped and stumbled – her heart missing a beat – but with her arms out wide and more focused concentration, she stabilized herself again.

Lan resumed her ascent.

Screams were leaking out from the inside. She could hear them faintly at first, someone wailing, like the call of the dead. *Are we too late?* Lan wondered. The noise spurred her on and she rose ever upwards, smashing in windows, always looking in to see if anyone was inside who needed help.

Then, with her foot on one windowsill, a hand suddenly

clutched her shin – it was a pale-faced, dark-haired woman garbed in white robes. Stitches arced across her forehead and she appeared to be phenomenally undernourished.

'Are you OK?' Lan shouted, prising the woman's fingers from her leg in case she stumbled. 'Do you need help?'

The woman simply stared back at her, wide-eyed. Lan climbed down and angled herself into the grim room. Inside was a bed, a desk and a bucket. The metal door at the other end was locked and, Lan noticed, possessed a barred grille at eye level. Smoke began to drift down, so Lan turned, grabbed the woman, who simply became rigid as if expecting Lan to beat her. Lan dragged her to the window and, using all her strength, edged the woman up onto the sill; with an almighty heave, Lan jumped into the air with the woman clutching Lan in a death grip. Together they tumbled onto an adjacent bridge.

Loosening the woman's constricting hold, Lan grabbed either side of the woman's face and stared into her eyes. 'I'll return to see if you are OK – I promise.' With that, she dashed back through the air, onto the side of the building, and continued further up.

The smoke was pungent now, and Lan thought there were probably a whole host of fabrics being combusted inside. At this height the cityscape opened up around her, in full panorama, little lights in the various nearby rooms, people standing at the windows, people on the bridges – there was no doubt that Villjamur could be a beautiful city.

Then above was a distinct scream.

Lan smashed in another window and smoke billowed out. *Oh my ...* Lan wrenched her gaze away in shock, but forced herself to look inside, holding her hand across her mouth because of the fumes.

A corpse lay on the floor in a large pool of blood – it was a woman with her throat slit and a sharp chunk of glass in her bloodied hand. She was clothed exactly like the woman a few floors below, and again the room was furnished in the same way.

Lan headed further up the side of the building.

As the wind ravaged her, she managed to reach the penultimate floor. Again smoke billowed out when she kicked in the window. She waited to let it clear, gripping the edge of the window frame for support, but the smoke kept on spilling into the evening air.

Eventually, holding her mouth, Lan climbed inside.

This wasn't a room like the others. It was a mezzanine, with once-grand stairways and an opulent lobby, decorated in shades of grey and purple. A layer of smoke was crawling across the ceiling, and the heat was intense, even though she couldn't see the fire.

Vuldon's voice: he was shouting for people to exit the building.

Lan plunged further inside to locate him, and a stream of people drifted past her with a dreamlike reluctance to escape the flames she could now see roaring away in a vast chamber just beyond. Vuldon's hulking figure was practically flinging people out and down the stairs.

Suddenly one of the supporting frames behind him gave way; the ceiling began to buckle, one floorboard at a time snapping under the strain. Vuldon lurched forwards, and the fire upstairs collapsed down with an enormous noise, then began to spread. The room was now blocked by blackened and burning wood.

'Don't just stand there, you stupid bitch!' Vuldon shouted, 'help me get them out!'

Lan glided to his side, the smoke starting to infiltrate her lungs. They had to be quick, so with Vuldon she began to smash the blockade with bits of furniture – metal stands and chairs – and soon there was enough of a clearing for her to squeeze through. Flames engulfed her, but she concentrated on channelling the effects within, and the fire began to respect some abstract boundary around her body. Absurdly, Lan was now repelling the flames, and inhabited a bubble of her own making.

Focus . . .

There, under a hefty workbench in the centre of the room: a group of people with frightened faces were huddling together. Lan finally reached them, knelt down and extended one arm, and tried to coax them out.

They wouldn't come. Frustratingly, they simply looked away, some shaking their heads.

'I'll help you!' she shouted. 'We're here to get you out.' Still they wouldn't come. She tried to pull one of them, but they resisted.

'Magic person,' she thought she heard one of them say.

'No, I'm not a cultist.' But it was no good, they weren't going to move.

Vuldon crashed in behind her and lumbered to her side. She told him of the situation. To her shock he lifted their workbench shelter, toppling it backwards. 'Come on, you fuckers, get yourself out of here. Move!'

He violently heaved them forwards, and they screamed at him. Lan didn't know what to do, but followed Vuldon's lead, and pushed them outwards.

'Look out!' she yelled. Another support fell, smashing two of the group through to the floor below with screams, leaving a gaping hole. Lan watched in despair. She felt out of her depth. She wasn't made for this, wasn't used to seeing such horror close up.

Vuldon was bellowing at her to move but all she could see were the two frightened faces that had plummeted down. She heard him swear then flinched as he grabbed her by the scruff of the neck and hurled her out past burning timber, where she finally came to her senses and began guiding the survivors down the stairs.

A stone spiral staircase lined the way down, and as they

moved past various rooms – cells – Lan peered in to check for other victims or survivors, but there were none. Just what was this place? It was cell after cell, not exactly a prison, but it was no place of freedom.

Heading down the stairs, they all drifted away from the heat. She couldn't see Vuldon any more, but trusted he would have the skills to survive. Finally, she guided the remaining survivors out through the smashed main door, a sign of Vuldon's work. She heaved in the sharp air, and then realized that she had been crying – either from the smoke or the intensity of the incident, she didn't know which. She composed herself.

Twenty-four survivors shivered in the cold. Each of them was wearing an identical, shapeless pale gown. They trudged around in circles, always looking down to the ground, never at each other. Two of them vomited against the wall, three sat down cross-legged in a vaguely child-like gesture. She checked some of them for injuries, and each bore strange markings around their heads. Scar tissue blossomed visibly on at least half of them. Whenever she looked in their eyes she saw only distance, or vacancy, or a disturbed mind.

A few minutes later, Vuldon exited the building, caked in black dust, carrying a large book under one arm. He brushed himself down as he approached her, the picture of nonchalance.

Lan said, 'Are they—?'

'That was fucking awful, Lan,' he snapped. 'You should be fucking ashamed of yourself, just standing there like that while everything was burning.'

Lan stopped herself from replying angrily, and considered what he was saying whilst she recalled her embarrassing slowness.

She had failed.

'I'm sorry, Vuldon. There's just no excuse. I messed up.' She knew he was right, but he had a special way of making her feel insecure again. His presence was intimidating, and she didn't know how she was going to continue.

'Least you admit it.' Surprisingly he simmered and walked away. He addressed the survivors individually, examining what was going on, checking everyone was fine.

Soon Vuldon returned to show her the book he was carrying and in one large hand offered it to her. 'What do you reckon of this then?' His tone suggested he already knew the answer.

She opened up the tome, a heavy leather object, frayed around the edges, clearly something that had seen better days. Inside was a list of names with descriptions of behaviour and treatments. 'Is it some kind of patient record? Maybe this place was a hospital.'

'Not quite. It housed the mentally ill—'

There was a boom above as the fire began to move down the building, collapsing floor after floor. Vuldon looked back at her and continued, 'And even with that in mind, something's not right. There were relics in there – the kind you used to see back in my day. Diagrams on the wall suggesting there was research going on. If I didn't know better . . .'

Vuldon marched over to one of the male patients and nonchalantly gripped his head. The man's body became utterly limp in his hands, and Vuldon examined the scars around his head before releasing him.

'It's a fucking research centre!' Vuldon shouted, returning to her.

'Research – for what?' Lan asked.

'Cultists literally poking around in people's heads. I haven't seen one of these places for decades. Fucking disgusting.'

'What shall we do with them?' Lan tilted her head at the patients.

'We'll lead them to the Inquisition headquarters. Other than that, there's nothing else we *can* do. They're helpless. They were made to be helpless. Transformed into a bunch of walking experiments. Cultists often use humans for research purposes, testing out the technology of the ancients to further their knowledge.'

Lan asked, 'But who do they get to work on?'

Vuldon replied, 'Those at the edge of society, mainly, so long as they're all quite healthy specimens. Usually not even from Caveside, because not everyone there eats well. No, they used to take those who committed petty crimes, or who were creating a bother for the Council, or openly rejected the will of Bohr, or they were queers, whatever was flavour of the day.'

Lan cringed at Vuldon's coarseness, and the fact that homosexuals were also abused here. How could a city act in such a way towards its inhabitants simply because of their private lives?

'Come on,' Vuldon said. 'We'll round this lot up and march them somewhere less cold than out here. That's all we can do for the poor shits.'

'OK,' Lan replied. 'I left a woman on a bridge and I need to bring her here, with the others. I made a promise.'

'Well hurry up then,' Vuldon sighed. 'We've not got all night.'

EIGHTEEN

The barracks hadn't been used for years. It was a conclave of abandoned, ex-military shacks – seven, in all, and surrounded by a tall wooden fence. These basic structures were set up in a line in the far east of the underground, in a district that, on new Imperial maps, was now declared unimaginatively as Underground South Three, but which was named, according to the Cavesiders, 'Freetown'. The cavern that formed one half of Villjamur was enormous, stretching across for miles, like the stomach of a stone god. The plates of glass that lined the cavern ceiling like a sparkling, monstrous ribcage, brought some elements of reflected daylight into the caves, but only stretched so far. Freetown was spawned in one of the many regions of gloom.

Here, Shalev promised, there would eventually be light.

Due to the crime levels in the outer city, such 'dark' zones were now patrolled by a cursory guard unit of just one old-timer, who spent more time sat in his little shed catching up on sleep, possibly dreaming of the military glories of his youth, than engaging in genuine surveillance work. And these days the army was out mounting big operations across the Boreal Archipelago, freeing the locals from oppression in the name of the Empire. Shalev had explained that, in reality, this meant clearing islands of tribes, shattering communities, and forcing open trade and slave labour markets in order to fuel Villjamur. On islands where the Empire could not go, Maour,

Dockull, even the Varltung Nations, Villjamur armed and funded tribal warlords to slaughter the resistant locals so that trade routes could, at the very least, become established.

That was why barracks like this, which could be found in several districts of Caveside, stood empty: the soldiers were out preparing the roads where industries would travel.

All these buildings did now was emit putrid smells and spawn urban stories. But they could be more than this. The Cavesiders needed to make a statement, something that would add to the frustrations of the ruling elite. Here, in these abandoned barracks, was shelter and relative warmth and hope for the refugees camped outside the city's walls.

That was where Shalev was now, outside, smuggling in dozens over one of the walls at a location known by only a handful of Cavesiders. Caley had heard there were to be ropes, ladders, subterfuge and decoys, but most of all there were to be *relics*. Shalev had enlisted the help of other cultists and they were erecting a momentary wall of invisibility to hide the refugees' movements. It was incredible what Shalev had done for these people – for Caley. She had given him a will to exist. His life suddenly had purpose. For a few years he had lived with an unemployed uncle who practically scavenged and begged to get by. Caley would willingly have worked for a living, if there were any jobs to be found, but as there weren't he instead chose more illicit paths. But now, thieving had become his work. He was making a contribution with it.

People down here were no longer an afterthought of the Council, no longer just criminal gangs running through dirt tracks around poor housing estates and ugly architecture. They had become a concern for those in the outer city, who wouldn't look twice at someone from Caveside. They were *noticed*. Caley enjoyed causing havoc out there, but not running into those fuckers, the Knights.

He waited until one of the Jorsalir bells rang out six times.

A moment later, when the sun was just setting outside, the glass that refracted in the light suddenly stuttered and cast the caves into darkness.

He ruffled his hair to look the part. He was dressed in fine clothes – black breeches, white silk shirt, embroidered cloak – too fine for a typical Cavesider, and filched from the outside. Mentally he rehearsed the better accent of someone from the upper city; he stumbled forwards across the dirt road to the guard hut, which was made from metal sheets. There were windows on each side, and a lantern burned within. Caley kicked on the door, and shouted through the window.

'Hey!' Caley screamed, and the guard sat up startled, brushing down his moustache and doing his best to pretend he had been anything other than asleep. 'Hey, come quick! Some men have just taken my mother into an alleyway. I'm from the second level of the city and I do not know anyone. Please, you must help her. They're going to ... going to ...'

The soldier's eyes narrowed, as if he'd waited years for such a moment. 'Worry not, lad.' He leapt up, grabbed his sword, pushed open the door and shuffled out after him.

'This way,' Caley said with pseudo-desperation, and trotted down a network of streets, surprised that the guard could keep up, especially with all that armour and the heavy uniform. He rattled behind and, breathlessly, Caley led him behind an old slaughterhouse, where the others were waiting.

The old man was surrounded on three sides by dozens of masked, weapon-wielding anarchists who were still bleeding out of the gaps and from rooftops. A granite wall stood behind him preventing his escape. He peered around, a desperate man, whilst Caley backed off behind his comrades. Torch flames flickered mellow light across the yard.

A voice called out, one of the women – one of Caley's sisters. 'Do you yield, soldier?'

'Never!' the old man crowed, and brandished his sword

like a magical enchantment. 'I represent the Emperor's name. What do you want?' he demanded.

'We're reclaiming them barracks,' she replied. 'Whether you live or not – doesn't much matter to us.'

The soldier pressed his back against the wall, shaking now, his gaze darting this way and that, his shortness of breath apparent. Then, quite calmly, he bellowed, 'In the name of the Empire!' and charged forwards.

Two shots from crossbows impacted with his face: his head snapped backwards and he crumpled into the dust.

'Nice one, Caley,' one of his brothers muttered, while the gang moved to help dispose of the body. Caley breathed heavily as he watched the old man so casually dragged into the rear of the slaughterhouse. 'You all right, kid?'

Caley breathed a 'Yeah.'

One of the brothers placed a hand on his shoulder. 'You got to remind yourself of what's gonna happen now. Gonna be dozens brought in from the ice, you hear? Dozens of lives saved. This man, he's happily gone for nothing more than an image on his uniform, that seven-pointed fucking star – he went how he wanted to go. That star means nothing to us, but meant everything to him, you hear?'

Caley reminded himself of what was at stake here. He swallowed. He accepted. They set to work preparing the barracks for their new inhabitants.

*

After an initial assembly meeting, in which roles were established, an hour passed, two, then three, and before they knew it they had made the barracks hospitable. Fifty-five Cavesiders scrubbed the buildings, removed debris, washed floors, whilst several artists painted cheerful murals across the walls to make things attractive. They brought in bedding, clothing, stoves, utensils, tools – luxuries acquired from the outer city and provisions they had grown themselves, utilizing cultist relics, in attic rooms or vacant patches of dirt.

Even though he was used to the amazing levels of organization that Shalev had brought with her, Caley was staggered at how quickly and thoroughly they were revitalizing this dead zone of Villjamur.

Caley himself helped to accumulate any ex-military junk metal, which would be wheeled out to skilled smiths for them to reclaim for a better use; it wasn't glamorous work, but it was to help other people. It seemed more satisfying somehow – all the jobs he'd ever held had been performing dreary manual labour, or running errands, or whatever he could get his hands on, so to be doing all of this for the community brought him a strange kind of sensation, and he wasn't even sure what that was.

He was constantly peering over his shoulder, wondering if the military would come and interrupt them, but no one came, no soldier, no politician, no one from the outer city. Most importantly, there were no Knights.

*

The faces of the refugees would forever haunt him. Gaunt and malnourished, their stares went right through Caley, in a worryingly passive way as if they had already given up on life. Wearing muddied and bloodied rags, reeking of shit and piss, they filed past meekly, steered by his brothers and sisters through the dark passageways, groaning and moaning in a variety of dialects, women and children and some men following. They needed medical aid – quickly. Caley guided about twenty into the farthest cabins, and they were willing to do anything he said. The level of power he had over them made him feel immensely uncomfortable. They had come from all over the Empire, from distant islands that he had heard mentioned perhaps once or twice. Broad and tanned faces, heavy accents, some that could not fully speak Jamur.

'Are you Caley?' a woman asked. She wore a plain yet expensive-looking shawl, and her blue eyes and bright blonde hair startled him. The thickset grey-haired man beside her was equally well dressed, in smart green cloak and tunic. He carried a black leather bag.

'Yeah,' Caley replied.

'We are here to help,' the man declared, his accent refined. 'We're both medical practitioners, and we are skilled in herblore . . .'

Caley had heard tell of this couple, who lived on one of the high, fancy levels of Villjamur, but were willing to help those in need even, it seemed, Cavesiders and refugees. Caley felt intimidated by their presence, but tried to recall some of Shalev's lessons. 'Couldn't have come soon enough,' Caley muttered. 'It's pretty dire.'

'We'll get right to it.' The couple instantly began dressing wounds: open sores and frostbite.

The place stank. He leaned by the blonde woman and whispered, 'I'll leave you to it – we need water here.'

'That's OK,' she replied, adding, 'brother.'

He left her, feeling bad that he had not asked her name.

*

In the darkness of one of the cabins, he gathered several of his own people and suggested that a system be put in place to bring water from the docks, sanitized with relics. People ran out to spread the word, and Caley felt proud then that his input had been noted. He watched them leave and gazed at the hubbub outside the barracks, at the people who marched back and forth distributing supplies, then he felt a hand on his shoulder.

It was Shalev. She was beaming. His nerves got the better of him, and he found that he didn't know what to say to her.

'How is everything going here, brother?' she asked, in that thick accent.

'Good,' he mumbled. 'Well, as good as can be hoped, I think. Yeah. Did you, uh, have any trouble?'

'Of a kind,' she replied, eyeing the scene at the barracks with pride. 'One of our invisibility shields collapsed, bringing some of the city guard to our side, but we ... despatched them efficiently.'

'Were the Knights out?' he asked, with awe.

Shalev shook her head. 'We had decoys, of course, a cluster of incidents on the other side of the city.'

'Wow, you had it all planned, Lady Shalev,' Caley replied.

'Sister will suffice,' she replied. 'No titles. There is far too much elitism involved. No, I do not think these Knights are even aware of their situation. As individuals they are no problem to me. As a group – as a symbol – they are little more than something in which the populace can place their hopes. They are merely for political gain – unlike us, they have no substance.'

NINETEEN

The next morning, back inside their clifftop residence, the Knights' tempers were heating up. Lan wanted to rant at the old, skinny cultist with grey hair in front of her but remained calm on the surface. The woman's skin sagged visibly, and the bags around her eyes said she hadn't had an easy life. With a copy of *People's Observer* in his pocket, Investigator Fulcrom paced back and forth behind her as she explained what had happened at the asylum and, though he tried not to show it, he cringed at her words. Feror stood in the background for a while, pretending not to make notes, eyeing the female cultist with casual disdain.

'So', Vuldon accused the cultist, 'you just abandoned the place.'

An experiment had turned sour: a fire broke out in their rooftop laboratory, but they did not know the cause. It was thought that substances exploded out of a relic killing one of their own, and soon it had seeped into the floorboards. Highly combustible, it ravaged the whole of the top floors, so the cultists had simply vacated.

'It's not quite like that,' the cultist replied.

'No, we tried to get some out, but then we weren't sure how long we had.'

'The fire wasn't that bad,' Vuldon declared. 'That material wasn't as flammable as you make out. You just ran because you're cowards, hiding behind your damn magic.'

'It isn't magic,' the cultist hissed. 'It's research.'

'We could do without that kind of research,' Vuldon said. 'Just how long had you been farming zombies, eh?'

'Well, without such research,' the cultist explained, 'we wouldn't have been able to provide *you* with such powers. The whole facility was set up for the purposes of research in order to generate various powers that the Knights could use – you were, in fact, just the start of things. They were all quite necessary, as I'm sure you'd understand. To damage them was, in some way, to benefit you – and therefore the city.'

Behind, Feror closed his eyes, nodding softly.

If I didn't already feel guilty about my position...

Vuldon marched towards her. 'You lying, patronizing b—'

'Easy, Vuldon.' Fulcrom stepped between the two of them before things could get any worse.

Eventually Feror and the other cultist left them with their guilt. Lan wasn't sure if she could do this any more.

Vuldon and Tane stormed off into the city, and as they closed the door, she grabbed Fulcrom's sleeve and said, 'I want to get out of all this.'

'OK, let's get a drink,' he said. 'I know of just the place.'

'No,' she urged, 'I want to get out of the Knights.'

'I know what you meant,' he replied coolly. 'I still think we should get a drink.'

*

At that point between breakfast and lunch when the bistros of the city experienced a lull in activity, Lan and Fulcrom entered one such establishment, taking shelter from a sudden snowstorm.

On the upper levels of Villjamur, only those without jobs, yet with enough money, could be out drinking at this hour. That usually meant retired landowners or those on a military pension, or youths drinking away their parents' wealth.

The bistro was one of those wood and metal joints that

you didn't often see in Villjamur any more, and Lan found its bookshelves, thick tables, pot plants, log fires and candles to be utterly charming. Three smartly dressed old men sat in warm silence at one table by the stained-glass window, and a red-haired girl was behind the counter cleaning the glasses from the morning rush.

'I come here when I need to think.' Fulcrom parted his robe as he sat down.

Lan sat opposite him, keeping her thick black cloak close to cover her uniform. She didn't want fuss being made right now – twice people had come up to her in the street, and all she could do was smile politely and move away. The serving girl came to take their order. In here everything seemed so cocooned, so comfortable, and she felt she could really talk to Fulcrom. 'I'm not cut out for this,' Lan began. 'You should find someone else, someone who can cope better. Our group – it isn't what I thought it was. I don't want to be some tool that the Emperor can use to make people feel safe.' She explained how useless she had been the previous night at the asylum.

'Lan, you should stop feeling sorry for yourself,' Fulcrom replied. 'You've been given a wonderful opportunity. Don't waste it on angst.'

'Do you have any idea', she snapped, 'what I've been through in life?'

'I can't pretend I understand your pain, but I've read your file. I know your secrets, sure, if that's what you mean.'

She leaned back in her chair, unnerved by the unspoken threat of exposure. Even the hint of it was like a slap in the face.

Fulcrom reached forward to clasp her hands in his. His dark rumel skin was thick and tough, and for some reason she felt intensely feminine being touched by him, enjoyed the sensation, and refused to feel bad for enjoying it.

'I'm sorry,' he said. 'Look, don't worry, I'm not going to

tell anyone – as far as I'm concerned, the past is the past.' He began to speak with great tenderness. 'The threat of your exposure is from them, the cultists, and the Emperor and his agents. Which is to say – you've really no choice in any of this. You've been given this change, and a job to do, so you have to accept it.'

What do you really think of me? she felt the urge to say. Lan was so vulnerable all of a sudden, at this junction of life in the middle of nowhere. All she could do was sigh.

The serving girl brought over their drinks and left.

'I can barely look after myself – let alone anyone else. I'm just not very good at being a hero.'

'Well, you'll have to be one,' Fulcrom replied. 'The city needs you.'

She reflected on this. 'I'm scared of so many things. The dangers, falling from the air and dying. And I'm scared that you know so much about me and ... well, what do you *think* of me?' She whispered the words whilst looking around at the other tables, just in case they were overheard. 'I need to know, do you even consider me to be real? Does my past affect how you treat me?'

Fulcrom gave a beatific sigh. 'The world isn't black and white, I know that much. You get feminine men, masculine women, and a whole bunch of in-betweens. So I can well understand you're worried. But – really – you've no reason to be.'

It seemed the right answer, even though he didn't say what she wanted him to say. 'The danger here is that I'm trusting you with who I am and I know next to nothing about you. You never talk about yourself.'

Fulcrom appeared stunned for a moment, and she wondered if she'd ventured too far into uncertain territory. Embarrassment began to creep over her. 'I didn't mean to be forward and cross some professional line ...'

'No,' Fulcrom said, still wide-eyed. He gave an awkward

laugh. This wasn't going well. 'No, it's just that it's taken me so long to work out something.'

'What?' she asked. A moment passed as he stared at the table. 'Come on,' she teased nervously.

'You remind me of my former – now dead – wife. She would always say that she wanted to know me, that I kept myself to myself, that I was more interested in cleanliness than her.' A glance came, in which he was clearly gauging her trust, 'And you have remarkably similar eyes.'

'Oh.' What was she supposed to say to that? Was it even a good thing? *Similar eyes ... She must have been human.* 'You're entitled to a secret or two yourself, you don't have to tell me.'

He stared into his drink. 'No, it's OK. You're right: how can you trust me if you know nothing about me? She passed away several years ago. She was killed by a crossbow bolt at the scene of a robbery.'

'I'm ... I'm sorry to hear that. Was she in the Inquisition?'

'No, she was just in the wrong place at the wrong time. For whatever reason, probably because they found her on the scene, she was labelled as an accomplice – I know, the partner of an investigator, too.'

Fulcrom moved on quickly. He spoke of trivial things, then of his work for the Inquisition, of crimes he had solved and, due to his dedication, he talked of a lonely existence. In between ruminations, he sipped his tea with care, and used a napkin with grace. He'd joined the Inquisition because he liked the stories about it that his family used to tell him. Rumels, it seemed, were proud of their association with law enforcement.

'This is no consolation, Lan, but this world of ours constantly throws things at us, mostly horrible events, and it never stops. Some people choose to look away and focus on their own lives, but as it's our job, we have to face it day in, day out.' A pause. 'But I guess your life's been pretty tough already, hasn't it. I suppose being a Knight is one of the more comfortable positions you've been in?'

'Well, my most pressing concern, other than the reasons I'm doing what I'm doing, is that I'm scared of being who I am, being in the public eye, being so recognizable.' Lan paused. 'I knew one or two other transgendered people from my entertainment days. It seemed a good community for us to hide in. We didn't exactly see eye to eye, but we didn't completely hate each other.'

'What happened to them?' Fulcrom asked.

'One of them was murdered,' Lan said. 'She was murdered because a group of men sexually assaulted her, then found her out. She was dragged into a nearby marsh and stabbed repeatedly – just for not fitting into a category; or perhaps more specifically, that she was not what they were after. The men were repulsed by her. Sickened because she was different.' Lan was aware she was speaking in a drone, but she was consciously washing the emotion from her mind – a self-preservation tool. 'This was in some small town that the circus travelled through. The other girl, she saw the assault, but didn't report it at first – she was in hiding. By the time the circus moved on it was too late to do anything about it. You yourself must know how these disconnected communities can be sometimes.'

'How did you find out – about the murder, I mean?'

'The other girl – well, she eventually caught up with the show. That was many weeks later. She pleaded with our owner to return, to report the crime to military installations along the route, but he wasn't interested. Said he'd had a lot of his retinue die on him, what was one more? I was too scared to force anything to happen. The other girl, she ran away. I never saw her after that. I still feel guilty about it, and such shame, but I wanted to hide myself as much as I could. I didn't want the same to happen to me.'

Lan peered up at him, and he seemed uncertain of how to react. He shook his head and held her hand. 'I'm so sorry, Lan.'

Lan didn't know about that. Life was certainly easier than before.

'People fear what they don't understand,' Fulcrom continued. 'I'll freely admit it is difficult – and more so – for your . . . you . . .' He shook his head. 'Even I struggle. I understand, to some extent – not that it helps – since my family spent a year in one of the smaller towns, which was hell if you were a rumel. We faced threats, our doors were kicked in during the night, my father had eggs thrown at him when he went to work in the mornings. They didn't welcome what they didn't understand. They thought we were bizarre monsters, so we came back to Villjamur, where there's a great mix of peoples – garudas, rumels, humans – people seem to get on better. There's more understanding here, for all its sins.'

'At least you can freely be a rumel and be accepted by law,' Lan said. 'Hell, you lot are mostly the law – why is that?'

He laughed at that. 'A quirk of old doctrines. Rumels live far longer than humans, and experience is required for the job. That's what we tell ourselves, anyway, but it's also because thousands of years ago, so the history goes, there was a great tension between the species. We rumels were given high positions of legal office to placate our needs against the many human rulers. It forced us both to be civilized to each other – and I guess it worked.'

'There's not much in the way of legal protection for the people I used to be. The law doesn't even recognize shades of gender – it's very black and white, but luckily our culture is such a wreckage that anyone can change who they are in a heartbeat with a forged document in their hands. No one asks questions, no one wants proof – apart from getting into Villjamur.'

'You can make your mark, here in the city,' Fulcrom concluded. 'Life is tough for all of us, in our own ways, and if it wasn't you who received these powers it would have been someone else eventually. You've been chosen because of your proven adaptability: you're well known in cultist circles – they knew they could rely on your body. And those people who were used for research – there's nothing folk like us can do about it. Choose your battles, but stay with us, Lan. You can choose to be a force for good.'

She didn't say anything.

Fulcrom announced that it was time to go. He said something about having business with a priest, and smiled earnestly. Before he left, Lan – conscious she was going to do it – gave him a peck on the cheek and whispered her thanks. It seemed to disarm Fulcrom totally, and as he stuttered away through the snowy streets, she felt shocked at how forward she could be.

She liked the sensation.

*

Ulryk was waiting patiently on the steps of the Inquisition headquarters as fat flakes of snow drifted down around him. Fulcrom marvelled at how peaceful he seemed to be, despite the flurry of citizens and the bustle of Villjamur.

'Good afternoon, Ulryk,' Fulcrom called out.

The priest turned and gave a welcoming smile. 'A most delightful day, investigator.'

'You can tell you've not been in the city long. The citizens are sick of all this cold weather and snow.'

They moved across the city at a leisurely pace, and Fulcrom showed him where some of the smaller libraries were, as they headed to the largest in the city, around the corner from the Astronomer's Glass Tower. Ulryk gasped as they entered a vast courtyard of glass flowers, in a variety of colours, but mainly blues and purples. Giant petals and heart-shaped leaves were glittering.

'This is phenomenally beautiful!' he sighed, clasping his hands together. 'How old is this garden?'

Fulcrom chuckled at his reaction. 'A few hundred years, more or less. They were built before the great Varltung Uprising.'

A couple were walking arm in arm to one of the benches at the far end of the courtyard, where they sat enveloped in each other's attention. Rising up around the scene were some of the finest buildings in the city, limestone houses with vast windows that overlooked the glass flowers. Some were glowing warmly with firelight, and it highlighted just how cold it was outside.

'Here it is,' Fulcrom said. At the far end of the courtyard was the central library of Villjamur, indicated by a wide-arched entrance at the top of a stairway.

There was a member of the city guard standing at the bottom, blond-haired and round-faced, clutching his sword with one hand and gazing sternly at some point in the distance.

'Sele of Urtica,' the guard said.

'Sele of Urtica,' Fulcrom replied, flashing his medallion. 'I didn't realize they were guarding this place as well?'

'Every major landmark in the city is being guarded now,' the officer replied. 'Someone's here day in, day out.'

Fulcrom nodded and continued up the steps with the priest. 'This is the place you'll find the oldest books in the city,' Fulcrom said to him. 'There are a thousand legal texts going back thousands of years, which we in the Inquisition are forced to use from time to time. But I'll see that the librarians treat you right – they can be a brutal bunch.'

*

Four storeys high, and banking into the distance over an uneven topography, the library was intimidating in size and bewildering in its layout. Lit by glass lanterns, spaced regularly at every fifteen feet, it looked like a settlement all of its own. Thousands of books bound in varying shades of leather were stored here, and among them Ulryk seemed more relaxed than usual, as if finally having returned home. A few custodians shifted intermittently like ghosts between shelving units and smaller, more concealed vaults of books. Fulcrom knew of many more rooms underground, too – sepulchres containing texts sacred to the Jorsalir church, as well as tomes in which the foundation of the Empire had been detailed. Some were said to hold clay tablets and books written in rare script that no one alive could decipher.

Fulcrom flashed his Inquisition medallion at the main desk and had a quiet word with the librarian. Presently, Ulryk was granted access to all areas of the library including sensitive areas normally open to only those in the Inquisition or those attached to the Council. But when offered a custodian to guide him around, the priest declined. Ulryk's only question was the location of the scriptorium, the room in which texts were copied from language to language, and distributed across the Archipelago.

Fulcrom followed Ulryk around the first floor. Any expectations of revelations or dramatic magic suddenly being uttered from the priest's lips rapidly diminished, and it wasn't long until he became bored with constantly loitering, prodding the spines of books, or blowing away dust to read the various titles:

Languages of the West, The Second Book of Poetics, Voyniches.

'So what exactly are you looking for?' Fulcrom whispered. He leant on one of the rails from which he could see the tiers above and the level below, where a handful of Villjamur's citizens were either milling about or seated at dark wooden desks, studying by lantern light.

'I told you, the other copy of *The Book of Transformations*,' Ulryk replied, not annoyed at all at having to repeat himself. 'It's the only text that I desire, but I don't expect to find it easily. And I have a casual interest in most other texts, theologies of course, to see if there are any deviations to aid my own research.'

'So,' Fulcrom gestured at the sheer expanse of the place, 'you simply start at the bottom and work your way up, through a million books?'

The priest chortled quietly. 'That could be the case, though I suspect I will be heading downwards, not up. No, for now, I am merely browsing – I feel so at peace here, amongst all this . . . recorded knowledge, this history.'

'Didn't you say most of it was fake?' Fulcrom teased.

'Oh, yes, some of it is, some of it isn't. Each text should be studied in isolation. And each will bear the stamp of the author and, if one knows how to look, the way it has been constructed will reveal its origins. But none of this concerns me currently. Tell me, there are hidden rooms, I take it? Sections where the public are not permitted?'

'There are, yes. And I've seen that you have free access – if you have any more trouble I can help you.'

'If I may be so bold, I doubt you will be able to help.'

'Sorry?' Fulcrom asked, raising an eyebrow.

Ulryk closed the book he was scanning and came close to Fulcrom. 'Do you think, in a repository of knowledge, you will know where everything is kept? The power in such words is immense. There are barriers everywhere to stop the uninitiated from accessing such information. Why, you yourself know that the citizens of the city are limited in what they can see in terms of political goings-on. Do you think that this isn't a tiered system of access?'

'I'd never thought of it like that, and I'm still not quite sure I follow.'

'We had such a system back at Regin Abbey. Even most of our own clerics were not permitted access to the more sacred texts, and those who were could not read them. Barriers to knowledge exist everywhere – it is one of the greatest methods of information control.'

'So what do you plan to do?'

'Find what I am not allowed to find,' Ulryk replied mysteriously. He picked up a book nearby, closed his eyes and inhaled the aromas from the leather and then flicked through to smell the paper.

*

Fulcrom decided to leave Ulryk to his personal crusade to find his book. He was experiencing a sudden doubt about what the priest had said concerning the history of religion. Against so many books, so many opinions, there was a lot to overturn, despite the magic that Ulryk had shown him the other day.

Keep an open mind, Fulcrom told himself. *The moment you shut out the improbable is the moment you fail as an investigator.*

Fulcrom stood at the top of the stairs waiting for another bout of snow to ease off. Footprints littered the courtyard like dark entrails, and at the far end of the glass flowers someone was in the process of being helped to their feet, presumably having slipped on the ice. The couple on the bench had departed. But something was out of place.

The soldier on guard ... Fulcrom thought, looking around. *He said, 'Someone's here day in, day out.'*

Fulcrom walked quickly down the steps of the library and, to one side, he spotted a group of twenty or so people huddled in a close circle. Some of them were clearly in distress, and one man was holding back his young child from seeing something, but the kid kept pushing through the coats and robes to get a better look.

'Stand aside,' Fulcrom called out as he approached. 'Villjamur Inquisition.'

As two women parted, Fulcrom squirmed through the circle to see a dozen expressions of disgust, a body on the floor, and a slick pool of blood under the head and abdomen.

It was the guard who had been posted on the library steps.

His throat had been severed in a clean cut, the sign of a

professional, and there was an open wound from his left shoulder to his right hip. His sword still sheathed, his hands were stain-free: the man had probably not even seen his attackers, probably wasn't even alive long enough to clasp at his wounds.

Fulcrom immediately called everyone back, but he knew it was far too late to find any footprints. The public had long since trampled on any clues. *Shit*.

Back to the body and blood was still pooling. This was recent, very recent.

'Did anyone see anything?' he demanded of the crowd.

'Sorry, mate.'

'No.'

Then nothing but shrugs and silence and morbid curiosity. He moved among them, searching for blades or a guilty glance, but nothing seemed out of place. 'No one is going anywhere. I want you all to remain here so I can get statements.'

He ignored the following groans from those whose routines were about to be interrupted. People seldom looked at the bigger picture, even with the blood before them.

Fulcrom pushed through the throng and commenced jogging in a wide arc, his cloak floating like wings as he scrutinized the perimeter of the courtyard and between the glass flowers, staring through the falling snow to see if anyone was perhaps running from the scene or acting suspiciously.

'Shit,' he breathed, the word clouding before his face. Why kill a member of the city guard here? This was clearly meant to be seen as a statement, a signature in blood.

He headed back to the scene of the murder under the gaze of at least thirty people now, and noticed, tied to the stone rail of the steps, a black rag, the token of the anarchists. This confirmed his hunch.

As he ordered the citizens all to stand clear, he drew out

his notebook from his pocket then began to jot down the details of the crime and sketch the position of the body; and, with a deep patience, he began to interview members of the public.

Any serenity to be found in this garden of glass flowers had been shattered.

TWENTY

Tane and Vuldon, it seemed, could get in anywhere with their new-found identities. On a rare evening to themselves, they decided the best thing to do was go for a drink, get to know each other a little better. Vuldon was fine with that. He knew that it was important to form a good relationship with someone who might, one day, end up saving his life.

They strolled through the sleet to one of the new silver and glass bars that were becoming more common in Villjamur. Cultist-enhanced lights and coloured lanterns made the place look surreal. A weird green glow fell across the shiny cobbles. A couple of young girls ran by laughing with a wax coat raised up above them to shelter from the wet, and they headed inside. Two soldiers stood either side of the doorway, dressed in military colours that Vuldon didn't recognize: sleek, dark-red uniforms, with a white belt and hefty black boots.

Vuldon stepped up to the two men. 'Interesting uniforms you got there, gentlemen.'

The one on the left spoke, 'Colours of the Shelby Corporation Soldiers. Sir.'

'Private militia?' Tane queried.

'Emperor's allowed private companies to offer military services in the city, sir. What with the current military being overstretched.'

'Looks as though you're kitted out well,' Vuldon said, nodding towards the fine-looking blade at the man's hip.

'What kind of business is Shelby in?' Tane asked.

'Ores, mainly. Based in Villiren, sir.'

'He make those swords?'

'Yes, sir.'

'Well, doesn't that work out well for his ore business, soldiers of Shelby?' Vuldon said. 'I take it you're not going to deny us entry?'

'Absolutely not, sir. Knights are most welcome indeed. Sir.'

Vuldon and Tane glided past the soldiers and into the bar. Vuldon had to crouch a little to fit under the lintel, but eventually found himself in a cavernous room that looked as though it had once been something like a factory, except now it was polished metal and lurid coloured lighting.

'Now this is more like it!' Tane enthused.

'It's horrible, is what it is,' Vuldon muttered.

'Now there is nothing wrong with a little progress in design. You'll get used to it. And look at these women!'

Vuldon peered about the joint. It was full of youngsters moving in spasms on a central floor, while all along the edge were musicians on tribal drums and weird nasal-sounding instruments. 'There's too much noise. I want a drink.'

Vuldon muscled his way to the bar and asked the barman for two rums. He looked back at his own reflection, at the logo on his chest that seemed to glow in the weird lighting. He tossed over a coin, took his drinks and was, almost instantly, surrounded by people.

'You're . . . you're a Knight!' someone gasped.

'I've heard about you.'

'I saw you only yesterday helping someone.'

The compliments rolled in; these people were in awe. He smiled awkwardly, thanked them, and pushed back towards Tane, who accepted his drink.

'You know what, old boy? These powers have their advantages. I heard everything those fellows said to you.'

'Tell me something I don't know,' Vuldon mumbled.

'How about, I can hear what that group of women are saying about you.'

'You shouldn't listen in to conversations like that, cat-man.'

'Really? The one with red hair thinks you're a fine-looking specimen. But the thing is, I can listen to what the ladies like, and direct my charm offensive accordingly . . .'

'That's . . . creepy,' Vuldon said.

'Nonsense, it's streamlining. Take that lady over there – she's just broken up with her lover, and hates men. That's not worth pursuing.'

'*She's* not worth pursuing.'

'Over there – the brunette in the blue dress – it's her birthday, and she's feeling the need for change in her life.'

'And you could bring that about, yeah?' Vuldon asked. 'You could have a meaningful relationship and respect her?'

'Now steady on, chap. I'm merely suggesting what these powers can offer. I'm talking about the lady there, the blonde in the black dress.'

'Cute, but too young for my tastes.'

'Not for me, old boy. Not for me.'

He took a sip of his drink. 'What's her story then?'

'See you *are* interested. It can't be helped, can it? So her story is – I think – that she hates her father, and her mother doesn't even know she's out tonight. She is your classic rebel – and I'm an admirer of such qualities.'

'You're a predator, is what you are.' Vuldon felt the eyes of everyone in the room on him – not helped by the fact that he towered above most people. And he couldn't help but think it was all a waste, that while refugees were dying outside the city's gates, people here were planning to drink or sleep their way into forgetting about the ice age.

'I'm merely being efficient,' Tane replied.

'We're getting enough attention in here as it is,' Vuldon said. People were gathering around them, young faces smiling, little waves, everyone hoping to catch their eyes – and all for what, helping out citizens in distress?

'Vuldon, Vuldon, Vuldon,' Tane laughed. 'Don't you ever accept the notion of a challenge?'

'You complicate life too much, cat-man,' Vuldon replied, and downed a shot of rum. A curvy brunette sidled up to him and placed her arm on his waist. She said something about liking a hero. Vuldon turned to Tane, but the other Knight was already ploughing a furrow through the throng to his chosen girl.

Well, what harm could it do? he thought, glancing casually at her. *It has been a long time. So much for getting to know Tane.* 'Evening, miss.'

*

Lan awoke bleary-eyed, with sunlight bathing her room in hues of orange and pink. She ached, as she did every morning after a night patrolling the city. She had volunteered to go out on her own last night, whilst Vuldon and Tane were permitted a rare evening of relaxation. They'd decided to go out and drink in the taverns on the lower levels of the city and, when she returned at some ungodly hour, they were still out, so she went straight to bed.

Intermittently during the rest of her sleep she heard a distant, female voice.

As she climbed out of bed, the thick blankets and sheets slipped to the floor. Her room was beautiful and minimal, a far cry from the cluttered rooms she had shared with the girls at the circus. Cream sheets and white stone walls, with a marble floor and a vast window overlooking the sea. A table to one side with incense, an elegant wardrobe with geometric mock-Máthema motifs, a small log fire containing only ashes now – though with her augmentations she didn't feel the cold as much as before.

To have her own space was a luxury she had dreamed

about for years. No more having to hide herself, no more self-consciously getting dressed. Aware of being different, every slight detail, every movement, every glance could have opened up terrifying consequences for her. Now that she didn't actually have to be aware of such things, it didn't alter the fact that she wasn't able to relax fully, even in her own room, and Lan realized then just how many ghosts from her past were walking alongside her.

Sometimes she felt guilty for having undergone so much of a transformation. She knew of other women who would have killed to have been given her opportunity to match their anatomy with their gender.

She stood naked before a full-length mirror, smiling, a method of reminding herself every morning of who she was. She extended her arms out either side and connected with the powers given to her by the cultists, feeling a vibration deep within her core, as if a strong wind was carving a channel through her insides, and gradually she lifted into the air, hovered a foot above the ground, fine-tuning the sensations.

It was useful for her to do this, to practise using the technology.

Slowly, she lowered herself back to the ground, lost her connections with her body, and felt a sense of deep relaxation. She got dressed into one of her black uniforms, though left the top few buttons undone since they irritated her around the neck. They might make the three of them look like some elite force, but these uniforms annoyed and chafed at times.

As she headed out into the main lounge, Tane's door opened, and a beautiful young blonde girl tottered out, garbed in what she must have been wearing the night before. She couldn't have been more than nineteen years old. She was pretty and slender, with thick curls, red lips, dark eye-liner, and a wonderful black dress. Tane beamed at being caught in the act.

Tane picked up her fur coat from one of the chairs outside his room and placed it around her shoulders. The girl peered shyly at Lan, and Tane made a protective, almost patronizing gesture, by placing his arm around her shoulder as he walked her to the door, where she stood on tiptoes to kiss him goodbye.

'Will I see you again?' the girl asked.

'I'll find you,' Tane whispered.

One of the sentries on the door ushered her out, and Tane whispered for him to keep a safe eye on her. Just then Feror strolled into the room with as much zest as Tane; though perhaps he achieved his happy state through more honourable means than Tane.

The old, green-cloaked cultist made his usual checks on the Knights whilst a terse conversation raged in the pointed glances exchanged between Lan and Tane. And while Feror began to warble on again about his daughter and his wife, Lan was fit to burst at Tane's indiscretions.

Eventually, after he seemed satisfied with Tane and Lan's meagre, one-word answers to his questions, Feror left. Then Tane peered around wearily, strutted back into the room and clasped his hands. 'So. Breakfast?'

'You're not supposed to bring people back here,' Lan snapped. She was furious. The idiot was jeopardizing their security by showing the girl the way to their sanctuary, but he didn't seem to give a shit.

'We're not jealous, are we?'

'You're a dick. You were out chasing women last night then? Glad to know you made the most of your evening off.'

'On the contrary, dear lady. Those women were chasing us – they love us. We were showing off in some of the bars down on the first and second level – Bohr, I'd never known such attention. I say, being a Knight really does have its perks, doesn't it?'

'And as for keeping a low profile?'

'Well, we must be out there to reassure the public of their safety, so we keep being told.'

'Not like that.'

'Our presence was essential, one might say,' Tane replied, apparently oblivious to any point she made.

'You're trying to convince yourself?' Lan asked. 'You were just abusing your power so you could be a cheap slut.'

Tane leant back to fold his arms, quite proud of his new moniker. 'Perhaps I could have that name stitched on the back of my uniform. You think that might work?'

A moment later, Tane's gaze lurched to the door, his senses heightened. He seemed to sniff the air before relaxing with a smirk. 'Now it's your turn.'

'What?'

'Your lover boy is here.'

'What the hell are you on about now?' Lan frowned, her heart skipping a beat.

A knock on the door and Investigator Fulcrom entered the room, relaxed and well mannered, as always, his tail waving this way and that, elegantly cool.

Tane leant in and whispered, 'Perhaps you might swoon a little less obviously?' before walking forwards to Fulcrom. 'Good morning, investigator. And what news do you bring on this fine morning?'

'Tane, who was that girl walking out of here?' Fulcrom enquired.

Just then, Vuldon's door opened, and the big man escorted two young ladies out, one with brown hair and wide curves, the other skinny with coal-black hair. They, too, were dressed as if they'd just come in from a night out in the city, with fancy clothes and jewels sparkling on their chests. He paraded them nonchalantly through the lounge, completely ignoring the others, guiding them to the exit. 'See you soon, ladies,' he mumbled.

'How *on earth* did you manage that?' Tane demanded as Vuldon closed the door. 'You don't even *have* a personality.'

'Some of us don't need to yap their way into bed with a woman,' Vuldon replied coolly.

'Vuldon,' Fulcrom snapped. *'For fucksake.* You are *not* supposed to bring anyone back here. What if one of them works for the anarchists? If you want to bring people back, they must be vetted thoroughly.'

'I already did that,' Vuldon grinned. 'They had nothing to hide.'

'Oh please . . .' Lan said.

Fulcrom lowered his face into his hands.

'Lighten up, old boy,' Tane said, full of energy. 'We were heroes down there. People loved us – they love everything we stand for. Whatever the Emperor wanted, it's working quickly. We really mean something, in such a short space of time. Women kept coming up to us, and men slapped us on the back. We meant something to the people of the city, Fulcrom – it's intoxicating, so allow us a little fun.'

'Well, while you were enjoying yourselves,' Fulcrom said, 'the rest of us were trying to solve the murders of three members of the city guard – brutal killings, and each of them in plain view of the public.'

'Oh,' Tane said.

'Oh exactly,' Fulcrom replied.

'One in front of the library, and two more on the gateways to the third and fourth levels, and there're still no leads to finding the killers of them or the councillor.'

'Sorry,' Tane muttered, 'but we didn't hear about them.'

'Don't you know any better? The more of a reputation you get, the more you have to lose. You've all got a past, things you'd rather weren't shared about – you're playing into the Emperor's hands even further. He wants you to become stars so it binds you further to your job. You'll be a Knight for life at this rate, no chance to get away from it all when our work is done. How much more vulnerable are you all to being exposed when you're celebrities?'

Nothing but silence. Fulcrom was right, he was always right.

'Exactly. Before you had nothing to lose. Now, you've much more, and every time you invite people back here, that risk of not only exposure, but of fucking up the efforts of so many people looking to reduce crime, all gets greater.'

'All right,' Tane sighed. 'You've made your point.'

Fulcrom paused, and eventually calmed. He took a deep breath. 'Good. So, while people were busy getting killed yesterday, where precisely were you all?'

'I was out, but there were only a couple of petty thefts – they were quite open and shut though,' Lan told him.

'Open and shut,' Fulcrom replied. 'Right.'

'Do you think I'm lying?'

'No – it's just that these petty crimes, they might be an effort to distract you while something bigger's going on elsewhere in the city.'

'I didn't realize,' Lan replied.

'It's OK,' Fulcrom said. 'I'm only just working these things out for myself.'

'You expect us to be everywhere at all times?' Vuldon remarked bitterly. 'There are hundreds of thousands of people in this city. We can't stop every murder.'

'I'm sure Fulcrom didn't mean that,' Lan said.

'Well, you would take his side, wouldn't you?' Vuldon muttered.

Tane mouthed the words 'Lover boy' at Lan, and Fulcrom glanced to each of them in confusion.

Lan knew Fulcrom was smart enough to know what was going on, to read the silences, the conversation that wasn't being spoken here. She felt incredibly awkward and embarrassed and shy, yet there was something about having her affections implied that offered some relief – because she sure as hell wasn't going to say anything about her growing feelings for the investigator.

'These murders,' Vuldon said eventually, 'what can you tell us?'

'Each of them was committed in a public location,' Fulcrom said, sitting on one of the plush settees. 'Each victim was a soldier in the city guard, on a highly visible location. There was a note by one of the bodies, scrawled by the culprits – who we believe to be the anarchists.'

'What did it say?' Lan asked.

'It said "You put symbols out here, with deeds we will be removing others".'

'A retaliation,' Vuldon declared. He sat next to Fulcrom, his bulk making the investigator look like a child. 'Which means you – or the Emperor – will want us to retaliate back.'

'Exactly,' Fulcrom replied. 'Because they won't stop until more people are dead. We're dealing with a strange psychology here.'

'What do you want us to do then?' Lan asked.

'As soon as you're all ready, we're heading into Caveside. The Inquisition has handed over to me the names and addresses of those we think are crime lords of varying effect – those who manage guilds on this side of the city, ones who are known to have their claws reaching deep into the caves. We visit them one by one and see what we can find, see what they know. It's essential we find Shalev, and the Emperor is growing more demanding by the day.'

'And if we don't find her by this method?' Lan prompted. 'It seems unlikely a criminal would just hand over an ally.'

'We try something else. But even if this doesn't work, we'll hopefully be able to put the fear into some of Caveside's shadier characters.'

'And it's a chance to visit some old friends,' Vuldon added, smirking.

Fulcrom reflected on his words. 'I don't want anything to get out of hand. No old vendettas.'

'You forget that my secrets aren't like yours,' Vuldon protested. 'I was framed for something I didn't do, and I know there were some of these so-called crime lords involved in that, or their families were. I was set up and I—'

'Want revenge,' Fulcrom finished. 'That's understandable. But for now, Vuldon, please – you have a job to do. Virtually no one remembers what happened since it was covered up by everyone involved. To the public you simply disappeared. You're just Vuldon now, someone with greater powers and responsibilities. There are several paths you can choose to making amends, and I suggest you simply get on with helping the people of the city.'

'You've a smart answer for everything,' Vuldon muttered, and Lan couldn't discern if it was a simple statement or the start of a threat.

'I'm not concerned with smartness,' Fulcrom added, 'just getting the job done.'

*

Fulcrom was in a morose mood as he marched them towards the crime lords. He hoped that Tane and Vuldon were sulking, or reflecting on their deeds. Their excessiveness was to be expected, perhaps, but they needed to know those actions would be a liability. Lan seemed to be the only one he could fully trust, and his fondness for her grew each day. He was drawn to her introversions, to the world of emotions beneath her surface – it made a change from the brashness and arrogance found with many of the investigators.

They wore dark hooded cloaks. Moving through the snow along the fourth level of the city, he watched Lan closely – she walked with an amazing grace, a lightness of step that must have come from her years of acrobatics. They headed down a network of small alleys, where the walls were actually chunks of rock smothered in dripping lichen, and every now and then there would be a small, steamed-up window, some- times with a face behind pressed up against it. The snow ceased, filling the air with tension and light. Caught on the breeze, a couple of abandoned issues of *People's Observer* skittered along the street.

The Knights were silent as they progressed further into what Fulcrom knew to be dubious territory: they arrived at a large, metal door set into a whitewashed wall of an expensive-looking house. It had been constructed so the owners could see over the lower levels of the city: rooftops sparkling in the sunshine, the spires and bridges casting bold shadows and, over the walls, in the distance was nothing but murky tundra, much of it trampled by the passage of refugees.

Standing next to the house were two men, each nearly as tall as Vuldon. Shaven-headed with dark cloaks flapping from their shoulders, each bore the scars of combat, and by each of their sides hung a fat sabre.

'What can we do for you gents?' one of them asked gruffly.

'Three gents and a lady, to be precise.' Tane indicated Lan, and one of them took a closer look at him. He slid back his hood to reveal his cat-furred face and weird eyes, but the thug didn't seem concerned. Not even at the sharp claws he'd used to point at Lan.

'Heard about you lot,' one man declared. 'Knights or something or other. Funny costumes, like them MythMaker sketches.'

'That's right, the Villjamur Knights, and I'm Investigator Fulcrom of the Inquisition. We're here to have a word with Delandro.'

Vuldon glared at Fulcrom then, and the rumel turned away. 'I didn't know he was still alive,' Vuldon hissed.

The two thugs consulted each other, and one went inside while the rest of them stood in silence. Vuldon seemed to be in the grips of a barely contained rage.

The first thug returned and bid them enter and the Knights followed.

*

Every bit the signature of a man who had more money than taste, it was a dark yet garish abode, with gold-leaf cressets, black-painted wood, wide arches, full-length mirrors and erotic paintings. Each room was larger than Fulcrom's own apartment, and smelled of some expensive fragrance.

They were escorted into an antechamber with a skylight shadowed by snow. A handful of logs burned in the huge central fireplace. A frail-looking man shuffled into the room, wearing a dark-green robe with neat stitching, a simple, costly elegance that was fitting for an emperor. He moved silently to the fire, where his bodyguard helped him into a large wooden chair akin to a throne. He remained there, the light of the fire warming one half of his face and casting the other half in darkness.

Tane leaned into Fulcrom and whispered, 'This is one of the most violent men in the city? He doesn't look like he's capable of wiping his own behind.'

'His power is all in his wealth,' Fulcrom breathed. 'He funds organized crime – though that's something we've never been able to prove.'

'Enough of this whispering.' Delandro cleared his throat and continued in a frail voice. 'What brings these famous celebrities to my house?'

'We were wondering if you could help the Inquisition with some enquiries,' Fulcrom said.

'And you bring these – ' Delandro raised a hand to gesture wildly at the others ' – enhanced thugs for added persuasion.'

'It wouldn't be all that different from your own business operation, now would it?' Fulcrom challenged. 'The deals which you've done with your men's hands around people's throats? Intimidation and bullying? The deception, the theft?'

'You can prove nothing, investigator. Besides, I have friends in the Council who will vouch for my clean record.'

That was true, and didn't Fulcrom know it.

'This one, the brute, he looks familiar.' Delandro indicated

Vuldon, who was loitering in the shadows, by one of the paintings.

Fulcrom could hear Vuldon's heavy breath even from this distance. He could sense the tension. 'You met him in a previous life,' Fulcrom said. 'You probably remember his old name, though.'

'I'm not so sure.'

'The Legend,' Fulcrom replied.

Delandro was visibly taken aback and examined Vuldon with cautious interest. 'Oh.'

'Oh indeed, fucker,' Vuldon growled, stepping out of the shadows.

Whether or not Delandro felt any remorse, he didn't reveal it. 'I believe the Inquisition were also implicit in your demise,' the old man offered, his tone radically changed to one of reason.

'True,' Vuldon replied, 'but you're the cunt who made sure the events panned out in their favour. Your men rigged that wall, your men set up the false crime so that I'd turn up – because you wanted rid of me too.'

Delandro sighed. For the first time in his measly existence of lies and corruption, he spoke a truth: 'I'm old, I have no reason to hide parts of history where you're concerned. The Council needed help. I was told Emperor Johynn wanted rid of you because you had uncovered evidence that Johynn had in fact killed his own father Gulion to claim the throne. You were ready to expose that, so they set you up. It was that simple, and I'm sure if you make enquiries through official channels, you will still find that no one will let you press the issue any further.'

'Why kill those children?' Vuldon should have been enraged, but there was a break in his voice. 'Sixteen kids died because that wall collapsed on them – that was set-up by *your* men, and timed so that I would be there – too late to do anything about it, but right on time so that I could be set up for supposedly knocking down the wall. There was no escaping it.'

'You were offered retirement in exchange for keeping everything quiet,' Delandro said. 'Or that was the plan. You kept your reputation intact where possible, and so did the Emperor. It worked out best for all concerned – it was a simple business transaction. The children ... yes, that was a tragedy admittedly. But sometimes we must make tough decisions.'

'You ruined so many lives,' Vuldon murmured.

Fulcrom knew what happened to Vuldon next: the fall from grace, the spiral of depression, the alcohol and drugs and his wife choking on her own vomit after a drinking binge. The Legend fading into legend.

Fulcrom couldn't bear to watch Vuldon like this for much longer. 'Shalev,' he said. 'We're looking for Shalev. You must have heard of her in your circles, surely?'

'Ah, yes, our anarchist queen.'

'You know her?' Fulcrom pressed. 'Have you met with her?'

'Do you honestly think you can all waltz in here simply for me to tell you these things?' Delandro chuckled.

'We can give you money,' Fulcrom offered.

'Fuck your money,' Delandro spat. 'I have all the money I need.'

Fulcrom signalled to Vuldon; Vuldon lurched towards Delandro. One of thugs came in out of the darkness to intercept him, but Vuldon turned, lashed out, shattering the man's jaw, then delivered a blow to the stomach, hunching him over. Vuldon grabbed the scruff of his neck and slammed him down on a table right in front of Delandro. The wood exploded as the thug collapsed on the ground.

Delandro sneered at the ruined table and the stilled body. Four more bodyguards in red tunics stumbled into the room and, in the dull light of the fire, the Knights spun to challenge them.

It happened quickly, in the firelight, and in relative quiet. As the bodyguards drew their swords and lunged forward, Tane raked his claws across one man's face with two further blows to the side of his head and he was down. Meanwhile, Lan leapt, hovered then kicked at another – first a blow to his arm sending his sword clattering to the ground, then to his stomach. As he doubled over she grabbed a vase and exploded it on his head – he collapsed pathetically.

As the action continued, Fulcrom strolled nonchalantly closer to the now-panicking Delandro.

'Impressive, aren't they,' Fulcrom commented calmly.

'They're monsters,' Delandro told him as he watched Vuldon put down another two attackers with ease. The Knights turned their attention to Delandro, and waited for Fulcrom's word.

'I have done nothing wrong, no crime,' Delandro spluttered, sitting back in his chair, then laughing awkwardly. 'Please, you would not hurt an old man.'

Vuldon lunged forward but Fulcrom held out a palm. 'We've no reason to hurt you at all – well, Vuldon has, of course. Just tell us what you know of Shalev and we'll be on our way.'

'In all honesty, I know nothing.' The old man stared glumly into the fire, before resting his head in his hands. 'She comes to this city, she gets the proletariat on her side. It makes things difficult for businessmen of my standing.'

'I get it,' Fulcrom said. 'You mean people from the caves, they've no need for your types of crime when they're working for her.'

'Crime, indeed,' Delandro muttered. 'Where I once gave hardworking men and women in my employ food and drink, trinkets and coin, she now provides them with such things for free. I hear she has done things to grow food in the darkness, and it is in plentiful supply. I hear they have no need for coin with her ways. If they have their desires met they do not wish to work for me. How can I compete with that? In what ways can I tempt them? No, I am done with it all. I have enough, and I am too old for this game now.'

There was nothing for them here, no new information. 'Let's move on,' Fulcrom announced.

'I'll follow you out in a moment,' Vuldon said, looking down at Delandro.

'Don't abuse your powers, Vuldon,' Fulcrom warned.

'I won't abuse my *powers*,' he replied, pushing his fist into his palm. 'I just need a quiet word with an old friend.'

Fulcrom knew what might happen, but felt that, all things considered Vuldon probably deserved this time. Turning reluctantly away, Fulcrom steered the others out of the house.

*

Outside in the wintry chill, Tane and Lan discussed what Vuldon had been through – it was as if they had a new understanding for him, and that pleased Fulcrom.

Vuldon joined them a couple of minutes later, leaving the door to the property ajar. Tane peered inside then quickly turned back.

'What did you do to him?' Fulcrom asked, shivering in the wind.

'Told you,' Vuldon replied calmly. 'I had a quiet word, is all.'

'Have you finally released all those years of suppressed anger?' Tane offered.

Vuldon glared at him. 'If you'd been through what I have, because of that man, you wouldn't hold back.'

'Fair enough,' Tane replied, looking away. 'My apologies.'

'Did you kill him?' Lan whispered.

'He's alive,' Vuldon snapped, pulling up his hood. 'Let's just leave it at that. So, where to next, investigator?'

*

The Knights stood dumbstruck at the sight of Caveside. Apart from Vuldon, Fulcrom realized that, like much of the outer half of the city, the other two Knights had never visited the underbelly of Villjamur.

Despite its underground location, the place was bright, with light from the sky above channelled through strips, and down the underside of the massive cavern and adjoining catacombs, that were the under-city. Ancient, cultist-crafted glass captured light in a central hub and distributed it. This architectural magic meant that the people down here could dwell in almost similar lighting to the grand city of tier after tier of Imperial glory on the outside.

From their position of height, entering from the third level of the city, they could see across the buildings.

'Place still looks fucked-up,' Vuldon said. 'Like a god vomited a hundred styles of buildings on top of each other.'

From Underground North to East, there were two-, three- and four-storey houses, in clusters and scattered randomly, and the rest of the miles-wide indoor plain comprised of crude stone constructs or half-arsed metal-and-wood shacks. Some houses were weirdly decorated, with marbles or shards of glass pressed into surfaces. They were utilitarian structures, for warmth, shelter – not things of beauty. There was nothing grand here, no styles to be proud of. Washing lines hung between some of the taller buildings, underneath which children played and mangy dogs and cats chased one another. And weirder things dwelled in the underground, animals that cultists had messed with, half-bred with lizards and birds and creatures that should not dwell on land.

A heady fug of chimney smoke formed a layer near the top of the cavern, like an artificial cloud. Down to one side, the underground docks were restless as tiny boats ventured along the long, thin channels to the sea.

People milled around the streets, talking, even occasionally laughing. Certainly more life than Fulcrom could ever remember, which surprised him, because the place had never been exactly vibrant. There had to be two, maybe three hundred thousand people living down here and further into the catacombs, but the surveys seldom stretched that far. It was difficult to tell how big these underground tunnels reached. They'd been gradually expanding for centuries.

Shalev is out there. Someone here has to know where she's hiding.

*

For the hours they spent patrolling the Caveside populace, the Knights caused a hum of discontent to arise. From underground dens to the corners of dubious taverns, the group trawled major venues but found only the dregs of humanity. Under the Emperor's instruction they marched brazenly, openly, making their presence known, so that those who had something to hide would be fearful.

They kicked down doors and slammed suspects up against the walls of empty taverns. In dark alleys there were quick and futile retaliations at the heroes of the city stirring up trouble; and it was followed by brutal punishments from the Knights – or at least Tane and Vuldon. Lan sometimes looked away, choosing to fight only when challenged.

Again and again, Fulcrom interrogated known leaders of the criminal underworld, whilst Lan, Tane and Vuldon took care of the physical work.

Fulcrom repeated himself: 'Where was Shalev hiding?'

A partial drunk: 'You can't fucken come here doin' this, fuckers.'

A squat lady who dealt in knives: 'Fuck should I know where she is?'

An ex-tribal thug: 'Yer get the people under 'ere angry, they'll come ta get yer.'

A refined gentleman who had fallen on hard times: 'You're simply not welcome around these parts. Push these people too hard and they will come for you – because if you know where to look you will see they are ready to claim their city back.'

Fulcrom's frustration grew by the hour, and even the Knights began to sense the futility of their endeavours. No one seemed to know anything or wanted to give any details on Shalev. Each time a lead proved useless, Fulcrom closed his eyes and pictured having to tell the Emperor about the lack of progress. Threats, bribery, even Vuldon's less than subtle techniques resulted in nothing. The people down here had hope now, Shalev had given them that and in return they gave her their loyalty.

It was no surprise that the Cavesiders weren't going to hand her in, no matter how hard they were pushed.

*

Fulcrom had to admit: things weren't as bad as he remembered around here. It didn't smell as rancid, and there weren't as many people living on the streets – no, in fact, there was *no one* living on the streets, and there were few signs of the poverty he was used to.

Suspiciously, they found carts full of vegetables: carrots, courgettes, potatoes. How did they get hold of such items, when the prices were phenomenally high in the outer city? When Fulcrom quizzed the owner of one such cart, a chipper old fellow with a beard, the man replied, 'We grow them ourselves, mate. Got a few cultists helping us out, let us grow crops in all manner of ways.'

'I'd like to meet these cultists,' Fulcrom said.

'You and me both!' the man laughed. 'They never show themselves, we just get the seeds from 'em anonymously. I ain't complaining, though – just like to thank 'em, is all.'

One last unpleasant surprise came as the Knights finally called it a day and started heading upside, strolling along one of the main streets that eventually connected with the first level of the outer city. Behind were thirty, perhaps forty men and women from Caveside marching peacefully in unison,

227

shadowing them, but now and then someone would shout out insults.

'Likes of you ain't welcome here.'

'You should stop pestering us, we's done nothing to deserve rough treatment like this.'

'You Knights should get away from us.'

They don't understand, Fulcrom thought, *yes things are tough, but they have a psychopathic killer living amongst them, someone who makes life hell for the decent, law-abiding citizens of the outer city. This is what makes the job hell.*

Vuldon turned to confront them, but Lan and Tane both restrained him.

'Calm down,' Tane soothed.

Some of the Cavesiders formed a silent line and stood their ground as if to challenge them. Vuldon turned to Fulcrom, who merely shook his head. This was a situation that could get very ugly, and he did not want to turn the Knights against the populace on so large a scale. Perhaps he had been insensitive to the new underground culture, but he was stunned that they had formed enough spirit to stand together like this, and so peacefully.

'I think we should go,' Lan said.

'I agree. This isn't our kind of battle,' Fulcrom said, turning to walk away. 'This is not our front line.'

TWENTY-ONE

Ulryk's Journal

To be within a library again was a great boon, the smell of the books
and vellum and leather, the years of dust.

As I suspected, there was a system at work there of which not even
the librarians were aware. Within many of the ancient libraries across
the Boreal Archipelago, there existed a code: various sections – histories
and geographies mainly – are spaced at precise distances from each
other, and no librarian had ever been able to explain why this is the
case.

I knew why, of course.

The system was created as a way of guiding Jorsalir wayfarers to
specific texts within the library, journals of previous wayfarers and
pilgrims, as a way of secreting progress in spreading the word of Bohr
and Astrid. But there were deeper and darker codes that only those
most senior in the church knew of, guides to hidden regions. Codes that
guided those in the Jorsalir religion to forbidden texts, translations of
works hidden from the general public. The section of rare tomes – those
in public view – was a surprising treat for me. Kept in protective cases
are doctrines written (supposedly) in the time of Vilhallan, and critiques
of King Hallan Hynur who established the original colony. I allowed
myself a chuckle at the commentaries on the Rumel Wars, a great
mythological battle between tribes of that race, but I know that this is,
as is most of the history in this library, likely to be a lie.

I found a bizarre section buried deep within the section on fauna, a tiny nook on the third floor. This particular room was of little consequence, save that I knew such chambers existed and they were not sealed off, and I considered this progress. Where there was one, there were likely to be many others.

*

Maps! The great cartographers of the last thousand years had each left original works here, carefully preserved and rarely examined, it seemed. There was evidence of lands beyond the fringe of the Boreal Archipelago in all directions, and some of the librarians had barred me from investigating further into the map room. It suggested a control of information. There was one particularly shifty custodian, a leering fellow with a forest of eyebrows upon his head, who saw it as his duty to stop people from even walking by the cartography section. He piled up great tomes and built a wall of books to prevent access. I entertained myself for several minutes by visibly showing I was contemplating different routes and I enjoyed watching him haul books to the other side of shelving units to block my way. He was old and greatly unfit and if I had continued all week I would be confident that his back would be put out.

*

Despite my urgency, I felt I was not in a great hurry this week. I did not feel watched. I awarded myself the luxury of several days settling into the library and its books in order to do my job properly, and perhaps by soaking up the atmosphere I could perceive new depths.

What was certain, though, was that the wayfarers of the ages had . . . struggled here. They were frustrated, even troubled by some of the presences deeper within the library. They spoke in rhyme and a deliberate confusion of old tongues; these were codes which intrigued me, but in my darker moments I suspected that those who came to understand the books in the library descended into insanity. One wayfarer called Jorg repeated the word 'Acheron' several times in his final entry. I could not be certain, but I suspect I would be dealing with forces new to even me, and this caused me both vexation and excitement.

The dead – that is what the entries referred to. According to my own studies of the very oldest texts, Acheron is a river to, and of, the world of the dead. Many wayfarers talk of the dead under the city, the dead stirring beneath the library, at the very least. Was Villjamur constructed upon the souls of the dead? I have seen the dead walking during my travels to the city, however they were not sentient as these texts suggest. It has long been known that many of the great ancient ley lines all intersect here, but ley lines tell us nothing, and much of this history is truly unreliable.

Perhaps the ancient occultists were guiding people here, to this spot?

It is certain that the city needs exploring further, though where I hope to go maps will be of little use. I will head down, into the depths of the city. I could be gone many days.

Acheron.

TWENTY-TWO

Nestled into a private wooden booth at Bistro Júula, behind two giant potted ferns, Fulcrom and Lan stared at each other across the half-dozen tea-light candles. Fulcrom was in his finest woollen tunic, a dark green number with rural motifs in the stitching, an outer-cloak he'd been saving for as long as he could remember, and his boots were so clean he could see a reflection of himself in their gleam.

Lan, in a high-collared long black dress with ornate lace patterns around the hem, was an impressive presence. He wondered vaguely why she didn't make more of her athletic figure, but he assumed she was still in the habit of concealing herself.

'So should we be doing this?' Fulcrom asked.

Lan shrugged. 'We're just discussing how to find Shalev, that's all, while the boys entertain themselves with lower-level ladies.'

'Right,' Fulcrom replied, noting her emphasis on the word lower. 'They're not going to be out *all* night, I hope? I mean, they must know about the indoor iren opening tomorrow?'

'Yes they do, stop being a control freak,' Lan mocked. 'Despite their bravado, they do take it all seriously, especially since your lecture to them.'

'I know, I know.' Fulcrom leaned back in his chair. 'It's just that it's only you guys and the city guard there, and I don't think they're particularly good at looking after themselves let alone protecting the event from Cavesiders.'

'You're starting to sound like one of the characters from a MythMaker sketch.'

'You read that rubbish?' Fulcrom asked.

'Sometimes, I do. You must admit they're funny.'

'I've never read one.'

'Then how would you know if they're rubbish?'

'A valid point,' Fulcrom confessed.

'Besides, the children of the city seem to love it. I vaguely remember talk of them from years ago, but they went underground. There seem to be a lot of them about now though.'

'So I've noticed,' Fulcrom grumbled. 'I guess children need their heroes?'

'Even adults,' Lan remarked. 'So it appears, at least.'

Fulcrom made a vague wave of his hands. 'These are uncertain times,' he said. 'What with the ice age really settling in, the reports of genocide, and the war that's going on in Villiren, people need to believe in *something*. That the Knights exist gives them deep comfort. It gives them a focus. Did you know, people even stop us investigators on the street to tell us how appreciative they are of you.'

Lan gave a cute smile, and there was something about her manner that said here was affirmation that she was doing more than just fighting crime, that she was happy to be a symbol.

*

Fulcrom came from a long line of extroverts, and found being around others to be hugely comforting. He could absorb their energy, enjoyed observing their quirks and mannerisms and making huge generalizations about their lives. Throughout his childhood, his mother and his father would constantly guffaw across the dinner table, make jokes with pats on backs and discussions of the day. They were a tight-knit and outrageous bunch, Bohr rest their souls. And it made sitting across from

233

Lan all the more interesting, because clearly she had spent much of her life trying not to say anything – doubly interesting, because he noted how with *him*, she was the one initiating conversations, prodding him on his past and his tastes. She laughed when he spoke of things he knew weren't *that* funny.

If he read people as well as he thought he could, these were encouraging signs.

But Fulcrom also felt uneasy for any number of reasons. Of course there was his private knowledge of Lan: she used to be anatomically male, and no matter how liberal and open-minded Fulcrom considered himself, no matter how good the cultists had been, that thought existed. A lot of it was new to him, too – he had studied as best he could to understand notions of what made someone a man or a woman or one of the shades in between; he tried to understand how someone's gender and sex could be different, but found such matters to be amazingly complex. Could a person be so different from the one they were a year ago? Perhaps it was the investigator in him, but all he had were questions.

'You're thinking about the *issue*, aren't you?' Lan asked.

'Not at all, no.'

The waitress brought over some soup and spiced bread, then left them alone again. Lan held her hair back with one hand as she leant over the dish. Whenever she looked up at him, something resolute inside him melted. He'd been shutting out such feelings for so long he didn't know what to think any more.

'Aren't you going to eat?' she asked. 'I don't want to look like some starved pig compared to you.'

Fulcrom didn't need telling twice, and tucked into the soup, letting the intense flavours of garlic and cumin spill over his tongue. A band started up, violins and drums playing old folk numbers, loud enough to be heard but not enough to ruin the moment.

In between mouthfuls Lan opened up. 'You know, it's pretty good being a Knight.'

'Finally adjusted to the life then? I knew you would.'

'You know *everything*, don't you?'

'No, but it's my job to at least try to know everything.'

Her raised eyebrow indicated she'd registered he wasn't being serious. 'Yes, it's good. For the first time I've found a niche for myself. I'm glad I was taken – not how I was taken, but that I've been allowed to be *something* useful. To make a contribution to the world. One thing I've learned is that it's very difficult being a woman in this world.'

'I *think* I know what you mean.'

'You don't know until you're actually a woman,' Lan said.

He was surprised at how matter-of-fact she was about the hidden suggestions of her transformations. He'd assumed she'd never want to mention it.

She continued, speaking earnestly and with passion. 'There are too few ways in which a woman from low birth can have an impact in society. There are next to none in the Council, few of them are landowners outright unless by marriage. Few of us have access to power. You know the other day when we were doing an appearance on behalf of the Emperor, afterwards a little girl trotted up to me in a makeshift black uniform. She was like a miniature version of me, and she told me that one day she wanted to grow up to be just like me. It was amazing. *I* was a role model for a young girl. I can never remember there being many female role models – apart from the Empress, and look what happened to her.'

Fulcrom said nothing.

'That was the point where I knew for certain I could be happy – being a role model for young girls. And what irony.'

'I guess so.'

'You don't like it when I hint about my past.'

Fulcrom shrugged. He wanted to say that he wanted to

know every small fact about her, because he thought her attractive and that she was gradually colonizing parts of his mind.

'I'm not going to shut it away,' Lan declared. 'Just because I led a hidden life didn't mean I was repressed in any way. It is admittedly easy never to mention it, but why repress it? That only grows your anger and your bitterness. I kept telling myself that I was above all that.'

'It must have been quite something to live with,' Fulcrom said.

'You have no idea.' Lan went on to describe how difficult her upbringing had been, but spoke always with a wry smile. 'It's easier for me if I forgive people, if I think about their needs, make excuses for them. I believe we're all still like children, just grown a little older. We still blunder around making mistakes, judging people based on our own limited experiences, lashing out at what we fear. We're all still scared of something. If I think of us all like that, it's easier to forgive.'

Lan was bewitching, holding his attention for longer than any woman in a long time, and he found her increasingly difficult to resist. It seemed those ghosts of his were growing fainter by the heartbeat.

*

Lan paid for the meal and drinks. She said she earned more than enough being a Knight, and she didn't quite know what to do with all the money. Begrudgingly, Fulcrom permitted her the gesture. Afterwards they took a walk along one of the bridges across the city – not one of the massive ones that horses trudged across daily, dragging wares from iren to iren and rattling the stonework to dust. This was one of the daintier, more ethereal structures, with tall arches and wooden trusses. Fulcrom tried to ignore the bitter winds and the plummeting temperature, instead dwelling on the things he'd not really had time for before: the stars, the way the moonlight skimmed across the slate tops of houses, the graceful arcs of hunting pterodettes, the deep black tundra beyond the city walls.

The tenderness of a hand in his own.

He'd offered his cloak to Lan, but she said she couldn't feel the cold since she had become a Knight. The fact was he found her remarkably attractive. He always had a thing for human women: their softness, their gentleness. Their vulnerability brought out his protective side, and a bunch of psychologies he didn't care to analyse.

In hushed and broken conversation they discovered a little more about each other. Then they remained in silence for a while longer, looking out across the city, growing used to the feeling that they were alongside each other. Only once did he see how scared she was, too, a look in her eye, a nervous laugh, a shaking hand. Fulcrom had concluded that it didn't matter who she had been – it had all served to present her as she was: as a beautiful woman, standing by his side.

Later, Lan walked Fulcrom home, an irony that wasn't lost on him. She kept on jumping up the sides of buildings, showing off, a little excited by alcohol perhaps, but he liked her sudden childlike tendencies, a playfulness.

Outside his building, they held each other's gaze and hands. She was in control now. She knew that he liked her, and she was enjoying the moment. It impressed him, to see her so confident. Gently, they moved their faces closer together, and she kept her lips slightly away from his own, so he could feel her breath on his face. It had been so long since he'd felt like this, been so long that he'd almost forgotten how to do it.

Lan kissed him with such a softness that it sent a warm shudder through him, and then applied passion, pushing him back against the cold wall of his building.

She removed her lips as quickly as she had placed them on his, and smiled saucily. 'Want to see what else I can do?' she asked.

They kissed again and she seemed to vibrate, and suddenly whatever powers she had activated slipped into him, fizzing down every nerve in his body like a static shock. She began to laugh. After a peck on his jaw she turned to walk down the street. A moment later he saw her running up the side of a limestone hotel, and up onto a bridge, vanishing into the night.

He headed inside, up the stairs, into his empty apartment.

Alone, he got changed into thick nightwear and folded his clothes neatly on the chair by his bed. His tired, beatific mind didn't want to shut off, and he lay there for a few moments staring at the ceiling, and he couldn't stop smiling.

Suddenly, a wind gusted into his apartment, and for some fathomless reason, he felt he wasn't alone.

A voice, definitely female and coming in a whisper, was calling out his name. It seemed to linger in the air like a plume of smoke, slowly repeating itself, and then, much harder, in the centre of his mind: 'I saw your new fancy woman.'

'Who's there?' Fulcrom lurched out of his bed and stumbled bleary-eyed around the room, trying to find his way around in the dark. A beam of moonlight pierced his curtains, scattering shine on the glossy objects in his room – the polished wood, his boots, the picture frames. He stood with his hands out wide, ready to grapple with his intruder. His tail darted back and forth in anticipation beneath his nightshirt, and through the echoes of sleep he tried to remember where he kept his spare blades.

The voice, a blur, came from all sides: 'What, you don't remember me?'

'What the fuck is going on?' he spluttered. 'Where are you? Who are you?'

'I'm insulted,' the voice said, and laughed. 'I'm in the bathroom.'

Fulcrom stumbled across his room, guided more by mem-

238

ory than vision. He could feel his pulse racing. He placed his shoulder to the door frame, and glanced around for an object: there, on the shelf, the candlestick. He cautiously lifted the heavy brass object and brought it in front of him.

Tentatively, he eased the door open . . .

Even in this small room, Fulcrom could see no presence, no figure, just the metal bath and a small white cupboard. The grey and red tiles were cold underfoot. A chill went through him.

'I . . . I can't see anyone.'

'Try the mirror, sugar.' Another chill, this one deep in his core. He recognized this voice, or at least he thought he did. *It's not possible* . . . For a long while he didn't turn around.

Eventually he forced himself to look and there, in the wide, circular mirror a person stared back at him – and not just any person.

It was Adena, his dead wife.

Twenty-Three

Dumbly, Fulcrom dropped the candlestick, and it smashed one of the tiles, but he wasn't distracted from gaping at the image in the mirror. 'You're ... you died.'

Almost completely white-skinned, with lank black hair and a heavy fringe, and with a wound at her neck that must have come from the crossbow bolt that had hit her on the day she was killed, Adena didn't look particularly alive. Seeing her now confirmed just how much Adena looked like Lan – or would have done if Adena was, in fact, alive.

'I did,' Adena said.

'So how come . . .' Fulcrom gestured wildly at the mirror. 'How come you're here? Is this still a dream?'

'For you? I don't think so. For me, I have no idea. It kind of feels like I've woken up from a really long dream though.'

Fulcrom struggled to believe what was happening. He stormed out of the room, flung open a window to let the bitterly cold air wake him even further. Clouds of his own heavy breath drifted away into the evening. After a moment he turned and walked hesitantly back into the bathroom, confident that the phantasm in the mirror would be gone.

Adena was still there, smiling meekly. 'Hi,' she said. 'Still here.'

Fulcrom snapped into full analytical mode.

On a closer inspection, she was glowing, ever so slightly, as if washed in moonlight. She wore thin white rags, and her skin seemed a little blue and unhealthy. There was nothing behind her save the reflection of some items in his own bathroom. She was just there, in the mirror – an apparition. He questioned whether or not he was dreaming, whether or not he had been drugged or taken hallucinogens, but he didn't think so.

'She seems nice, the new girl,' Adena declared. 'I like her.'

'Lan?' Fulcrom spluttered, feeling a sudden and irrational bout of guilt. 'How could you *possibly* know about her?'

'Oh, well . . . You can kind of see stuff when you're in this state. But, I guess you are allowed to see other women. I mean, I am *dead* after all.'

'How did you get here, in the mirror?'

'The priest set us free. I don't know what he did exactly, but after the priest's visit, some of us seemed to be able to get out of there.' She gestured down below. 'Though, it has to be said, most couldn't be bothered – they'd had enough of the living – it was those who just wanted to come back with unfinished business, that kind of thing. You're looking well by the way, sugar.'

'The priest,' Fulcrom said.

'Yes, Ulryk,' Adena replied. 'Nice man, if a little silly when he gets excited. He means well though.'

Ulryk . . . how is he behind this? 'I don't understand. You were killed, not put in some gaol – so how could he *free* you?'

'I wasn't burned, remember?' Adena said. 'The authorities thought I was a criminal. They thought I was in on that robbery and refused to burn me. They buried me – you must have watched them lower my corpse into the ground? Don't you remember?'

'Well, yes, I . . .' Fulcrom perched on a stool and pressed his face into his hands, recalling the faces of the mourners and the rain splashing on the mud as her coffin was lowered into the earth. After a moment he looked up again. 'I did try to explain to them that it was a misunderstanding – even tried to pull strings behind the scenes.'

'I know, my love.' Adena's face was serene, if a little ethereal. Very faintly the texture of her skin altered, tiny patterns moving just beneath the surface.

'What happened after that?' Fulcrom asked.

'My soul was trapped beneath the city, just like every other soul who wasn't burned on a pyre and set free.' She chuckled. 'I suppose it means the Jorsalir priests were right about something. And you know what, there are a surprising number of us down there, and not just criminals who aren't allowed to have their souls freed – although even most of them say they were innocent anyway. So we are all there, underneath Villjamur, doing what we've done for as long as any of us can remember, and Ulryk manages to gain entrance to wherever it is we were . . . I want to say living, but that's not quite right, is it?'

Fulcrom was amazed at how light-hearted she was taking all this. She never did take anything seriously, even when she was still alive – *Snap out of it, idiot. This doesn't prove anything.*

Adena continued. 'Ulryk gave his best religious mumbo-jumbo to set us free, but I think he meant to some kind of heaven. He did some spells, I think, from a book which he was carrying, and I'm not sure what happened, but we all just followed him right out of the underworld and through some strange passageways and up to the city. It took us a while, but previously we'd never been able to leave the underworld. All of us were trapped there, somewhere under Villjamur.'

Fulcrom tried to process all of this, trying not to laugh at how ridiculous it all sounded. Worst of all was that he was inclined to believe her.

'I came straight to see you,' Adena said, 'though at the moment I only appear in mirrors. Some of the others are able to move about the streets – I'm hoping maybe I can, too. So then, tell me all about Lan.'

Fulcrom turned away. 'I don't want to talk about Lan.'

'Why not? She's important to you, and you're important to me.'

'I just don't want to talk about it.'

'Oh, come on, I don't want us to argue on my first night back. That's all we used to do towards the end.'

Fulcrom was hurt. 'We did not.'

'You probably don't remember, burying yourself in your work. My memories are preserved, once they returned to me. They say, in the underworld, that the living have a habit of killing reality. As soon as something's happened, it's distorted from what it used to be.'

Maybe she was right. He was always forgiving her for something or other, always letting her get away with whatever she wanted. He was a pushover, and he remembered now.

'Are you just stuck there, in the mirror?'

'Sort of,' she said. 'For now I can't go any further than this. You don't just appear back in this world, apparently – you make slow transitions. Perhaps I can take more of a physical form soon.'

'And who exactly gives you such information?' Fulcrom asked, exasperated. 'Is there a clinic you all go to where you have a nice chat about coming back to life?'

'Now don't be sarcastic, sugar. You were always a perfect gent when I was alive.'

Again a sigh, again staring at the floor, the wall, anywhere but at the girl he'd tried hard to let go of for all these years. Eventually he faced her only to say, 'I need to sleep.'

'Of course you do – you go ahead, and I'll be back soon.'

'Knock before you do,' he replied, but her image was already beginning to ebb away. The room suddenly lost one

chill when he noticed another from the window by his bed –
and he walked over to close it. But, just before he did, he
swore he could see a couple of pale-glowing figures progressing across the bridges.

He couldn't be bothered to explore that. He was tired,
upset, and he was struggling to suppress his memories.

*

Lan lay awake on her side, glancing out of her bedroom
window. Huge columns of snow drifted across the sea, like
white banners floating in the breeze, and behind that slate-
grey skies extended into the distance.

Despite the weather, she was in a good mood. No, a great
mood, in fact. Last night, with Fulcrom, she felt as though
she'd overcome a major obstacle on her journey through life.
No matter how organized and skilful he was as an investigator, with her he seemed just as useless in the arts of being a
couple as she herself felt, which made everything seem so
normal.

She washed her face in the basin in the corner and got
changed into the black outfit of the Knights. Her finger traced
the encircled silver cross, their symbol, the one she'd noticed
graffitied on walls near Caveside, like a warning. The same
symbol that was featured on banners and flags drawn up for
sale at the Emperor's request, that little girls were stitching
into their own costumes as they pretended to be her.

For a moment Lan paused in the mirror, brushed her hair
and, with a pair of scissors, she straightened her fringe. A
little make-up next. Without the bustle of the show, without
other women around her, she enjoyed these little morning
rituals. No awkwardness, no glares loaded with meaning.

After she finished, she headed out of her room, where she
found that the boys were up, dressed and eating oats for
breakfast.

'What, no women this morning?' Lan asked, strolling past
the large window overlooking the sea.

'Turns out,' Vuldon said, in between mouthfuls, 'that Tane's conversational skills are a bit of a contraceptive at times.'

Lan didn't even want to know what he'd said.

'How did it go with your lover boy?' Tane leapt up off the chair and sauntered to her side, his tail swishing playfully. His irises flared with a feral streak. 'Did you let him ... you know?' He wafted a hand towards her loins.

For some reason Tane's blunt charm completely circumvented any awkwardness, and it didn't hurt to think about it when he was so matter-of-fact. 'I'm not going to let your lack of personality ruin something nice,' she said. 'But no, if you *must* know, nothing happened.'

'Lan, you need to tell us if you two are intimate.' Vuldon lumbered over to the corner to stoke the fire and add a couple of logs. 'Just lay it straight. We need to know – conflict of interests and all that.'

'We kissed, all right, there's nothing else to say,' Lan replied with a frown. 'And don't worry, I won't let it get in the way of the job.'

'Good, because we've got a heck of a task ahead of us today.' Vuldon stood up and folded his arms. 'Everyone who's *someone* in Villjamur is going to be at this damn opening,' he growled, 'and all eyes are on us, seeing as though we're the city's darlings. Let your concentration fall, and you could fuck it up – which means we're done for.'

'I'm not going to fuck *anything* up.' Lan wished he would show her just a little more faith sometimes. Was it the fact that she had messed up one night previously, or did he not trust women to do a decent job?

*

All along the Maerr Gata, the largest street on the fifth level of the city, people were stirring. Hunched in their shawls and cloaks and furs, under gentle flakes of snow, men and women trundled towards the new indoor iren, the first covered

245

market installation outside of the caves. At first they came in ones and twos, the early trinket-seekers, and then they swarmed like beetles, scurrying out of cobbled passageways and across buckling bridges to join in with the main crowd.

The air was laden with expectation. This wasn't just another iren, it was a statement against the ice age, a defiant gesture that life *could* go on. Not just that, but the grand opening had been hyped beyond all belief, so much so that the people of the city could well believe that they were about to witness an event on a par with the birth of a god.

Boards advertising the event had been erected about the city; banners of new insignias rattled from metal railings; criers stood broadcasting against the tide of citizens.

'These people,' Tane remarked, with a gesture down below, which for all Lan knew could have referred to some hell realm, 'they really ought to get a hobby. This simply can't be the centre of their world.'

Lan couldn't help but laugh at the look of mild despair on Tane's furred face. The Knights had gathered, in advance, on top of the main structure, keeping an eye on the crowd, and as a visible deterrent against anyone wishing to disrupt the event.

'Says the guy who spent his life throwing fancy parties,' Vuldon grunted.

'Networking, old boy – it's a different art entirely.'

Lan had to hand it to the architects: the iren certainly was impressive. Whilst not mirroring the aesthetics of the surrounding buildings, it had been designed with the future in mind. The three-storey facade was crafted from a green mica, so it shimmered like a monstrous emerald and scattered on its surface were deliberate patches of limestone that made the structure appear as if it was suffering from a disease. Arched windows were placed at regular intervals on each floor with a rigorous attention to geometry.

Whether or not it would be popular was yet to be determined, but people were pausing before it, cooing or gesturing or beaming. Lan knew then that its intention to offer a distraction against the ills of the world would probably be a success.

'Vuldon,' Tane called above the wind, 'did you have to perform such chores back in your glory days?'

Vuldon perched on the outer wall, peering down with a bemused expression on his face. He rubbed his broad stubbled jaw. 'After a while it became posing for one thing or another. I tried to fight it off but people just seem to want something to believe in. It happens to soldiers, too – those that come back from big campaigns, especially the commanding officers, become a point of interest.'

'I don't know,' Lan said. 'I think we're of more value than this.'

'I quite agree,' Tane declared. 'You're a miserable sod at the best of times, Vuldon.'

Vuldon shrugged, stood up and brushed the back of his uniform. 'I don't care, cat-man, that's just how things are sometimes – and I'm fine with it. We've got a good income, a good lifestyle, and a little attention.'

'A little?' Tane said, prancing about the rooftop. 'A good slice of the populace treat us like we're gods.' To prove the point he waved to the people below, who responded with waves and cheers.

'The Cavesiders don't treat us like gods,' Vuldon said.

'Neanderthals, the lot of them,' Tane replied.

Two city guards appeared further along the rooftop – four, six and soon a unit standing in sharp rows, forming a path. They snapped to attention as Emperor Urtica arrived, his aureate, purple robes fluttering in the sharp wind. He was wearing thick leather boots, a purple tunic and a rich fur cloak. He approached the Knights and only when he was close could Lan smell the musky aroma of arum weed smoke on his clothing.

'Sele of Urtica,' she remembered to say.

Tane and Vuldon shuffled into line beside her.

Urtica issued a professional grin, and an obviously rehearsed speech. 'My Villjamur Knights, how splendid you look.' His voice was richer than she remembered. 'You have been instrumental, if not the sole reason, in reducing crime in this city in such a short space of time. Your citizens hold you in high esteem, as does the Council – and as do I.'

'Thank you, my Emperor.' Lan could sense Vuldon's snort of disdain, even though no one else appeared to notice.

'Today, as you know, is important. I am about to open this incredible iren – what a structure! There are soldiers from the city guard and men from a Regiment of Foot stationed on every floor of the building, but I have been receiving certain ... threats of late.' His voice betrayed him and Lan could suddenly see the sleepless nights in his eyes. 'The anarchists seem to think today represents everything they disapprove of. I cannot allow such a rogue minority to ruin this for the good people of Villjamur. This iren is to be a symbol of our wealth, status and pride.'

Lan smiled but inwardly questioned: who exactly was the majority? The people starving outside the city gates? Those trying to make a life for themselves Caveside? Or those privileged few crowded below them to celebrate the opening of a building created for the sole purpose of pleasure and image?

*

Fulcrom stormed across the city, through a light shower of snow.

All around this region of Villjamur, the city was in the midst of being reconstructed. Horses dragged gargantuan carts of stone and wood precariously across the cobbled roads. Scaffolding webbed over and across buildings as if woven by some monstrous machine, whilst masons and labourers climbed up into celestial mists.

Fulcrom arrived at the hotel where Ulryk was lodging, a rickety, whitewashed building typical of the lower levels. Fulcrom banged on the door to his room, but there was no reply. In the small, tastelessly decorated lobby, decorated in deep reds, with old furniture and garish paintings, Fulcrom enquired of the landlord of the hotel if he'd seen the priest.

'Nah, not seen the guy,' he replied.

'Have you heard anything strange from his room perhaps?' Fulcrom pressed. 'Or have there been any visitors?'

'He's a quiet one, aye, keeps himself to himself mainly. No friends, no visitors. Don't eat with the other residents in the dining room – who'd want to, mind, they're a freakish lot – but he's always smiling whenever I pass him.'

'Are his movements strange?' Fulcrom asked.

'What, like the way he walks?'

'No,' Fulcrom sighed. *Idiot.* 'I mean, the hours he leaves and returns, are they strange?'

'Up and down with the sun, mainly. Though I've not seen him return for the last two days.'

'Thanks for your help. If you see him, send word by a messenger to the Inquisition headquarters. We'll cover the cost.'

'Will do, sir.'

*

Fulcrom headed to the Inquisition headquarters. There, in the sanctuary of his office, he sat upright at his desk for nearly an hour, staring into space, turning things over in his mind.

Warkur poked his head in through the doorway, then knocked on the frame. For a big rumel, he certainly moved with surprising stealth. 'Fulcrom, got a minute?'

'Of course, sir, come in.'

Warkur closed the door carefully, then approached lugging a thick bundle of papers. He dumped them on the desk in front of Fulcrom.

'What are these?' Fulcrom asked.

'Statements from last night,' Warkur ventured, although he seemed disturbed. 'You're in charge of weird shit. Well, here's a big pile of weird shit.'

'I'm not sure I follow.'

'We got a stack of witness statements last night, and they're from people who . . .' Warkur leaned in as if ashamed to speak the words '. . . who claim that the dead visited their houses. If it was one or two people, I'd have slapped them in a cell and let the silly fuckers sober up. But we got over forty declarations that the dead – or people *believed* to be deceased – were up and about, hassling the citizens of this damn city.'

Fulcrom breathed out slowly. 'Right you are, sir, I'll look into it.'

'Don't let this get out anywhere, and don't put too much effort into things. We don't want to be seen to be wasting our resources on shit that might not even be real.'

'Understood, sir,' Fulcrom reassured him.

Warkur retreated from the room. At the door he paused. 'I know you're not their babysitters, but are those damn Knights of yours prepared for today?'

'I believe so, sir.'

'Good. I never trust it when matters the Inquisition should be overseeing fall under the control of the city guard just because the Emperor is present. They're an arrogant and unsubtle bunch. We should be there – feels like a threat whenever they suggest we don't get involved.'

As Warkur left, Fulcrom lowered his forehead to the desk. Things were no longer looking so good.

His problems would not go away. He had loved Adena more than life itself, and it took him weeks to even speak to another person after her death. Her life gone, Adena had been framed for a crime she didn't commit. It was a savage end for such a beautiful, delicate human.

People began to talk about him behind his back – sentiments of sympathy at first, and then something more serious, questioning his fitness for the job of investigator. Fulcrom threw himself into his work assiduously, and discovered it was the only thing that would keep him from thinking about her. Eventually the pain diminished, but he was left with a residue in his mind that he couldn't scrub away, no matter how hard he tried to force the matter from his thoughts. Then years later, there was Lan with her eccentricities and her charms and her differences from anyone he'd met in a long time. Something close to hope had reared itself in his mind.

And then last night, of all nights to visit, *she* came back . . .

Fulcrom glanced through some of the reports from the previous night.

'My Jed was there – it's been nearly twenty years, but he was there,
still a boy, at the foot of my bed.'

'I was in the bath and this presence crept behind me and tried to kiss me!'

'Two of them – the ones that robbed me blind last year, standing there all glowing white and with the knives they carried that same night. They taunted me and my wife and we didn't sleep at all afterwards.'

The stories were very similar to his own – visitations and phantoms haunting the living of Villjamur. *What the hell had that priest been doing?*

*

The path inside the iren was lined with numerous ornate cressets that each held a fat-based flame. Across a white marble floor, with mica-covered walls and ceilings, the place was assiduously clean and gleaming, and across such surfaces the echo of their footsteps ricocheted down the corridor.

Lan felt nervous as the weight of expectation dawned on her.

Not only were the Knights celebrated by the people of the city, but they would be in the public eye once again. If something should go wrong, the people would not look to the city guard for assistance, they would look to the Knights – the manufactured symbols of hope.

The corridor didn't turn at right angles, it curved gently, implying the vast size of the structure. Soon they found themselves at the top of an iron spiral staircase and, together, they descended, passing portraits of the great icons of the military dressed in various regalia. At the bottom of the stairs the city guard boxed around Urtica, obscuring him with their crimson and grey colours, guiding him forwards, their dull steel shields held aloft as if they were heading into a fracas.

Then a lower level, wider, lighter, with skylights, wooden rails and gold cressets. Everything here seemed to glitter, as if they were in some heady dream.

People, who Lan guessed had something to do with the iren, were loitering. Wealthy types, judging from the looks of them, in regal tunics and dresses. All of them desperate to meet the new celebrities. 'This is bizarre,' Lan whispered to Tane.

'I love it,' Tane replied, shaking hands with some of the traders. 'It's why I love the taverns so much. I can't quite get enough of the adoration.' Then, to those gathered to one side, 'Nice to meet you. Sorry, must be on my way.'

'Tane,' Vuldon snapped, 'watch them closely. See anything remotely strange act on it.'

'I am, big guy, I am. I can hear dozens of conversations. I can do this stuff without even thinking about it, and meanwhile I'm still on the lookout.'

'You good, Lan?' Vuldon demanded.

'Yeah.' Lan was now peering into the deepening crowd as their noise swelled to fever pitch.

A shaven-headed man in his thirties, wearing a dark-brown hood, came to her side – and he was pleading with Lan for a kiss; an admirer. She ignored him at first, didn't want to make a scene here, but he laughed perversely.

'You look jus' fine in that outfit,' he drawled, then groped for her breasts.

Lan grabbed his outstretched arm, punched his stomach, and he buckled over. Finding reserves of strength that surprised even herself, she grabbed him by the hair, yanking him back, and clutched his throat. She snarled into his alcohol-reeking face: 'You leave me alone, right?'

The man squirmed a nod, and she pushed him away. Clawing his throat, he vanished into the masses.

'Well handled,' Vuldon said, without a hint of sarcasm. 'Bet being a woman in your position surprises you somewhat.'

'Fuck you.'

On through the horde, shadowing the city guard, who opened out behind a platform overlooking the lower floors in this vast atrium. Above there were two huge skylights, latticed with wood, and made from the most remarkably clear glass Lan had ever seen. The building felt as airy as an outside iren. A faint cough of a pipe as the new fire-grain heating system imported from Villiren continued to pump warmth around the place. *This is simply stunning . . .*

Upon seeing the Emperor above them, the audience fell into a hush.

He cleared his throat and paused. 'This is a momentous day. One of progress . . .'

While he recited a prepared script from memory, the Knights moved into position behind the city guard and across to the opposite side, gaining a better perspective on the events. Shops were layered on three floors, nearing a hundred units in all, mainly clothing-sellers and milliners, but also everything from designer carpenters to weapon-smiths, with a few bistros scattered about.

'. . . from the latest materials developed with the assistance of cultists, utilizing the great ancient technologies of millennia past . . .'

Around the sides of this highest level, marksmen crouched with loaded crossbows. One of them glanced her way and nodded, before allowing his gaze to settle on the throng below. As the Emperor continued his oratory, Lan, too, began scanning the crowd for any signs of trouble.

It seemed impossible to know what signs to look for. Everyone had been searched on entry and any weapons confiscated – an act all the more ironic considering that expensive blades would soon be on sale here. Lan noticed personnel sporting the new Shelby Corporation colours, white belts bright against the dark-red uniforms. It seemed they were guarding some of the more impressive-looking shops.

She focused on people's hands, whether or not they were in pockets, about to draw out something, people nudging those next to them, people gesturing across the atrium.

Through the glass, she saw something up on the roof. Possibly a pterodette or a garuda on patrol?

A noise below caught her attention. Someone had knocked over one of the grand portraits. Laughter frothed up around that corner and a man was hauled to his feet, peering around sheepishly whilst members of the city guard restored the work to its place on the wall. He was escorted from the premises.

The Emperor continued his speech with no pause, his voice carrying across the distance of the atrium. People stood listening in earnest. Again, Lan caught movement – something on the roof.

Moving through the press of guards surrounding them she reached Tane and Vuldon, who were scanning the crowd below.

'I'm going up onto the roof,' she said. 'Is there a way to get there without drawing too much attention?'

'Only the way we came,' Vuldon whispered, his gaze flitting about the iren. 'You need support?'

'I don't know. Just a hunch.'

'Fine. Well, we'll stay here for now.'

*

Lan peered back up over the doorway, and could see the roof extending back overhead, so she gripped the frame and, using her circus skills more than her powers, she quietly hauled herself up to the higher level.

Crouched by the guttering, wind pummelled her, sending her dark hair flailing around her face, and she pulled the strands aside and under control. Ahead in the distance, the towers of the city soared into a fine mist.

The roof was curved slightly, banking upwards, con-structed mainly from a slate-like material, but one which possessed more grip. Some distance ahead, Lan could see the two vast skylights which focused light into the iren. Each must have been twenty feet across.

And there, crawling along the outside of a skylight was something ... some kind of *creature*. She shifted along the perimeter of the roof to gain a better perspective, being careful not to catch its attention. From behind she could see its body, a brown and leathery skinned beast, twice the length of a human, with four squat legs, a stub of a tail.

Lan's foot caught a loose tile and she slipped; the creature froze, then turned to face her, an image of surreal horror: there was nothing but a vast mouth, no eyes, nose or ears that she could discern, just layered rows of teeth set in a slobbering maw.

The thing tromped on the spot, rotating its fat body. It snorted thick gloop by its feet. Then with a surprising, lumbering speed it charged towards her. When it was less than a few paces away Lan leapt up hovering in the air. The creature reared up, chomping at the air, but couldn't stop itself from sliding over the edge of the roof and, moments later, came the sound of its mass slapping against the cobbles below.

Lan lowered herself and looked over the edge of the building. Down below, in a vacant alley, the thing had become a purple aggregation of blood, offal and pulp.

What the hell was that?

Lan scanned the rooftop but could see nothing else. She scurried along the edge of the roof, peering over the side.

At the rear of the iren, a small huddle of figures dressed in dark clothing with scarves across their faces were surrounded by buckets of water. She watched as they placed a hand-sized, dark lump before them, and poured one of the buckets of water over the top. Suddenly the small mass began to lurch and convulse, contorting itself in all directions, and swelling into something altogether larger.

It ballooned into the precise form of the creature that had attacked her moments earlier, then one of the three – now clearly holding a sword for protection – kicked it so it tottered forwards, out of the alley, up a wall and out of sight. The figure returned to the others, who tilted up a sack to empty out one final dark mass, only to repeat the process.

Screams and manic calls for help started to erupt from the inside; she could feel the hysteria through the roof.

Lan took a leap off the edge of the building. She hung in the air – positioning herself – and then she allowed herself to fall at a velocity that wouldn't be quick enough to injure her, but certainly hurt the three down below. She collapsed into two of them, catching one on the back of the skull, another in the chest, and they both lay still, dead or unconscious. The third figure swung wildly with a sword, but Lan tuned into her powers to funnel out a blast of energy, repelling the weapon and sending it clattering behind. She followed up with two swift punches to the stomach, kicked the figure's face, and her victim collapsed backwards.

Her left leg ached from the fall, but she ignored it, removing the scarves of the strangers – two men and a woman – and recognized none of them. The female did not fit the description of Shalev at all. They were all still alive, so she heaped their bodies in the corner and ripped the now empty hessian sack into strips. She bound them tightly around their wrists and ankles.

Scooping up the discarded sword she sprinted around to the front of the structure, where citizens were pouring out from the iren's main entrance and into the wide Maerr Gata. Three of the recently spawned beasts were attacking people as they fled.

Lan drew on her reserves of energy, and projected herself into the air. She made a huge arc and came down on top of one of the beasts, driving her sword through the back of its skull: the thing heaved, groaned and shuddered into stillness. As she stumbled around to its front, people lurched away in horror – there was a human leg hanging out of the beast's jaw, and four corpses lying around in close proximity, each with a limb missing. At least the military was present and they were busy escorting people away to safety, apparently unconcerned with stopping the beasts.

Another beast was dispatched in the same way: a sword to the skull, blood pooling across the cobbles, and this time blood beetles arrived in their droves. Rarely up this many levels of the city, the insects were a glossy black tide devouring chunks of flesh and feasting on blood.

The final beast gave more of a fight. It threw itself at her; Lan jumped, drew up her legs so she was almost horizontal and thrust the sword into the side of its head. It wasn't quite dead; she hadn't used enough force. With a gaping wound, the creature hobbled in a circle, unable to control its movements. Spasmodically, it snapped at anyone nearby. Lan skipped up onto its back, fell to one knee and drove the blade through the thick hide on the top of its neck. The thing collapsed with a thunderous wheeze. She faced the front of the iren, this glorious structure of modernity, and she noticed that two black banners were now fluttering down from one of the windows.

How have the anarchists got there, too?

She ran towards the entrance, shoving her way through the crowds and, when it became too congested, stepping up through the air to run above them. She descended to land by the main entrance, by two sets of open double doors.

Lan paused in shock to regard the horror.

The opening event had been turned to carnage. Blood pooled thickly on the ground whilst crossbow bolts showered down from the tiers above, hitting innocents and the ravening monsters alike. There was screaming and chaos as the surreal hellions lunged and surged across the marbled floors, snapping at any pieces of moving flesh, sliding in the blood, and tearing apart whatever they could fit into their maws.

Vuldon was making his presence felt. He was at the far end of the ground floor, a sword swinging in each hand, lashing out at the vile freaks. Tane seemed to be everywhere at once, using his speed and agility to haul people out of the way of certain death, and raking his claws repeatedly through the beasts' thick hides to render them useless.

The creatures, while vicious, succumbed quite easily; they possessed little awareness or control, nothing in the way of guile. The creatures died, one by one, and very quickly there was just the aftermath, people sobbing, the injured calling for aid and a mass of blood and bone scattered across the once pristine floor. There were around twenty of the monsters, each considerably bigger and broader than Vuldon. He dragged the carcasses into a heap while Tane stood idly, drenched in blood that wasn't his, contemplating the event with something akin to disbelief on his face. Up above, Emperor Urtica stumbled forward from his military shelter overlooking the blood-soaked scene.

Although some distance away, Lan could tell how horrified the man was. A skylight suddenly shattered. Glass buckled and fell in large shards to disintegrate on the marble surface, while purple light flared in the gap; and down came a solitary figure, a woman with no hair, her dark cloak fluttering as she drifted softly to the floor on a line of light. Shalev.

On his lofty tier, Urtica recoiled into his metal shell and Lan sprinted towards the criminal cultist, desperate to intercept her. Vuldon and Tane were already running to protect the Emperor, yelling 'Get him the fuck to safety!' and urging the guards back, whilst snipers fired at Shalev to stop her.

The woman crouched to one knee, drew up a bent arm as if for protection, and then flicked some device with her other hand. The bolts pinged off an invisible field, and pausing on their rebound, as if time was stilled, they fell harmlessly to the side.

Lan darted in front of Shalev, around thirty paces away, the Emperor somewhere above and behind. Shalev stood up and pointed a relic at the protective box of soldiers. Lan tuned into the apparatus installed within her body, the same field that pushed away fire, allowed it to layer and accumulate within her until she felt she would burst, and waited.

As Shalev detonated her relic, Lan jumped upwards and held out her arms and released all her pent-up energy, shuddering in mid-air.

An aggressive pulse spat out from her hovering form and intercepted the flash of light extending from Shalev's relic. Lan felt as if her breath was being sucked from her body. She convulsed, allowing the internal, implanted mechanisms to take over.

Lan saw purple sparks.

Heard screams.

Her world faded to black.

*

Fulcrom found the priest later that day. A messenger brought immediate news of his return to the hotel, and Fulcrom sped across the city on foot, under brooding, darkening skies.

'Ulryk,' Fulcrom said from the doorway of his room. 'What the hell have you been doing? You set the dead free.'

The priest seemed unsurprised, and sighed. 'You have noticed, I see.'

'Damn right I've noticed,' Fulcrom snapped, 'as have a good slice of the populace.'

The priest turned away sheepishly, meandered back to stoke the fire. He waved Fulcrom in, and the investigator closed the door behind him.

Bizarre pieces of vellum were scattered about the room, as were half-melted candles wedged into bottles. Fulcrom glanced at some of the parchments, many of which were nailed to the wall, some stuck to the window, but he couldn't even recognize the text on them let alone read them. He was no expert on such matters, but the ductus of the script seemed utterly alien on some pieces, yet on others was vaguely familiar, a distant echo of Jamur. Arcane symbols and sketches and woodcuts crowded him.

Ulryk continued poking the flames absent-mindedly.

'Why the hell did you do ... whatever it was you did to bring such spirits to the city?' Fulcrom demanded.

'It was not, admittedly, my original intention,' Ulryk replied. 'I hope I have not done anything illegal. You are not here to arrest me, are you?'

Fulcrom chuckled glumly. 'I'm not sure what I'd arrest you for exactly.'

'Very well,' Ulryk replied. 'If you are not here to do so, would you at least like some tea? We make it quite differently out in the east.' Ulryk moved towards a small pot kettle hanging above the fire.

'Tea, yeah,' Fulcrom said. 'And then you can tell me about what you've done and how you've done it, because I thought I just showed you around an old library, not to new levels of existence.'

'That shows how much the people of the city know about their own libraries,' Ulryk replied. Eventually, with a cloth covering his hands, he carefully lifted the pot to one side, and poured the tea into small porcelain cups.

He handed one to Fulcrom, who took a sip. It was one of the tastiest drinks he'd ever consumed, warming and soothing. Fulcrom was forced to let his inner rage calm a little.

Ulryk certainly liked to do things at his own pace. Slowly, the priest eased himself into a battered leather chair, and sipped his tea.

'It's difficult to explain where I've been and what I've done. Perhaps it would be easier to show you. These things are best seen for yourself, given how analytical you like to be.'

'You mean the underworld?' Fulcrom asked. 'Is that where the dead are spilling from?'

'Under the city, underworld ... To be quite honest with you, I am not sure any of the names I have heard are accurate, but they'll do for now. Yes, the realm under the city, where the trapped souls reside, into which five rivers flow.'

'Rivers under the city? That's ridiculous.'

'Of all the things you've witnessed recently, the presence of flowing water under the city is perhaps the least ridiculous.'

'True,' Fulcrom admitted. He no longer had suitable points of calibration for the bizarre. But as he was in charge of such matters for the Inquisition, he had a duty. 'Go on then, I'd like to see this place.'

'So be it,' Ulryk replied.

*

A sudden snow shower hit the city, bringing with it huge flakes that whipped through the ancient streets. Late afternoon, and most of the citizens were sensibly indoors, avoiding the bad weather – all apart from packs of children hungrily staring at new sketches issued by the MythMaker that morning, devouring the artwork and the story scribbled to one side.

Above, thousands of windows glowed with the warm light of lanterns, candles and fires. Pterodettes perched on ledges or under gutters, the avian voyeurs peering into apartments until a military garuda flying past on patrol scattered the little reptiles across the city.

Through the garden of glass flowers, past the scene of the first city guard murder, up the steps, Ulryk and Fulcrom headed to the library, and into the vast chamber which was illuminated mainly by oil lanterns. A couple of stained-glass windows allowed coloured light to fall on some of the higher floors, but it was too dreary outside for any noticeable effect.

Ulryk knew many of the staff by name already, and before he spoke to each of them he placed his palms together, fractionally bowing his head in acknowledgement of their presence. One of the clerks kindly handed Ulryk a large lantern to guide them on their way, and the priest thanked him profusely.

'They are very good people here,' he whispered. 'Most of all they love the books, which is an admirable quality in any person, no?'

They passed along an off-white and ornate balcony. It overlooked the scriptorium, a vast stone chamber, where row upon row of cloaked young men and women were hunched over lecterns, working on parchments under the light of thick candles.

'The poor fellows,' Ulryk lamented. 'Over the years their eyes will dim. Their backs will knot permanently. Their bodies will ache. There is pain in the pursuit of knowledge.'

Someone from below regarded them sternly and placed a finger to his lips, waving for them to move on.

In the dark corridor Ulryk said to Fulcrom with some urgency, 'This is the first scriptorium I have ever known outside of a Jorsalir building. The poor young scribes are not of the church, but work on behalf of the Empire – many seem straight out of school. I have, in quiet moments, seen some of what they work on – they are copying political messages and threats into the various tribal languages. Some are writing instructions on how to speak Jamur. It is a systematic homogenization of tongues.'

The priest gazed expectantly at Fulcrom.

'There's nothing illegal about that,' Fulcrom replied. 'It might not seem right to you, but the savage peoples abroad should be guided to our ways.'

'Have you been to these islands and spoken to these *savage* people?' Ulryk demanded, a brief flash of temper showing for the first time.

'Well, no . . .'

'Then do not utter such ignorance. They are simple, peaceful people being exploited, investigator. The lies of your Empire ruin them. Such actions only go to repress them further, and to diminish their identities. Look at your own city; the refugees outside the city gates starving and uncared for, the Cavesiders below, oppressed and desperate, fighting for equality and their right to live. Villjamur – a city where the needs of the many are ignored for the comfort of the few. Do you honestly have the right to call other people *savage*?'

Fulcrom considered his words. Ulryk reminded him a little of his old mentor Inspector Jeryd and his words echoed uncomfortably.

*

Vuldon's gruff voice.

The shuffle of footsteps somewhere, idle background chatter, the smell of perfume.

With great effort, Lan forced open her eyes.

Row upon row of glittering glass bottles surrounded her, their contents coloured, some with labels upon them. They were arranged neatly on shelves, or in cabinets. Behind a counter, there were jars containing powders, by the look of it, and she realized the perfumes she could smell were probably from some of these vials.

In this dreary room, Tane was kneeling by her side, concern on his furred face. 'The lady wakes,' he announced.

Vuldon thundered over and crouched beside her, one hand down on the floor for balance. 'How are you feeling, Lan?' he asked, uncharacteristically gentle.

'Like shit,' Lan replied.

'You look it,' Tane commented, smiling at last – a gesture that reassured her.

'Thanks,' Lan sighed.

A cultist arrived – not Feror, but another one she recognized who worked near their clifftop retreat, a blond man in his thirties, and he injected something into Lan's abdomen, but she was too tired and numb to notice anything. Soon she began to feel sensations, the cold floor beneath her aching back. She felt like she'd been wrestling a bear.

'What the hell happened?' Lan asked.

'Shalev happened,' Vuldon said, rubbing his wide jaw. He moved out of the way to let the cultist make a quick assessment, then the man nodded his unspoken approval for them to continue, and shuffled out of sight. 'And,' Vuldon added, 'it seems *you* saved the Emperor, least that's what he seems to think.'

'I don't remember that part,' Lan replied.

Vuldon went on to explain the series of events. Shalev had tried to use a relic on the Emperor, to hit him with her magic, and Lan's intervention bought them enough time to usher him to safety. Vuldon and Tane made sure he got away to an escape tunnel, then returned quickly to find Shalev limping away, shell-shocked, before she vanished into a coloured mist, though her apparent injuries did not stop her killing two snipers on her exit.

'Urtica might want to make another one of those presentations to show us off again, you in particular,' Vuldon concluded, with a rare smile. 'You did good, lass.'

She liked that, gaining his approval at last. To her it seemed important that Vuldon could have faith in her abilities, and so her thorough exhaustion had been worth something at least. 'Where are we?'

'An apothecary,' Vuldon said. 'We're still in the indoor iren.'

'We didn't get Shalev then.'

'We will,' Vuldon said. 'We know she's not invincible, and that's more than we knew before. We know she's also predictable, seeking a big show – that's all useful knowledge.'

'Then why does it feel like we failed?' Lan asked.

Vuldon stood up, groaning. 'That's a glitch with your own personality. Can't help you there. Just bask in the extra fame and attention, like Tane.'

Lan tried to push herself up, but felt too exhausted. She fell to her elbows and laughed, slightly giddy, slightly drowsy. Then sprawled onto her stomach, feeling the bruises and the agony inside.

Vuldon helped her stand, and Tane suddenly turned his gaze on somewhere behind them.

Someone rattled into the doorway, a young soldier in full battle regalia. Gripping onto the door frame, in breathless gasps, he said: 'More trouble, this time Caveside. We need your help, all of you. It's getting out of control.'

Vuldon squared up to the soldier. 'What's happened?' he asked despondently.

'The anarchists,' the soldier panted. 'They've been leading

a march out of the caves. Thousands of them. Protesters. Threatening to riot. It's chaos.'

Vuldon sighed and glanced down at her. 'Lan, you up for saving the day again?'

TWENTY-FOUR

Some entire bookcases were built around doors, and others were themselves doors. They might open up into hidden enclaves, showing texts bound in different materials, from different ages. Most of the books were covered in centuries of dust. Rats scurried away from the light, spiders tottered backwards into corners. The more of these rooms they travelled through, the worse the quality of the architecture became – these were more basic zones, rooms for primitive collections or almost-forgotten tomes.

'Do the staff permit you this far?' Fulcrom enquired.

'I doubt they are even aware that most of these rooms exist,' Ulryk replied cheerfully. 'If you have noticed from our rather convoluted route, we have entered a labyrinth of sorts. It is quite a common arrangement in ancient libraries, which leads me to believe that they were all constructed, originally, by the same architect or designer. Such creators intended there to be hidden regions, for the protection of certain tracts of information, for those in power to maintain their grip on the populace, even to rewrite histories. I suspect, though, there were powers greater than mere emperors at work, areas to which even the ruling kings and queens were blind. That is the thing about knowledge: there is no discrimination over who owns it, or who may abuse it.'

Room after room, each one different. Corridors turned this way and that, with no apparent design. For much of the next hour, Fulcrom saw only the lantern and the soft glow it cast upon the side of Ulryk's face. Occasionally the priest would pause at some dark intersection, with the possible paths ahead denoted only by their utter absence of light. Once, Ulryk raised the lantern to the wall to show Fulcrom the graffiti of yesteryear. There were names and directions written in a script that hadn't been in common use for over two thousand years. Other languages here were even more *alien*.

'Is it going to take much longer?' Fulcrom asked, aware of how petulant he must be sounding.

'We are about halfway,' Ulryk replied.

'Is this the route the dead took?'

'I have . . . little idea of their methods,' Ulryk confessed. 'It seems that although I pretend to hold great knowledge, there are many things strange to me.'

'You and me both,' Fulcrom muttered.

*

Their placards argued for a peaceful resolution to their claims, though their sheer mass was an implied threat. In the late afternoon sunshine, thousands of people marched out of the caves, men, women and children, human and rumel, and old garudas with broken wings. Underground radicals and change-seekers, all were unified on this march. It seemed a critical mass had been achieved.

Perched on a wall alongside several of the city guard in their crimson finery and slate-grey armour, the Knights watched the unfolding scene.

'Fucking inbred scum,' muttered a soldier in the red uniform of the Shelby Corporation Soldiers.

'Aye,' another said, leaning on his sword. 'Bad enough that they leech on the rest of us, now here they come spreading their diseases.'

'Why do you hate them so much?' Lan asked.

'Cunts come out here and steal things for their own

decrepit culture, is why,' the first soldier said, putting on his helm ready for combat. 'Take food from honest hard-working folk, steal whatever trinkets they can get their filthy hands on, rape women.'

Lan had a flashback to that period a few years ago, after she had left home. She tried to remember what the people were like in the caves, but she realized she had been drunk or on drugs for the most part. All that came to her was a visual echo of the girl who just about cleaned her up, their friend-ship born out of an urgent desire for secrecy.

People flowed out towards them in their thousands, a river comprised of years of pent-up resentment. They blocked the cobbled streets leading from the caves, dressed in the general Caveside fashions, cheap-looking breeches and shirts, over-alls, shades of greys and browns. Lan couldn't help but notice that the women were dressed just like the men. She was not sure what to make of all this, or even if the Knights would be of any use in a situation where surely diplomacy was the key.

She focused on the details, tried to discern the chants and the scrawls on crudely painted boards:

The Cavesiders called for respect. For better jobs, for investment in people's health and housing, and not pretty irens for the rich. They wanted food for the refugees outside the city walls. And better rights for women, for acknowledge-ment of tribal cultures and religions, and the right for all Cavesiders – even those with unregistered addresses – to vote. They called for the end of brutal conduct by organiza-tions like the City Guard and the Knights, and a halt to the endless victimization of Caveside dwellers. To Cavesiders, these authorities of the city were feared and despised. There were slogans suggesting oppression. Wooden boards were held aloft with the symbols of the new anarchists.

All strands of concern had been brought together and Lan stood agog at the sheer energy they created, the challenge they presented. There was a hatred towards her that was different from any she had known previously – and she had known a lot.

'Get down there then,' ordered one of the soldiers.

Vuldon turned his bulk steadily. Lan for once appreciated his potential temper. 'Who the fuck', Vuldon growled, 'do you think you are, talking to us like that?'

The fear was obvious in the soldier's eyes. 'I didn't mean no harm, like. I just meant for you to help us. Honest . . .'

'We take our orders from the top.' No sooner had Vuldon spoken than a messenger came directly at the Emperor's request, asking for the Knights to stand before the front row of the protest.

'The front?' Lan asked.

'It's our job,' Vuldon snapped. 'This is what we do. Come on.'

They set to work. Tane and Vuldon shuffled off the wall with the soldiers, while Lan simply stepped off and glided down to the cobbles. They criss-crossed through a series of narrow alleyways behind tall, granite walls and taverns. As they moved towards the front, soldiers from the city guard and the Dragoons had already lined up to block their passage. Lan guessed they were facing off against the protesters.

'What do we do?' Lan asked, turning to Vuldon.

Vuldon could see over the sea of grey helmets. The chants and buzz of the crowd were threateningly loud down on street level.

'The road banks down towards the caves, so I can only see the tops of the placards.'

Tane said suddenly, 'Look at who's lining up.'

Archers in green and brown uniforms were scrambling over the precarious rooftops on each side of this wide street. They negotiated the wet and hazardous angles of slate, until they had positioned themselves perfectly with a view of the Cavesiders' protest.

Lan felt remarkably uncomfortable at the fatidic nature to

the event, even more so because Vuldon and Tane didn't have a clue how to handle the situation. She had no doubt that the military ranks on the front row had their weapons drawn and were prepared for combat.

Against their own people? This shouldn't be happening. They're not rioting at all, they're not causing any damage, this is just a simple march.

'Who's in command here?' Vuldon bellowed.

The back rows of the guard peered back to regard Vuldon, and soon word rippled forward. A few moments later and a senior officer, a thickset veteran, shuffled through his own ranks in order to speak to the Knights. They walked sideways until they were in the shadow behind the back of a bistro, out of the potential conflict zone.

'I want you to tell me in simple terms,' Vuldon ordered, 'what the fuck is going on here.'

The soldier removed his helm, revealing a weathered face, a wide nose, and a thick greying beard. The look in his eyes betrayed his uncertainty. *Not even he knows what to do.*

'Military orders, issued from the Council, are to stop this march from progressing any further. They're spread out for half a mile up from the caves, causing havoc. Citizens from this level have been evacuated – they're in fear of their lives.'

'It's just a protest,' Lan said, 'not a war.'

'You conspiring with them, eh?' the soldier said fiercely, then laughed. 'Course you're not, love. Best you leave this to the men, eh?'

She turned to Vuldon, who signalled his permission. Lan grabbed the soldier by the throat and slammed him against the wall; using her powers she raised him only a few feet in the air. His sword and helmet clattered down on the stone and one or two of the other soldiers turned in response, but Tane, now displaying his claws, cautioned them back.

To the veteran, Lan said, quite coolly, 'Do not call me *love*, and do not treat me as if I'm some useless fucking dress-tart.

We've done more for this city in a few weeks than you probably have in your entire life.'

'All right, lady, I was only kidding . . .' he spluttered.

Lan lowered him, but let him drop the final foot. He stumbled to his knees amidst scraps of food and murky puddles. His glance was full of disdain as Vuldon hauled him back upright, and dusted him down theatrically.

'Now where was I?' Vuldon said breathing into the soldier's face. 'Oh yeah – we got orders to defuse the situation.'

'So have we,' the officer replied. 'Look, we can let you pass through, all right, but that's all I'm doing for now. You wanna go to the front? Fine. Rather you than me.'

A few quick orders and a line parted in the gathered ranks allowing the Knights through. There were men and, surprisingly, a few women, from units of the Dragoons, Regiments of Foot and city guard; their shields raised, their swords in hand, their helms fixed in place.

As they approached the front, a row of protesters could be seen stretching in a rough line the full width of the street, which was perhaps fifty paces wide. Thick, granite walls boxed them in – surprisingly bland structures for Villjamur – and the buildings they had passed were mostly terraces. This meant there was no route for the protesters to move out of the street.

There was only backwards or forwards.

Towards the military, or back to the caves.

A few people leaned out of the windows to hurl abuse at the Cavesiders, some chucking rotten food on them. The archers were numerous, silhouetted against the bright sky. A few garudas swept over the scene, and would probably be relaying details back to the commanders.

The Knights presented themselves to the Cavesiders, who had stalled about twenty paces from the military in a stand-off, and as soon as they arrived the protesters began to hurl abuse and obscenities.

Lan was mortified. Why couldn't these people see the bigger picture? There were signs that declared her presence was an act of oppression, that the Knights victimized Cavesiders, that they worked only for the rich and served the privileged. Was that even true? Had she sold her soul to the wealthy?

Vuldon and Tane moved forward and tried talking to some of the protesters, but this seemed to raise the aggression towards them.

When they eventually returned to her side, Vuldon gave a huge sigh. 'There's not a lot we can do here. We're part of the reason they're protesting. We'll make things worse by being here.'

An object flew by – a bottle – and it crashed down a few feet to one side, then burst into flame. A pool of liquid was on fire. Lan could swear that it had come from behind, from the Empire's soldiers, and not the Cavesiders.

A ripple of clattering metal: in an instant, the front row of the military surged forward past the Knights, and locked their shields. Another bottle exploded further away. This most definitely came from above – *one of the archers?* What were they doing? Black smoke began to rise and the snow suddenly intensified.

'I see now,' Vuldon said, his head turning left and right as he analysed the scene. 'Oh shit, I can see.'

'What? What do you see?' Lan demanded.

'They're planning to slaughter their own people!' Vuldon snapped.

'Shouldn't we stop this getting out of hand?' Tane asked, peering around hurriedly. The abusive chants amplified around them.

Vuldon shook his head in despair. 'What, cat-man, do you suggest we do? The military has already made their decision. There are hundreds of them and only three of us.'

'We can't,' Lan pleaded. 'We're meant to look after the

people of the city – and that includes Cavesiders, surely? They deserve our protection, just like anyone else.'

Movement above: the archers were now readying their arrows, and taking aim.

'Get away from this,' Vuldon ordered them both. He pointed his finger down at their faces, like they were children. 'We walk away or this will haunt you for years. Do not involve yourselves in this massacre. We won't stop the military and the Cavesiders won't listen to us – even if we could get to them. I can do dirty work now and then, but I've found my backbone, and I won't be involved in a massacre. These are my orders now. Walk right away immediately.'

More bottles exploded around them. Instructions were being barked from somewhere within the massed ranks, and soldiers edged closer into position.

Lan felt shame and hopelessness, and an overwhelming urge to remain there, to do something – anything – but Vuldon was now pulling her back, back through the lines of soldiers, away from those she wanted to help, to save, to be the hero she believed herself to be.

Soldiers pulled into ranks, obscuring her view of the scene on the ground. Lan was aghast: arrows commenced raining down on the Cavesiders, whose screams rose up from the streets, shrieks of hysteria drowned out by the sounds of the Imperial soldiers continuing their assault upon the Empire's own subjects.

*

Fulcrom was getting bored. There was only so much he could take of seeing one dusty room after another, hearing his own footsteps shuffling on the stone, and following the light clasped in Ulryk's hands. Only the occasional downward stairwell broke the monotony of their location. The corridors were oppressing, the centuries of darkness and decay closing in on them like a fist.

Some of the rooms possessed statues of humans: bronze

busts or full figures, covered in dust and cobwebs, gazing lamentably into some distant realm. Fulcrom speculated at who they might be, but they bore no resemblance to the paintings and statues of Villjamur's leaders of the past few hundred years. 'How far have we come?' Fulcrom asked. 'I've counted well over fifty sets of stairs going down.'

'I suspect we're far beneath the city. The floors are gently sloped; we have entered rooms that open out onto lower levels – though do not ask me how they have been constructed.'

'And you've been this precise way before? How can you be sure you're not going a different way?'

'Why, my footprints are in the dust,' Ulryk observed, and lowered the lantern to prove the point. Within the next hour, though, the books were no longer present on the shelves, and soon the empty shelves vanished, and the rooms became caves, then vast caverns. Beneath their feet, flagstones capitulated to loose gravel, fine pebbles, larger, moss-strewn chunks that were hazardous to navigate over in the light of one lantern, and their feet no longer tapped but crunched.

There was suddenly a change in the quality of air: it wasn't still and confined, but stirring, bringing with it a damp aroma. And Fulcrom heard the water before he saw it, a vague dripping sound. The ground grew uneven, rising then dipping, and Fulcrom followed Ulryk's lantern until it reflected off the surface of the water. Its intense pungency made Fulcrom question its origin.

A small river, perhaps ten paces across, was flowing.

'Before you ask,' Ulryk said, as if reading his thoughts, 'no, I do not know where the river flows from. But if we follow it, you can see where it runs to.'

'Are we *under* the city?'

'Directly under the heart of Villjamur,' Ulryk beamed. 'Although we are probably now in a different part of reality than where we walked from. We have been travelling down for hours, yet . . . no paths from the outside lead here. We have gone through secret room after secret room, and travelled through a labyrinth designed specifically to keep people away. And we may – though this is merely an assumption, given what you are likely to soon see – not be in the same realm of . . . our usual time. So you need not worry about being late for any further investigative work.'

The priest was too cheery for Fulcrom's liking. If Ulryk was used to this kind of weird stuff then fine – but for Fulcrom this was difficult to comprehend, even to believe. There was no logic.

'You see,' Ulryk continued in the darkness, 'Villjamur – or rather, this location – predates this Empire. The city itself is a mere eleven thousand years old, and within this cave system lies the remnants of something greater. Many ley-line maps of the Archipelago have suggested there is something to be found in Villjamur, where the lines all converge. It is no surprise to find activity here that one may never expect. You seek answers to what happened on the surface last night, investigator – well, I will show you where the dead have come from. They're not far away now. They never were.'

Silence seemed the best answer. All Fulcrom could do was absorb the information and process it steadily, like he had always done, sifting through it for some sense. Had Fulcrom not seen his dead wife in the mirror the night before, he might have dismissed the priest's crackpot suggestions in an instant. As it was, having her haunt his room, he decided to maintain an open mind.

They continued, their feet crunching on the stone for some way before Ulryk sat down beside the river.

'What's wrong?' Fulcrom asked.

'Nothing is wrong. See over there . . .' Ulryk gestured with the lantern, and even though the light was weak, Fulcrom could make out an utter blackness filling an arch. 'We must continue along in the water from here.'

'I'm not swimming in that!' Fulcrom said.

'Oh, investigator. You do amuse me. We are not swimming, we will be sailing.'

'In what?' Fulcrom demanded.

'Patience.' Ulryk said, drawing out his book – that book he always used, the one which produced *magic*.

'Before you start, what *exactly* is that book?'

'It is one version of *The Book of Transformations*.'

'I know that, but what does it do – what do they both do?'

'There were two, both written by Frater Mercury. This is not the one I seek, however, though it does nicely in disaggregating the world when such talents are required. The one I seek is much more powerful than this, I believe, though I don't quite know how much they differ; but when they come together, real magic should begin . . .' Ulryk flipped open the book and began to recite some words, hypnotically, and Fulcrom stood agape: the pebbles around the shore were slicking and slinking across each other, coalescing until they formed a flat, rigid platform beside the priest. A moment later, he pushed it to the water's edge.

'It's quite safe,' Ulryk urged.

Fulcrom did as he was bid and climbed aboard, stunned that it didn't sink on its own, let alone with their added weight. The cold stones held firm, and the two eased out further into the water, until they were caught in its flow and began to drift forward. Ulryk simply crossed his legs, placing the lantern alongside him. Fulcrom drew his knees to his chest, preferring not to get wet.

The two sailed through the cavern, further along the river.

'All will be revealed shortly,' Ulryk declared portentously. Fulcrom seriously doubted that and felt foolish for having come this far: why was he even here, following the whim of this priest? Perhaps it piqued his curiosity, fulfilled his desire for learning new things. Was he escaping his dead ex-partner, or was he trying to find a way to make sure she would leave him alone? Of course, there was the matter of the other dead folk walking the city, and Fulcrom would have to find a solution to that.

Well, if the priest caused all this, then maybe he can give some answers.

There seemed to be more ambient light here, and Fulcrom could just about make out ruins – no, a crippled city – in the distance. Ahead were some glowing forms, tiny white phantoms, and a few more along the bank of the river to their left. Another river flowed in from the right, causing the current to alter slightly. There seemed no colour here, just monochrome shades of grey, black and white.

'I believe,' Ulryk announced finally, 'that this passes for an underworld of sorts. And the little glows you see on the shore? Why those are the dead, dear investigator. This is the thing about Villjamur – it isn't just the hub of the Empire, it's the centre of more than that. Things we do not understand. There are gateways and connections that I cannot fathom – there were even dead portals in that labyrinth. And I believe it is here – in this rubble-strewn city – where my quest needs to continue. Somewhere, here, is the original copy of *The Book of Transformations*. I am sure of it.' Ulryk's tone changed to a more conversational one – as if he was turning ideas over in his head. 'I have been tracing mentions of this place through my research, and all the metaphors turned out to be quite real. Rivers I took to be representative of Time, for example, but no – here they are, all flowing to this one place. Having traced my notes, I am convinced my quest will be resolved here.'

Fulcrom watched as the figures on the shore waved to them. 'Once you get this book – what are you going to do with it?'

Ulryk remained silent. The stone raft drifted closer to the shoreline and a few of the white glows took their human and rumel forms more clearly. They stood in groups of two or three, gazing as the raft came in. The dreary, dreamlike silhouette of a broken city lay behind them – the rising towers in decay, half crumbling, if not already a wreck; walls with notable damage; black, windowless frames. Before the city, running down to the water's edge, was a dark pebble beach.

'My quest,' Ulryk finally replied, 'is simply to use the book to return its author to his world.'

'This Frater Mercury guy?'

'You have a fine memory, investigator. It does you credit.'

'And just what is Frater Mercury going to do when he is back? Do you even know if he's anything more than a myth? I get the impression a lot of this is based on faith.'

'Much of all we do is based on faith, investigator. I have been . . . conversing with him. Through various methods and rituals. Through dimensions. He is quite real. His world is spilling through into ours, and you know already of the genocides and wars in the north. Here is evidence.'

'That's not evidence of him, though.'

'I have seen what I need to. Not everything can be proven. We need faith in the things we cannot see.'

Fulcrom was stunned. How could anyone communicate through dimensions? Then he realized by his questioning he actually believed everything that Ulryk was saying. *Just because you've seen the dead doesn't mean all he says is true.*

They sailed to the shoreline, where a white figure – with a much gentler glow up close – helped them up.

'Back so soon, eh, Ulryk?' he called out, much to Fulcrom's surprise, in a traditional dialect. The man was bald, tall, muscular, wearing ancient fashions, high collared shirts and a knee-length tunic. His nose and chin were thin and long, giving him an almost bird-like appearance, and his skin was dark like dusk – no, only the right side of his face, because the other was pale, and no matter how hard Fulcrom looked, he could not see the bisecting line down his face. 'Brought a friend this time, I see.'

'This is Investigator Fulcrom,' Ulryk said, climbing off the raft.

'Oh, aye. We've some Inquisition members here who still fancy themselves in charge of law and order. Not that there's much point, heh. Anyway. Welcome, sir. My name is Aker.' The old ghost offered a hand, and Fulcrom, pushing himself upright, didn't know whether or not to take it, whether he would grip onto nothing. He did take it, in the end – and the grip was quite real. A moment later and two huge waist-high cats padded down across the stones to Aker's side and, when seated, eyed Fulcrom suspiciously.

'Don't mind these two,' Aker said. 'They just ain't too fond of the living. Sets 'em off.'

And I'm not too fond of the dead, Fulcrom thought, watching one lick its paw. 'Do you get many of the living here?'

'No, I'll give you that. Just Ulryk here.'

Fulcrom and Ulryk were guided further onto land where more of the figures greeted them.

'These are all the dead,' Ulryk whispered on approach. 'Many followed me back to see what the world was like again. Some had unfinished business, you see, or people they wanted to see. I can only assume the rest here didn't want to leave.'

The dead appeared much like the living, but wore the wounds that had finally killed them. They also possessed an ethereal shine, similar to the one that Adena had possessed. Clothing spanned history, and Fulcrom noticed various costumes or styles from tapestries or paintings he'd seen over the years. In groups, they came and went, seeing the spectacle of the living visit them. 'How many are left here?' Ulryk called to Aker, who was following with his cats weaving around behind him. Then, to Fulcrom, Ulryk whispered, 'I think this fellow is some kind of gatekeeper.'

'Oh, I would say around a hundred or so,' Aker boomed. 'People prefer to stay around for the most part. Living ain't what it used to be. Besides, a few who tried to cross the river felt too weak – didn't have the determination to go on, so to speak.'

'I do not suppose you bear news on the location of the book I sought?'

'Aye a few of the locals were thinking about this. There are old libraries down here, too, though wrecks these days. Much like the rest of the place. But nothing yet, I'm afraid. They'll keep looking. It keeps them busy, since life can get dull round these parts.'

They passed through a massive iron gate set into dark stone walls. Huge cracks penetrated the stone, splitting it completely in places, and Fulcrom noticed how the design of the walls was much like Villjamur, as if it mirrored its style, yet had suffered from the impacts of some apocalyptic event.

Fulcrom shook his head in disbelief. The city was laid out similarly, roads banking up either side in a circular route. The buildings, tall and narrow, were leaning precariously upon each other, crumbling or ready to break. It was unnaturally warm. Two dead men were playing cards on a table in the street, one with a knife protruding from his back. There were plazas and courtyards, parks with dead trees, and the dead were everywhere. Fulcrom felt an overwhelming and unexplained sorrow, which was met with his refusal to accept what he was seeing. Nothing made sense any more, nothing at all. Were these genuinely the remains of those who had died from the surface world?

'I've seen enough,' Fulcrom said. 'I ought to return to my duties on the surface.'

'Ha, typical of the livin', that,' an old man said. 'Always concerned with duties and jobs. Try enjoying life a bit while you still got it, yeah?'

'I enjoy my job,' Fulcrom muttered. 'I make a difference.' There was more defensiveness in this final statement than he would have liked. Then to Ulryk, 'Please . . . I can't stay here. I can't bear to look.'

Ulryk placed a hand on each arm as if he was going to shake Fulcrom. 'You wanted explanations, investigator. And I wanted you to *believe*. I will need your help, most definitely in the coming days. I know a man of logic when I see him – and you needed convincing. This, I feel, has helped. Have faith in me and what I am doing – your world is about to change greatly.

'I know that the church has ordered creatures into the city. When I find the other copy of *The Book of Transformations*, I will need to conduct rituals upon the surface. It may take me a good while to ascertain the details, and in this time I will need your protection, as much of it as you can offer. I will require your *faith* in me. There are few who will be able to believe in what is going on here, few who can offer such loyalty.'

'I think', Fulcrom whispered, 'that you can relax. I believe in you.'

The smile on the priest's face was tinged more with relief than happiness.

'Though tell me,' Fulcrom began, forcing his mind back towards logic, 'what about the dead who have gone to the surface? They need to be returned here, don't they?' All the time his thoughts were on Adena, and how to rid himself of her ghost.

Aker interrupted them. 'The thing is, any of those who have gone up need to be persuaded to come back down.'

Fulcrom breathed steadily, his eyes widening.

Aker laughed, rubbing the ears of one of his cats. With a face of pure contentment, the beast crooked its neck to allow further scratching.

'What's up, sir?' Aker asked. 'You look like you've seen a ghost!'

TWENTY-FIVE

On the south coast of Tineag'l, the remnants of the Order of the Equinox discovered yet another abandoned town. The absence of any residents heightened Verain's sense of fear.

They had to wade through the snow in order to get along its streets, which had so clearly and so recently experienced carnage. Streaks of blood were splattered across the facades of wooden buildings. The heavy layer of snow probably hid much of the gore below.

There was little wind today, and the sunlight was stronger than the far north of the islands, where the Realm Gates were located. It was warmer here too – just a degree or two, but enough to raise her spirits.

'Tuung, why can't I remember his name?' Verain pointed to one of the other cultists who travelled with them, a young blond man who seemed physically fit and who spoke with an optimism she herself was lacking. 'Did he accompany us when we left Villjamur?'

Tuung frowned. 'Of course he did, lass. You honestly don't remember?'

'No.' She *felt* she recognized his features, though searching beyond that yielded little. 'It's Todi,' Tuung replied, his expression changing from one of amusement to something more serious. 'We're good mates, me and him.'

'I'm sure it's just the cold,' she lied. 'Yes, his face is very familiar. Todi.'

'Good thing we're stopping for the night, lass. If we can find a room that hasn't got a corpse in it, we can maybe get a good fire going and get some food down. You look as though you could do with a good meal.'

Houses bordered the two main streets, which ran parallel to the coastline, and there were a few other lanes trailing out like vines into open country. The buildings had been painted garish colours: yellows, blues and greens, as if to brighten what was, otherwise, a desolate community.

A street backed onto a large harbour, one filled with towering industrial vessels with old fishing boats jammed between. This was a small port town, Verain realized, one used to export the ore that was the lifeblood of the mining island. It was probably once a bustling area, with stevedores and blacksmiths and enterprise.

Now it was a ghost port. There was no life here, no community, only the lingering sense of what once had been.

Though her memory was betraying her, she could remember that they had passed through settlements such as this on their way north in search of the Realm Gates. So many towns and villages had been cleared of their inhabitants. Farmed for their inhabitants, in fact – only the corpses of the very young and very old remained. *Yes, I remember Todi now. He was the one who threw up when we found the corpse of an old lady in her bathtub. That's right.*

The recollection gave her some relief. Perhaps it really was the cold that was fogging her memory. The cultists had surveyed the town and, unlike the others, they found few bodies at all. The houses looked like they'd been vacated in a hurry, with doors open and food left on stoves.

From further along the docks, Dartun came marching towards them, effortlessly kicking up snow. A couple of the dogs bounded behind him. He looked so normal just then, simply a man walking animals by the sea.

'I've found a good vessel,' Dartun announced, full of

optimism. 'It's ideal – a small, military longship, with ample shelter for us all. We might have to leave the dogs though.'

'Did you see if there were any of . . . you know. Them?' Verain asked. 'They could be hiding somewhere for all we know.'

'They don't concern us,' Dartun said coolly.

'How can you say that?' Tuung snapped. 'You know what they're doing to these people around here, and we saw it with our own eyes when we passed into their world.'

Verain's memory sparked:

The cities beyond the gates were hideous. There had been meat factories through which naked humans were herded like livestock. Verain had seen men and women scream as they were forced through great, mechanical devices, never to be seen again. They were processed for their materials – flesh and organs were used for food, their bones were used for construction materials. Smoke filled the skies, leaving a chemical taint in the air, the sun barely seen through the pollution, and it was cold, colder than she had ever imagined . . .

'They will leave us alone,' Dartun replied, bringing Verain back to the here and now. 'They have no interest in us.'

'How do you *know* that?' Verain asked. 'They could be hiding behind any of these buildings' – she waved to a row of abandoned houses – 'waiting just to murder us.'

'Nonsense,' Dartun laughed. 'If you remember, we walked away from the Realm Gates, right past those who are responsible for the harvesting of these islands.'

There was something accepting about the way he said *harvesting*. As if it didn't seem at all cruel to him that there had been a mass genocide.

'And why was that, Dartun?' Tuung demanded. Verain held her breath waiting to see what their Godhi would make of such boldness. 'Why did they just let us stroll back from their world?'

The other cultists had gathered behind Verain and Tuung

now, all facing Dartun and waiting for an answer. Whilst they were relieved to have escaped that other world, they wanted answers to why they were free. Why they had been permitted to leave when so many others had not.

'Not only that,' Tuung pressed, 'but how come you're enhanced? How come you've got a fancy new arm, the one you used so well when you murdered *a whole other band of cultists*?'

Their leader didn't respond with his usual confrontational statements, nor did he inspire them with his passionate rhetoric. He just ignored them. 'We rest tonight,' Dartun said finally. 'I've located a house with a dormitory. We can shelter safely together, light a fire, and be warm and relaxed.' He reached down to ruffle a dog's neck, and the animal sat up excitedly. 'It's around the corner, a white two-storey building with a green double door. I'll be in there if you need me.' And with that he tromped away through the snow.

The remains of the Order of the Equinox looked at each other, and in their silence waited for someone to say something, anything.

Tuung muttered, 'Since when has he been so concerned with our safety, eh?'

'You're thinking of splitting?' Todi asked, a worried look on the young man's face.

'Well, I mean he marches us up to the top of the world just to march us back again. Into hell and back out again. I've no complaints with where we're going now. I just want to get home to Villjamur. If he wants to keep us warm and safe all of a sudden then . . . well, that's fine with me. I'm not going anywhere, but I don't like the stuff that's going unsaid. What about you, lass? You're closer to him than anyone else.'

All eyes turned to Verain. 'Maybe I can have a word with him tonight, and find out what's going on.'

Although she didn't hold much hope. Dartun had changed.

And not just physically. She wasn't sure there was anything left of the man she had once loved.

*

They sprawled in a school room. It was the first night that they had not all huddled together in one large, canvas tent. All six cultists sat around a wood-burning stove, staring into the flames, letting the heat bring them back to some kind of conscious state and, for a long time, no one said a word. This was luxury.

After witnessing the horrors of the otherworld, Verain felt surreal looking at the crude and innocent paintings that adorned one wall. There were brightly coloured toys and books at one end, and a few tables at the other, everything muted by the soft orange light of the fire. Tuung had located well-preserved provisions in a kitchen. They had eaten ravenously. They had not seen so much food in . . . she didn't know how long. Two men were in a blissful state of satiation, in a deep state of slumber, and Dartun simply stared into the flames, barely moving. There were questions she wished to ask, but not here, not in front of the others.

She wandered upstairs into a tiny, decrepit library. The light of the moons passed through shutters and slanted across the desk. She had spent the last few days with five other men around her, where even simple tasks such as urinating became an embarrassment. Alone, finally, she could gather her thoughts. If she was honest with herself, she wished Dartun would join her up here, just so she could see if there was any slight chance she could do something to make him change back to how he had been.

Using a drawstring, she opened the shutters fully, and gazed through the murky glass. *That's odd* . . . The horizon to the east revealed a strange line of light, a thin orange glow pressed into the dark distance, and now she felt – very slightly – that the room was shuddering.

Was this some geological phenomenon? It didn't look like it.

The line of light was shifting. It must have been some way off, but it was definitely moving, and drifting towards the coast. She allowed her eyes to adjust over a few minutes, but nothing more could be gleaned from the sight.

Footsteps up the stairs . . .

She spun back, her heart beating furiously, as Dartun pushed open the door.

A sigh of relief, a surge of adrenalin that she could now press him further. *I care for him – I'm not going to let him grow into some . . . monster.*

'I trust you will be better company than those downstairs,' he said, more gentle than she'd heard him speak for a long time.

'They're well fed, for once, and very tired.'

'Yes, I forget just how exhausted the human body can get.'

'That implies you don't have a human body,' she suggested, tracing the scars on his face, the exposed metal. 'I saw what happened with Papus – we all did. That wasn't normal, Dartun.'

Now that she had voiced her concerns, she feared what might happen. Silence stretched out before them. He seemed quite inert, as if he was incapable of formulating an answer.

'Dartun, what happened in that otherworld? We were lovers before we went away, and now we're back I don't even know where we stand. But I'm not saying this for me – I care about you.' She took his hands in her own. In the moonlight, his scars muted by the dim light, his face regained much of its handsomeness. His expression was contemplative. 'What happened, Dartun? What did they do to us . . . to *you*?'

'I can't remember, Verain. I really can't.'

'You're lying. The rest of our order was wiped out – I remember that. The specimens of the undead you took with us – they're gone. There's just a few of us left now and you're dragging us halfway across the world without any explanation. You *must* tell us something, Dartun – you can't force people just to follow you again without some reason to.'

His face darkened and his breathing quickened. 'I wanted immortality,' he said, 'and I think I've found it. You remember the cages in which we were kept?'

'As if I could forget.'

'We were there for weeks, Verain – it was days here but weeks there. We were kept alive, we were special. They found us more intriguing than average human stock – we knew how to use aspects of their technology and it mystified them.'

'Who's *they*?'

'Can't you remember? You just said you couldn't forget being in the cages.'

'I remember being in them. That's all.' She wondered if she had forced many of the horrors from her mind of her own will, or whether there was something genuinely wrong with her head.

'Our captors comprised of many races, bizarre creatures – much worse than the shell-based life forms we passed on the way in, and only a few of them could communicate with us in anything more than grunts. Some individuals knew our tongue, and our culture was vaguely understood. And we few – we survived. We managed to negotiate. We're heading back to Villjamur with a message, to visit our rulers and negotiate.'

'What, exactly, are we negotiating?' she asked, eager now she gleaned some information.

'They wish to enter our lands. They wish to occupy our islands. You must not yet tell the others – I will do this in my own time.'

Verain gestured to the window. 'Is that them, out there? Is that their armies?'

Dartun took a cursory peek, before returning his gaze to her. There was a tenderness to his voice now. 'Indeed it is.'

'Who are they?' she breathed.

'They are part of the Akhaioí. Do you remember their war? Those military machines that were constantly droning in the distance?'

She shook her head.

'They have been seeking access to our world for years, and they will take it by force. But to minimize loss of life, I am to . . . negotiate with the powers in Villjamur. That's why I have been modified. They've given me augmentations so we can travel safely back to Villjamur. I only know half of what I can do. And I'm struggling to cope, if I'm honest.'

He had never been this candid in all her years of knowing him. His vulnerability touched her. She moved in closer and held his forearm tenderly. For a long while it seemed he had forgotten what to do, but eventually his arms closed in around her.

*

The dormitory was vast but minimalist, with little in the way of decoration. The beds were too small so they had to be pushed together in order to be of any use, but, still, this was opulence compared with what they had gone through recently. A night spent under a solid roof was more than a relief.

The rest of the order dozed off, eventually finding a deep state of rest, but Verain could not sleep at all. She had been thinking long and hard about the consequences of what Dartun had told her earlier. One detail didn't sit right in her head: why were the other cultists not killed with the rest of the order?

The army passing on the horizon also prompted her concern. Where exactly was such a large body of beings heading? Images flashed again, of the otherworld, her inter-mittent memory teasing: vast columns of troops marching across decimated landscapes. Hideous beings covered in blood.

She pushed herself up and out of bed. Dressed in thick layers, she headed down to the kitchen, the stairs creaking beneath her cautious, night-blind steps. Clouds had obscured the moons, which left the kitchen quarters in utter darkness. The musky smell of cooked food seemed more prominent as she sensed her way by touch, her eyes gradually adjusting to the oppressing gloom.

She wanted to make herself a drink, something warm, so after stumbling about for several minutes, she eventually lit the stove and the fire seemed to heighten the blackness at the edges of the room. For a moment she thought she could see eyes looking at her, but it was a decorative metal handle on one of the cupboards. Other items glimmered, thick blades and whisks and ladles.

She heard something outside. A faint movement, snow crunching underfoot, the rattle of a stifled breath.

Verain felt afraid and alone. She had no relics with her, so she moved across to the other end of the table, grabbed a massive knife from a rack, shut the door of the iron stove and pressed her back against one of the walls. From here she had a view of two windows either side of the kitchen, one of them being right next to the door. There were no shutters here – just thick, cheap glass.

Something brushed against the outside of the building: she heard it clearly. Perhaps one of the dogs had escaped? No, this was a much slower noise, like something scraping down the wall.

Her heart froze.

Moonlight came, and through the facing window a silhouette was defined. It was . . . human. Yes, definitely human, just standing there a few paces back from the door, in the middle of the street, peering in.

Cautiously, she stepped across the room and flipped down a hatch on the wide door to the building; a rush of cold air followed. Outside, the man was facing her, silent and still, arms by his side – he reminded her of the undead humans that Dartun had reanimated.

'What d'you want?' she whispered.

'You speak ... Jamur,' he stuttered. He stepped forward presenting his hooded face, long stubble and haunted eyes. His accent was heavy on the vowels. 'You're not one of them?' He seemed desperate and breathless.

'One of *whom*?'

'You ... know who. Those ... those things that came here.' He was freezing, rubbing his arms vigorously and shivering in his thin, ragged clothing.

'No, I'm not one of them,' she replied.

Behind him, the street was deserted, but he kept gazing about him, scanning the area.

'How did you survive?' Verain asked, debating whether to invite him in. 'We've been through several settlements and we never saw a soul.'

'We've been hiding in a tavern cellar – seven of us, and we have been surviving with next to nothing. I came out to see if they have gone ... Where are you from? How did you get to the –' he searched for the word in Jamur '– educational facility?'

'We're cultists.'

'Thank Bohr! I never thought I would be relieved to see a magician.'

We're not magicians, she wanted to say, but it seemed pointless. Was she even a cultist without her relics? 'We're only passing through,' she replied. 'We'll be gone in the morning.'

'Take us with you,' the man pleaded.

From the other side of the house came a sudden raking noise, harsh and staccato. Verain turned to the wall and then back at the man, into his wide brown eyes. Days of dirt and tears and snot had turned his grimace into something entirely primitive, and she could smell fish. 'Let me in, please.'

'I'm not sure I should. Tell me where you're staying and we'll come and find you in the morning. It's probably safer if you—'

A stifled wail, the man vanished from the door, thumped on the ground and was dragged around the corner of the house. Moments later she could hear a terrified scream from further along the street.

Guilty now that she had not let him in, Verain grasped the knife more firmly and hurried in the direction of the man's wails.

Moonlight gave an odd texture to the scene, highlighting the snow along the main thoroughfare, though leaving the buildings in utter darkness. Anyone could have been looking out from behind shutters or windows, and she would not have been able to see them.

A trail cut through the snow, an erratic path of blood. She staggered on and then she saw it, in the doorway of the adjacent building: a creature several feet tall, a glistening, bulbous shell, hunched over the corpse of the man.

It faced her. She froze, her fear rooting her to the spot.

'Verain!' Dartun's voice, from behind. 'What the hell are you doing out here? You're too valuable to put yourself in danger like this.'

She couldn't take her eyes off the gruesome-looking shell-creature. It was like the others they had seen on their way north.

'Get back to the house,' Dartun commanded.

Just then, the thing moved towards them, abandoning the corpse and leaving it splayed across the steps.

'What is it?'

'Cirrip,' Dartun breathed. 'It's only a Cirrip.'

Another flashback: that was their name in the otherworld, these foot-soldiers of the Akhaioí.

'It's not connected to their hive-mind,' Dartun said. 'This stray shouldn't be out here alone. It should not have killed this man either, it should have taken him back with the others through the Gates.'

The beast staggered with an awkward yet strangely fluid gait towards the two of them. She could see it clearly now, its hideous claw-hands, the intense musculature beneath the armour, the flaring tendons, the deep black gloss of its skin.

Dartun moved forwards, cautiously manoeuvring so he stood between Verain and the creature. He tried speaking to it in its own language, something that she found profoundly bizarre, but it was to no avail – the thing lashed out with a claw. Dartun held up his arm to block the blow; the contact producing a brittle crack. At first she thought his arm had broken, but, instead, Dartun was rising from the ground, two feet up, four feet, then above the rooftops, his arms held outstretched for balance, his body slowly rotating on a vertical axis.

The Cirrip, still on the ground, began to click and hiss, craning its head as it watched Dartun proceed ever higher and then – like a bolt of lightning trailing purple light – Dartun dropped to the ground feet first and drove his boot into the head of the creature.

A jet of blood spurted out of the Cirrip's eyes, and it toppled backwards to the ground, its face imploded. Dartun tumbled forwards over its spasming form.

'Your knife, Verain,' he demanded, regaining his poise.

She stumbled over to offer the blade. Dartun took it, and slit its throat.

'It must have broken free from their pack,' Dartun said, quite calmly, wiping the blade in the snow. 'They possess a connected sentience. They tend to swarm.'

'How could you talk to it?'

'Something I gleaned from their world,' he replied sharply.

'The army is marching down to raid another island, isn't it?' Verain gestured to the alien corpse. 'These things are going to continue until they wipe out every city on the continent, aren't they?'

'Which is why it's vital we get to Villjamur so that we may establish a more peaceful resolution.'

'You could always fly there,' she suggested, 'given this apparent new ability.'

'I didn't even know I could until recently. I wonder how far I can go?' He paused momentarily and scanned her face. 'No, I must ensure you're all protected.'

He trudged through the snow to the remains of the man who the Cirrip had been toying with moments earlier. Verain followed him.

'He's dead, all right,' Dartun announced.

The man's body was broken in two, his torso no longer fully connected to his legs. Bones jutted from the open wounds.

'He told me there were more people in a cellar under the tavern,' Verain said. 'He was looking to see if we could help them.'

Dartun shook his head. 'The best thing for them to do is stay in that cellar.'

'But we can take them with us – escort them to another island.'

'We haven't got the time,' Dartun replied.

'At least help them to a boat—'

'We *haven't got* the time,' Dartun repeated forcefully, and she knew when to stop.

She understood that they needed to get to Villjamur as quickly as possible but regretted that this necessitated leaving these innocents to fend for themselves. She only hoped that Dartun knew of some way to stop the ongoing bloodshed. Otherwise, she feared, this was just the beginning.

TWENTY-SIX

For hours the next day, the Knights sat in their lounge area, in silence, uncertain of whether they should go back onto the streets. They had received no instructions. Instead they gazed at the black pall of smoke hanging over the city: vast funeral pyres, carrying away the souls of the deceased; this was the limit of respect the Cavesiders had received from the authorities.

Exhaustion filtered through every fibre in Lan's body. She stretched out across the floor beside the fire, into which Vuldon was gazing intently, prodding it now and then with a poker. Tane emitted the odd sigh, but was otherwise sprawled forwards across the table like a drunk. They avoided eye contact with one another. 'It could have been worse . . .' Tane finally offered, but a grunt from Vuldon terminated that conversation.

Lan felt immense guilt over what had happened but tried to find a logical explanation for why it had occurred. 'They targeted the Emperor's new trading area with violence – true. But this was a peaceful protest. Maybe the anarchists are just an extreme faction of the Cavesiders, but the majority want a more peaceful solution?'

'It would explain the military's heavy-handedness,' Tane agreed. 'They probably expected the worst after the events in the iren.'

'And those bombs the soldiers were throwing,' Vuldon

suggested, 'they were either to control the crowd or to incite violence. The cynic in me needs no persuading, I'll say that much.'

'I can't believe they turned on our own people,' Lan breathed. 'It's inhuman.'

'It's politics,' Vuldon muttered. 'No matter who's in charge of this damn city, it's always the same. Things going on behind the scenes. You can bet right now that—'

A polite knock on the door and Feror entered the room.

'Not now,' Vuldon told him.

Feror seemed not to notice, walking in distractedly without so much as a glance in their direction – he seemed a completely different man from his usual, cheery self. Nervously he began asking questions, the usual, but this time his voice was monotonous, as if he was reading badly from a script.

Vuldon muttered 'Fucksake' and gently steered him from the room. 'Not now, old guy. We're not in the mood.' The cultist gave him a defeated look and quietly closed the door behind him.

'What do you think was that all about?' Lan asked.

'Who gives a shit?' Vuldon replied. 'We've bigger things to worry about.'

'Where is Fulcrom?' Tane asked.

'Maybe I should go and find him,' Lan offered, pushing herself upright.

Tane snorted a gentle laugh. 'Maybe you should.'

*

He wasn't at home, so she walked to the Inquisition headquarters, giving no displays of her power, no signs of her abilities to step out across the air. She pulled her thick woollen cloak so tight that her Knights uniform – and its symbol – could not be seen. She was used to being despised for what she was, but after witnessing such overwhelming hatred when she thought she represented something good . . . that was different. Being a Knight had given her something on which she could construct a more positive existence. Having it called into question was difficult.

Taking two steps at a time, she headed into the Inquisition headquarters. A couple of officers tried to halt her as she entered the building then, on noticing who she was, allowed her through.

Continuing down the corridor, she examined the office doors for Fulcrom's name. Finding it, she knocked on his door repeatedly but there was no answer. *Why can't he be here?*

As she was about to turn, he opened the door. 'Lan, I didn't want to answer but I thought I heard . . .'

She entered the office and noticed the bags under his eyes, the set frown. 'You look worried. What is it?'

'I've had a hell of a night.' Fulcrom sighed and picked up a note from his desk. 'And I found this on my return. It claims to be from Shalev, saying that she wants revenge on the Knights for scuppering her plans. It's probably nothing. We get threats here all the time.'

'She may be a bitch,' Lan said with a sigh, 'but she may have a point.'

Fulcrom looked at her with surprise. 'I heard the opening of the iren was . . . eventful. You saved the Emperor. Everyone is impressed. You're the talk of the town again.'

His words of praise pleased her because they were coming from him, but the content of what he said did little to raise her spirits. While he perched on the edge of his desk, Lan paced, her hands brushing her hair, relating the events of the iren to him, then the attack on the citizens.

His face darkened. 'That's not what I heard,' he said. 'I was told by the senior officers that there was a minor, violent uprising from the caves, but the military managed to stop those responsible with,' he paused, and stressed the final part as if it had been read from a statement, 'minimal loss of innocent life.'

Lan couldn't believe that such crap was being spread. 'I wouldn't call it minimal loss,' she said. 'That isn't how it happened. That isn't what we saw.'

*

The city walls of Villjamur were no place for a stroll, but the long grey platforms, nestled behind crenellations, were at least somewhere where they could be alone and talk without being overheard.

On one side was the refugee camp, more sparsely populated than when she had arrived, and on the other archers of the city guarding the walls. She looked at them and shivered, remembering the flights of arrows loosed upon the people. She explained what had taken place, and what the Knights suspected. Fulcrom said nothing, merely allowing her to relate her story. She could see his mind working, weighing up the information, assessing where it fitted in with the bigger picture.

After she had finished, he told her there was nothing they could do. There would be an official statement, and that would be the one that was recorded, issued, discussed, and already trickling through to the future.

'I'm too tired to be angry,' Lan said. 'But just so you know, if I had the energy, I would scream.'

At that point she gazed across at the refugees – those who had been abandoned by those inside the walls. Including herself, she thought guiltily. A raw wind rolled in, deep and chilling, settling ice further into the city.

'Why do we even bother?' she asked. 'People say the world is dying. Seems to me like this culture is already dead.'

'Because there's always something worth fighting for, Lan,' Fulcrom told her. 'So we don't have the guilt from having sat around doing nothing while the world caves in. Come on, let's get a drink.'

*

The tavern was a tiny, two-up two-down affair that had been converted into a cheap but charming salon. Lined with old fishing and agricultural gear, with cheap candles melting slowly onto ancient wooden tables, it was usually a quiet place, though tonight there was a bawdy bunch in the adjacent room. These days it seemed there was a lot of heavy drinking going on.

Fulcrom swirled a beaker of malt whisky, whilst Lan sipped a warming wine. There were contented, pleasant pauses in their conversation. Occasionally there was eye contact loaded with potential meaning. Where did their tentative plans for romance fit in with all the recent violence?

Fulcrom was nervous. He was terrified that he might see his dead wife – or indeed any other ghosts – at any point. He hadn't yet reported his findings to anyone – not that he had any findings really. If only a few dead had surfaced, then maybe he could find them one by one, and persuade them to go back down again.

He wanted to share his burden with Lan, this woman who was becoming increasingly more beautiful to him.

'I shouldn't stay out too late,' Lan told him. 'Vuldon will just get frustrated if we don't get back to work before long. Have we any plans for how we deal with the anarchists now? We're loathed by the Cavesiders – who knows what damage the massacre has done to the people there?'

Fulcrom peered into his glass. 'We stand up, brush ourselves down, and carry on. We have no choice. You take your brief glory for saving the Emperor – and you will have to ignore what happened with the protesters.'

A short man with a ginger beard stood by the end of the table and asked to shake Lan's hand. 'Sorry to disturb, lass, but jus' wanted to say ta for doing a great job keeping us lot in business. Things'd be a lot worse if it weren't for you Knights.'

Glancing to and from Fulcrom, she obliged, took his thanks, and said little else. An awkward silence came and went, and the man trotted off happily enough.

'This fame,' Lan said, 'I'm not used to it. Somehow it doesn't feel right. It's like I'm being thanked for nothing. I don't feel like I've protected anyone.'

'People are grateful for what you've done,' Fulcrom said sincerely. 'Enjoy it.'

'All I've done is enforce the law – and I saw what that meant this afternoon. The law is geared up to protect the people in here from the people out there.'

'I guess so,' Fulcrom confessed. 'Depending on where "here" and "there" is.'

'The Cavesiders, the poor – they have just as much right to our protection as the rich do.'

Fulcrom frowned. 'You need to be careful who hears you talking like that. That's what the anarchists' new slogans say,' he said. 'Walls are being whitewashed daily to remove such sentiments.'

Lan sighed and leaned forward to take Fulcrom's hand. 'I know. Let's not talk about work. Can we go back to yours?'

Don't let her see you react, Fulcrom thought, dreading that Adena might be there waiting for them.

'We don't have to if you don't feel you want to,' Lan said.

Fuck, now you're caught between the ex-wife and exacerbating Lan's deepest fears. 'Sure, we can go to mine,' Fulcrom said. 'I'd like that. Though, are you sure you're not too upset about the events yesterday? I wouldn't want to be seen to be taking advantage . . .'

Lan just smiled and kissed him.

*

They held hands as they ascended the stairs to his apartment, kissed against his door, and all the time Fulcrom feared letting her down. As her lips gently pressed down in tender ways across his neck, he couldn't help but worry if his dead ex-wife would be waiting to berate him on the other side of the door.

He held his breath as they blundered into his apartment . . . but there was nothing, just the empty silence of his room.

301

He sighed with relief and lit the fire in the stove, perched on the end of his bed, then he noticed how Lan froze. Again he thought of a ghost, but then he guessed that this one was probably her own.

'Are you OK?' Fulcrom asked softly.

'Yeah, of course. Yes.' Her words were almost to herself, but he didn't mind that, and didn't even mind the hunch that he was helping her move on somewhere in her own head-space. In many ways, she was providing the same relief for him, too. He removed his cloak and she laughed as he folded it neatly on the chair to one side. 'How spontaneous,' Lan whispered with a sarcastic grin.

'I like to be neat.' Fulcrom chuckled and sat down next to her.

They kissed. There were tentative gestures of exploration. He could feel her tense up, then gently unfurl, offering herself to him. Surprisingly he found that his desire to help her through whatever issues she herself might be suffering, her anatomical-based fears, overtook his own concerns that this was the first woman he had kissed since the death of his wife.

Half-clothed and worried she had forgotten how this sort of thing was done, Lan laid him back and straddled him. He fixated on the symbol on her Knights uniform. She peeled it off, joking, 'No one's going to save you now.'

Please not my dead wife . . .

He moved his hands inside underneath her uniform, helping it off. Again she became still.

'What?' he asked.

'Cold hands,' she replied.

'Oh, right.'

After losing the rest of her clothes he could tell she waited for his reaction, so he was quick to show her that she was – as indeed she was, and *damn* she was – a fine-looking woman.

'You're beautiful,' he breathed against her neck, kissing her gently, and inhaling her fragrance. He whirled his tail around and ran it down her spine. She arced her back like a crescent moon. Lan seemed so small above him, in the gentle glow of the fire, so vulnerable. Something inside of him melted. He could not help himself. He wanted her.

He spun her over, unleashing years of introverted agony. He levered off his breeches with his tail whilst running his lips against her legs.

Lan made it clear she didn't want anything more than this. They lay under the sheets for an hour, embracing, curling, fondling, learning each other's quirks and preferences. And he simply enjoyed having her soft human skin against his tough rumel hide.

Whenever she shuddered he paused to check it was because he'd done something good, and not disturbed a memory – and she told him to stop worrying, laughing it off. There was something so wonderfully free about all of this, about having waited so long, about the not knowing, and it filled him with so much adrenalin, so many emotions, that it was an exquisite agony.

After their passions had ebbed, they lay there, a pleasing tangle of legs and arms and tail.

Eventually, breaking this monumental sense of peace, Lan said, 'I shouldn't fall asleep here.'

He agreed and after another long, slow kiss, she climbed out of bed. He watched her like a voyeur dressing in the half-light.

Reluctantly he roused himself, pulled on his breeches, and moved to see her out. He kissed her at the door and, as they parted, he noticed how she seemed a different person – they both did. Barely a word was uttered – and there was no need, because the warming look in her eyes told him enough. She brushed back her glossy black hair and sashayed sleepily down the corridor. By the top of the staircase, one hand on the rail, she blew him a kiss.

Beaming, he glanced away and strolled casually back inside—

Where his heart nearly stopped.

Adena was there, fully formed, with an ethereal sheen and a black-bloodied neck, sitting on the chair next to his bed. The room felt colder than it had previously, the fire had gone out. The darkness was more oppressive than before. He peered around anxiously.

'Fuck,' Fulcrom declared, agog. He felt guilty, a sinner, a cheating spouse, in the midst of some ridiculous love triangle between the living and the dead.

'How long have you been there?' he demanded.

'Enough to see that you're still the attentive lover you always were.'

Adena was wearing some kind of dress – though it was more or less in rags – and her dark hair contained bright silver streaks, her scruffy fringe hanging lankly before her eyes. The bones of her body seemed to jut out more than usual, darkness pooling in sunken skin. Her presence still sent a shiver through his body, and his tail was rigid with fear. Now more than ever there was a sinister air about her, although her expression remained muted.

'Where were you when . . . ?' Fulcrom faltered, his voice was weak, as the world around him tried its best to reduce him to pure insanity.

'In the corner of the room,' she replied. 'I chose not to be seen though.'

'Why didn't you say something? I don't know, spook us, slam a door, flip a book across the room. Why did you just watch something so obviously painful?'

'I don't know,' she answered flatly. 'Because it didn't affect me the way I thought, I guess. When I first watched you, through the mirror, everything seemed intense.'

'I . . .' Fulcrom faced the floor and closed the door behind him. 'I've no words for this situation,' he continued honestly. 'What can I say? I thought you were – are – dead. I know you are a ghost at least. I even went down there, and saw others like you.'

'To the underworld?'

He placed his hands on his hips and tried to gauge his situation, to remain logical amidst this madness. 'Yes, I was told all about the escape from the priest himself, and I followed him to the city beyond the river.'

'Would you go back?'

'It's not exactly top of my travel destinations. There's no way to return you there forcibly, if you were wondering. You have to go back by your own will.' He found himself being remarkably stern, harsh even, perhaps a panic reaction, but what was he to do? He was talking to a ghost. There were no rules for such a discourse.

'You've kept well,' Adena said, ignoring his not-so-subtle request, and only then did he realize he was semi-naked, showing evidence of his betrayal.

'You shouldn't have stayed,' he said.

'I had to see it through, Fully,' Adena muttered. She seemed to curl in on herself as the conversation continued. 'I had to know if there was a chance of us ever getting back together.'

The emotions came from somewhere, and he found himself on the verge of tears. 'There couldn't be, Adena. You're not alive. It was never possible.' He knelt before her on the floor and tried to take her hand. It was colder than a frost and he released it in an instant. 'We've been allowed a rare moment to see each other, but you have to realize that out here – in the real world again – time goes on. I can't just stand still, though there was a time I contemplated . . . joining you. But that was long ago.'

Adena glanced up and gave him a deathly stare. She didn't

mean to frighten him though, and he knew it – it was just the way she was now. *When will the madness stop?* he thought, logic suddenly visiting him. *Get a grip on this, immediately.*

'You know, it isn't as bad as you think,' she said. 'Everything still hurts, but it's . . . Look, I've had a few years to get used to coping without you, too. That makes it a little easier.'

'What will you do now?' he hinted.

'You've made it clear there's nothing for me here.'

'There's a world down there that you can make your own, surely?'

'No. It's pointless to have much ambition there, Fully. When you have all the time in the world, nothing seems to happen. Did you notice time dragged by so slowly while you were down there? Well, it's the pressure of dying, I think, that makes you do things quickly up here, whether or not you lot realize.'

They talked a while longer, he didn't know how long, didn't bother looking at the clock. He was too drained to care any more. His eyes were sore, and he was exhausted, mentally and physically. This had been the most bizarre day of his life; and a healing one, too. Now old wounds were being poked at, but he forced himself to be mindful that he was more than a pile of emotions.

Adena spoke of wishing she could visit him, but she thought as soon as she crossed that river once again, that was that, she would never speak to him again. Awkward silences grew now, he suspected, because they were waiting to find something profound to share in that final moment, the last sentence they would breathe to each other.

He consciously tried to hold her again, but she flinched. 'Just because I might move on, doesn't mean I won't think of you. The reason it's taken me this long is because I couldn't get over you.'

'I know,' she agreed miserably. 'It's just me being selfish and I should leave you alone. There were only a few of us up here, the dead, but a lot of those have gone back now. The fun wears off pretty quickly when you can't feel much.'

'I loved you. I just have to make the most of what time I have here.'

'*Loved*,' Adena whispered. 'Look after her, Fully.'

I'll do my best, he thought, welling up again, feeling the lump in his throat becoming unbearable.

Adena stood up from the chair and again he noticed how similar she was to Lan, something about the face shapes, the body; and whether or not his subconscious had been at work, he didn't care at all. Adena walked – drifted, almost – into a wall . . . and then the ghost of his wife was gone, just like that.

The fire in the grate sparked into life and he jumped. Warmth erupted, dissipating the chill her ghost had left.

Glancing over his shoulder, he climbed and then collapsed onto his bed, where he cried himself to sleep.

Twenty-Seven

Ulryk's Journal

For two days I walked among the dead.

Their city had no name, though there are several districts. Woe, Wailing, Fire, were the more palatable labels; Aaru and Duat being names with which I was unfamiliar. They were deserted places, though comprised of distinct cultures and architectures. Some were classical structures, others more elaborate and baroque; some utilized straight lines, others domes. These districts were vast and seemingly endless.

I spent some time in the district of Woe, where there seemed, ironically, to be large numbers of healthy specimens of the dead. Ragged clothes were washed and strung up to dry, draped over lines that extended betwixt high, grey-stone walls – it appeared that even the dead had codes of etiquette and cleanliness. There were crude irens that traded in colourless gemstones, faded metals and dreary items of Art; though I had not found anything that resembled a market in food, a common centre-point of surface world cities, and there were no bistros either. Thus the dead congregated around places of entertainment: crude board games; or impromptu poetry recitals.

Experimentally, I tried summoning Frater Mercury just the once down there, but was unsuccessful. The necessary elements in the text, or possibly even speech, simply did not work. As I suspected, in my very last transmission to him, in the real world, I must raise the other copy of the book to the surface, and there I shall continue my rituals.

What might I unleash when I summon him here? I often wonder.

Still, if indeed creations are spilling into our own world, then it can only be a good thing to bring him back for our defence. I can see evidence in everything else he has done or said, enough to allow me to have faith in the things I cannot see.

*

The underworld beneath Villjamur does indeed fit with Jorsalir descriptions, what little there is, though the state of one's soul after death is a complex business. There are hell realms, of course, where we are said to go if our lives have been conducted in an unfulfilling manner. There are realms of gods and demigods, who are said to bicker and fight constantly over status, wealth and power. But the dead here were in limbo, so it is said, souls who were trapped. Yet, they were not in stasis.

For instance, they were very helpful in my search. It seemed that several of them were utterly bored and my predicament gave meaning to their lives, a way to spend their endless days. I was, I suspected, of great amusement to them.

Whenever I managed to communicate with Frater Mercury, and I sought the precise location of the tome, he spoke only of the 'House of the Dead' and 'artificial realities' and up until now I thought that it meant the underworld, where the dead roam free, but what if he meant something else: a specific location. A house, indeed, within the house.

I spoke to some of the locals about this 'House of the Dead'. I questioned them, but was met only with silence, faces that responded as if I was barely even there – as if I was the ghost.

*

Perhaps, I thought to myself, libraries were houses of the dead, with voices speaking from beyond the grave, throughout the centuries. I, too, know that when I am gone these words will linger.

Aker has enlisted Pana and Ran, two frail-looking fellows with strange gaits, and who seemed more insane than useful, to help my search. They sauntered off throughout the Unnamed City to locate any libraries in which the other copy of The Book of Transformations *may reside.*

But there were great challenges. We knew that there are obstacles, buildings in which there are traps that even the dead fear. Why? I did not know – they seemed ethereal things that could even ensnare spirits. The dead did not fear dying – they feared only an eternity of nothingness.

I felt certain that the agents of the church could not hunt me down. They did not know what I was doing, but were merely trying to stop my knowledge from reaching far places, though of course it was too late. The church had propped up their own myths and I could wait no longer.

*

Back in Villjamur, it was still daylight and I breathed the air of the living. Only when I returned did I realize how oppressive it is to walk among them, the countless faces that have died through the ages. I became mindful of life. Even in a troubled city such as Villjamur, I realized there was much to be appreciated.

Stand still and look around. Be conscious of one's breathing. Come back to oneself and new worlds are revealed: the smile on a young child as it picked up a tundra flower growing between two cobbles; two old men contentedly watching the world go by; a girl handing her lover a cake she had just purchased from the bakery.

Sometimes I felt I was ignoring real beauty.

*

My room had been ransacked! What little belongings I carried were cast about the floor. Lanterns lay on their sides, books sat open on the bed – clearly someone had been reading these, though there was nothing too sacred. After a quick analysis, nothing of value had been taken.

By the door were two scratches in the wood, not caused by a sword, nor as a result of the door being kicked open. Creatures had clearly found my whereabouts.

Was I being watched still? I will need the investigator's protection more than I thou—

TWENTY-EIGHT

From a bridge spanning between a church and a dancehall, the two Knights looked across the evening cityscape, regarding the gentle ambience of a calm, cold night in Villjamur. A pterodette skimmed the edge of the bridge before disappearing somewhere.

'I don't like it,' Vuldon grunted. 'Not even the dance is making that much racket. It shouldn't be this quiet.'

'Why ever not?' Tane replied. 'There is a lot less work for us to do on a quiet night. Even criminals take time off from time to time.'

'Maybe.'

A well-to-do couple walked by, the man in a very regal purple cape, the woman wearing a beautiful gown. They nodded their greetings to the Knights as they went on their way, their footsteps echoing. In the distance he could see the warm light of the dancehall and the heads of people busy mingling.

'Don't you ever feel just a bit of a fool out here?' Tane said. 'Not that I'm complaining, ultimately.'

Vuldon turned to look at him. 'What d'you mean?'

The cat-man gripped the brickwork as he regarded the empty streets below. 'I know that the Emperor wants us to be visible, to be seen by people, and I'm fine with that, really. But should the time come – and we're required for some major operation against the anarchists, say – would people genuinely look to us, and could we cope?'

'I could,' Vuldon replied. 'I get what you're saying though. But what else would you do in the Freeze? I don't relish getting drunk in a darkened room again. My rep is good these days. I'm happy to give a little hope. This lot up here don't think beyond their own lives, so there's no point in wanting more from things.'

'A little cynical, but I see your point.'

A harsh screeching noise suddenly shattered the calm. Tane placed his hands to his ears, cringing as he crouched down behind the wall.

'What the fuck was that?' Vuldon scanned the city but could see nothing out of the ordinary. Then to Tane he said, 'Get up.'

'Blimey,' Tane replied, 'that hurt my head.'

'Which direction did it come from?' Vuldon once again looked around the city and after a moment Tane leaned forward next to him.

'A few streets to the east,' Tane said.

'Are you sure?'

He shrugged. 'As much as I ever am.'

*

They ran along the bridge and through the empty streets, taking side routes and down crumbling stairwells, all the while checking around them for any signs of where the scream had come from.

'Do you have ... any idea ... what it could be?' Vuldon spluttered through huge intakes of breath.

'Possibly a fight, I can't really tell.'

They sprinted down-city, using Tane's senses to guide them, and being careful not to skid on the cobbles.

Eventually they reached a tiny viewing platform that over-looked a small stone courtyard between closed shopfronts.

'There,' Vuldon snapped, and the two paused. 'What the hell is that?'

Down below a huge, skeletal creature in a hooded cape

312

was towering over an elderly man. The thing held up a huge iron morningstar, a bulbous, spiked weapon. Two blue eyes glowed from within the hood, and its movements were eerily fluid. The old man managed to scurry out of the way of the blows, which sounded like those of a blacksmith's workshop.

Vuldon heard a word hissed loudly between the high stone walls: 'Heretic.'

The old man seemed to pause for a moment and chant something. Vuldon watched in disbelief as a sword materialized in the air before the man who, gripping it firmly, commenced sparring feebly with the creature.

There was no quick way down, and the fall would likely injure Vuldon, so the two Knights were forced to run around the perimeter path, then down a stairway that led to the courtyard. Luckily, Vuldon saw that a member of the city guard was already moving to the aid of the old man. That would buy them some time.

As they navigated past the detritus in front of a bistro, Vuldon looked at the scene in annoyance. The young soldier was of no use: he pissed himself as he stood before the monster. Paralysed with fear, he meekly held his sword forward, muttering something to himself. The bony creature with perverse and unlikely musculature and tendons flaring underneath its crude brown outfit pulled back the morningstar behind its shoulders and with one swing smashed the soldier's head. The man's body remained upright for a moment longer before crumpling in a heap.

The skeletal creature plucked the hunks of flesh that had adhered to its weapon, then turned to face the old man. 'Heretic,' it hissed once again. 'I have been ordered to stop your blasphemous lies, priest.'

It leered, swinging its weapon through the air in an attempt to kill the old man and struck the ground so fiercely that sparks skittered upwards, and in places the cobbles themselves were removed in twos or threes.

Tane and Vuldon arrived to intercept the assault.

Tane immediately began to attack behind and around the demon, which could not bring its weapon down in time. Tane's extended claws drew across the back of the monster's legs, hamstringing it, and while it fell, lowering the morning-star for a moment, Vuldon barged in and stomped a boot into its chest, sending the weapon clattering to the ground. He grabbed the demon's bony arm while Tane drew his clawed hand down the creature's back, ripping its already flimsy outfit – the creature let out a sinister hiss as if deflating. The waxed overcoat and cape fell away, revealing its repulsive body, a bony form with bulging flared muscles. It screamed, then lashed out; Vuldon smashed down on its arm, then slammed it face-forward to the floor, before he reached down for the morningstar. Then he whipped the weapon down on its head with a crunch: its legs kicked out, its arms flailed, but then it became quite still.

The old man, his sword no longer to be seen, shuffled over to the Knights and began expressing his gratitude. 'Thank you, thank you, my saviours. Please, who are you? Let me know your names.'

'We're the Villjamur Knights. I'm Vuldon and he's Tane. Now, who the fuck are you?'

'I am but a simple priest – my name is Ulryk.'

'Well then, priest, what was that thing and why was it after you?'

'It is called a nephilim,' Ulryk replied, slowly edging away to regard the corpse. 'It was a demon created in secrecy, and sent with a purpose to kill me, but to explain why could take many hours.'

'We've not got all night. We're going to have to log this with the Inquisition,' Vuldon replied. 'You'll have to come with us, I'm afraid.'

*

A new day, a new beginning. Cleansed of his past, though still a little raw, Fulcrom felt like he had been reborn. He was up early, felt a little groggy, and splashed water on his face. With a towel thrown across his shoulder, he scanned his apartment, contemplating the scene from the night before.

Lan dominated his thoughts. There were so many qualities about her which made him smile: her confidence, strong-mindedness, the life she'd led, the way she'd note down interesting names she saw on signs or conversations she overheard, the way she played with strands of her hair, all of which formed the content of her soul. Fulcrom didn't commit himself often, he decided, but when he did he was certain it was the right thing.

He shaved with all his usual meticulousness and checked his face in the mirror. He slicked his white hair to one side. This time, it was because he wanted to be on best form in case he ran into Lan. He picked up the folded clothes on the chair but realized Adena had sat upon them and, though he was not a superstitious man, he decided to put on different attire: a black undershirt, a green tunic, Inquisition outer robe.

Out into the bone-piercing cold. From the front door to his building he watched the snow begin to settle once again on the city, despite the best efforts of the city's cultists. Cobbles were obscured. The undersides of bridges formed bold black streaks across the sky, like print on paper. People hugged the edges of buildings, cocooned in thick and heavy clothing.

Around one corner Fulcrom saw an old ritual under way. A dozen women dressed in warrior garb, a design worn hundreds of years ago – padded red and blue garments, bascinets and aventails, and bright chain mail across their torsos – were parading beneath a flag bearing a red leaf and a flame. The women were dancing in a circle around a fire in a barrel, throwing stalks of various crops into the flames whilst reciting – in an almost scream-like pitch – a poem, a lament for those who had lost their lives in crop failures three thousand years ago. Crowds had gathered to watch the procession, parents drawing children closer to them, a whispered word in their ear explaining the reasons for the ritual. It was said that the incident brought the Empire to its knees, to the point of collapse. Fulcrom rarely thought of the cultists who had provided farmers with free seeds treated to survive the extreme temperatures across Jokull, and which arrived by the boatload in Villjamur. He prayed history would not repeat itself anytime soon.

As Fulcrom carried on his way to work, something dark streaked past above him and landed to one side.

Lan crouched down to absorb the impact, and rose to greet him. 'I wasn't stalking you, promise,' she said with a smile. 'I was just passing.'

The winter cold seemed muted by her presence and penetrating gaze.

'Well, as far as stalkers go . . .' he joked. 'I see you're up early.'

'Yeah, having worked late last night, Vuldon and Tane are both still asleep. Vuldon seems to spend a lot of time either in his room or out on the streets anyway – so I wasn't going to hang around waiting for those two to wake.'

Cautiously, Lan stepped into his embrace and their lips brushed. He held her there, small and fragile, vaguely aware that citizens, as they parted around the couple, were watching them attentively. But he didn't care. Right now, it was about this girl on his lips, and to hell with what others thought.

*

Barely able to keep their hands off each other, they kissed openly on the steps of the Inquisition headquarters. Afterwards, under the impressed stare of many investigators, aides and administrative staff, Lan sprinted up the red-brick sides of the building and, with her final step, pushed and walked across a fifteen-yard gap onto the roof of the adjacent structure, her feet narrowly missing a gargoyle.

To those closest to him, Fulcrom explained, 'It's not *just* for show. There's not as much ice on the side of a building so she gets a better grip.'

One of the younger investigators was grinning like an idiot. 'Fulcrom, she's famous. It's been years since you've even talked about a woman and now you're dating one of the Knights?'

'I'm sure that'll disappoint a lot of ladies,' said Ghale, the human administrative assistant. Her expression was one of mild disdain, and he wondered if Lan's showy exit had upset her somehow.

No sooner had Fulcrom set foot in the building, than Warkur grabbed hold of him. 'Fulcrom, my office, now,' he growled, stomping away.

Fulcrom sheepishly followed, speculating on the reasons behind the old rumel's sour tone.

Warkur's office was Fulcrom's worst nightmare. Papers were heaped up in haphazard piles that leaned on each other for support, documents with handwritten notes scrawled all over them. Legal texts were scattered across the floor, opened, and stained with rings from cups of tea. How Warkur managed to navigate his way through the Urtican Empire's ancient, baroque and sometimes eccentric legal system was a mystery to Fulcrom.

The walls were cluttered, too, with framed documents or certificates, various titles he'd been awarded over the years, and none of them were parallel with any other, but pinned up at all angles. Obscure weaponry was heaped on the shelves, maybe illegal repossessions, maybe his own collection. In one corner lay a blanket and pillows, and a storm lantern stood on a table. There was the faint aroma of something gone off, but Fulcrom couldn't deduce a thing beyond the mess.

'Sit down,' Warkur sighed thunderously as he sat behind his own desk.

Fulcrom tiptoed across the apocalyptic office and perched opposite his superior officer. 'Is anything wrong, sir?'

'You're damn right something's wrong. We're now down to one arsing printing press.'

'Has the other one broken as well?'

'I wouldn't know. It's been stolen.'

'Stolen?' Then the irony hit him. 'You saying that someone has *stolen* a printing press from the offices of the Inquisition?'

Warkur's expression said two things. The first was that he was a very tired man. The second was that if anyone breathed a word of this outside this building, he would personally sign their execution order.

'Any leads as to who might have taken it?' Fulcrom asked.

'There was a small flag which we all know and love,' Warkur said, 'and that would have been left by our friends, the anarchists.'

'Oh.'

'Fucking "Oh" indeed,' Warkur muttered. 'Aside from that, where were you yesterday? There was a stand off between the military and the anarchists, and you weren't to be seen.'

'I thought the conflict was between the military and the Cavesiders, *not* the anarchists, sir.'

'How could you know if you weren't there?'

'Lan told me.'

'Lan told you.'

'Yes, sir. We were . . .'

'I know what you were doing,' Warkur said. 'I saw the two of you outside, all over her like a kid licking a sweet.'

Fulcrom looked at his boss steadily. 'It won't get in the

318

way of our project – there will be no conflict of interest, and we're well aware of the issues.'

'Good. And meanwhile the official line is that the military *engaged with anarchists*, simple as that. There was trouble, and it was dealt with.' Warkur's gaze became distant, his mind drifting elsewhere. 'It never lasts, you know.'

'Sorry, sir?'

'That passion,' Warkur declared. 'Never lasts.'

Fulcrom's eyes settled on the blanket and pillows behind Warkur, and though he concluded much, he said nothing.

Warkur changed the subject by demanding a status report of everything Fulcrom had been working on, and if he was any closer to finding any figures involved with the anarchists.

Fulcrom confessed it seemed as if they were chasing shadows. The Knights were always one step behind – responding to crime rather than preventing it in the first place. None of the known, established criminal families were involved – the anarchists were offering something different to the people, and money wasn't of interest any more. They were highly organized and they were networked. Little had been heard about Shalev outside of the confrontation between her and the Knights, at the indoor iren.

'The Knights, having interrupted the majority of the major planned offences by the anarchists,' Fulcrom concluded, 'are holding the city together.'

Warkur was absorbing the information. 'Well, I've some information for you on a related matter. That priest who called for you a while back – the man's been brought in by Vuldon and Tane last night.'

'Ulryk was arrested?'

'No, not arrested. He was kept here for his own safe keeping, apparently. They brought in a weird-looking corpse, too. You'd better take a look.'

*

Satisfying her occasional preference for isolation, Lan surveyed the cityscape from a high church roof. For the very first time in her life she could admit to feeling a happy person. People around Villjamur took on a new form. There were smiles where previously she saw none. There was laughter where previously she heard only morose grumbling or discreet whispers between underworld figures. Even the garudas, as they sailed through the air, were no longer imposing; they were now graceful creatures, possessing a freedom she had once envied, a symbol of everything that was out of reach.

Was she really a bundle of clichés all of a sudden? Was this what actually happened when you fell for someone? *Get a grip!*

Lan shook herself into a more focused state. She was a Villjamur Knight and she had a job to do.

She closed her eyes to listen to the sounds from the street for any signs of trouble. Much of the job distilled down to this simple act: an inspection of the city, waiting until she could offer help. And despite her new-found happiness, despite her tendency today to err on the side of optimism, something seemed wrong. She didn't for a moment believe she had some kind of extrasensory perception, but Villjamur itself seemed primed for something.

From the east of the city, a woman's scream came to her ears. Lan pushed herself to the crenellated edge of the roof and jumped across to the opposite building, a gap of ten feet, and then up onto the rim of a cultist-treated bridge. People looked up startled as she sprinted past them, following the echo of the scream.

She crossed over several streets, actively enjoying the rush of speed. She was utterly comfortable with her powers by now – completely attuned to their nuances, harnessing the forces inside that altered her sense of balance and maintained her position in the air.

She settled down to the ground on the second level of the city, the furthest point from the caves, and paused to filter the sounds of the city. Villjamur's endless passageways provided a huge frustration: they played havoc with sound, and had completely wrong-footed her on several occasions. Becoming a little out of breath, Lan's sprint became more of a jog.

It wasn't long before she located the crime. In the shadow of tall buildings, at the back of a narrow brick alley, two men had pressed a blonde woman up against a wall.

'Hey!' Lan called over as she approached.

The two men were shaven-headed, looking like brothers. Both stood over six foot tall and were wearing long wax coats. One thrust an iron bar against the woman's throat; her thick coat lay discarded on the cobbles, exposing a heavy brown dress and hefty leather boots. Underneath the grubbiness she was pretty, and the tears streaking down her face left little to the imagination as to what had been going on.

'Leave her alone,' Lan ordered, confidently entering the dark alley. Her voice reverberated between the stone walls.

One of the men turned towards her and spat at her feet. His voice sounded raw, as if he'd been drinking all night long. 'Piss off, bitch. This needn't worry you, unless you want to join us.'

Lan pushed her left leg against the wall to lever herself upwards, then she leapt to close the gap between them before they could do any more harm to the woman. She landed a few feet from them and, curiously, both men backed away to the dark dead end behind. *Are these thugs scared of me?* Lan immediately checked that the woman was OK, whilst she kept an eye on the men.

The victim hid her face in her hands, shaking, and Lan looked towards the two men who had paused—

In an instant, the girl reached up and grabbed Lan's hair. She pulled it, and slammed her head against the wall.

Lan shambled backwards in a daze.

A whistle came from somewhere. At the open end of the alleyway, several figures quickly closed in, silhouetted against the light, each carrying a weapon. Though her vision was hazy, she noted that the men at the dead end were smiling. The woman she was meant to have saved laughed as she kicked at the back of Lan's knees, sending her sprawling forwards onto the ice-cold stone.

Lan's hands and face stung from the impact. She wiped grit and blood from her chin.

'Wait,' Lan held out a hand as she climbed to her feet, 'I was only trying to help.'

One of the skinheads spoke. 'We don't need no fucking help, bitch. We're sick of you fuckers ruining things. You represent authority and power – you're of no use to us. Can't you see it's best for the people if you just stay out of our business?'

'You work for Shalev?' Lan spluttered.

'We don't work *for* her. We work together.'

A blow to Lan's stomach, an iron bar across her back, and she collapsed to the ground as a useless ball of agony.

A squat man with bird-like features poked a wooden club into her ribs and asked, 'Is this the he–she one?'

'Apparently. Fancy taking a look to see?'

Crude laughter.

'See what? S'all changed by cultists, innit?'

'Fair point.'

Distantly, Lan wondered, *How could they possibly know?* She tried to come to her senses and her feet, but only managed to rock herself to her knees. She needed to tune into that quality within, to tap that force which she had been given, but the kicks and punches had knocked any concentration out of her system. Clawing at the force within, she pushed her arms aside, the blows knocking back two of her attackers, and they stumbled against the wall. That effort in itself weakened her and she allowed her judgement to drop.

Distances seemed artificial. Suddenly her head felt incredibly heavy. The gang crowded her.

Weapons rained down upon her skin, and she felt them as light taps. One to her stomach: she hunched again. One to her forehead: she flipped gently backwards. One to her hip: she sprawled forwards on the ground.

Gentle strikes to her back and skull, like brutal raindrops . . .

*

The corpse lay stretched out for them all to see.

Measuring almost seven feet in length, its feet drooped over the edge of the polished granite table in one of the old quarantine sectors of the Inquisition headquarters. Formerly a cellar, the room featured a domed brick ceiling with several open arches for doorways, meaning the place could receive an unusually large amount of traffic, if it wasn't for the fact that people knew dead bodies were often observed down here. Cressets burned along the wall, as did a huge log fire at the far end of the room, and within these simple confines, Fulcrom, Ulryk, Vuldon and Tane were attempting to make sense of the alien body.

The specimen reeked. What clothing it once possessed now lay in a heap in a metal container by the wall. Sinewy dark skin was taut across jagged bones, which, at the joints, were formidable-looking structures that seemed set to burst through.

It was hominid, as much as they could tell, possessing two pairs of tightly muscled arms and legs, and where its skin had been torn by Tane's claws, black blood had bubbled upwards to seal the wound. Much of its head had been reduced to mush, as Vuldon proudly pointed out, but what remained now were barely more than fragments of a malodorous skull.

Fulcrom had never seen anything quite like this, and he had seen some strange things bred by cultists in his time. No, this was entirely an alien entity, and one he was glad he hadn't encountered personally.

'It is called a nephilim.' Ulryk muttered the word as if it left an acidic taste in his mouth. 'It is a demon of the church.'

Tane whistled, leaning over to take a closer look. 'Ugly chap, isn't he? Vuldon, do you *swear* this isn't one of your girlfriends?'

Vuldon ignored Tane and prodded the priest for further information. 'Why was it after *you* specifically?' he asked. 'From a distance, we saw it went after you alone.'

Ulryk peered imploringly at Fulcrom, and he knew just how difficult it was for Ulryk to explain his past once again.

'You can trust them, Ulryk,' he encouraged him. 'They're here to help.'

To his credit, the priest encapsulated his story as much as possible, avoiding the questions of altered histories, of politics within the church. He mentioned that the church merely considered him a heretic for his views, and had placed a bounty on his head. His mission in Villjamur was one of great urgency, and the nephilim was sent to prevent him from succeeding. Fulcrom wondered just how much the church knew of the priest's intentions.

'Your mission, priest?' Vuldon stood as ever with folded arms, showing little sympathy for this old man who had fled across the breadth of the Empire simply because of his beliefs.

Ulryk told him he was looking for a copy of a book that would betray the church and everything it stood for.

'Sounds fair enough to me,' Tane said cheerily.

'Idiot,' Vuldon grunted. Then, to Ulryk, 'Will you be causing any other incidents that are going to threaten other people's safety?'

Fulcrom was impressed at how well Vuldon had developed

a sense of dedication to his job. If only Tane would at least sound responsible, just once. Every time he spoke, Fulcrom cringed.

Ulryk contemplated those words, closed his eyes, and said something Fulcrom deeply suspected was a lie. 'The populace will remain undisturbed.'

'Fine,' Vuldon replied. 'Make sure that *is* the case.'

Fulcrom had put his faith in everything the priest had said up until this point, though he had not fully committed to a belief in him. An open mind was one thing, but here, right before them, was yet more physical evidence that everything Ulryk had said up until now was utterly true.

Yet Fulcrom had never considered just what would happen when the priest obtained his other copy of *The Book of Transformations*.

'Investigator,' a voice came from one of the arches – one of the aides. 'We've another incident. This is urgent.'

'Do we need the Knights?' Fulcrom indicated Vuldon and Tane, who were now alert and focused.

'I think it's best,' the aide replied, 'since it involves the other.'

*

She was strung up by her left foot, dangling from a vast, arched bridge that crossed over one of the busiest irens in the city. Hundreds of people clustered underneath and pointed upwards as she spiralled on the spot in the wind; and from windows, many more silently watched.

Fulcrom managed to remain surprisingly calm. He knew instantly that it was Lan – she was garbed in the iconic uniform of the Knights, and her notable, dark hair drooped down below her head. For the second time in his life, the woman he loved had been taken from him.

In a state of numbness, the following moments became a blur.

He remembered sprinting up a stairwell, slipping on the

first three steps and hurting his thigh; Vuldon knocking him aside to charge past him; Tane taking a more complex route via rooftops. Fulcrom vaguely remembered the gust of wind that almost knocked him over when he reached the bridge at the top.

Pushing through the crowds, tears in his eyes, praying to gods he didn't believe in.

Vuldon and Fulcrom ran to the centre of the bridge, where the rope was tied tightly around a crenellation. Vuldon leapt up onto the edge, his bulk causing a vast shadow and, as Tane arrived alongside, the Knight began pulling in the rope in great lurches.

Fulcrom stood watching Lan's ascent, her hair all over the place, so isolated and so vulnerable, his tail gripping the side of the wall for security. Below, the crowds were still gathering, their movements gentle and fluid from this height. Morbid curiosity had caused many more to gather near them on the bridge, and Tane and Fulcrom shoved them aside as Vuldon gently lowered Lan's body down to the cobbles.

Vuldon used his own mass to push the crowd back.

She was covered in blood. Her face was bruised and bleeding, there were cuts to her eyebrow and chin, and the back of her hands scuffed from being dragged along the street. Fulcrom instantly placed his ear to her chest and ... could hear a faint beat. 'She's not dead,' he spluttered, then tried to calm himself. 'She's unconscious, but *she's not dead.*' He forced himself to think logically. 'Tane – we'll need the cultists immediately. Fetch them. Please, we need your speed.'

Tane didn't need telling twice. The cat-man vanished into the crowd.

'You,' Fulcrom demanded – it was a small boy in smart robes, who looked startled at being brought into this affair – 'will you fetch me some water and a cloth? This is a Knight of our city and she needs help.' The boy looked at Lan, nodded eagerly and ran. A few minutes later he returned with them. Fulcrom began tenderly cleaning Lan's face.

'Get a hold of yourself.' Vuldon shook his shoulders. 'You can't cry in front of these people. It ain't manly.'

Fulcrom hadn't even realized he was crying until he wiped away his tears. 'Fuck you, Vuldon,' Fulcrom replied, 'and fuck being manly. This isn't the time for your cheap machismo.'

He continued treating Lan, cleaning her up, aware of Vuldon's burning gaze.

'You genuinely care for her, don't you?' he asked gruffly.

Fulcrom watched the water leak from the clenched cloth, carrying blood down the smooth lines of her face, and ignored him.

*

Lan was still unconscious when Tane and the cultist, Feror, arrived carrying a stretcher.

'Her bones really ought to have survived the incident,' the old man advised quietly, 'but this is merely a precaution.'

Fulcrom and Vuldon lifted her gently onto the stretcher, still with people milling around them – why would they not just leave? They carried her along the bridge, then into a beautiful plaza on the third level, where a horse and immense black carriage stood waiting for them.

They lifted her inside the carriage and laid her on the floor.

'I'll stay with her,' Fulcrom said, an order, not a request.

*

In one of the many drearily lit chambers near the clifftop residence of the Knights, Lan was stripped of her uniform – something that made Fulcrom distinctly uncomfortable – and her nakedness revealed painful-looking abrasions and bruises on her body. He could only imagine what brutality created them. A team of cultists half-immersed her in a bath of brine on a surgical platform. Wires were lowered into the solution, and machines were activated. Metal artefacts hummed and sizzled into life.

He paced back and forth outside, listening to the bubbling and buzzing and spluttered gasps, trying to piece together what was developing behind the metal door, but his imagination soared with variants on how Lan was being dismantled. Instead, he focused on what had happened.

Tane and Vuldon were not much help and, happy that Lan would survive a little longer, had headed back out into the city to see if they could find witnesses or clues. Fulcrom doubted they would find much.

The anarchists were frustrating, militant and smart people. They weren't just a step ahead, they had whole plans sketched out, and he had virtually nothing to show the Emperor apart from showcase heroics. And he had no idea just how many Cavesiders considered themselves part of the movement. Though the Knights had given the rest of the city something to talk about, managed to prevent many crimes and put offenders into the hands of the Inquisition, Fulcrom realized that all they were doing was trying to plug holes in a dam. There was only so much they could take before the force would become overwhelming. The rest of the Inquisition were overworked with increasing numbers of criminal cases and leads that went nowhere.

What could he do, order a purge of Caveside? Who were they even fighting? Anyone brought in for questioning said nothing. Either they genuinely had nothing to say, or Shalev had inspired such loyalty that they would not give anything away. No, a purge would do no good, and besides the military had already slaughtered civilians.

For the first time in his life, Fulcrom began questioning his purpose as an investigator. Not even when he helped Investigator Jeryd free the refugees, only for them to go straight back into the decrepit camps outside the city walls, did he feel as low as he did right now. His choices were limited: the

Emperor would have him killed if he failed or walked away. All he could do was press on.

*

About an hour later they let Fulcrom in to see Lan. She was lying with a blanket over her body like she belonged in a mortuary. But she was, at least, breathing. Miraculously much of the bruising had vanished from her face and, from what he could see, her neck and shoulders.

'What did you do to her?' Fulcrom asked the room. Three of the cultists in the corner, busy tweaking bits of equipment, glanced at each other, as if deciding who could be bothered to give such a long-winded answer.

Feror stepped in alongside him. The old man was a reassuring face, as much as a cultist could be. 'It was me, mainly,' he said. 'I guess it's nice to know I'm not completely letting everyone down.'

What does he mean? Fulcrom thought, observing his nervous mannerisms that contradicted his confident words. 'Go on.'

'We essentially bathed her in a solution that speeded up her recovery at the . . . cellular level.'

'What?' Fulcrom demanded.

'The little building blocks, which make us all.'

'If there are any secrets you're keeping from—'

'It is well known in cultist circles. A lot of the enhancements we'd given her, particularly the skeletal alterations, protected her. If she was a normal woman, she would be dead.'

'What do you mean by *normal?*' Fulcrom snapped.

'Without our rigorous enhancements,' Feror corrected, and Fulcrom contemplated the sudden silence between them.

Feror continued, 'So, what should have taken months of recovery, will now take hours.' Feror talked about obscure things like oxygen flow, and to Fulcrom the science could have been magic for all he knew.

The important thing was that Lan was alive and would soon be back to normal. The cultists' work done, Fulcrom was allowed to be alone with her. As they closed the metal door behind them, Fulcrom pulled up a leather chair alongside the surgical platform on which Lan was resting, and slumped into it.

And waited for her to wake.

*

When she was fully conscious and her drowsiness fading, with a beaker of water in her hands, Lan described the attack in full detail to Fulcrom, who stood alongside her bed and affectionately caressed the back of her neck.

'It was a trap,' she told him. 'And it was definitely the anarchists. I remember them arguing how far to take the beating. Someone asked if they should actually kill me, but the woman in the gang – it wasn't Shalev – she said that they wanted the city to see how vulnerable it is, and how normal the Knights are. That they had the upper hand. They wanted the *bourgeoisie* to feel scared again, to give people something the *People's Observer* couldn't twist into propaganda. She said they were using me as a symbol.' Lan took a sip of water. 'Which explains why they dangled me off that bridge, I guess.'

'Feror told me if you weren't enhanced, you would probably be dead,' Fulcrom said.

'Oh,' Lan replied and appeared to contemplate the statement. 'Perks of the job, I guess.'

Fulcrom smiled. It was reassuring, under the circumstances, to see she still possessed a sense of humour. 'Apparently your recovery is going to be quick, because of these cultists. You've considerable value to the city, you know.'

'I feel a little guilty, if I'm honest. Especially after seeing so many people slaughtered by the military, for me alone to receive such privilege just doesn't feel right.'

'The Emperor has invested heavily in the three of you.

He's simply protecting his interests. Nothing personal, I'm sure.' Fulcrom winked.

'You're full of love this . . . afternoon?'

'Nearly. It's early evening now. You've spent a few hours in bed.'

Lan pushed herself so that her legs hung off the edge of the platform, and Fulcrom pulled the blankets up over her to keep her decent, should any of the cultists return to the room.

She gave him an intense look then, and he knew that there was a deeper problem, one that the cultists couldn't fix. 'What is it?'

'I'm . . . I'm pretty sure they knew my past.'

'Nonsense,' Fulcrom reassured her. 'I promise you, no one outside of the highest echelons of the empire have the slightest clue, and even then the background of the Knights is hugely confidential – just one or two cultists, perhaps; security is tight on this. They wouldn't gossip.'

Had she imagined it? Her head was hazy from the beatings and the treatments. Maybe it wasn't true. No one was treating her any differently, were they? And in fact the cultists had just spent their resources repairing her. She felt she should just keep quiet about it.

'From now on,' Fulcrom said, 'I want the Knights only to work as a group, or at the very least patrol the streets in pairs.'

Lan creased her face as little fluxes of pain moved around her body. 'I feel a little drunk. What did these cultists do to me?'

'Saved your life, is what they did,' Fulcrom reminded her. 'It was Feror's work mainly.'

'Good old Feror.' She gently eased her feet to the floor, Fulcrom clasping his arm behind her for support as her legs took her weight.

She let him prop her up for a while longer, and he walked her around the room in slow circles.

Soon he realized she was walking normally. 'Do you actually need my arms around you?'

'No, I can do this on my own – I just didn't want you to let go.' She smiled, stood upright, faced him, then with a sigh she held him, burying herself beneath his robes.

For someone who'd nearly been beaten to death, her grip was remarkably strong.

*

When Lan was well enough to return to her living quarters that evening, Fulcrom guided her home, taking care not to be too patronizing with his gestures. He found Tane and Vuldon in the company of Ulryk. *Of course*, Fulcrom realized, *the priest has not yet found a new place where he can shelter. What better place than this?*

He didn't think there would be a conflict of interests – he was overseeing 'weird shit', as Warkur so aptly put it. It seemed more efficient to lump all the weirdness together.

None of the three stood up at the couple's entrance. Tane and Vuldon were hunched over a table. The pages of *The Book of Transformations*, Ulryk's copy, was the focus of their attention. The tome was surprisingly large under the mellow lighting, at least a foot long, and three or four inches thick. Sometimes Fulcrom wondered why so much fuss was being made over a simple book.

'Investigator,' Ulryk announced, 'I was explaining what it was that got me into so much trouble earlier. I considered that such brave and skilled people might be able to help me . . . where we both visited.'

'I was thinking something similar,' Fulcrom agreed. 'Though I'd only be able to spare a maximum of one. No more, I'm afraid. Maybe it's something Lan could do?'

Lan nodded as she joined the three of them at the table. Somewhere in the distance, Fulcrom could hear the sea droning against the base of the cliff.

The tattered sheets of vellum were turned slowly, one after another, as Ulryk revealed some amazingly incomprehensible scripts and diagrams. There were weird woodcuts, parodies of real-life objects, creatures in perpetual states of change, and unexpected juxtapositions – couples bleeding into flowers into houses.

'To the trained eye,' Ulryk explained, 'there are numerous glyphs, none of which are to be found in any other text in our world, and no more than seven per word. This is a special script, a special language, comprised of special letters, written in intricate code. It is an artefact of huge importance.'

'Who wrote it?' Lan asked.

'Frater Mercury,' Fulcrom said. Then, aware of everyone's surprised expression. 'That's what Ulryk told me before. I've no idea who he really is.'

'The wars you have heard about, where creatures have come from another world into ours,' Ulryk said. 'They come from warring civilizations, ones created by Frater Mercury. These civilizations he created millennia ago, in this very world. He is responsible for all you see – for life as we know it – and within *The Books of Transformations* we can be witness to some of his secrets. I think, also, that he has left such texts for wayfarers to discover, people such as myself, should he need to return to our world. I am convinced it is so. Now he needs to return. As islands of our realm are cleared of human and rumel life, as alien cultures swarm into ours to destroy it, we need him. And, as I understand it, things are far worse where Frater Mercury still resides.'

Though the news of the wars on the fringes of the Empire came rarely, Fulcrom was aware of the threat. He was convinced that what reports *People's Observer* did publish were heavily censored so that the information wouldn't be detrimental to the population's peace of mind – or, indeed, threaten the current regime.

Was it some ancient conflict coming to fruition?

'Frater Mercury – the man who wrote this – you're saying he's still alive?' Lan asked. 'How old is he?'

'Who knows?' Ulryk sighed. 'He is responsible for creating much of our culture. As his influence grew, and his creations began to dominate, he was forced into another dimension – a choice he took in order to preserve his work.'

'Is he some kind of god?' Lan asked.

'Gods are crafted by mortals, dear lady, so that may have been the case at one point. I believe that he was a scholar, a theologian, a scientist, a philosopher, a linguist. A world-changer.'

'What kind of *things* did this Frater Mercury make?' Fulcrom enquired.

Ulryk sat back with a beatific grin. His shoulders rose and fell as he chuckled. 'What didn't he create?' Then with sudden urgency, he returned to the book and pointed out a section which seemed to feature wings ... Garudas. They were definitely draft sketches of garudas, with tables of incomprehensible script to one side.

'Here,' Ulryk gestured with the flat of his hand, 'lies the method in which garudas were constructed. And here' – he skipped backwards two pages, where a diagram of other animals upon which large wings had been grafted – 'here is where primitive experiments at creating flying beasts failed. I have trouble reading much of the notes, but I have little doubt that garudas were as a result of experimentation deep in the past. And Frater Mercury had repeated this process for hundreds of other creatures, many taken from our own stories, made real – merely because he had the knowledge to do such things.'

The group stared dumbly at the pictures, not quite understanding, but not quite disbelieving either.

'It is my conclusion, from years of study, that cultists – who for thousands of years said that they rescued and perfected ancient methods of technology – were in fact merely resurrecting the tools of the author, Frater Mercury. I believe that the still undiscovered companion book to this unites the two texts; and that, together, they contain a ritual for the restoration of Frater Mercury in this world. Given the great disasters about to ensue, his return might well prevent a catastrophe.'

Vuldon seemed to take a deep interest in the pictures. With reverence, and a delicate gesture, he turned the pages, smiling when he came to an elaborate sketch. 'This is a recipe book for life itself, then.'

'It is indeed, my dear Vuldon,' Ulryk sighed.

'The pictures – do they come to life or something? I mean, is this magic?'

'No, though there are techniques I know where pictures can have an extra dimension added to their purpose – pictures that can influence minds.'

'I'd really like to see that.' Vuldon seemed impressed. 'Fulcrom, Ulryk can stay here for the evening if he wants.'

Fine by me, Fulcrom thought. *Better to keep an eye on him than have him summoning anything else into being.*

TWENTY-NINE

Their ship ran into trouble: the seas were rough, rolling at four times the height of their vessel, and none of them had the skill to sail or navigate.

Dartun was forced to steer them to the western edge of the island of Folke, and it took them some time before they found a stretch of coastline that satisfied their needs. They had run out of provisions and were desperately hungry. Verain was so exhausted, physically and emotionally drained, that nothing in her life seemed to matter any more.

Eventually, they ran their ship into a wide estuary, surrounded by high, snow-smothered valleys, with a scattering of buildings nestled into the nooks and crannies of the landscape. Smoke drifted up from chimneys, a sight that generated some optimism in Verain's heart: here was a signal of domesticity, an indication that life was perfectly normal for some people.

Up ahead was a reasonably large port. A few dozen boats of various sizes were moored, most of them equipped for fishing. Slick slate roofing and grey granite structures created a dreary ambience, but at least this side of Folke was untouched by the invaders pouring from the Realm Gates.

Snow and winds buffeted them as their craft approached the quay. A local harbourmaster strolled out in a thick coat and hat to meet them as they alighted on the quayside.

Verain's determination to survive had somewhat diminished since they'd left Tineag'l, but it felt good to be on land again, to have something solid beneath her. She did not have the legs or stomach for sailing.

'Sele of the day, strangers,' the harbourmaster called out loudly in heavily accented Jamur. 'Not from these parts then.' A declaration more than a question.

Dartun strode forward to meet him. 'Morning, sir. We were passing through, on our way to Villjamur. We seek lodgings for the night.'

'You, uh, got a licence for that vessel of yers? 'Fraid we've a tax for those who ain't registered with our community, like.' He had small button eyes, narrowed tight against the weather. His skin was sun-blemished by years of working outdoors, his close-cropped beard was grey.

'We're cultists,' Dartun announced.

'I see . . .' the harbourmaster replied. 'Well, I'll let it be known to yer, we don't welcome the likes of magicians here.'

'Sir,' Dartun continued, 'we will be no trouble. We need simple lodgings, that is all. We've little in the way of money, but I'm sure I can lend my hand to something that requires fixing in exchange.'

The harbourmaster appeared to think about it. Seagulls called out across the distance, and boats rattled against each other in the water behind. 'After last night's storm, a wall on one of our churches has collapsed, four streets away,' he said. 'Road's blocked and we ain't any spare horses to clear the rubble. Whatever magic yer have, keep it hidden – but if yer can clear our mess, I'll guarantee lodgings.'

Dartun nodded curtly. 'Consider the road cleared.'

*

The roads were very narrow, the houses tall, so the rock was piled not just over a wide area but high, too. Dartun worked with his bare hands, tossing aside boulders as if he was playing a game and eliciting admiration from the gathered locals. Verain wondered what they'd feel if they knew the truth: that he had transformed, that he was *inhuman*.

While he single-handedly hauled chunks of granite, more locals congregated. But awe soon changed to fear, and soon Verain could hear sinister accusations about them being cultists, people of magic. Most didn't trust cultists: they thought they were abnormal, artificial, ghosts, monsters, whatever – anything other than welcome guests.

A grunt drew her attention to Dartun once again, as he laboured with a hunk of granite the size of his torso. Verain could only watch in awe: she knew what he was doing was not possible for a human. Rock by rock, Dartun slowly cleared the street, piling the rubble neatly alongside the remains of the church, and eventually traffic could now flow along the cobbles with ease.

Having lost interest the locals drifted away, resuming their routines. In the distance a pterodette's cry rose above the sound of the sea.

Dartun sat on a rock and his cultists gathered around him. He was breathing heavily, showing that the labour had, at least, required some effort. Verain threw his cloak around his shoulders, whispering, 'You'll need to keep warm.'

'Thank you,' he replied, and gave her such a look of tenderness that she almost hoped him capable of returning to normal again.

'We could've helped you,' Tuung muttered.

'You wouldn't have been able to lift any of this.' Dartun gestured to the stone. 'The locals couldn't, and you don't have any relics.'

'But why do this on your own?' Verain asked, laying a hand to his shoulder. 'At least you could have let us try.'

'No. You each need safe accommodation for the evening. You need food and warmth if you're to survive the journey home.'

Tuung didn't seem satisfied by that, and if she was honest with herself, neither was Verain. Their exchanged glance revealed that they weren't buying Dartun's reasoning, but she knew better than to press him.

They were rewarded with cheap lodgings in the local tavern, which was more like an impressive drinking warehouse overlooking the harbour. A large and spacious building, with several rooms available for rent, the group were the only guests – although the word guests implied an element of hospitality, whereas their stay was negotiated in one swift, urgent conversation between the harbourmaster and the landlord.

This was the only tavern in town, so the place remained packed with mouthy locals until late. Not that it mattered: they ate well, and Verain was sitting so close to a log fire she thought she might burn. That was all that mattered, to feel some heat in her bones, to feel . . . *human* again.

The landlord didn't let the locals get near them. The harbourmaster had said that they should keep their heads down. A line had been drawn with the fug of weed smoke and ale, and Verain was fine with that. Dartun slumped silently in the corner of the tavern, in the lantern light; and, as he impassively regarded this vast hall, which was an excellent opportunity to discuss their plans, Verain remained too scared to say anything. Now and then the locals would direct fierce stares at Dartun, but when he returned their gaze without response, they quickly looked elsewhere. Two citizens even spat on his table as they passed, but he did not move an inch. Dartun's inertia disturbed her.

In between sips of the strong, local ale, Tuung whispered to Verain, 'I don't know about you, lass, but I reckon your fella is up to something.'

'He's not my "fella" any more,' she replied solemnly. 'I just want to get back home.'

She longed for Villjamur again, for the comfort of the ebb and flow of the city.

*

It wasn't until they were about to go to bed that the trouble started.

A group of locals loitered just beneath their window. Songs broke out, crude and vile lines. Raucous, they began throwing stones, little pebbles at first, and then larger rocks that clattered against the wall and eventually broke a window. Cold air and bitter voices washed into the room. Verain huddled on the floor along with the others, next to the fireplace – no one spoke about their situation, as if they might be able to ignore it completely.

A firecracker smashed through their window, landing by her foot; she leapt up and kicked it against the far wall before it exploded. Everyone in the room cowered back in shock. They turned as Dartun suddenly stood.

Without looking at them he calmly walked out of the room, closed the door and they heard as he walked down the stairs. A few moments later, a quarrel erupted outside.

Verain tiptoed to the window, navigating her way carefully around the broken glass. She peered down to see Dartun had emerged down below, and the crowds began surging towards him. There must have been nearly a hundred people there, packed in along the quayside, where boats gently moved against each other in the strong breeze.

A few at the head of the throng steered towards Dartun and began hurling abuse at him. He moved out of sight, back towards the tavern, but a gurgled scream followed – then another.

'What's going on?' Tuung asked, grabbing her elbow and trying to glimpse past her.

She tugged herself away from his grip, threw on her wax coat, ran out and rushed downstairs to the front door which was still open, but it was too late . . .

340

A dozen bodies already sprawled at Dartun's feet, their forms bent awkwardly, limbs severed in places. Blood was pooling on the wooden veranda, glinting in torchlight. Still people came at him, brandishing swords and maces. Someone fired an arrow, which pinged off Dartun's chest, he caught another in mid air. The locals gasped.

Verain screamed his name, but he ignored her.

She stepped outside but slipped on the spilled blood, collapsing uselessly to the ground. Looking up, she saw Dartun heave his arm into someone's stomach, their eyes bulging as they hunched over, more than winded. Another man tried to hit him with an axe but Dartun grabbed it at the handle, pulled the attacker forwards, and smashed the weapon backwards into their own face – cracking their skull with a simple ferocity.

Two, three more bodies fell, six, eight, ten – it was hideous, but she was too scared to move. This was beyond her control, beyond her scope of understanding. Why would these people not move away from him?

Eventually the immediate crowd dissipated. Someone hurled a firecracker by his feet but he didn't flinch. Where it exploded, it should have ravaged his leg. She followed his still-emotionless gaze to a line of townsfolk, who were standing by the corner of a street, each carrying a bow. They fired at him and he stood there, arms out wide as the arrows rained down.

Verain clawed at the door frame as she scrambled back inside, shuddering as the arrows impacted on the tavern wall. When silence came she peered around the corner. Moonlight broke through the cloud, revealing the massacre in full. Dartun was standing still, arrows imbedded in his body – he strode forwards, plucking them out one by one, happily gesturing for the archers to try once again, but they looked at what was approaching them and retreated around the corner.

Verain joined him outside, where under the light of both

341

moons she surveyed the scene. Her hand across her mouth, she gazed on the wreckage of the community: the corpses and dismembered limbs were everywhere. Where bodies were still moving, she longed to do something to help them, to call for medical attention.

Dartun began to hover then, as before, raising himself above the ground.

'Dartun, what the hell are you?' she screamed. 'Just . . . This is *your* doing. You killed all these innocent people.'

'Verain . . .' He looked down at her, his face twitching. 'I'm discovering something . . . new.'

Dartun's arms fanned out wide, and a gentle trail of purple light radiated below his toes. He drifted away from her, many yards above the harbour and – in a sudden burst – he rocketed skywards, becoming an arc of light ascending to the heavens.

*

It wasn't even midnight when people began returning. Verain feared for her life, feared for all of their lives. Dartun had suddenly abandoned them to face the aftermath. They held a rapid meeting in their room.

'We've nothing but a few clothes,' Tuung said. 'No weapons, no relics, no food, nothing.'

'The townsfolk will be wary of us at first,' Todi replied. 'It might permit us an opportunity to get out.'

'Aye, the lad's right,' Tuung said. 'If no one objects, I say we get our stuff, get on our boat and move up the coast.'

'It's pitch-black,' Verain observed. 'I don't know about you, but I'm not optimistic about our chances of navigating at night.'

'We've got no choice, lass. Either that or get lynched.'

They packed, then crept through the darkness of the tavern, seeking a back window or door to get through. Verain heard wailing and crying from the front of the building, where families must have been picking through all the flesh in an effort to find loved ones. She felt sick because there was nothing she could do.

*

Unobserved, deliberately or otherwise, they managed to make their way through the narrow streets to the boat. They set off.

Moonlight glittered across the water up ahead, broken up by the waves. For a long while no one spoke or didn't know what to say. Their purpose was as before, simply get to Villjamur, only now there was no one driving them like cattle.

They might have been sailing for an hour – maybe two, Verain couldn't be sure – when there was a trail across the night sky, a purple jet of sparks and, moments later, there it was again, except moving the other way. *Is that him?*

'Tuung,' she called.

'What is it?' he replied from his position at the tiller.

'Come and look for yourself.'

'You come here and tell me.'

Verain stepped cautiously across the deck towards him, then pointed up past the sails. 'There was something up there. It was moving across the sky.'

'Meteor?' he asked.

'It could be, but there – no look! There it is again.' Sure enough, there was another trail, this time curving much closer: it zigzagged then hovered, approaching the boat very slowly, like some inquisitive firefly.

Then, a final rush and it clattered aboard the boat, rolling and skidding to a stop at the far end.

'Dartun!' Verain called, and instinctively rushed towards him before remembering what he had just done. She paused, waiting for his reaction to define the following engagement.

Dartun brushed himself down and limped around to face her. His face was bizarrely pale, even in this light, and his clothing was almost non-existent.

'The moon,' he declared, 'is not a moon.'

'What the fuck?' Tuung called out. The others had stirred from their rest now, and sluggishly moved to Tuung's side. Verain was between her order and Dartun, uncertain which way to go.

'What do you mean?' she said.

'One of the moons,' Dartun replied, as if nothing had happened. As if he had not just slaughtered dozens of people. As if he had not just flown around the sky like a human comet.

'What about it?'

'It isn't a moon!' he replied again, exasperated. 'It's an immense city. Or rather, it was an immense city – however long ago.'

'You aren't telling us you've just come back from there?' Verain enquired in disbelief.

'I am,' he said, watching them now with great sorrow.

'Why did you go up there?'

'Because it is in my nature, Verain. You of all people must know my tendencies to push the boundaries of knowledge. I . . . I could not help myself. I found these new abilities and, perhaps selfishly, I simply flew higher, and higher, until all I could see was the moon. I'm sorry I abandoned you.'

'Never mind that,' Tuung spluttered, 'what the hell was up there?'

Verain glared at him.

A groan of wind passed through, and in the following silence Dartun continued. 'It was one long, sprawling city. Metallic street after metallic street, all abandoned to time. There were immense numbers of dwellings, small units, large units, all of an equal mass. There were burn marks . . . charred elements, blackened zones around the edges of structures, as if a fire had engulfed the place.'

'How big was it?' Tuung asked excitedly, and for a moment Verain thought they could just forget everything, just blank out what had happened, and return to their old state of happy exploration of sciences and the unknown.

'A thousand metal Villjamurs, all bleeding into one another,' Dartun replied. 'It was not a moon, most definitely not. Whatever it is, it was designed by no civilization that I know of. The closest I had seen was the architecture of the Máthema, but it wasn't quite right. It is artificial. There were substances I've never seen, fabrics I cannot even begin to comprehend. With the aid of my transformation, I stood on the highest level of their tallest structure and stared out. All I saw was lane after lane, road after road, spiralling around each other with precise symmetry. There were lattices, grids of sunken metal streets. It shimmered so greatly that, as I flew invigorated across the crest of our world, the detail caught my eye. It reflected the light of the sun as strongly as the other moon, which seems quite real, and did not possess the appearance of streets or cities.'

Tuung was evidently in awe. 'What do you think it was built for?'

Verain was on the verge of breaking down. *This is what we'll do then. We'll ignore his brutality. We'll ignore that he just slaughtered a crowd of innocent people. We're tired and need to return home. That's fine with me.*

'I do not know,' Dartun replied. 'Perhaps our cultures sought out to live among the stars. The project did not, it seems, end well.'

And neither will ours, Verain thought.

THIRTY

Lan followed the priest for what seemed like miles. Would there be no end to these passageways? Feeling raw and vulnerable, she was at first reluctant to leave Fulcrom's side, but he persuaded her that this mission with Ulryk was the lesser of the evils available.

A good night's sleep had left her with stiff legs and aching muscles, but despite this she felt reasonably fit again. Part of her wanted to go out and find the people who caused her pain, but she had her instructions, and trusted Fulcrom's intentions.

'Ulryk,' she said, after what must have been an hour, 'where are we?'

He articulated his detailed explanations, most of which she didn't understand, and she felt he might be trying to bore away her curiosity.

Several times on the route down, the priest stopped to assess a blocked doorway, whereupon he would chant in an esoteric language. She could not quite perceive what was happening, only that the blockage was no longer there.

Rooms trailed into a sequence of holes, which in turn led into an underground cavern. At this stage, they entered such complete darkness that she had no sense of where she was, what time had passed or how Ulryk could discern where they were going. Guided by his voice, she listened as, now and then, he softly informed her in some small detail of where they were, but none of it had any context. More to the point, she couldn't see how she could help. She wanted to be doing something, anything, using her powers and skill and judgement, not shuffling her feet through the dark. But that was all she did, for hours.

Eventually, she watched in awe as the priest constructed a raft from stones by using only speech, and navigated them through the darkness.

Finally they approached the second city, the city under Villjamur, the city of the dead. From the exponential decay, it looked as if a disaster had struck, and the sky – if she could see it – was utterly black, with no stars or moon, nothing to denote there was anything but a void above them.

Ulryk explained to her the logistics of the place, who the people were, and what he had discovered so far.

'How long have you spent down here?' she asked him, as they walked along the crumbling streets. Shutters and doors opened as they passed, though she could see no figures beyond.

'Time is different in this location, though I estimate it has been several days' worth of work.'

'And you've found nothing?'

Ulryk shook his head and sighed. 'I have been searching for something that may or may not be called the "House of the Dead", for that is how Frater Mercury referred to it. I once assumed this whole world was what he implied, but I have my suspicions that there are buildings down here that defy time and imagination.'

She could see, for the very first time, the exhaustion in his expression and the wariness in his eyes.

The dead were friendly enough, merely curious to see someone from the realm of the living. At first she was afraid to go anywhere near them, but she could see they meant no harm. The initial cluster of civilians faded to just a couple of Ulryk's helpers.

They passed a plaza, where the dead roamed the streets in vague exploratory arcs. Whispers echoed towards her from all directions, as if the citizens were talking about them, but she couldn't see them looking their way. They just went about their business – whatever business there was down here.

A young, attractive woman – with a remarkably similar appearance to Lan, though her face and hair were alarmingly pale and she had neck wounds marring her throat – wandered over to them with a determined look in her eye. 'Priest,' she called.

Ulryk turned to face her and listened earnestly to what she had to say. In a hushed, formal voice, she continued, 'I've heard of your quest. You're a friend of the investigator, Fulcrom, aren't you?'

Ulryk's face lit up, and Lan couldn't help but be charmed by his determination. 'Please, continue.'

'You said "House of the Dead" right? We suspect it could be a region that we ourselves can't get to. It is dead to us, as we are to it. That's what they say, but I wonder if it's some way out of here for us, too.'

'We may have found what we are looking for. What is your name, young lady?' Ulryk asked.

'Adena.'

'Well, Adena, can you show us the way?'

*

After acquiring two torches, they passed along a huge, labyrinthine path that cut between rock faces. Lan noticed how, on the journey, the young woman barely acknowledged her, discussing the route and making eye contact with Ulryk only. She was so similar to Lan that it made her uneasy.

It could have been the better part of an hour before they arrived at the front of a temple. Half of it was constructed from brick, and the other half from the rock. It had a vast classical facade, with pillars hacked into a towering cliff and, set directly ahead at the top of a broad stone stairway, a simple square doorway, framed by pillars.

Adena paused at the bottom of the stairs, either unable or unwilling to go further.

Lan and Ulryk climbed the steps, waved their torches over the fine detail, examining the intricate stone carvings. If there was anywhere that *should* be the House of the Dead, this would be it: skulls and complete skeletons could be seen breaching the surface of the stone, as if bones were somehow imprisoned within geological structures. As they were the same colour as the rock, it was difficult to tell if they were stone or real.

Lan turned, casting light on the backs of the pillars, and jumped back: she was face to face with an angled skull, its mouth open, cobwebs covering its eyeholes.

'Weird building,' Lan said. 'Do you want me to go first?'

She pushed aside the notion of the skeletons here – they could have represented anything, a ritual, a sacrifice. It did not mean she herself would be joining them.

Ulryk nodded and motioned for her to continue forward, but looked back as their guide called to them from the bottom of the stairs.

'We ghosts have no knowledge of this place that can help you. I've seen kin go in there, never to return. This temple is part of the old city. No one knows anything about it. I'd . . . like to see more, though. It may bring me peace. May I come with you?'

'Of course,' Lan said, but Adena did not want to notice her.

'May I?' the girl asked again.

'Yes, please,' Ulryk replied.

'Come on, Ulryk,' Lan said. 'I want to get back home. Let's see if this book of yours is in here.'

Lan entered the doorway . . .

. . . and found herself in a woodland glade. *What?*

A moment later, Ulryk stumbled alongside her, followed by Adena, who seemed to possess more clarity now.

It was night, wherever they were, and thick trunks of trees extended as far as she could see. She could hear the sound of running water in the distance. All around the glade were rocks – no, remains of buildings – smothered with moss. Their torchlight caught the edges of beautiful heart-shaped leaves, and smooth trunks.

She turned round to see where they had come from, and the doorway was still there, without a frame, simply a presence in the air.

'Where the hell are we?' she whispered. 'What is this place?'

Ulryk seemed delighted for some reason. 'It . . . it looks precisely like a series of woodcuts I have observed in a primitive Jorsalir text. And also . . .' He removed his copy of *The Book of Transformations* from his satchel and opened it to one of the pages. The drawings were crude, but one page showed a location undeniably similar to the one they were in.

'A paradise,' he mentioned, 'of sorts.'

Lan scanned the page. 'So we're probably in the right place. But this book you're looking for, it could be anywhere here. Does it say in your copy where the other might be?'

Ulryk shook his head and closed the book with a snap. 'No, but I suggest we follow the river first, then we may have a clearer understanding.'

With the book tucked under Ulryk's arm, they continued through thick grass towards the heady smell of the river, and soon located it, a column of slow-flowing water, which was around twenty paces wide. Further along the bank, strange lights were floating out of the vegetation before sinking back into the undergrowth. She wasn't entirely sure, but there seemed to be other people watching them: pairs of eyes glittered from the other bank, fading in and out of her sight.

'This place doesn't seem like a paradise,' Lan whispered. She tuned into her powers then, just to make sure she could tap them – and sure enough, whatever worked in Villjamur and the ghost city worked down here, too.

The girl, Adena, moved out towards the edge of the river and began to walk slowly down the bank, hitching her ragged dress above her knee while she descended into the water. She seemed to be cautious at first and then, when her feet were submerged, she looked up with a smile on her face.

'I think . . . I think I can be free now. This is where the others must have come.' Suddenly she glared at Lan – acknowledging her fully this time. 'You'd better look after him,' Adena said.

'Who?' Lan replied.

Adena turned away and plunged face-first into the water without a sound.

'Ulryk, shouldn't we help her?' Lan asked, moving to the edge of the bank.

The priest scanned up and down the river, but there was no sign of the girl. 'It seems there is no one left to assist. And I'm not entirely certain that this is water.'

Lan remained utterly confused. Could ghosts die or pass on elsewhere?

*

Lan and Ulryk continued along what certainly looked like running water for some time, heading towards its source, Lan constantly searching for visual markers to help them on the return journey. She did not want to be abandoned here, wherever it was.

'This is useless, Ulryk,' Lan muttered more than once.

In the dark canopy, she heard something rattling, shifting between the leaves. Vines began trailing down, slithering towards her. Skipping from side to side, out of their grasp, she urged Ulryk onwards. And eventually they reached another clearing, this one glowing as if moonlit, but she couldn't see any of the moons in the sky. There was a macabre ambience to the place. Grass had been flattened in various directions, and in the centre of this wide clearing lay an object.

A book, in fact.

With his torch in one hand, Ulryk rushed forward to see if it was the other copy of *The Book of Transformations*, but beneath the surface of the grass something began to move, knocking Ulryk backwards. His torch fell to the grass, inert.

Lan dashed towards the priest and helped him to his feet; and, at the periphery of her vision, she saw movement coming from behind the trunks. Creatures began unfolding themselves from behind the trees, gleaming in the dull light, and bulbous things began bulging from beneath the surface of the bark. Not a sound was made as the strange wood constructs began presenting themselves, malicious-looking entities with serrated branches and blades, no two the same.

These things lunged towards them.

Lan could feel Ulryk shivering with fear beside her. 'Use one of your fucking spells,' she said, tuning into her powers and beginning to tread air as quickly as she could. She traversed the gaps between the tree-things, and on impact, she drove her heels down into the branches, snapping them, drawing their attention away from the priest.

Eventually the monotone of Ulryk's chanting became loud.

The tree creatures began combusting, flames taking to the wood and leaves with brutal effect. Lan dropped back to where Ulryk stood chanting and forced a barrier around them both where the flames could not reach. Kneeling, she watched branches tumble to the forest floor, withering and crackling with heat, an alien wail rising from within – and from here it was obvious the woodland wasn't quite real. The flames emitted a slight purple tinge; there were sparks spitting outwards, too.

A few moments later, once the flames had burned down, she released the forces surrounding them.

Foliage still smouldered, and Ulryk was panting.

'Are you OK?' she asked.

'I have', Ulryk observed, 'felt better, but thank you.' He was still shaking, and there was a burn mark across his robes.

'There's no logic to any of this,' Lan said. 'It doesn't seem real. The weather doesn't seem to exist, the forest seems to act abnormally. I could be in a dream for all I know.'

'The same could be said for the world above.'

'Don't get meta with me. So, do you want your book then?' Lan gestured to the tome that lay in the grass, untouched and unharmed.

Ulryk stood with a steady dignity and began hobbling towards the book. Something, though, didn't seem right: half of the sky was black, half of it a distorted grey, and the forest canopy seemed to be ... irregular. Instead of the natural curves and edges to the trees and leaves, things were comprised of hundreds of little squares, an abnormal, mosaic forest.

As soon as Ulryk lifted the book from the grass the world fell apart – quite literally. The squares multiplied, sweeping across the forest with a rush of wind, changing from dark browns and greens to the colour of rock, the images distorting.

They found themselves inside a large stone chamber: it had all happened so suddenly.

Ulryk turned around, gasping. He fumbled until the two books he was carrying were safely in his satchel, and then he hurriedly pointed to the hundreds of equations etched deep into the walls, whereupon he began to mouth things in a language she couldn't quite recognize.

Confused, she turned her attention elsewhere. There was a

square doorway, but nothing within the room itself, save for the numbers and letters and lines. Lan moved to the door and poked her head out, confirming that they were in the temple surrounded by skulls.

'OK . . .' Lan said, then back inside to Ulryk. 'Hey, what the hell just happened?'

'It was an artificial reality,' Ulryk marvelled. 'The lines on the wall, they're a language that I've only seen in a few texts. If you look carefully, there are thousands of minute mirrors constructed within the brick. We passed through an artificial reality! You were quite right, Lan – it was a dream, more or less, but one created by Frater Mercury – who must have used his technology to store the book in a safe place.'

'Why?'

'So only those who deciphered his code could understand where he had hidden it? So it left a connection to him, but one almost impossible to find.'

'What happened to the ghost, Adena, if it wasn't real?'

'I'm here,' a voice said.

The priest moved around the room trying to locate where the voice came from. 'Adena?' he said. 'Speak again.'

'I'm in the mirrors this side now. Look closer.'

Faintly, in a cluster of the small mirrors, a shape took form, broken up by the stonework behind, and it began to resemble the girl who had guided them here.

'So many mysteries,' the priest muttered. 'So little time.'

'I'm fine now,' the ghost said. 'There's more, so much more on this side . . .' And with that, the form faded, leaving the room in utter calm.

'So now what?' Lan asked.

'I need to return to the surface, reflect upon the texts and compare them, then I must conduct the rituals.' Ulryk paused for a moment, as if the weight of expectation dawned on him. 'Then I suppose I must see about bringing Frater Mercury into our world. I am ashamed to admit that I have not thought much about the realities of this: merely finding the other book. For years I thought it did not exist. And now . . .'

'Let's get back,' Lan said. 'There's plenty of time for speculation later.'

PEOPLE'S OBSERVER

The Secret History of the Villjamur Knights

The famed heroes of the city of Villjamur are frauds. They are not what you think they are. They are weapons of the elite, trying to suppress the poor. Would you let these people protect your city?

Here be secrets:

The one called Lan – the female of the group – used to be a man! Cultists have turned her body from a man to a woman by using the evils of relic technology. Would you let your children roam the streets with such a monster claiming to be their protector? This is not right!

The one called Tane – he is famous for having huge amounts of wealth. Tane is the son of Lord Chattel, who owned the most vicious slave business in the Archipelago. Slavery, though frowned upon in this city, still goes on in the corners of the Empire, and Tane is an inheritor of a vast fortune. More! He has earned much of his wealth in his own lifetime. He is a man who trades in death and

yet parades about the streets as if he has the moral upper hand. This is not right!

The one called Vuldon is no stranger to these streets: he is the Legend, the so-called hero from our city's past. Those with long memories will remember the Legend as being responsible for a tragedy whereby many children were killed. He escaped into hiding, but deems himself now suitable to return to this city. A child-killer is loose and unpunished. This is not right! Would you let this brute see to the safety of your child?

Documents signed by cultists associated closely with the sinister Knights will be produced as proof in the next issue. People of the city, you have been fooled. These people are monsters. Do not let them get away with this. Reject them. We call for them to be harassed from the streets for the safety of ourselves and our children. Do not let these perverts and abusers roam free.

THIRTY-ONE

Fulcrom found the article in the afternoon, as it fluttered about the streets, and he picked it up only because he'd seen more than a few citizens eagerly reading their own copies.

Time stood still; even the snow seemed to linger hesitantly. He could feel his pulse quicken as the words filtered through his mind. Things connected there. He realized that the anarchists would have used the printing press stolen from the Inquisition to make this and that somewhere along the way, someone had betrayed them. But these were his final thoughts – his first concerns were for Lan.

Immediately he stormed back to the clifftop hideaway to find the other Knights, but they were out, and Lan was, of course, still with Ulryk. Fulcrom fumed and stomped about the complex, shouting at whoever was around. He ordered every available cultist and staff member into a brick-ceilinged antechamber, whereupon he held up the faked copy of *People's Observer*, and read it aloud.

That was when Feror broke down in tears; all eyes turned towards him.

Fulcrom moved over to the cultist, and dragged him by his collar into the Knights' quarters. He slammed him up against the cold stone wall. 'Talk,' he snarled into his face.

Feror slid down the wall, drew his knees to his chest and began to sob.

'You have one minute to tell me why I shouldn't kill you!' Fulcrom shouted.

Feror was merely the sum of his emotions then, nothing more, nothing less. 'They . . . they made me.'

'You know,' Fulcrom said, 'we hear that excuse all the time. *They made me*. Who the fuck *made you*, and what did they make you do?'

'They took my family – my *daughters*, they've got them hostage. Still have. What was I to do? It was my family, investigator . . . Y-you understand, don't you?'

'You should have come to us *first*. We could have helped. We're the fucking Inquisition, if you hadn't noticed.'

'They said they would kill them in an instant,' Feror blubbered, 'if I so much as breathed a word about it to the Inquisition. They just wanted background information. I didn't see it as a big issue, just a little information.'

'Have you seen *People's Observer*? This forged rag that has now spread about the city like a plague?'

Feror nodded, and he closed his eyes with more tears streaming down his face.

'There's your big fucking issue. The effectiveness of the Knights depends upon the population's favour now. I've no idea how they'll react, but I'm guessing it won't be kind – especially to Lan. They'll probably want to lynch her.'

'I know,' Feror sobbed. 'I know.'

Fulcrom stared at him for a while longer, and kicked at Feror's legs to release some aggression. 'What do you know of the anarchists' organization? I want addresses. I want names. Otherwise I'll hand you over to the Emperor's *special* forces and let them deal with you.'

The distraught cultist revealed only a handful of facts. He didn't know any leaders, had never even seen Shalev. The anarchists – such as they were – operated in splinter cells, virtually independent of each other, united only in their hatred of the rest of the city.

Feror had seen his family one member at a time in the top floor of a backstreet tavern, and only for a few minutes at the most, enough to ensure his loyalty to them. He'd pleaded for their return but they refused until they'd bled him dry of information.

'Are they still with the anarchists?' Fulcrom demanded.

Feror nodded.

Fulcrom's rage ebbed, and mental clarity returned to him. Could he have acted any differently than the old cultist who was protecting his family? What if they'd taken Lan? Fulcrom hauled him to his feet and stood toe-to-toe with the man.

'We'll get them back for you.'

'How?' Feror's eyes brimmed with hope.

'We'll use the Knights while we still can.' *Wherever the hell they are.* 'Presumably you had a contact, someone to go to when you found something useful?'

'A landlord at the tavern. I'd go to him and he'd send word. We'd meet in his upper room.'

*

Tane and Vuldon returned to their quarters, finding Fulcrom and Feror sat across a table from each other, in a contemplative silence.

'Which fucker told?' Vuldon demanded.

Cautiously, Fulcrom explained what Feror had done while the old man stared at the table, not daring to meet their eyes while his guilt was aired. Neither of the Knights made a move to threaten the man, which either showed how much they'd grown into their role, or revealed how stunned they were.

'Now what?' Vuldon asked.

'We go to get his family back for him,' Fulcrom replied.

'Are you fucking kidding me?'

'Vuldon, we get his family back. You of all people know how important his children are to him.' He wished he didn't have to mention that fact, but it seemed to hit Vuldon where required.

'Where's Lan?' Tane enquired, padding around to Fulcrom's side.

'Still with Ulryk.'

'I suspect it's easier for the old girl to keep away for now.'

'You don't hate her?' Fulcrom asked. 'You didn't know her history.'

'Oh, we knew everything, old boy,' Tane replied with a wink, much to Fulcrom's surprise. 'These cultists yap like hounds to please us Knights. Who knows, the amount of information I took from those show-offs, I might have made a decent Inquisition aide after all.'

'And it never bothered you?'

Tane shrugged.

Fulcrom glanced to Vuldon, waiting for his response. 'I know what it's like to be judged,' Vuldon grunted. 'She proved herself. Only thing that matters is a job well done.'

'Whether or not the people of the city think that's what matters is something else entirely,' Fulcrom said.

'No good crying over spilt milk,' Vuldon declared. 'Action's better than us sitting here wondering what they think of us.'

'What,' Tane said, 'we're just going to ignore any of this happened?'

'I'd say so.'

'But we're nothing more than the Emperor's tools for propaganda and now that opportunity has gone.'

'No,' Vuldon snarled. 'Well, yes, that's true, but what else d'you expect from politicians? We've also done fuck-loads for this city, saved dozens of lives and halted just as many crimes, and I'm not giving up because of this. I'll only stop when I'm dragged away – you can bury me in this outfit.' Vuldon pulled at his shirt before turning to Fulcrom, who felt a spark of pride. 'So,' Vuldon continued, 'do we get this joker's family back or sit here like idiots?' Vuldon tilted his chin to indicate the cultist, who was silent but wide-eyed.

'We get his family,' Fulcrom replied.

*

They headed into the caves undercover, an hour after Feror had gone ahead with his request to deliver information. He had given them an address across the road and been told to wait. It was a run-down shell of a room that overlooked the street alongside the Dryad Tavern, a three-floor joint deep in the new territory of Underground North. It was night, and the glass that lined the roof of the enormous cavern cast no light in the darkness. The street was empty and something didn't quite sit right with Fulcrom: there was an absence of activity. With a couple of hundred thousand people within this cavern, he expected to see some of them.

According to the cultist, Feror was always taken to the top floor of the Dryad Tavern by hooded Cavesiders, where he would then reveal any information about the Knights: their movements, their general status – and, of course, their pasts.

'How do you feel,' Fulcrom asked the two Knights, 'about the anarchists hijacking the *People's Observer*?'

Tane wore a pained and tired expression. 'It wasn't fully correct, not that the people would really care. I don't have any dealings with my father's business. I frittered away all the money deliberately, because of where it came from, and I . . . Oh what's the point?'

Vuldon mumbled, 'I suppose in this case, the *People's Observer* is generally closer to the true facts than the shit the Emperor's been hawking around.'

'Are you fit to put this aside and carry on?' Fulcrom asked.

'If you think the public will be fine with us,' Tane said. 'Let's face it, most of what we were about was image and now look at it.'

'Then maybe we can replace that with some substance,' Fulcrom replied.

After that brief exchange, they focused on the window opposite, waiting for evidence of life on the top floor. Finally lanterns were lit and figures stirred on the inside, three or four of them.

'Time to go,' Fulcrom declared. 'Tane, search the side rooms. It's unlikely they'll show him his family at first, but they'll be nearby.'

Back into the streets. Tane followed the route up over fences and along the rear of the adjacent building, searching for a high entry point, while Fulcrom and Vuldon took the more difficult and obvious route of heading through the tavern.

The spit and sawdust joint was quiet inside, maybe five customers staring into their drinks at the bar in a fug of weed smoke, while the man behind it – a thuggish-looking brute dressed more like a bounty hunter, with close-cropped hair and earrings – tried to stop them from reaching a doorway leading upstairs.

'Out of bounds, lads,' he warned, jumping over the bar with a surprising athleticism.

He made a move to grab Fulcrom, but Vuldon intercepted him, grabbing the man's fist in his own and punching his jaw, snapping his head back to one side. The man didn't make a sound as Vuldon, with a pugnacious rage, jumped up and kicked him in the chest with so much force that the man flew backwards and smashed into the bar. Only a couple of the drinkers peered up from their pints to observe the racket.

Fulcrom and Vuldon headed up the stairs with stealth until they were on the top floor. Around the rim of one door, at the end of the corridor, Fulcrom could see light leaking from the room and, as they approached silently, voices beyond became prominent. One of the speakers was Feror.

'Go,' he whispered to Vuldon.

The Knight took a few steps back, then charged forward, aiming his shoulder at the door. It exploded open, revealing Feror at a table, surrounded by two men and a woman in dreary-coloured tunics, and who each instantly drew their swords.

'I got 'em,' Vuldon announced.

Fulcrom ran over to Feror and pulled him out of the ensuing ruckus.

'Any idea where your family might be?' Fulcrom asked, as Vuldon did something that caused one of the men to shriek in pain. Fulcrom didn't wish to see what he was doing.

Feror, with a petrified look about him, could only shrug. 'They must keep them nearby. They only let me see one of them at a time.'

They tried a couple of the other doors until they found a sparsely furnished room occupied by two young girls and a middle-aged woman. On closer inspection, Tane was at the far end of the room by the window, with his arm hanging out of it.

'Go on,' Fulcrom encouraged. Feror peered around cautiously before hurtling towards his family and pulling his daughters to him. They collapsed together on the floor in tears of relief.

Fulcrom permitted them a brief period of privacy.

'What've you got there?' Fulcrom asked, walking over to Tane.

'Take a look, old boy,' Tane replied.

Out of the cheap glass window, Tane was dangling one of the hostage-takers by his collar, and pressing one claw against the back of his neck. The man's feet kept kicking the side of the building in fear – it must have been at least a thirty-foot drop below.

'I'm debating whether or not to let go,' Tane declared cheerily, and loud enough so that the man would hear. 'Any thoughts?'

The man outside whimpered.

'We might get some answers out of this one,' Fulcrom suggested. 'I'm guessing Vuldon might not have been so kind to the others.'

As if rehearsed, Vuldon's stomped into the doorway, a single fleck of blood on his cheek. 'All done,' he grunted.

'Did you leave any alive?' Fulcrom asked.

'You didn't say to,' he replied. 'Sorry.'

*

Feror and his family were returning with the Knights to the clifftop hideaway, in case the anarchists returned for revenge. The group started the return journey with their captive in tow, choosing more obscure routes to avoid detection. Fulcrom was aware that, as more time passed by, the scandal in the faked issue of *People's Observer* would be having a greater influence on the people of Villjamur. Vuldon lugged their prisoner in a large hessian sack, deliberately dragging him along the cobbled roads, and doing his best to be as careless as he could.

They entered a small stone courtyard on the third level, and came across a religious ritual, with a priest of Bohr blessing a small crowd rammed between the high buildings, in front of his church.

'Hey, stop!' someone shouted at the rear of the gathering, peeling off to block their route. It was a man in his thirties with a thick leather tunic, stout boots and grey cloak. 'Aren't you lot the Knights?'

Fulcrom raised his Inquisition medallion, which glinted in the firelight. 'Sele of Urtica, citizen. I'm afraid we're in a hurry.'

'It is – I recognize that one's cat face,' the man gestured towards Tane.

More people at the rear of the audience drifted nearer, surrounding them. Fulcrom turned to Feror and whispered, 'You know the way. Get your family back.'

'What about the others there – the cultists?' Feror asked. 'Will they lynch me for my betrayal?'

'I'd revealed what had happened and said you weren't to blame. You'll just have to hope for the best in human nature.'

'But—'

'Just go!' Fulcrom snapped, and the cultist guided his family away.

Fulcrom turned back to see that the crowd were now in their faces. Tane was stepping away, but Vuldon stood his ground. They were shouting things at him now. Someone held up a copy of *People's Observer*, demanding to know why it had been kept a secret.

A young woman in a shawl asked Tane, 'Is it true?'

Lie, damn you, Fulcrom thought.

'Yes.'

'Tane – you don't have to tell them that.'

'It's been hanging over me for ages. I'd wager it's better out in the open.'

You don't know what people are like. They're not interested in the truth, just being told what they want to hear.

There must have been thirty or forty in the mass, crowding just the three of them. They started to shout things at Tane: about his deception, blaming him personally for his parents' role in slavery, saying he had no right to be here. Tane kept trying to talk his way out of it, to justify himself, but it was no good – there was no way he could be heard against their chorus of accusations.

And to Vuldon, who was still holding the captive in a sack, they simply spat at him and cursed him, blaming him for being a child-killer, saying he wasn't fit to do his job, that he should just clear out.

Fulcrom watched the man-mountain stand there silently, not moving, barely responding – his vision had fixed onto some point above them, as he chose to ignore the torrent of abuse.

Or at least that's what Fulcrom thought. Suddenly Vuldon screamed – an immense, bass roar – and everyone was stunned by his eruption. As people stared dumbly at him, Vuldon pushed through the crowd, knocking several of them to the ground and a woman cried out as her head hit the ground.

Oh shit. Fulcrom followed the gap Vuldon had created in the throng, steering Tane along with him. He kept apologizing to the citizens on his way through, palming the air, keeping his head low.

They found a quiet area in one of the many quarters of the city currently in development. They huddled under a massive viaduct surrounded by scaffolding. Overhead a horse and cart rattled across over the arches. City lights extended into the distance.

Vuldon dumped the sack containing their captive, who squirmed within, pleading to be let out. Vuldon kicked him until he fell silent.

'Now what, investigator?' Vuldon asked.

'Do you have control of yourself now?' Fulcrom demanded.

For a moment Vuldon strolled along the edge of the work area, his feet crunching grit into the stone. 'It just got to me.'

'You're not to take it out on the people, Vuldon. We're all just grown children, especially in crowds, and sometimes people act on emotions, without much thought.'

'I know. I know.'

'Tane, how are you feeling?' Fulcrom enquired of the unusually silent werecat.

Tane sighed, crouching and rubbing his face. 'I had hoped to keep it all hidden just a tad longer.'

'Yes, well, this changes everything now,' Fulcrom said.

'How do you mean?' Tane asked.

'The Knights are only effective with public support. You were created for that very reason – to assist the populace, to reduce crime, but most of all to give them something to believe in. A symbol.'

'Propaganda,' Vuldon grunted.

'Of a kind,' Fulcrom admitted. 'But at least you were out there helping people feel safe, and you were recognized for that.' *Which is more than I've ever been.*

'So what now?' Tane asked with a look of expectation on his face.

'We get this guy back to the Inquisition headquarters, and we'll question him there. Meanwhile, I suppose I should really see if I can meet with your employer tomorrow.'

*

Fulcrom didn't sleep well that night, worrying about Lan, if she was all right in the underworld, and struggling with how to explain the recent developments to the Emperor.

Fulcrom had put in a request to see Urtica and, unsurprisingly, the Emperor wanted to see him anyway regarding the publication of the Imperial newspamphlet. After addressing minor administration, and avoiding conversations with the other investigators as best he could, he made his way to see the Emperor.

Level after level, the streets were becoming deeper with snow, as if the cultists couldn't keep up. Morning traders were fewer each day, and the irens were hollow experiences now. There was less to sell, but there were increasing numbers of bric-a-brac stalls, or more innovative traders who restyled the waste and accoutrements of the city into more appealing delights: swords melted down into cutlery or metal and glass sculptures.

His mare took her time, the poor thing, trudging up the hazardous cobbled roads, the cold air whistling around them both. He left her at a guard station on the fifth level, where only registered horses were permitted – which was news to him, but he wasn't going to argue with the military. At each guard station, at least three men searched him thoroughly,

367

despite his Inquisition medallion. They asked him questions and were sceptical even when he showed the papers for his appointment.

'This level of security is ridiculous,' he said to one of the guards.

'Sorry, chap – captain's orders. Every few days we add to the list of questions. Just the way of things.'

Fulcrom eventually plodded on by foot, up the gently sloped road that led to Balmacara, wary of what he would say to the Emperor.

*

The Emperor peered back at Fulcrom as he finished his explanation of what had happened: of the printing press being stolen from the Inquisition headquarters, of being betrayed by Feror, whose family had been taken as hostages. Fulcrom could see in his eyes that he was a tired man – redness and dark rings around his eyes indicated a lack of sleep, his bitten nails seemed to suggest it might be down to stress. What's more, Fulcrom could smell the musky odour of arum weed on the man, and his breath stank of some disgusting alcoholic beverage.

If Urtica was using substances, Fulcrom expected some backlash, an outburst perhaps, and given what Fulcrom had seen himself of the Emperor's decision-making – for instance, the attempted slaughter of refugees – there was no one in this city Fulcrom feared more. But the Emperor merely acknowledged his acceptance of what Fulcrom was telling him, now and then gazing out of the vast, diamond-shaped window across the spires of the city.

'But,' Fulcrom continued, 'we have captured a member we're sure is close to the key figures of the movement in the caves, and I hope to have the names of those involved very soon.'

'Yes . . .' Urtica muttered.

Fulcrom paused and looked nervously at the man sat across

from him. 'My Emperor – forgive my asking, but is everything all right?'

'I have', he sighed, 'been better.' Then he slid his chair back, which was no small effort for him, and from a drawer to one side he retrieved a map and a handful of pebbles. As he unfolded it before Fulcrom, the Boreal Archipelago, creased and under a grid, was presented.

'We have reports from garudas,' Urtica started, 'of the war in Villiren, and of the invasion force attacking from Tineag'l. This is common knowledge.' Urtica placed a pebble in the island of Y'iren, where Villiren stood.

'Is the combat going well? I see the occasional article in *People's Observer* . . .'

'That news outlet aside, I believe we are on course for victory,' the Emperor replied, with a momentary glimpse of enthusiasm. 'Now, however, there have been reports of incidents here, here and here.'

He placed a pebble in three locations, on various islands, each one closer to Jokull. It was only then that Fulcrom realized the Emperor's hands were shaking.

'Incidents, my Emperor?'

'Massacres, of varying degrees. The first was the remnants of the Order of the Dawnir.'

'The Dawnir?' Fulcrom asked, surprised. 'Does that include the famous Papus?'

'Indeed. She had been dispatched to track down a rogue cultist. It was a minor affair, and between us both, ridding this city of two major cultists was no bad thing.'

Sly, Fulcrom thought. *Thus allowing you more influence over the rest of them* . . . 'How was such a . . . legendary order wiped out?'

'Probably a clash between her order and another. The other incidents are more concerning. All of them indicate something is heading right towards our island. Possibly to Villjamur itself.'

'Is it related to the war in Villiren?'

The Emperor shook his head. 'None of us are certain what it is, but there has been violence in several towns. What few eye witnesses are still alive have suggested that magic has been used.'

'Cultists, then,' Fulcrom suggested. He couldn't hide the allure of this mystery.

'Whoever it is,' Urtica concluded, 'they are heading on a path here.'

'And this causes you concern?'

'Nearly a thousand people have died at the hands of this . . . this thing, this cultist. Do you have any idea what such a presence could mean for this city?'

And that's why you're not that concerned about the Knights being exposed, Fulcrom thought. 'My Emperor, I wonder if the Knights would be in a position to offer some resistance to this threat.'

'The Knights . . . but aren't the people turning against them?'

'We've had just one minor incident, but it's too early to tell.'

'I've had nearly a hundred of the most influential citizens in the city register their disgust at the Knights.'

'They can't help their own pasts, my Emperor. Part of why they were chosen was because of those pasts. This is the reason they were created.'

'They were created to protect the citizens of the city, investigator, no more, no less. Their secrets were their security to us. If the people fear them for being monsters of whatever kind, then they are of no practical value. Feror, of course, we will execute for his betrayal.'

'But his family—'

'We must stay strong, investigator, until the very end. Feror will be used as a warning to others, and a symbol to the anarchists that we will not tolerate their ways.'

Fulcrom clenched his fists behind his back, and allowed the Emperor to continue. 'My Emperor, I'm pleading with you, don't—'

'Don't plead, investigator, not in my company. It isn't decent.' Urtica leaned forward and ran his hands through his hair. 'Given that their secrets are out, especially Lan's, it makes us all look like fools – particularly me. Is something wrong, investigator?'

'No, my Emperor. However, whatever you believe Lan was before, she is now a committed member of the Villjamur Knights. I have a wonderful record that I can write up for you on the way she's served the city.' Fulcrom could feel his mouth becoming dry.

'That may well be, investigator, but given the crises faced by this city, the people need to look up to the Knights. They've certainly cost me enough money. We can rebuild Tane's reputation, perhaps. Vuldon's too – a few articles in the *People's Observer* can do that – but Lan ... well, I have contemplated the issue in some depth and decided that it's just not natural, is it? Already I've been receiving messages from councillors and various moneylenders to the Treasury, as well as the senior officials from the Jorsalir church, all expressing their concerns about what Lan is. A little slavery is OK, it seems, but I won't gloss over her past. I rule strongly, investigator, but I need people on my side in times of a crisis.'

Fulcrom swallowed, felt hot. *Don't say anything that could get you executed.*

'Now,' Urtica continued, 'Lan is beyond salvation. Consider her decommissioned—'

A banging on the chamber door interrupted them. Disturbed, Urtica snapped: 'What is it?'

A senior military official poked his head around the door sheepishly, with his helm under one arm. 'My Emperor, I bring grave news.'

'Out with it,' Urtica ordered.

371

The officer stepped inside and took a stance as if he was on parade. 'Combat has broken out from the caves, my Emperor.'

'What kind of combat? Can't your lot deal with it?'

Fulcrom noted the concerned look on the soldier's face. 'We believe we will have the situation controlled within a couple of hours.'

'Hours? What the hell is going on?' Urtica demanded. Fulcrom felt lucky: the Emperor's tone with him had been remarkably mild. To this officer, it was filled with venom.

'It seems that a significant number of citizens have armed themselves with weapons. What's more, I suspect there're relics in use.'

'How many is *a significant* number?'

'About four thousand, give or take, my Emperor.'

Urtica sighed, and glanced down at the maps before him, his fingers slowly scrunching up the corner. He suddenly stood and walked over to the soldier. With the pathetic effort typical of someone not trained in combat, Urtica struck his face with the back of his hand. The soldier showed only surprise; he lowered his head and muttered his apologies for delivering the news to Urtica. A silence lingered.

'So, how many military personnel are there now?' Fulcrom enquired of the soldier. 'All ranks. Three thousand?'

'Two and a half,' he replied, cautiously eyeing the Emperor. 'Skilled fighters, mind – not like those Cavesiders.'

Fulcrom nodded. 'Sounds like it'll be in hand then.'

Urtica began to walk away, the tension began to drop, but before he sat down he snapped, 'I want a report every hour, on the hour, is that clear?'

'Yes, my Emperor, of course.'

'Get out.' Urtica sat down then peered at Fulcrom, more tired than before, more desperate. 'Return to your post, investigator, and await further instructions.'

Fulcrom stood, but dared the Emperor's wrath one more time. 'And Lan?'

'We'll decommission ... her. I'll send notice soon for her powers to be extracted.'

*

Fulcrom stomped back to his office, nearly starting fights at each guard station. He didn't have the time to deal with pedantic idiots any more.

Insane. That's what he was – an unhinged individual. How that man can lead this city – let alone an Empire – is beyond me.

How could the Emperor be such a fucking fool? Lan was immensely valuable to the city. She was – and had always been – a woman. It was as simple as that. Why should she have to suffer because of everyone else's small-mindedness?

After he arrived back at the Inquisition headquarters, settled back at his desk, he looked at the walls and desperately tried to form some kind of strategy.

Warkur opened the door then knocked on it gently.

'You got the stare, Fulcrom,' he said.

'Sir?'

'The stare. Seeking that distant place, wishing you were anywhere but where you are right now. Be fucked if I don't know that well enough myself. Can I sit?'

'Sure,' Fulcrom grunted, indicating the chair opposite his desk. He lit another lantern to brighten the room.

'What's eating you, Fulcrom?' Warkur asked with a thunderous sigh as he slumped in the chair.

Since when have you cared? Fulcrom thought. 'A few concerns.'

'How did it go with Urtica?'

Fulcrom explained the situation with the Knights, and his meeting with the Emperor, and his thoughts about how to move from here.

Warkur listened in unusual silence, offering no pearls of

wisdom, no sarcasm – not even when Fulcrom mentioned that the Emperor reeked of drugs. *Something's wrong with you as well*, Fulcrom thought.

'These, uh, Knights of yours,' Warkur started. 'So the Emperor is fine for Tane and Vuldon to continue as normal?'

'More or less, yeah.'

'And the other?'

'I'd rather not dwell on that, sir.'

'You see, that's a little tricky, Fulcrom. Some of the fellows in here have registered a complaint about your relationship with this Knight.'

'She has a name, sir. It's Lan.'

Warkur's face betrayed his discomfort. 'I, uh, yeah ... You're a good investigator, Fulcrom. One of the best lads here. You're young, what fifty-odd? You've got a big career ahead of you, well over a century of good investigative work. Don't piss that away because of some *woman*.'

Fulcrom stifled an incredulous laugh. 'Misogyny aside, sir, I take it that you have a problem with my relationship with Lan? Perhaps it's not so much my relationship – your problem lies with Lan herself.'

'Not me personally, you understand,' Warkur replied, breathing deeply.

'Then who?'

'It's ... well, the others say she's just not natural, and if I'm honest, there are some people here who have – there's no easy way to put this – raised speculation over your sexuality because of this. That this Lan figure is some kind of he–she, well – you know the laws of the city as well as I do, Fulcrom. You don't want to face the executioner on those city walls, so come on, have a think, yeah? It just can't be permitted if you want to stay in this role. Relationships, they come and go – trust me, I know about them.'

'With respect, sir, you know nothing about relationships,' Fulcrom replied, glaring at his senior officer.

'No, I guess I don't.' Warkur stood to leave, his mannerisms full of uncertainty. He inched towards the door. 'Fulcrom, don't be foolish – just think about it, yeah?'

'Let me get this clear: you're threatening me with dismissal, because of my relationship with Lan, and what you don't like about her is that she does not fit into your neat little view of the world?'

'It isn't like that, and you know it. It's about perception, it's about the law.'

'The law', Fulcrom growled, 'says nothing about a situation like this.'

'They're saying once you're a man, you're always a man no matter what cultists say. That means you'll be drawn into this. Get out of it while you can.'

'You're right – I'll get out of it,' Fulcrom said, sliding back his chair. He rummaged around his neck to unhook his medallion and sent it clattering across the floor by Warkur's feet.

'What're you doing, Fulcrom? Don't be a fool.'

Fulcrom gathered his cloak and bundled a few items in a satchel while Warkur assaulted him with trite reasons as to why he should reconsider this move.

'You'll regret it,' Warkur concluded.

'No,' Fulcrom replied. 'All I'll ever regret is working with people I no longer have faith in. It's been a pleasure, sir.'

Fulcrom offered his hand, but Warkur merely gave him another world-weary look. 'Fulcrom, you're our best investigator.'

'Will you get the others to reconsider their views? As my superior, will you help to find clarity in our legal system?'

'Those things can take years . . .'

'Will you?'

Warkur sighed and shook his head. 'The others, they've dug up old Jorsalir texts about the souls of men and women . . . I don't think it could ever happen.' He stared at the floor, and Fulcrom pushed past him, through the old, dusty hallway, past the offices of the other investigators and past the receptionist, Ghale, who was staring dreamily over her desk at some other rumel, and he headed right out of the door, past the guards and down the steps into the snow, where he wondered just what the hell he was going to do.

THIRTY-TWO

Tired and relieved, Lan strolled back with Ulryk out of the library, down the main steps and into the beautiful courtyard. It was daylight, though she didn't know which day it was, and the snow had just ceased, leaving a light dusting that had yet to be absorbed into the warmth of the buildings, be cleared by cultists or trodden into mush.

Ulryk hugged his books in his satchel while Lan was watchful, concerned for his protection. It wasn't long until someone called out to her, the words echoing around the stone. 'Hey, Lan! You're Lan, one of those Knights, right?'

'Yes!' she shouted back, trying to find the person speaking.

'You fucking freak, man–woman!' the voice called. 'We know about you now. We've seen the truth. You're *disgusting*.'

Like a bolt through the heart.

Her world ready to implode, Lan spun round to see three middle-aged men in thick coats, one of whom was shaking daggers from his sleeves.

'What the—?'

'I am assuming this recognition is not always a good thing?' Ulryk cautioned.

The three men moved closer, continuing with their obscenities. She began to shake. She could feel her heart beating at an incredible rate, suddenly bringing her to a state of alertness. She closed her eyes and blocked their words, then located her powers once again.

Opening her eyes at the sound of feet scuffing stone, she saw one of them – a heavily built man with long hair – run at her, a long blade in his hands. She lunged back and allowed him to fall forwards. The other two, skinnier, followed suit, attacking simultaneously. She side-stepped, air-stepped and stepped over them, their knives narrowly missing her feet.

'Get down, weird bitch,' one snarled.

'Man–woman!'

She landed hard, spun, and realized she had had quite enough of this. She ran at them – burst into an absurdly quick sprint – shouldered the thickset one and sent him tumbling over on the cobbles, cracking his head. The other two came at her then, viciously swiping this way and that. She grabbed one arm whilst shoving her boot in the other's stomach – and while he buckled over, muttering 'Certainly fights like a man', she broke the arm she was holding over her knee, sending his blade skittering across the ground.

Then a blow to the back of his knees sent him face-first into the stone.

The final assailant regarded her with such an expression of disgust she was taken aback. How could anyone look at her like that?

You're not a monster, she reminded herself. *People like him are.*

He tried one final attempt to lash out, but she jump-kicked him, sending him tripping over the bodies on the floor – not dead, but certainly out of action.

Ulryk stared at her in surprise, but never questioned her. 'Come on,' she said. 'We should find Fulcrom.'

And maybe I can find out just what the hell I've missed.

*

Lan entered the Inquisition headquarters but was blocked at the front desk. Guards asked her – politely but with caution – to wait.

The black-skinned rumel called Warkur headed out to meet

her, his face cracked with stress, his tail wafting about with agitation. She knew something was wrong when he tried to get her to step into his office.

'Is it Fulcrom?' she asked. 'Is he dead?'

Warkur laughed nervously, eyeing the priest, the guards behind, never seeming to look her in the eye. 'Nah, Fulcrom's not dead. But he's no longer part of the Inquisition.'

'What?' she asked. Ulryk's peaceful face could offer nothing.

'He quit.'

'Why?'

Warkur reached into his pocket and gave her a crumpled-up copy of the *People's Observer*, and thrust it at her. When she took it he put his hands in his pockets and waited for her reaction.

Lan read it and stood there shocked. More than once she opened her mouth as if to say something, but couldn't. There were bad things about Tane and Vuldon, too, but she couldn't help but think of her own problems the most. 'I . . . I—'

'You can't believe it,' Warkur said. 'I get it.'

'But why did Fulcrom quit?' she asked, wary now of the scene presenting itself: the presence of several investigators and aides, the bulky looking guards looming ever closer.

'That doesn't matter,' Warkur said. 'What matters is that you get yourself back to those cultists who gave you a bunch of powers you don't deserve.'

Her thoughts connected quickly: she was exposed and she was to be stripped of her position in the Knights, but Ulryk seemed a step ahead: he was chanting something, slowly, the words seeming to hang in the air. Suddenly the gathered throng on one side began to grip their ears as if hearing a deafening noise, and some began to scream.

Ulryk, still chanting, tugged at her sleeve and pulled her away and out of the building.

*

They found Fulcrom in his apartment, and when he opened the door Lan buried herself in his chest, almost in tears. He held her there for a moment, while Ulryk lingered without comment in the doorway.

'We went to the Inquisition but they said you quit,' she said, as he guided them into his home.

Fulcrom turned to Ulryk, eagerly asking, 'Did you get it – did you find the book?'

Ulryk patted his satchel.

'Good.'

Lan looked around the room. Everything was in boxes, his clothes, his personal items, and paintings were off their hooks. 'Were you planning on running?' Lan asked.

'Not exactly, no. I was going to put all this in storage,' he gestured around the room, 'but I have a suspicion I'll be a wanted man, so it's—'

'Why?'

'For not doing my job,' he replied. 'I take it you're aware I'm required to hand you in to the cultists?'

Lan signalled her understanding, trying not to reveal just how upset she was. 'Why did you quit?'

A pause, while he gazed into her eyes. 'I quit because I worked for a bunch of Neanderthals.'

'Will they come for us?' Lan asked.

'They will, but they have other concerns at the moment.'

'What concerns?' Ulryk enquired.

'The anarchists are leading an uprising.'

'Should we do something?' Lan asked.

'No,' Fulcrom replied.

She grasped his arm. 'But I want to help.'

'The Knights are over, Lan.' He held her gently by her wrists. 'I'm sorry. The anarchists have exposed everyone – but it seems the Emperor is still happy with Tane and Vuldon to continue with their duties . . . but he refuses to accept you.'

'Because . . . ?'

'Yes, because of that,' he whispered, low enough so Ulryk wouldn't hear.

'So what happens now?'

'Good question.'

'I'm not going to hand myself in to be "decommissioned" – whatever they mean by that,' Lan said. 'I don't want that. I like who I am now.'

'I know – I don't want it either.' Fulcrom sat down on the bed, Lan perched alongside him. Ulryk considered the view out of the window.

'And because of that,' Fulcrom continued, 'they'll want to arrest me, too, for obstructing the Emperor's commands, for protecting a criminal, because that's what you'll be if you're not handed in.'

'We'll be fugitives,' she said with a surprising eagerness. 'We can leave the city.'

'It's a possibility,' Fulcrom replied. 'To be honest, I've not thought it through.'

'That doesn't sound like you,' Lan muttered.

'This time, it really is. My whole existence has been based around the Inquisition, so I'm a little lost right now. First, though, I want to see certain jobs through, and I know that the uprising is going to buy us some time.' His gaze turned to the priest. 'Ulryk, will you want to do . . . whatever it is you'll be doing, then?'

'I will,' he replied. 'That building, is it what I think it is?'

Fulcrom stood up to move behind Ulryk, following his line of sight. The priest raised his arm, pointing to the structure that crested the immediate rooftops, reflecting what little light there was.

'That's the Astronomer's Glass Tower,' Fulcrom said. 'Why?'

'Is it used any more? I haven't had time to find out. But I will need access to it.'

'I don't think so. It was originally used for predicting

phenomena, but back in Johynn's rule the Jorsalir church finally convinced him it was blasphemous and it was shut down.'

'That is no surprise,' Ulryk chuckled. 'Such glass structures can be found across the Archipelago, most of them in forests or along coasts. They're ancient buildings, constructed on top of channels of ... I'm not even sure what the right word would be in modern Jamur. Ley lines, perhaps. I wish to visit it and conduct my rituals from its rooftop.'

'I didn't even know it had a rooftop,' Lan said, joining them. 'I thought it was a sheer face of glass.'

'There will be a rooftop,' Ulryk declared.

'Lan,' Fulcrom said, 'will you ensure Ulryk's safety? You must be careful though. The streets are starting to become extremely dangerous with the clashes and I'd change from your uniform if I were you – or at least cover your head, and that symbol.'

Lan rummaged around Fulcrom's wardrobe until she found a hooded jumper. Once she was wearing it, she accompanied Ulryk to the door and glanced back at Fulcrom. 'Are you coming?'

He shook his head. 'I can't yet. I need to find Tane and Vuldon and get to them before the Emperor or his agents do, and I could be a few hours.'

'How will you do that? If you've quit, you won't be permitted access to them surely?'

'I know. Look, for now, please just ensure that Ulryk completes his task, but return here if you can't get through the streets easily because of the violence – I might know of some alternative route. Whatever you do, don't risk your life recklessly.'

'And what about afterwards?' she asked.

He turned to her and took her in his arms. Tenderly in her ears he whispered, 'I'll meet you here. Whatever the hell happens, we'll do it together – just you and me. No one gives us orders any more.'

*

Stopping on the way to collect a case full of flammable fluids obtained from a cultist who owed him a few favours, Fulcrom headed towards the outer city, to an abandoned building.

Despite the population pressures, Villjamur was full of disused regions, which was part of its charm. There were chambers and catacombs dotted around the city, usually subterranean spaces where it wasn't unreasonable to assume people could scrape some kind of living. These zones occasionally harboured criminals on the run, the occasional drug addict or, before the ice became bad, Caveside whores looking for a quiet place to take their clients for a quick fuck, but today they remained eerily dormant.

Fulcrom had hoped that under Urtica's reign there might be a renovation of these urban spaces and that the authorities might permit some of the refugees to enter the city and be housed there. Alas, this was not the case, and security had been tightened further, denying most people access. But it wasn't the subterranean territories he was approaching right now – instead he sought a vacant hotel on the fourth level, one that had lost all its business long ago.

He strolled through the streets, head down to prevent the gusts of snow from skimming into his face. A couple of taverns had boarded up their windows here, and quite a few store premises were for sale. Eventually Fulcrom arrived at his destination and looked up at the broken facade of the enormous hotel, which was taller than he remembered, at least nine or ten storeys, which for Villjamur was significant. Three gothic arch windows sat each side of a central stairway, which led to a thick wooden double door. Several months ago these very steps had been the scene of a brutal double murder, and that – combined with the hostile weather – had ensured the owners were better off selling up to the Council, and since then it had stood empty.

Fulcrom slipped a dagger from his sleeve and prised open the lock. He headed inside, through the murky light, and up several flights of stairs that had been colonized by bulbous spiders the size of his hand.

He heaved the case of fluids up onto the flat roof, where he was struck by the chilling wind. There were a few discarded items here, a few dead hanging baskets, a table and chairs that hadn't seen action since warmer times, but all these items would help. All around him rose the spires of Villjamur, and he suddenly felt a pang of loss that he might have to leave this city he loved so much.

Fulcrom gathered the junk and spread it across the surface of the roof. Then he opened the case containing seven vials of transparent fluids and picked one out. He poured its contents across one side of the roof, away from the door to the stairs, being careful not to spill any on himself. In the distance, from the direction of the caves, came the sound of rioting – it was faint, a mass chorus of voices – but at that moment it wasn't his concern.

Satisfied that he had covered enough of the area, he poured one final vial containing blue fluid in a neat line between himself and the rest of the roof. He took out a piece of flint from one pocket and some kindling from the other. Sheltering in the lea of a wall, he struck the flint several times with the steel hilt of his dagger, and eventually a few sparks shot off onto the kindling. He blew gently, encouraging the flame, then, with great caution, dropped the burning bundle on the other side of the line of blue liquid, and dashed back towards the stairway.

Fire exploded across the rooftop, tearing into the heap of junk he'd prepared, and assaulting him with heat. He stumbled back, but was amazed at how well the fire respected the line of blue fluid.

He had saved one chair, of course – he didn't know how long he was going to be up there – and placed it by the stairway. According to the cultist's assessment of the liquid, Fulcrom guessed he had maybe three hours at the most. So he simply pulled the chair back towards the view of the city, and waited.

*

The priest said he needed an hour. Just an hour to work through both books to find the links required.

After Fulcrom had left, Ulryk stationed himself at the rumel's desk beneath a window with a distracting view of the cityscape, and set to work.

With reverence he opened both copies of *The Book of Transformations* and began examining them. Lan lay on the bed, her eyes half turned to the priest.

'What exactly are you going to learn in an hour?' Lan asked lazily.

'Shush,' Ulryk replied.

'Fine.'

He turned the books page by page, switching his gaze between them, assiduously comparing the detail within, and making notes to one side. By the seventh turn of a page, Lan was beginning to embrace the pillows on Fulcrom's bed. She had no idea how long in real-time she had spent under the city, though it had been a matter of a few of hours judging by the clocks in the library. She dozed off, catching up on some much-needed rest. Dreams flashed in her mind, images of warm and distant lands, leaving her with a craving to flee the city . . .

Ulryk made a noise that startled her awake. He rubbed his eyes and examined the pages with a new-found zest and a smile.

How long have I been asleep? Lan propped herself up on her elbows. She looked around in case Fulcrom had returned, but there was no sign of him. 'I take it you've worked it all out?'

'I have, yes!' His face betrayed his relief, his voice was full of an optimism she hadn't heard before. 'It was coded in the woodcuts, just as he inferred.' He chuckled to himself. 'Now come, we must get to the tower.'

And then maybe all this can be over, Lan thought as she stretched herself further awake.

*

Lan and Ulryk only had to head across a few streets. It was a simple enough task, but there were plenty of warnings she should have paid attention to: the lack of traffic through the lanes; the line of garudas stood atop the crenellated rooftops, silhouetted against the sky; the distant noises she wrongly attributed to city life.

Ulryk, clutching his satchel containing both copies of *The Book of Transformations*, steered her towards the shadow of a wall not too far from Fulcrom's apartment.

'What is it?' she asked.

'Something does not feel right,' Ulryk cautioned.

'We should just hurry – the Glass Tower is only over there.' Lan gestured to the glittering facade over a rooftop.

'Wait,' Ulryk said again. Then carefully he pointed at a street corner, behind which a unit of soldiers was waiting, and they were making whistles that she had previously mistaken for the call of a pterodette. From the open door of an adjacent building a dozen archers sprinted, joining the other unit. Two took positions on the corner, one standing, one crouching; they nocked their arrows, ready for whatever was coming.

'It appears,' Ulryk sighed, 'that the Glass Tower is the other side of this incident. Fulcrom was right about the violence.'

Soldiers were now lining up in the open street in two rows, one row kneeling just before a standing row, and they were facing towards her – but it wasn't Ulryk or Lan they were interested in.

With an effortless, fluid motion, the two archers on the corner released their arrows, pulled more out of their quivers, readied them and released them, repeating the process several times until they ran out of arrows.

The nerves they must have ... Lan thought, as a heartbeat later a surge of citizens rounded the corner, a few of them with arrows buried in their crude shields.

The line of archers loosed their arrows and wave after wave of civilians collapsed to the ground. People began to scream – both men and women – their voices intense between the walls around them, and Lan simply looked on, unable to help. People scrambled for cover in twos or threes, shouting for a retreat. Another cluster of civilians came to evacuate the injured, and pull back the dead from the bloodied cobbles, while the army coldly picked off whoever was left, one by one.

Ulryk was whispering a prayer.

Civilian militias were jogging in tight units, heavily armed; carts were being turned up on their sides to be used as crude shelters, spilling produce across the streets. Military archers were sniping from above, while youths with scarves pulled tight across their faces were beginning to launch their own attacks from street corners.

'It's so confusing who is fighting whom,' Ulryk said.

'Do you have to do whatever you need to on the Glass Tower?' she asked.

Ulryk opened his eyes slowly. 'I'm afraid so.'

'Don't worry,' Lan replied. 'We'll get you there. Somehow.'

*

How was it possible not to have an obvious chain of command and still form an army? The notion went against everything Caley had been brought up to believe, against all his instincts. No one was instructing them on what they should do, but there were those who were clearly more skilled than others, ferocious-looking people, those good with a sword, or rogue cultists who had been given a new lease of life. The rest of the Cavesiders clustered around these groups, looking for guidance or advice. *Almost* everyone wanted to help out – they knew they had come so far, and that they were on the cusp of achieving something significant: bringing down the Emperor and all those who had repressed the people of Caveside.

From the corner of Sahem Road and Gata Social, Caley could see a rim of real daylight where the caves met the city, and he swallowed hard. Surrounded by now-aggressive men and women, he didn't know what to do, and looked to others for direction. There were hundreds, probably thousands of them, and they seemed to follow each other, as an organic mass. Within the throng he had forgotten just how cold it was – the wind always blew in strongly at the mouth of the caves, as if the elements were aiding the segregation.

I'm in too deep, he thought. *I'm gonna get myself killed this time, for sure.*

Several individuals wheeled carts up and down their lines, issuing homemade weapons, rough blades that had been perfected in the dark, away from prying, Imperial eyes. Caley took a crossbow that looked pretty neat, and he already had a sword at his side. Another woman came past with a cartload of armour, so he took a crude helmet that didn't quite fit and was remarkably heavy, but he figured it was better than going without.

The energy here was incredible. People buzzed with nervousness and anticipation, but mostly with a genuine thrill that *this was it*, this was where they would take over the outer city. Several major groups had gone on ahead – some of the elderly and less able forming more peaceful lines of protest, unafraid of what happened previously because they knew the military would be busy enough; and there were more groups of youths looking to create agitation in almost random pockets of the city, sudden outbursts of violence that would cause chaos and distraction. To them, this was good sport.

A little deeper into this moment of anticipation, a message rippled Caley's way. It came via one of Shalev's runners, fast youths who were carrying information around the self-organized units. A letter was handed to him by a tall, grubby blond boy with a long face and a dagger at his hip. Caley unfolded it, then stared awkwardly at the meaningless script. He couldn't meet anyone's eyes as he handed it back to the messenger. ''Fraid I can't read much.'

The lad nodded back, opened the paper and, as a few of the Cavesiders came to see what was happening, he cleared his throat and read out:

'Caley, do you want to help me kill the Emperor?'

*

Eventually, as the flames began to eat into the roof to a now-dangerous level, Tane and Vuldon arrived, sprinting up the stairwell. They both stared at Fulcrom, who was sitting with his arms folded.

'What took you so long?' he asked.

'There's a war on, or hadn't you seen?' Vuldon replied.

'So I heard,' Fulcrom said. 'Is it bad?'

'Yeah, ridiculously so. Fuck're you doing up here anyway?' Vuldon demanded.

'The old methods of communication are not what they once were,' Fulcrom replied coolly. 'I needed to talk to you.'

'I don't get it,' Tane said. 'Why cause a fire? Has all the stress finally turned you insane? Why not just come back to our quarters like you usually do?'

Fulcrom informed them of everything that had happened since he'd last seen them. He told them about his meeting with the Emperor, and then with Warkur. He told them he'd quit the Inquisition. He told them of what was going to happen with the Knights.

'No more Lan?' Tane asked. 'Seriously?'

Fulcrom shook his head, stood up and leant on the edge of the building to observe Villjamur.

'But you and her ... you were close, right?' Tane asked. 'That must have made matters rather difficult.'

'Right,' he replied.

'No wonder you quit.'

Vuldon grunted. 'That's this fucking city for you,' he said. 'Asks you to give your heart and soul for it, and once you're no longer able to be exploited, it spits you out again.'

'The Emperor will keep you in employment,' Fulcrom continued, 'but since I've walked out of the Inquisition, I've no longer the same level of access to you. Hence the fire. You're on your own now, but it's likely they'll want you to consider hunting down me and Lan.'

'That's all right,' Tane replied, 'we can feign ignorance.'

'Shouldn't be too hard in your case,' Vuldon muttered. 'Don't worry, we'll not come after you.' Vuldon, in a gesture that was almost a show of emotion, placed his enormous hand on Fulcrom's shoulder. 'I'm not a fan of investigators, but you were all right. The rest of them can fuck themselves.'

'Thanks, I think,' Fulcrom said. 'Look, you'll still be required to work for the city, else they'll decommission you, too.'

'I'd like to see them try,' Vuldon replied.

'You can still do some good,' Fulcrom said. 'People still need you. The city's teetering on the brink of collapse.'

'Nah, it's just a skirmish, I imagine,' Vuldon muttered. 'The military will sort it out, then we'll be back to normal.'

'The military is heavily outnumbered, and ... there's something else heading to the city that the Emperor seems very worried about, and it's not just his paranoia.' He repeated his conversation with Urtica.

'We'll deal with that if it comes to it,' Tane said. He

suddenly turned away and began smelling the air. 'Trouble isn't far off,' he announced.

Fulcrom said, 'Look, I should get back.'

'Where to?' Vuldon asked.

'Good point,' Fulcrom replied. 'Somewhere, anywhere. Away from the law, and the Imperial hands – that ought to be enough.' It felt strange to say that: to run from the very thing he had represented all his life.

'Will you be taking Lan with you?' Vuldon demanded.

Fulcrom put his hands in his pockets. 'Yeah.' He glanced to one side, contemplating the flames and heat which were now dying down. 'We've a little extra business to sort out with Ulryk, but once we've helped him, that's it.'

'Look after her,' Tane said.

'She'll be looking after him if she's still got her powers,' Vuldon declared.

Fulcrom smiled at that. 'You might be right.'

An arrow narrowly clipped the rooftop, drawing their attention towards the city. Someone screamed. Fulcrom crouched and shifted near the edge of the building, Tane and Vuldon behind, ready for conflict.

There were calls from below, where a scene was developing.

'This battle,' Fulcrom said along the wall, 'just how big has it become?'

At least a dozen youths with black scarves covering their faces were strutting with intent down the street, kicking up puffs of snow. There was a guard unit of no more than two or three in front of them, armed only with swords, and another guard lay dead in the street with arrows in his body. Two of the youths were now firing crossbows, forcing the soldiers to cluster against the wall. Another few were busy drawing the strings back on their crossbows or loading bolts.

'Those soldiers are surely dead,' Fulcrom breathed.

The black-scarved youths surrounded the guards, with their crossbows raised to shoulder height, and the soldiers began to lash out with their swords: arrows and bolts thudded into their arms and legs, and they toppled to the cobbles, screaming, backing up against the wall. This was drawn out for enjoyment, not a swift kill.

Vuldon and Tane stood up on the edge of the wall but Fulcrom called, 'Wait!'

He indicated down to the left, by an intersection of three streets, where almost a hundred civilians – no, armoured civilians – were massing, carrying crude weapons.

Back to the soldiers now, and all Vuldon, Tane and Fulcrom could do was watch. The youths hollered and whooped like feral beasts as they executed the soldiers against the wall. A surge of civilians came round the corner and something more wilder than a celebration ensued.

'What were your orders?' Fulcrom asked.

Vuldon climbed down from the wall, Tane skipping back behind. 'We didn't really have any.'

'You probably won't get any either,' Fulcrom declared.

'What do you suggest?' Vuldon asked. 'We still want to help people. I don't care about what we were before – even if we were the Emperor's puppets, we still kept people safe.'

'Exactly,' Tane said. 'No matter what you do in this city, it seems someone's getting a rum deal. We might as well carry on trying so tell us, Fulcrom – tell us what we can do to *help*.'

'I'm not in charge of the operation now,' Fulcrom said.

'What *do you suggest*?' Vuldon demanded. 'I'm asking you as someone who knows what the fuck he's talking about, not as someone giving orders. What is our purpose?'

'Don't spend your time looking for a damn purpose.' Fulcrom gave an awkward laugh, and shook his head. 'All you've ever been required to do is make the innocent feel safe – and to protect the Emperor, of course.'

'Who knows where he is,' Tane cooed.

'Indeed,' Fulcrom said, contemplating the man's state earlier. 'You're still employed by the Emperor to protect people, and once this has calmed down you'll be required to do exactly the same. So all you can do now is protect the *innocent*. I'd advise you making your way towards Balmacara to offer your services – but on the way there, make sure any civilians you meet are not in danger.'

'Civilians hate us now,' Tane said.

'Don't pick sides,' Fulcrom warned, 'don't support the armed forces or the anarchists. You are not the military – this war is theirs. There will undoubtedly be civilian casualties, people who have no interest in fighting, and you need to prevent as many deaths as possible. You'll probably find that civilians will hate you less when they realize their lives are in danger.'

Vuldon offered his hand, and Fulcrom shook it. 'You speak more sense than seems possible. We'll take these as our last orders. You know, I hoped we could be better than this – be something more.'

Fulcrom repeated the gesture with Tane, who then rested a hand on his shoulder. 'Cheers, Fulcrom. We'll have a civilized glass of wine or something the next time we meet.'

Tane and Vuldon lumbered to the stairwell and down. A moment later, Fulcrom peered over the edge of the building to see the two of them jogging down the street.

*

Do you want to help me kill the Emperor?

If Caley accepted, he would be writing history. The notion was not lost on him: what Shalev was asking was important, and Caley had absolutely no hesitation in choosing to go.

Caley had followed the runner back along several side streets that were emptier than a few hours ago. Past taverns and shopfronts, behind surprisingly well-stocked gardens and structures he knew to be gambling dens, they eventually arrived at a terraced cottage rammed up against one of the cliff faces. Caley's pulse was racing.

Do you want to help me kill the Emperor?

It was just somebody's home, this place, a two-up two-down pile of wood that oozed a heady smell of arum weed. Inside, there was nothing in the dark room except a few candles and a solid table, but moments later several cloaked men and women stepped in from an adjoining room.

And then came Shalev.

'Caley,' she declared, 'you have made it. This, I am glad to see.' Shalev thanked the runner, who then stood in the corner of the room with his arms folded.

Shalev regarded Caley, who was so awestruck he could barely return an answer. 'It is all right, brother – we are all equals here.'

Her words didn't do much to settle him. 'You need me to help?' he asked.

She smiled and gestured to a spare chair. He sat down next to a pretty woman with red hair, who had lit a pipe. The heavy fug of smoke soon obscured the other faces.

Shalev began addressing them all. 'We are all of us equals, in Caveside, but you have all suffered a little more than most.'

No one said anything.

'I lost my family to the Empire,' Shalev continued in her weird and enchanting accent. 'I came from the island of Hulrr, but I was adopted by those on Ysla, which is where I learnt many of the techniques and organizational skills I have shared with you all. I was adopted because my family and most of my tribe were slaughtered by Empire soldiers who were trying to take another territory. For all my life I have wanted to kill the head of the Empire, whoever that may be, and to bring down its structures, to establish a truly democratic system like on Ysla, where people have control over their lives and don't surrender decisions to murdering ... scum. And I am not alone in having such a history, am I?'

Shalev sat down in front of them and glanced around the room, waiting calmly. The pipe-smoking woman next to Caley began to speak. Her name was Arta. She told a story of her own parents being evicted from their outer-city property for removing their funding from certain councillors when they were in the Treasury – namely Urtica. When her parents refused they had been hacked down with a blade in the night. She escaped, but was forced to scrape a meagre existence down in the caves.

They all had a story. Everyone in this room had been personally affected in some way, had their lives ruined personally by Urtica. It seemed to be a gesture from Shalev to allow them all to have the opportunity to kill the Emperor: to allow them to bury their ghosts.

Eventually it was Caley's turn to speak. He wasn't one for sharing his inner thoughts, he just wanted to get on with life, but reluctantly he cleared his throat, wanting to get it over with as quickly as possible. 'About a year or so after I was born, my dad was working in Balmacara as a cook when the Emperor – it was Johynn then – became increasingly paranoid that people were out to get him, so there were tough checks on anyone who worked there. According to my aunts, he'd come home complaining each night apparently. Anyway, one night Urtica and a few councillors began feeling really unwell and the blame was traced to a banquet the evening before. Urtica was the Chancellor at this point and so he sends soldiers to our house in the middle of the night to try to get my dad in for questioning. He was a stubborn one, so he resists arrest and a fight breaks out and before you know it he's got a knife in his back and Mum's outside screaming. She got killed too by the way. I get found the next day, by my aunt, but she was a lot older and she died a couple of years later. So I end up in the caves, like everyone else.'

He wasn't upset about it – he was too young to know anything other than what his relatives had told him – but he knew Urtica was the man responsible for taking away what chances he had in the world.

Seemingly satisfied, Shalev briefed them on what would now be required. Caley listened on, amazed that he would be playing such an influential role.

Shalev said, 'The military is going to be engaged in a constant conflict, and our overwhelming numbers will wear them down eventually. An initial ten thousand of us are up against their handful of units, which I believe to be two thousand. They will eventually bring in the Inquisition, and possibly seek the assistance of other civilians. The Knights are out of action for the moment, according to my sources. Everything is in our favour. And whilst erratic conflicts continue across the city, this true anarchism leaves Balmacara vulnerable. I can offer no training but I can offer weapons and guidance with relics. All of you may choose not to be involved, and it will not be held against you – you may rejoin the rest of the rebellion.'

Not one person in the room wanted to miss the opportunity.

Shalev smiled, stood. 'Then brothers and sisters, I shall return momentarily with all the tools we'll need.'

THIRTY-THREE

Clouds began to thicken above Villjamur. They brought a light snow at first, then it became heavy and relentless. The already hazardous streets became worse. Those civilians from the outer city not engaging in the combat locked themselves up in their homes and hoped for the best. A thousand lanterns were lit almost simultaneously in response to the bad weather and the wild cries of the anarchists' advancing army.

Tane and Vuldon sprinted through the streets of Villjamur, jumping over corpses left from skirmishes. Bodies lay in slushy snow, blood smeared all around them. Blood beetles flowed in weird spirals up the sides of walls in order to get to the corpses and then they tore into flesh with a ferocious appetite. There appeared to be equal amounts of civilian and military casualties, but those of the former group wore crudely constructed armour, giving them the appearance of soldiers, so it was often difficult to tell.

Now and then the two Knights checked to see if any of the bodies were alive, but each side had done well to look after their own.

In street after cobbled street, there were clusters of individuals either looking to find their way to safety or to despatch violence. More than a few arrows or bolts whipped near the Knights, highlighting their unpopularity. All they could do was ignore it, and Vuldon did his best to remember Fulcrom's words, to not let his anger take over again.

The city was – as he put it to Tane – fucked. There was no doubt about that. It didn't take much to realize that there were more Cavesiders than military, and they were organized and well armed. Small groups were stationing themselves by street corners, blocking access with upturned carts or crates or whatever junk they could find. The military, for the most part, seemed non-existent. As remarkable as it seemed, the city was gradually being taken over by the anarchists.

When they approached what was an empty iren, Tane urged Vuldon to stop. They pulled themselves behind a wall in time to witness purple light erupting from one end of the courtyard to the other. Between immense walls, and beneath two wide-arched bridges, four cultists were engaged in combat. In dark cloaks they dashed about this way and that, taking refuge behind disused stalls, collapsing awnings and sending wooden crates skittering towards their assailants. It wasn't at all clear who was fighting whom, or which sides they represented, but none of them fitted the description of Shalev. When two of them were side by side with relics in their hands they shot bolts of light at the other pair, and bricks exploded from the wall behind them, leaving gaping holes. Suddenly the other pair summoned the cobbles to rise up as if someone was flipping a rug, sending the other two up into the air, and the ground collapsed back into place, making the sound of thunder.

Tane whispered to Vuldon, 'Do we help these people?'

'No,' Vuldon grunted. 'They're not the innocent. We've no idea who's Empire or who's anarchist. We'll probably end up getting fried anyway.'

'Good point,' Tane replied.

They took another route around the scene, listening to the sounds of the cultists ripping up the city.

*

Then there were children.

Vuldon could only worry about them as they made their

way across a bridge over the iren where the cultists still fought. From one side he watched them marching across, about ten or so, with two adults guiding them. He didn't know which group they were – maybe schoolchildren trying to get away from the conflict – but when magic flared up from below, he knew they were in trouble.

Some of them gasped: and it was exactly the same noise as all those years ago. Vuldon froze as memories rose up from his past yet again. He had hoped he was over the incident, but their faces, their cries, they seemed identical to the ones who had perished and who he had been unable to save. With the magic beating the underside of the bridge, the children screamed and refused to move. They huddled and the two men who were guiding them across could not seem to budge them. One of the adults peered over the edge to assess the situation below and a vast blast of purple magic blew back his head. He didn't even have a chance to scream, and his charred face peered Vuldon's way before he collapsed in front of the kids.

I'll be fucked if I'm letting them go this time.

'Come on, Tane,' Vuldon said.

The two Knights sprinted across the bridge. All across the city there were streets burning. Smoke drifted up in a much greater volume than the usual chimney smoke, carried out across the tundra by the breeze. Snow skidded into his face, so he kept his head down. He approached the children, none of whom were older than ten. The remaining adult, a man in a wax rain cape and a tricorne hat, confirmed they were from one of the wealthier schools nearby.

'There's a safe house that a lot of families are sending their children to,' he said. 'They want shelter on school property – it's safer that way.'

'Seems like a good idea,' Vuldon replied. The children seemed pleased to see him. A few of them knew his name. Obviously the *People's Observer* had not yet affected their opinions of the Knights just yet. Vuldon explained that they should move and get to safety.

Three of the children were crying as they pointed to the charred corpse of their teacher as another blast of magic struck the bridge.

'We move now!' Vuldon shouted. 'Tane, stay at the back.'

Vuldon noted three children who were huddled on the ground dressed in their little rain jackets, unwilling to move, and he scooped them under one massive arm, then repeated the gesture with two more; all the while, magic raged upwards under the bridge.

He began running with the crying children beneath his arms; he looked back to see Tane copying him, a child under each arm and one on his shoulder, and the remaining teacher did his best to move the kids along behind.

Vuldon reached the other side and dumped the kids in a pile by the wall of an empty bistro. 'Stay here, all right?'

He didn't wait to see their reactions, and sprinted breathlessly back to the bridge. Tane passed him and as Vuldon surged forwards to collect the remaining children, the cat-man caught up with him again. Tane piled on three more children, two with frightened little faces, one smiling amiably as she played with the fur on Tane's face. There was just one more boy, and Vuldon picked him up under his arm and took him to the end of the bridge.

The stone surface suddenly buckled and swayed, and this movement was followed by a deep explosion from below. Purple light rose up on either side of him.

He sprinted but it seemed too late: he could feel the ground beneath his feet fractionally more distant, as if he was walking on air. *Keep going, fucker*, he told himself. His thighs pounded, pushing himself harder than he had ever done.

Twenty feet away from the end he paused, seeing Tane waiting with an open stance. He hauled the child back and threw him over to Tane. The kid screamed as he was launched through the air.

Magic raged up around Vuldon. The platform disintegrated. Tane – leaping high – caught the child before collapsing to the ground with grace.

Vuldon sighed his relief—

—and then tumbled alongside the crumbling masonry.

*

Lan mounted the walls on a row of tall terraced houses, Ulryk on her back. He might have been old, but he was still bloody heavy. She had to skip sideways along a couple of rows of houses, facing the sky, since Ulryk constantly pulled her towards the ground and she couldn't walk with the weight pulling her on one side.

Eventually they reached a rooftop covered in ice, and she slipped forwards, sending Ulryk tumbling over her head.

She pushed herself upright, 'Sorry – I couldn't help it – are you OK?'

Ulryk, as resilient as a boar, pushed himself up from the flat roof and rubbed his scalp. 'Indeed, I believe I am.' He instinctively checked his satchel, which contained the books.

From their position they could see more of the city, and the Astronomer's Glass Tower, which stood a few hundred yards away. In between them and the structure, the civil war on the streets of Villjamur was reaching something of a stand-off. Imperial troops had garrisoned themselves in one of the major taverns, extending a makeshift barricade of assorted city detritus, blocking off the route. Behind it, about a hundred soldiers were poised with crossbows, waiting for any anarchist surge.

The anarchists were less well organized and were hiding in buildings a few streets further along: she could see snipers leaning out of windows, waiting to fire at any passing military patrols.

Tension hung thickly in the air. After the initial set-tos, no one wanted to commit to a manoeuvre. The Empire soldiers were outnumbered, that was obvious, but the anarchists were not able to get the better of the highly trained men and women.

All of this lay between Lan and Ulryk and the Glass Tower.

'Are you sure you can't do the ritual here?' Lan asked.

'I suppose,' Ulryk breathed, 'I can try.' He rubbed his hands and reached into his satchel to withdraw the books. He walked to the centre of the roof and carefully sat down. There, he opened the books on various pages.

Lan strolled over to see what he planned. 'Are the books the same?'

Ulryk shook his head. 'They differ, many of the sketches and occasional tracts of script are dissimilar – deliberately so.'

He showed her two drawings of the same castle, which to her appeared to be identical. But he pointed out that figures were standing in the window of one drawing, and not the other. Ulryk suggested it was the equivalent of a prison. On another open page, there were different drawings entirely: one showed a small animal she'd never seen, another of a plant. 'This tract of text,' he explained, pointing to one edition, 'discusses the history of the islands and how they came to be. The other, well ... this is a panicked note explaining that the Jorsalir were attempting to have these works destroyed.'

'Why would the editions differ?'

'In case one got lost or destroyed. In one there are codes to explain what happened – a letter to a future generation.'

'That's some forward thinking,' Lan said.

'I am ready to attempt the summoning,' Ulryk announced.

Lan moved away, watching him rearrange the books before him. Ulryk brought out his own journal and began flicking through it until he discovered the correct page of notes. Cross-legged, hunching over the books, he closed his eyes.

Lan turned away to watch the streets again. Long shadows clawed their way over the city; sides of buildings were shrouded in darkness. Above, the clouds were clearing and she could see the red sun approaching the horizon. It was going to be a cold night.

Ulryk seemed to be in a trance now. His fingers were pressed down on certain pages but his eyes were closed, his head tilted up towards the heavens as if seeking extra help from above. He chanted things in tongues that didn't sound natural, let alone from the Archipelago.

The most important thing to note was that nothing happened. Eventually Ulryk looked up, not exactly disappointed. He gathered the books into the satchel and stood up.

Lan walked across the roof towards him. 'The Astronomer's Tower?'

Ulryk nodded, with an air of serenity about him.

THIRTY-FOUR

Their vessel approached the east coast of Jokull. The familiar snow-covered hills extended into the distance, and rocky outcrops of granite rose towards the cloud base, occasionally losing themselves within its mass. Gulls and terns screeched as they carved through the air in startling numbers; their presence was deeply comforting to Verain – they were home, there was life here. Trees littered the hills with their evergreen shadows, and stone walls marked the occasional – and probably abandoned – farm. Small plumes of smoke could be seen, originating from somewhere out of sight – probably from members of the Aes tribe who miraculously still survived in these extremes. When she saw them, she felt a yearning to join their primitive ranks and leave her situation behind.

For a moment, Dartun joined her on the quarterdeck, looking around as they passed along their home island. His cloak flailed in the strong coastal breeze. Where he had been injured on their arduous journey, tiny metallic patches were showing through. More than ever, he had the appearance of an artificial construction, as if made from relics and skin pasted half-heartedly on top. He said nothing, she said nothing – and this seemed to please them both. If he held answers, she no longer wanted to hear them.

They sailed for some time seeking an inlet, but couldn't find one. Eventually, frustrated with their search, they worked the sails, turned the ship toward the rocky shore and ploughed through the shallows.

The ship juddered and rocked: they had run aground, leaving a gap perhaps of twenty feet of water to the land. No one wasted any time. They took what little belongings they had gathered on their journey and jumped overboard.

Verain plunged into the icy water, which nearly took her breath from her body and froze her blood in an instant. The water only reached up to her thighs and, with her possessions above her head, she waded to the shore before collapsing on the rocky beach along with the others, some of whom were laughing like madmen. The young man, Todi, was shivering, rubbing his arms vigorously, and his breath was clouding before his face. Dartun stepped along beside him and placed his hands on Todi's shoulders: the young cultist relaxed suddenly, as if the chills had vanished.

Dartun then stepped behind Verain, repeating the gesture, and she felt warmth suddenly flow through her body. She shuddered. Dartun smiled impassively in return before moving on to the others.

*

The farmhouse they had spotted from the ship was indeed abandoned. It was a simple white stone cottage, surrounded by a scrub of trees and bushes that had died in the cold. Inside, a few pots and pans were sitting on the kitchen table covered in mould, suggesting that the owners had long since left.

After Todi and Tuung had gathered wood and started a fire in the hearth, the place felt like a home again. Verain changed into drier clothes. She sat by the fire, exhausted, relieved, empty. She wanted to stay there for ever.

Whilst she sat staring into the flames, Tuung moved in beside her, and pulled his cloak tightly round himself. 'I'm going to be leaving,' he whispered urgently.

'What?' she replied. 'Where are you going?'

'I don't know.' He shrugged. 'Anywhere but where Dartun goes.'

Verain looked around, but their leader was nowhere to be seen. 'I don't understand – why now?'

'We're almost home. I reckon I can find my way around Jokull all right. I won't head back to Villjamur, but to some of the towns up north maybe.'

Could I go with him? She was too lethargic, too afraid of what Dartun might do to her. Besides, Tuung hadn't asked if she wanted to go.

'If anyone asks,' Tuung said, still in a whisper, 'if Dartun asks, would you lie on my behalf?'

'And tell him what?'

'Tell him I've gone to scour the rock pools to the south for something to eat.'

'Do you think that will be enough?'

'It can buy me enough time, an hour or so, and then I can just . . . fucksake, I don't know. I'll find a road, or failing that I'll just keep heading north-west until I find a settlement.'

'Have you got enough to eat?'

'Fuck all, is what I have to eat; but I can identify enough from the land to get by. I've got flint to start a fire, and enough wits to trap a hare. I've found a blade or two in the kitchen. I'll be fine.' He took her hands in an unusually affectionate gesture. 'Best of luck, lass.'

She said nothing in return, but smiled softly, and turned back to stare at the flames as he disappeared.

*

Dartun returned with some meat he claimed was rabbit, but it tasted more like squirrel to Verain. Either way, she didn't care: it was food, and it could be eaten. There were some herbs drying in some of the cupboards, and she insisted on cooking dinner since it would be a task – something akin to normality.

'Should we not wait for Tuung?' Dartun enquired.

'He said he'd be on the beach, looking in rock pools for something to eat – in case you didn't find anything.'

'Hmm.' Dartun gave a short nod, and nothing more. He disappeared into the other room, allowing her to relax once again with the simple, pleasurable chore of cooking.

*

They ate with their fingers, in companionable silence, allowing the warmth of the fire to wash over them. They were seated in a semicircle, allowing Verain a good view of their faces – there was hardly a hint of humanity left in them. Here were morose and shattered individuals. There was little of the spark they used to possess as a group, none of the sparring discussions. It was like parts of their minds had been removed altogether.

Eventually came the question, and it was Dartun who asked again. 'Where has Tuung got to? Are you certain he headed to the coast?'

'That's what he told me, yes,' she replied.

Dartun wore a heavy frown, which was exacerbated by the firelight. He stood up and his chair flipped over. He marched out of the room and she heard the door of the farmhouse opening then slamming shut.

Wearily she eyed the others, and Todi looked at her with a resigned frown. 'I hope Dartun doesn't find him.'

*

Two hours later, the sun had set and the others were settled in blankets, listening to the snowstorm that raged outside. When the door burst open and a series of thuds and groans followed, she leapt up from her chair and headed towards the outburst.

Tuung was lying on the floor caked in mud, curled into a tight ball, his face creased in agony. Dartun loomed above him.

'He was nowhere near the coast.' His voice was loaded with accusation as he stared at her. Verain swallowed hard, too afraid to respond.

Dartun shut the door and stared down at the man's crawling form. 'No, he was a good mile or two north of here.'

'Did you capture him?' Verain eventually asked. 'Is he your *prisoner* now?'

Dartun seemed to consider these words seriously. 'No. No of course not. It is not safe out there – it is no place to be alone.'

Dartun stepped over Tuung and marched up the stairs. Verain rushed to crouch beside the prostate cultist, examining him for any injuries. 'Did he hurt you?' she whispered.

Tuung grunted his response. 'No, lass – he exhausted me, is what he did. He . . . found my tracks and . . . hunted me until . . . till I couldn't breathe. Then he dragged me by my feet across the snow. Took an almost manic pleasure in it.' Then, 'My arse hurts like you would not believe.'

Verain slumped against the wall beside him. 'We're trapped, aren't we?'

'Indeed,' Tuung said. He pushed himself up alongside her, grunting and groaning all the way.

'He's desperate to get us to Villjamur,' she said. 'What do you think he's got planned?'

'I have not a fucking clue, but I doubt it's going to be fun.'

THIRTY-FIVE

Fulcrom couldn't purge his sense of failure. He liked to finish what he started: complete cases, write up the notes and file them with his superiors. The fact that he would never find Shalev and never complete his mission was somewhat irksome.

No, it pisses me right off.

He was nearly done with Villjamur and only had a few final matters to sort out, but without having hunted down the troublemaker behind all the recent acts of terror he would never shake the feeling that he had let people down. It went against all his better qualities to walk away from it all; but, somehow, he felt he was doing the right thing.

Fulcrom approached his apartment building but could sense that something wasn't quite right. Opposite, he loitered in the shadows of an alleyway, watching a little longer as two of his neighbours scuttled out with urgency, peering behind them as they were leaving on some illicit business. Where they were going wasn't important; Fulcrom realized that someone had put them in this agitated state.

All I want to do is get back, pack, wait for Lan, and clear out of here. Now they *have come for me.*

Fulcrom heard a movement behind. Pretending not to have noticed, he reached down to his boot, as if to adjust the laces, though in fact drew out a blade. He felt a boot come down on his back and he tumbled forward across the cobbles, grazing his chin. He reached for his knife and leapt up, narrowly missing a moving fist . . .

Five figures in long grey coats, hats and scarves had him circled.

'There's no way out, not now, Fulcrom.' He couldn't tell which one was speaking, because of the scarves, and because they all seemed to blend into one unit without a hint of individuality.

'Just come along quietly,' another said. Maybe another, maybe the same one.

Fulcrom laughed. 'I know how you guys work. You think I'm stupid?'

'We only want to ask questions.' They inched ever closer, tentative steps, waiting for a response. Each was gripping a dagger.

'Sure you do.' Fulcrom spun his blade in his hand. Maybe bravado would buy him another minute or two. His tail became perfectly still in anticipation of their next move. At the end of the street, a small family had gathered to watch the scene.

Two of them attacked. Fulcrom slid to the floor and kicked the back of the nearest one's knee, sending the figure sprawling forwards. It was a dark-haired woman, and he grabbed her hair, tugged back her neck, held his blade to her throat. She pressed both hands to the floor, trying to push herself up.

Using her as a hostage, he gently hauled her up and positioned himself so the rest of the agents were one side of him.

'You're not an idiot, Fulcrom. Let her go.'

'I've killed for less,' he replied, breathing heavily through his teeth.

'No you haven't. You've no capacity for evil.'

'Don't be a fool,' another said. 'You're cut from a different cloth.'

Fulcrom's back pressed against the wall. With no direction

to go, no exit available, there was no point in wasting a life. 'What do you want – really?' Fulcrom released the woman and pushed her forwards. He dropped his knife to the floor with a clatter.

'We just have some questions regarding a missing Knight,' one of them said.

'I thought you might,' Fulcrom replied.

'You can help us then?'

Fulcrom looked down, sighed, shook his head. 'Not a chance.'

'We thought you might say that.' One of them lunged forward with a flash-punch to his stomach, but he'd tensed to absorb the blow. He didn't hunch, didn't show them the pain they would enjoy delivering. Another came, then one to his jaw, and one on the other side. He staggered forwards, and felt a blow to his head. He dropped to his knees on the wet stone.

They bound his hands and his mouth, hauled him to his feet and shoved him along the street. The only fear he felt was that he wouldn't see Lan again.

*

Vuldon regained consciousness and could hear Tane warbling away to someone in the distance. He noticed the curved brickwork typical of either a cellar or the cultist zones back in their own quarters. The background humming seemed to confirm this.

Breathing was a struggle. It felt as if he could only take in a fraction of the air he was used to. His muscles . . . they were numb. He expected some deep ache, but there was nothing to feel.

Cultists have treated me, then. Explains why I'm not burning on some fucking funeral pyre.

'Vuldon, old boy – you're awake then.' Tane approached him, his fur dappled in the lantern light. His claws gripped the end of the metal-framed table on which Vuldon was lying.

'Barely,' he replied. 'The fuck did I get here?'

Tane explained – with apparent glee – how he personally climbed down the wreckage to find him. Vuldon did not fall directly down because a rooftop had broken his fall. Instead, he burst through two floors of the house, which suffered minimal damage from falling masonry, due to its sheltered positioning against a support.

'You're rather lucky, I'd say.'

'If I was lucky, I wouldn't have fallen, idiot.'

'Well, we're out of front-line action anyway.'

'What do you mean?' Vuldon demanded.

'As soon as you're well enough, we'll be offering our fine powers to aid the Emperor in Balmacara.'

'I might just stay here and pretend to be dead then.' Vuldon glanced up at the brick ceiling.

'Now don't be like that, old boy,' Tane replied, as patronizing as he could manage. 'The war has meant we're rather ineffective down below. There's nothing we can do to help the civilians – that's in the hands of the military.'

'So we're to be nanny to Urtica.'

'On the contrary – it's a huge privilege. We're going to be there, guarding the inner sanctum.'

'That's not why we were given powers. We're to help people, not one person.'

'Orders are orders,' Tane replied.

'There's nothing else we can do?'

'Afraid not.'

'When do we go?'

'Whenever you're fit to work.'

*

Through gusts of snow, the cultists from the Order of the Equinox approached the gates of Villjamur by foot. Verain couldn't feel her legs any more. Each time she collapsed to her knees, Dartun would place a hand on her back and she would recover just enough to march on for another few hours. By now everyone realized they were prisoners and that there was no means to escape. It was futile. Verain barely noticed the conditions of the refugees outside, the mud-baths that had frozen up, the small pit fires, the skeletal dogs that trotted around the paths between crudely constructed tent homes. The place stank of excrement. But she would have given anything to join them right now, to be free again. Her memory was failing her. Her existence was being lost to a mental fog. The names of her fellow cultists were fading slowly from her mind. Verain was following Dartun – that was all she could do.

They trudged up the incline towards the first gate, refugees milling about their trail with a vague curiosity. Four soldiers in full battle regalia exited their small stone station and marched out towards them, their swords drawn.

'Sele of Jamur,' muttered a man with rat-like features. The others formed a casual line alongside him, eyeing the cultists with deep suspicion.

Dartun was silent.

'We'll need to see written reasons for entry,' the soldier drawled, 'and any associated medallions, before we can permit you through to the second gate.'

Dartun stepped closer and the soldiers held up their swords.

'Remain where you are,' the soldier cautioned.

Dartun chuckled without saying a word. He moved further forward and the soldiers slipped through the mud to intercept him; their swords clattered into his arm, pinging off its surface. They didn't know what to make of his immunity to their blows.

With the guards in a state of surprise, Dartun grabbed the nearest one, placed the palm of his hand on the man's back and the armour began glowing red hot. While the other guards looked on dumbly, the man screamed: his skin was burning, his face reddening and then, with a muted burst, the soldier exploded within his armour. Dartun discarded the bloodied armour to one side and, with a grin on his face, regarded the other soldiers.

*

Vuldon, with all the dignity of a drunk, lumbered groggily to his room. He lived abstemiously, never wanting to accumulate much these days. There was a bed, a chair, a cupboard of identical uniforms, and a desk, which he'd insisted on having installed. He sat at his desk, lit the lantern, and pulled sketches from a hidden compartment.

It was, more or less, the final scene.

MythMaker was about to defeat the king of the underworld, the crude parallel to Caveside, with a series of magical creatures he had summoned. This had been the culmination of the entire story, and Vuldon was wondering if he could say everything he wanted to say in the last picture. Moreover, ever since Ulryk had discussed with him the potential of actually bringing drawings to life, Vuldon had been struggling to incorporate this into his work. He wasn't even sure if what the priest said was true. Still, there was nothing to lose in trying.

MythMaker had been Vuldon's perfect coping mechanism. Ever since his withdrawal from public life, these picture stories had helped him to stay in touch with the essence of who he was – someone who wanted to do good, to please people. *That's what I am. I just want to please, to be accepted.* On these sheets of vellum, which were nailed to the various noticeboards and school-room doors about the city, he could continue saving imaginary lives. After he had pinned one up, he watched from a distance the reaction of children as they herded around to read the latest part of the story. Before the end of the day, youths might be re-enacting some of the scenes. He'd hear their innocent cries as they play-acted the defeat of Doctor Devil or the Unicorn Queen.

Now the city was falling down around them, it seemed that

MythMaker could be the one way of genuinely helping the children. If he was to protect the Emperor in these desperate hours – if he was to be away from the streets and unable to help people – then he would find a way of saving them: through MythMaker and using the priest's advice. Assiduously, with a remarkable speed that only practice could bring, Vuldon inked down the final acts of MythMaker.

A couple of hours later, Tane knocked on his door. 'Vuldon,' he called, muffled through the wood, 'time to go.'

Fucksake. 'I need more time,' he grunted. 'I need to head out before we see the Emperor.'

He heard Tane sigh. 'There's going to be no stopping you, I suspect.'

'Damn right there isn't.'

Vuldon opened the door with a bundle of the sketches under his arm and a purse of nails in his pocket, slipped past Tane, out of the building and into the night.

Snow was drifting across the city in thick flakes, but at least it wasn't raining much. He wore a cloak and a scarf across his face. For years he had paid others to do this job for him – that was, until the money ran dry, so he had taken to posting the work himself. Given his recent fame, he felt he had to be especially cautious not to be discovered.

Across the city – under bridges and viaducts, past the shadows of wrecked taverns and behind military lines, Vuldon pressed a nail through dozens of copies of MythMaker, fixing them to doors or noticeboards or any sheltered surface he could find. This sketch was special, he knew it, and had to be seen by as many of the city's children as possible.

The city was a depressing vision. Walls had crumbled, blocking paths, whilst militia groups prevented him from gaining access to certain roads, but he managed to target all the main thoroughfares on the levels farthest from the attacks. He couldn't get to the crude Caveside plazas, though, which was of concern – he wanted all children to have equal access to these sketches. Once he had finished he dashed back across the city to his headquarters. *Two hours late, but I don't give a fuck.*

When he came in he found Tane slumped on the couch, staring up at the ceiling.

'Ah, the traveller returns. What were you up to?'

'Never mind. Let's go babysit the Emperor.'

*

As they ascended the steps of Balmacara, past one unit of soldiers and heading towards another, they were presented with a panorama of the rise and fall of the city's rooftops.

'Wait,' Tane cautioned.

'What?'

'I can hear something.' He turned his head into the powerful wind trying to locate exactly where the noise had come from. 'There,' he said, pointing just as a flash of light soared up and struck the cloud-base, then a bridge collapsed somewhere around the third and fourth level. A cloud of dust rose up from the streets, and a sound of rumbling followed moments later.

'We should hurry,' Tane said.

Guardsmen, having recognized Vuldon and Tane, ushered them up the steps of Balmacara quickly, and led them into the relative warmth of the Imperial residence. A commanding officer of the Dragoons led them through the lantern-lit corridors, past a number of soldiers who were buzzing back and forth. They looked as if they were stockpiling food and weapons, ready for Balmacara to be a fortress.

'Wouldn't these warriors be better out there protecting the people?' Vuldon said.

'Aye, sir. I suspect they would.'

'You agree?' Tane asked.

'Sir.'

'Then why the fuck aren't you out there?' Vuldon demanded. 'People are dying.'

'Not our decision, sir,' the soldier replied, 'not our choice. You'll see.'

Vuldon looked to Tane, who simply shrugged.

Through layer after layer of security, through ever-darkening passages, and into an antechamber, they finally entered a vast room, with a desk maybe fifty paces away at the far end, and little else except a huge burning hearth and several vast windows that offered a remarkable view of the city. No lanterns were lit, no candles, so once they stepped away from the firelight, they were in a room of shadows. Flashes lit up the horizon now, booms of illumination that lingered and hovered, before scattering themselves throughout the cloud-base. Snow raked against the windows, wind rattling the glass against the frame.

A figure was silhouetted against the flares of magic in the distance, but as they marched closer, Vuldon and Tane realized that the person wasn't looking out, but facing towards them.

'The Knights of Villjamur,' the figure gasped. 'I am relieved that the two of you are now here. Those fuckwits behind you are about as useful in a war zone as a silk handkerchief.'

'You wish us to leave the premises and join the fighting, my Emperor?' the commander queried, with obvious sarcasm.

'No, no.' Urtica's tone was suddenly devoid of control. 'Get to your stations.'

As they retreated, Vuldon glanced across Urtica's desk, on which lay several maps of the city and the Archipelago, and there were more on the floor, too – enlarged, detailed plans of various sectors. On a small table to the left, there sat a platter of various meats on the bone, with a huge carving knife sticking out of it.

'What do you want us to do?' Tane asked.

Urtica observed him in the darkness. Vuldon could see the flicker of the firelight reflected in his eyes. 'They tell me that the city is falling.'

'Who?' Tane asked.

'Them,' Urtica made a vague gesture to the door. 'The soldiers. The military. The idiots should be able to handle a few Caveside yokels. They've got all sorts of superior weaponry – and all the reports I receive are of military losses, of streets overrun and claimed in the name of the anarchists.'

'What's the situation now?' Vuldon asked.

'We are withdrawing.'

'To here, I take it.'

'Indeed,' Urtica replied. 'All councillors and their families are now ensconced within Balmacara.'

'What exactly are you going to govern over, if there's nothing left of the city?' Vuldon demanded.

'Do not question my motives. I am the reason you are both still in employment – the reason you were first given your new lease of life.'

Like I give a fuck, Vuldon wanted to say, but even he thought better of it.

Urtica seated himself at his desk and ran his hands through his hair.

Tane looked to Vuldon then back at the Emperor. 'Do you really think the anarchists are going to come here to get you?'

'Without a doubt – they have been trying since that Shalev bitch came to Villjamur.'

'Then why bottle yourself up now?' Tane asked. 'Why not have as many soldiers on the streets, wearing them down?'

'It is not the anarchists I'm worried about.' Urtica slid back and gestured to the flares of magic. 'Do you know what that is?'

'No,' Vuldon grunted. 'Not really.'

'Neither do I, precisely. It is a cultist who has entered the city and, allegedly, begun a systematic destruction of Villjamur. Two garudas are taking it in turns to update me on his progress, and each time they return their news is even more disturbing. So far, much of the first level of the city has been destroyed.'

'What do you mean *destroyed*?' Tane asked.

'Reduced to rubble. Blood in the streets. People burned by magic. Houses collapsed. How precise a definition do you require?'

'Does he fight for the anarchists?' Tane asked.

'He fights for sport, so it seems.'

'What do you want us to do?' Vuldon asked. 'You want us to stop him?'

Urtica's face seemed to have aged massively – even in this light, Vuldon's acute vision could make out his tired eyes, the desperation etched on his face and the constant fidgeting of his hands. This was a man on the edge. There was none of the usual calm authority or resplendence that Vuldon had previously observed. 'Would you mind?' Urtica breathed, as if it now took all his reserves to form speech.

'The hell are we going to do against a force of nature like that?'

'You will find a way,' Urtica replied insistently. 'This is what you were created for.'

'Or what, you'll kill us?' Tane said.

Urtica leaned back in his chair and grasped the arms with bony hands. 'No. But I will kill the former investigator, Fulcrom, who is currently being interviewed by my agents. You ... you had a close bond with him, yes?'

Tane's expression revealed his concern. *Could he really have caught Fulcrom?* Vuldon wondered. The investigator said that he'd be a wanted man ... 'You're lying.'

'I don't need to lie,' Urtica hissed. 'But if you want proof, I could perhaps fetch for you a finger? Something more convincing, like his arm perhaps?' There was an almost manic tone to Urtica's rasping voice, suggesting that if his city was going down, then he was taking everything else with him.

'We might not be able to do anything,' Vuldon muttered. 'If this person's as strong as you say he is.'

Urtica began to snicker softly. Then he addressed the surface of his desk. 'My city is falling. Everything I worked for is failing. Those scum from Caveside need to be eradicated. And this cultist needs to be stopped. I don't care how – just get it done or I'll personally see to it that Investigator Fulcrom bears the full weight of my disappointment at your failure.'

Tane placed a furred hand on Vuldon's arm. 'We'll see what we can do.'

*

It was carnage. Verain watched through tears as Dartun threw his magic about the city without reason or rhyme. Like a man possessed, he drove his arm into walls, ripping through stone to collapse houses into the street. Men and women ran screaming into the streets and watched in slack-jawed horror as their homes were decimated.

'It's good to be back, no?' Dartun bellowed with a frenzied grin at his cowed order who shadowed his footsteps – too afraid to do anything.

The skies were darkening overhead, and lantern lights in windows indicated all the people looking on. She wanted to tell them to get out – evacuate – but knew they would think she was mad. Where else did people go when their world was falling apart? Home, of course. Citizens on the first level had begun to barricade themselves in, but the act hadn't done them much good – Dartun was somehow rupturing the very ground, popping up cobbles and flagstones in street-wide spurts. She was numb to it now, they all were. They merely watched, inert, as he ripped apart the city of her birth.

The first show of formed resistance came on the second level of the city. Standing at an intersection, where two streets banked up identical-looking slopes, two cultists from an unknown order had brought a crate of relics and tried to conceal themselves behind a wide grey-brick well. Filtering in alongside them were soldiers she recognized as being from the Dragoons. They fanned out to form a shield wall, while behind them about a dozen archers took position. In the dark skies above, two garudas moved in slow circles, their wings barely discernible.

Please stop him...

After some brief orders echoed across the street, arrows were let loose. Verain turned to face them, opening her arms in the hope that one might take her. She closed her eyes...

Nothing.

Dartun held up his hands, generating an invisible barrier that sheltered the members of the Equinox. Arrows weren't deflected, they were disintegrated. The archers turned and ran as they realized how utterly useless they were. The other cultists moved from behind their own relic-originated shield wall and planted a few objects just in front, before retreating. Safely alongside the military, they turned back to view their work. Dartun laughed and walked forwards. He bent down and lugged a stone at the invisible wall they'd put before him. He repeated the gesture with a handful of similar stones, all the time stepping closer and closer. Then, as if the wall had become water, he pushed himself through – much to the disbelief of the two cultists. The soldiers moved shields to one side and revealed swords before advancing on Dartun.

He crouched into a ball. Screamed. Stood and spread his arms like a prophet.

A wave of energy knocked every soldier back several feet, sending their swords and shields clattering about the place. The two cultists turned to run and Dartun caught one of them by his feet. He pulled slowly, dragging the man back. With one hand on the cultist's waist, Dartun pulled again at one leg.

Verain could only hear the screams, which faded into a crunch as Dartun ripped him in two pieces. The cultist passed out just after he saw his own ruined legs sail back over his head and into the path of the military personnel.

'Who's next?' Dartun bellowed.

THIRTY-SIX

Lan examined the army stationed between their current position and where they needed to be. Troops had perched on rooftops, and there were anarchist snipers firing at anything that moved on higher levels. Cultists were attacking each other, too, shown by the purple sparks of light that crackled between buildings. She didn't think she could make any successful leaps with the priest on her back without being noticed.

Damn.

Time was slipping away and there was no other choice available: the safest thing they could do was head back the way they had come, back to Fulcrom's apartment where they could work out another route or perhaps consult him on some alternative paths.

*

When they got to his apartment, they found the place was a mess. His door had been kicked open, his belongings had been ransacked. Papers and clothes were strewn about the place, drawers had been knocked over, pictures smashed.

Lan strolled down the marble-tiled corridor and knocked on the neighbours' doors. Every one of them greeted her with some fear, whether it was because of her past or her attitude, she didn't care. Only one apartment revealed anything useful. An interspecies couple, garbed in almost identical brown tunics said that people in long grey coats had started a fight with him outside the building.

Lan tried to hide her fear. *Emperor's agents.* 'How long ago was this?'

'About two hours,' the woman said.

'What happened at the end?' Lan asked.

'Well, they tied him up,' the rumel said. 'It seems pretty strange to do that to an investigator if you ask me, and then they took him up-city.'

They haven't killed him, she thought. *They just want answers.* Lan smiled politely and only then noticed the children running around in the room behind, that this couple had children – when rumel and human relationships could not produce offspring, and suddenly it hit her somewhere deep inside, a place she'd deliberately hidden away.

'We adopted,' the woman said, noticing Lan's gaze. 'In case you were wondering.'

'Oh no, I . . . No.' She composed herself. 'Thank you for your answers.'

Stifling tears, Lan turned back to Fulcrom's apartment.

'We hope you find him,' the rumel called out behind her.

Lan arrived back to the room to find Ulryk sitting on the bed studying his books once again.

'Ulryk, if I can get you to the Glass Tower, will you be all right on your own for a few hours?'

'Of course. Did you find out what's happened to the investigator?'

'I think so. He's been taken by agents working for the Emperor. If so, he'll most likely be in Balmacara somewhere, and I want to get him out of there.'

'Of course, of course.'

*

They set off once again with urgency, taking a different route, a circular one around the outskirts of the conflict. It was longer by far, but for some way there wasn't the slightest sound of military personnel. Much of the city had locked itself away. As night took a grip on Villjamur, lights began to define windows of numerous shapes across the city, and people could be seen looking out onto the streets below, marooned in their own homes.

Every now and then Lan would run up a wall and across rooftops to assess the route they were on. They managed to navigate furtive channels through the city, going backwards, and sometimes underground, in order to make progress past militarized pockets. It took them two hours to get somewhere that should have taken half an hour, and all the time Lan kept thinking that she urgently had to get to Balmacara, she had to break in *somehow*.

'There it is!' Ulryk exclaimed, pointing at the Astronomer's Glass Tower. It was an impressive structure, like that of a gemstone half buried in the cobbled streets. A circular path ran around the base, and the surface of the glass was incredibly smooth, so that she could see the lights of the city reflected in its surface. It had eight equal-sized facets, about twenty feet wide, but none of them seemed to feature a door or window, no method of entry.

'Do you need to get inside?' Lan asked.

'I don't know,' Ulryk said, sincerely. 'I could be near it, or on top.'

Lan looked up, but couldn't see the end of the structure. Somewhere not too distant were the sounds of skirmishing. Two rumels ran the length of the street behind, their footsteps echoing in the plaza before the tower. 'I can try to get you up there,' she said, 'just to be safe.'

Ulryk rearranged his clothing to check that it was tight. 'Over your shoulder?'

'There's no dignified way to do this,' Lan replied. She stepped forwards, leaned over and Ulryk tottered sheepishly towards her. She grabbed his arm and pulled him onto her back, tuning into her inner forces to push his weight off the ground so that he was as light as a kitten.

Lan took a run at the wall – gritted her teeth and forced

herself upwards. Her feet slipped on the glass and she was forced to run and skip and jump in order not to collapse to the ground. Every step made a strange thud, which resonated through the building. The wind came at her in thick gusts once she crested the nearest line of slate roofs, and she could hear Ulryk gasping.

'We're nearly there,' Lan called. 'Hang on.'

'What else can I do?' Ulryk replied.

She was beginning to feel the pressure in her legs, the strain of using forces that she wasn't supposed to have, but before she knew it they were approaching the top of the tower. As if blindly tackling a staircase, she sought the lip of the roof with one foot then, when she felt there was enough to take their weight, she pressed down, lifting the two of them over, and Ulryk was flipped across onto the roof on his side.

'Oh, I'm sorry,' Lan said. 'Are you OK?'

Ulryk showed more concern for the books in his satchel: once satisfied they were fine, he began assessing his own body. 'I am well,' he said.

'Good.' Lan pushed herself back up. The rooftop was flat, with strange, gold markings carved into the surface. They looked as if they formed an atlas of the heavens, with little flourishes of algebra and diagrams sketched in between weirdly proportioned islands. Ulryk was already marvelling at the detail.

Lan looked back across the city, towards the formidable sight of Balmacara, the Imperial residence. Somewhere inside, the Emperor and his agents were maybe or maybe not doing something to harm Fulcrom.

'Go, Lan!' Ulryk shouted, looking up from his hands and knees. 'You must help him.' He stood up and took her hands.

'OK, Ulryk, do what you have to do. If you succeed, what then? Should we arrange to find you? Fulcrom and I aren't going to hang around the city, and I've no idea where Tane or Vuldon are.'

'If on your return you could revisit this tower, then . . . that would be a boon.' Ulryk moved to face the rest of the rooftop. 'If I am honest, I do not possess the knowledge of what will occur from this point onwards.'

Lan smiled at him. 'None of us do.'

She leapt to the tip of the tower and sought out the nearest roof. Lurking in the darkness, fifty feet below, and twenty feet across, was a bridge that would lead her to the third level of the city. What was more important is that she could see no signs of combat.

She tuned in. She found a spurt of magnetism.

She crouched and believed she could make it.

She clenched her fists and jumped.

*

The iron door opened, a beam of light fell across his hunched form, and the agents filed in one by one, as they did on the hour, every hour so far, armed with knives and questions. Fulcrom's hands were bound in crude manacles, but he wasn't chained to the wall – there was no need for that in such small confines.

It all started off nice and gentle, with the typical fake offer of friendship, as if trading goods. A mutual deal. Then matters proceeded to a little roughing up, mock-arguing among themselves, suggesting that his fate was yet to be decided. He guessed accurately at their techniques, but suspected he only had a couple of days until they would commence full-on torture, which might be even sooner given the state of the city. Their beatings centred on his abdomen at first, then his legs, leaving his face in a fit enough state to talk comfortably – they required that from him. A fist to the stomach, an iron bar to the legs, it blurred into one numbing onslaught. All they wanted to know was one very simple fact: where was Lan?

'Why are you so bothered when the city is falling apart?'

'The Emperor was insistent,' one replied, and there followed an awkward silence.

'Look, we know where the other two Knights are but what about the third man? Come on, tell us where it is – then all of this will be over.'

That was a lie, and he knew it, but he was enraged by their subtly abusive references to Lan's gender. '*She* is long gone by now – if she's got any sense.'

'This Lan – does he possess senses like the rest of us?' one of the agents asked.

Drawing on surprisingly deep reserves of strength, Fulcrom stood to his knees, stumbling more than once as he staggered to the centre of the room. His body thronged with pain. 'Lan is a woman. Say what you will about me, but that woman has helped save numerous citizens of the city.'

The agents spoke amongst themselves. 'Say, if he's fucking a *monster* like that, does that make him a queer? Punishment by death, that kind of act.'

Fulcrom dashed forward and grabbed the nearest of the agents, pulling his manacles over the man's head and back down tightly on his neck. They fell to the floor, the man's screams choked by chains, and the agents swarmed over the pair of them, and Fulcrom remembered only being punched repeatedly in the face . . .

*

Lan stood atop the roof of Balmacara. The route here had been surprisingly easy. All the guards were now withdrawing into the complex, and preparing only for assaults from the ground. The anarchist threat was immense. Much of the city had been claimed, but elsewhere, at the far end of the city, a far stranger force was gathering. At first she thought that Ulryk had been successful, but this was nowhere near where she had left the priest. Fluxes of magic ricocheted across the first level, by the outer gates of the city. Out here, in the wind and the snow, it was like one of the glorious storms of old, when the weather was warmer and summer storms were intense.

Lan had made a decision: Fulcrom had given Lan her life back – no, he had actually contributed massively to allowing her a life that she had never known before. Whatever it took, she wouldn't leave him in there to rot. This was no radical politics, but amidst a crumbling city it seemed to be something worth fighting for.

She walked along the edge of the roof and, when she sighted a guard with a crossbow patrolling the upper levels, she dipped down and crawled along between the tops of windows and the gutters.

Something moved down below, in one of the small walled gardens: shadows fought urgent, silent battles – she saw guardsmen hacked down from behind, or collapsing with a bolt or an arrow in the chest, and then a group slid along the perimeter of this enclosed zone, some leaping over the walls and then guiding the others through. Were these the anarchists? She felt a primitive urge to stop them, but then came to her senses. *This is no longer your battle. Fulcrom is all that matters.*

Then two voices, two figures running down the steps – these she recognized. Lan turned and skipped across the window frames, nearly slipping a few times.

From under the lip of the roof, she watched Vuldon and Tane stomp down the front steps of Balmacara, towards a unit of guardsmen.

What should she do?

'Tane,' she whispered.

She saw the werecat pause briefly, and Vuldon halted alongside him. Tane looked about the platform, then appeared to be in dialogue with Vuldon.

'Tane, you idiot. It's Lan, I'm here. Please play along.'

Again, dialogue between the two Knights. Had he heard her? She could only hope so.

'Arrest me when I land, and tell them you're taking me in!'

Before she could reconsider she pushed herself from the wall and walked through the air, then down across their path, where she skidded to a halt on the icy ground. A unit of soldiers began to approach, but Lan looked up expectantly at her former colleagues.

Vuldon nodded his understanding, and waved a big hand towards the approaching soldiers, who clattered to a halt. 'If I were you,' he bellowed, 'I'd get back to your stations like the Emperor commands. We'll take her in. She's dangerous.'

Tane pretended to force her hands behind her back, and turned her around to face the steps.

'What's your plan?' he whispered in her ear. 'If we take you inside you'll be taken into custody.'

'I want to break out Fulcrom,' she whispered, blinking as snow whipped into her face. Vuldon was negotiating with the soldiers to one side.

'Do you want to join him in prison?' Tane said. 'They'll kill the both of you – or at the very least, they'll take away your powers.'

Vuldon marched over. He said quietly, 'I guess you want us to help break Fulcrom out.'

Lan smiled. 'Damn right I do.'

Vuldon said, 'Well, the Emperor expects us to see to that fucking blur of magic on the horizon – it's a cultist gone mad or something.'

'That isn't my concern,' Lan said. 'My concern is Fulcrom, and then Ulryk, who's at the Astronomer's Glass Tower right now, conducting his ritual. I've already seen the anarchists heading into Balmacara. They'll act as a distraction. We've got a finite amount of time.'

'Well, after we get Fulcrom, we should see what's left of the city and evacuate it.'

'Evacuate an entire city?' Lan gasped.

The two men remained silent as they marched her up the

steps, and it came as a relief to be out of the bad weather and into the ornate hall beyond.

'We're on our own from here I guess,' Lan said. 'No taking sides, no serving others, no orders. Just us, just the Knights.'

'Fine by me,' Vuldon replied. A young soldier slipped on the wet marble of the corridor in his hurry to check them, and Vuldon slammed a fist into his throat. Winded, the man collapsed in a clatter of armour.

'Vuldon,' Tane snapped.

'What? Lan said we're on our own.'

'One could be more subtle about such things,' Tane remarked with a sigh.

*

Caley followed Shalev and her revenge-seeking comrades through the black gardens of the Imperial residence. They scaled over the enclosed spaces, silent and rhythmic in their process. They flowed through abandoned guard stations, over beds of tundra flowers, ducked below ornate, iron-framed windows, and step by step they negotiated their way towards a particular window stationed by the residence's kitchens. Two members of staff from Balmacara had long ago defected to the anarchists, and Shalev had gleaned all sorts of useful information including the layout of the residence.

Garbed in cheap, lightweight armour, and looking like some primitive leather-clad tribal warrior, Caley's heart beat furiously as he watched his idol at work. Shalev held a relic underneath the vast window, activated it, and stood back as the glass melted into a pool of glowing purple slop on the sill beneath. Shalev grabbed the relic and stored it in her satchel. She leapt up, resting her knee on the edge, before man-oeuvring inside.

Shalev held out her hand; Caley was the first to take it. Careful not to tread in the liquid glass, he hauled himself inside. As the others gained entry, he shuffled around in the darkness. The place reeked of stewed vegetables and herbs.

He could see the shimmer of blades and utensils on one wall, beside two enormous stoves. Pots and pans were hanging above his head, and he swore he spotted a rat's tail disappear around one corner.

Eventually the Cavesiders were all assembled inside and drawing their weapons before following Shalev through the darkness. Caley found himself getting increasingly angry as they exited the kitchen and rounded the corner. If he had been asked to imagine opulence, he would have struggled to match the reality of this place. How was it possible that people could live like this? Why was there a need for so much gold, so many gemstones, such a finely polished marble floor?

One of the others tried to knock a vase from its pedestal, but Shalev spun on her heels and gripped the ornament. She whispered harshly, 'I know you want to destroy this place – but not yet, not now. First, we kill Urtica. With him dead, the fun can commence.'

Shalev led the way, having memorized the route from a crudely drawn map. She clutched a relic in one fist, ready to apply it, and Caley didn't have a clue what it would do, but he felt safe with the fact that something secret and advanced could be used against the Imperials.

They progressed taking slow, cautionary steps, suddenly pressing themselves against the wall whenever anyone passed. Some corridors contained a constant level of activity: Imperial missives being carried about the place, soldiers marching with some urgency. It surprised Caley, given the time of night.

They climbed the stairs and reached the third or fourth level – he couldn't be certain which it was – and they were presented with a vast, carpeted floor. Murals covered the walls and ceilings, though they couldn't be discerned properly in this light.

Somewhere outside, the wind still moaned.

*

Lan was following Vuldon as he searched his memory and led them further and further into the heart of Balmacara. No one had stopped them to question their purpose, where they were taking Lan, and ultimately it ceased to matter. The focus of all activity was on the all-out war flaring in the city.

Tane was invaluable. He walked alongside Vuldon with his eyes closed, with Lan steering him gently, in order to tune in his hearing as effectively as possible. They scoured a few holding cells nearby, but there was no movement inside, not even anyone sleeping. There were no guards stationed, nothing to denote use of the facility. 'I'm certain this place contains nobody at all,' Tane declared.

Down ever musty stairwells, the walls giving way to raw stone, the Knights moved through the darkness, not wanting to even strike a match or speak to each other, in case they gave themselves away. Lan felt vulnerable down here, in these confines, without the freedom to move vast distances. Her faith and trust was in the other two – who had never once questioned her intentions, or her past.

Eventually they reached the solitary confinement zone. Everything had been too easy so far. Would Fulcrom be kept down here, in the worst of the gaols?

Tane waved again for them to stop, and on each occasion the tension was drawn out so much that it began to hurt. 'Other voices,' he breathed. 'In the distance.'

Rounding the corner, she saw an area where a few torches were burning steadily. Further along the corridor two guards were sat playing cards. They must have been a hundred feet away. The shadows were bold, and Lan didn't know what they might conceal.

Tane whispered, 'Agents,' and within a heartbeat there were four of the grey coats walking in a line towards them. She had no idea where they came from, but Vuldon stepped in front of her – for once, she wasn't annoyed.

'Hand it over,' one of the agents muttered.

Vuldon grunted a laugh; here was a fight he wanted.

'The he–she – give it here and we'll say no more. You go your own way, we'll go ours.'

'The *lady* ain't going anywhere,' Vuldon declared. 'At least, not with you.'

'Lan is to be decommissioned,' another said, she couldn't see who.

Lan leaned forward to Tane and asked, 'Is Fulcrom here?'

'Indeed,' Tane replied. 'I believe he's up behind the guards. One of those corner cells.'

Vuldon waded into the middle of the room, and beckoned the grey coats forwards. They fanned out, each carrying a weapon. Tane angled himself in alongside Vuldon, his claws extended, waiting.

Lan moved along the edge of the room, feeling the gaze of the agents upon her, but Vuldon saw to them. 'Enough of this stand-off shit,' he called out. 'Give me a fight, wankers.'

They seemed to know enough about Vuldon to back off from him; in fact, they actively *fled*. It was absurd. Vuldon and Tane chased after them, hurtling through the shadows. Lan left them to it and sprinted at an alien speed to the end of the corridor, past the two guards. She peered in one cell: nothing, then another, nothing. She banged on the bars and heard a groan from the third.

Suddenly the two soldiers were upon her. She leapt up, hovered momentarily with her hands pressing up against the brick ceiling, then she kicked one of their heads. Stunned, the man fell to the floor, and Lan landed beside him. She looked up as the other brought his sword down – she rolled to the left, before she spotted more agents approaching.

'Vuldon!' she screamed. 'Tane!'

'Come here, you freakish bitch,' one of the agents sneered, reaching out for her while the remaining guard tried to grab hold of her. Tane arrived just in time, drawing his claws across the man's throat: it blossomed with blood and he collapsed. The second agent stepped back alongside the soldier.

As Vuldon arrived and started unremittingly thumping the face of one of the other agents just behind, Lan moved to gaze inside the last cell in the corner.

There, hunched up against the wall, Fulcrom turned his bloodied face towards her.

'Stand back from the door,' Lan spluttered, trying to force it open – unsuccessfully. It was made from some alloy, a good inch or so thick, and with a complex-looking locking mechanism. She gripped the bars of the tiny window set into the door, and shifted her feet up onto the wall to one side. Then she began panting heavily, seeking her reserves of strength. As the fight raged on around her, she reached deep inside herself ... then a few moments later released a burst of magnetism. In the blast, her heels piled into the stone, her arms stretched taut at the elbows and wrists, and she wrenched the door – still within its frame – bringing the two surfaces inch by inch apart. She relaxed and collapsed to the floor.

'Vuldon,' she moaned loudly.

The big Knight lumbered to her side and, with one palm against the wall, he instinctively pulled the alloy away from the stone – it seemed so easy to get in now that she had prised the surfaces apart.

Vuldon moved back to allow Lan inside, where she took Fulcrom's outstretched hand.

'How are you? Did they hurt you?' she crouched beside him and her questions were answered well enough by just looking at him. His face was covered in blood, one eye had swollen shut. And ...

'My tail ...' he spluttered. Down to one side was his thick tail – severed, like discarded rope. Lan felt the tears seep into her eyes. 'How could they do this to you?'

'They wanted to know where you'd gone,' Fulcrom said. 'But I wouldn't tell them.'

This was because of me? She gathered him in her arms and sat with her back to the wall, and she was careful not to squeeze him too hard.

From the doorway and silhouetted against the crack of light, Vuldon, completely unmoved, said, 'I saw to them, Fulcrom. I got them for you. Every last one.' She saw drips of blood fall at his feet.

'Much appreciated,' Fulcrom replied. He seemed unsure what to make of Vuldon's state.

'Are you bleeding any more?' Lan asked Fulcrom, stroking his hair.

'No . . . My tail . . . it's probably no use to me any more . . .' Fulcrom spoke between breaths, still with pride. 'What is the plan?'

'First we need to clean you up.' Lan then informed him of the rest: the rogue cultists, the anarchists being close to victory, Ulryk's position on the Glass Tower.

'Ulryk,' Fulcrom said. 'He's the important one here. Whatever he's doing, we must follow him. I have a suspicion that, if the city is as you describe, not a lot else matters.'

*

Caley had fallen to the rear of the group, cautiously looking back to see if they were being followed – so far, they weren't. Still they moved through darkness. Caley's inability to see anything made him even more nervous than he should have been. He wanted to see his enemies. As they reached the large, winding stairway that led up to the fifth floor, Shalev whispered for them to stop. Two soldiers were stationed on the next floor, either side of the top of the stairs. There was no way of passing without being spotted – and that would be it, their cover blown, attention drawn, the Emperor ushered out of the building.

Shalev ordered them to huddle and she drew out another

relic, threw it up – something flashed – and some weird netted material descended over their group.

Caley heard the guards at the top of the stairs.

'That thunder?'

'No, it's lightning that makes flashes, idiot.'

'That's what I meant.'

'Must have been.'

Through the material, Caley could see one of them move down a few steps to investigate. Caley's heart thumped hard. The guard peered about, then returned to his post. 'Nothing 'ere,' he replied. 'Urtica's mad as old Johynn was. His paranoia's getting to you.'

The Cavesiders shuffled up the stairs, smothered in the netting, and stood between the two soldiers. Satisfied there were no others around, Shalev rolled out under the netting and something else flashed on the outside. By the time Caley managed to squirm his way out, too, the soldiers were lying on the floor unconscious.

'This is the level we need,' Shalev whispered.

It was a vast place, full of wood-panelling and portraits of figures in regal clothing, and Caley was in awe of the ostentatious display. Shalev pressed her ears against each door as they passed, merely as a caution.

Around the corner: four more soldiers. Upon seeing them, the guards ran towards the Cavesiders but, using their crossbows, they shot the guards in the neck or face, while three of the anarchists dashed up to stop their bodies from striking the floor loudly.

Steering them silently to one side, Shalev pointed towards the largest door in sight. With a relic in her hand, Shalev tried the handles on the double door – with a remarkable quietness, as if she'd been well practised in the arts of burglary. To everyone's surprise, the door opened easily, and in a hushed manoeuvre they flooded into the chamber.

Shalev activated a relic, which radiated a soft purple light across the room. It was vast, with rich carpets and a hearth that had long stopped giving out any warmth. There was a tall window at the far end, snow rattling against it. The sky was lightening ever so slightly as dawn dragged itself forwards.

Caley stepped towards a desk at the end of the room, and there he saw a leg poking out from beneath it. He ran around to the other side and called Shalev over. Everyone approached.

On the floor, the other side of the desk, lay Emperor Urtica – his throat was slit, a carving knife loosely gripped in one hand. Shalev moved in to take his pulse, tears in her eyes – tears of rage, Caley realized.

'No!' she cursed. Then it became a moan, a lament that she hadn't had the opportunity to do this herself. 'No, no, no, NO!'

Caley stepped back, afraid. Surely all that mattered was that Urtica was dead?

She picked up the knife from the Emperor's dead hand, straddled his corpse and repeatedly hammered the blade into his chest and neck. Blood spat up as she withdrew the knife. 'My family! My life! You took everything . . .'

A couple of the others tried to pull her off – she had transformed from the cool woman who had led them out of the depths of the city. Shalev eventually regained her composure, realizing what she had become. The now-mutilated corpse of the Emperor vaguely disgusted Caley. Everyone else looked at the body and then each other and then Shalev, who was covered in the Emperor's blood.

A question lingered in the air, unspoken: *Now what?*

Caley stepped to one side, to where the Emperor's hand pointed. Something had caught his eye. There, splattered by blood and almost hiding under the desk, was a piece of paper. Caley picked it up and opened it, but, embarrassingly, couldn't recognize the letters scrawled across it. He noticed the official-looking insignias, and called for one of the others.

'What is it, brother?' The red-headed woman, Arta, came to his side, and examined it.

'It's been smeared in blood, but the rest – the rest seems OK,' she said.

'What does it say?' Shalev snapped, approaching slowly, her chest rising and falling in great puffs as she tried to calm herself.

'Hang on,' Arta said, squinting at the paper in the dreary light of the room. Someone lit a candle and she thanked them. 'Right it ... reads as follows. "... in Villiren. Furthermore, from what we have witnessed, with the presence of this otherworld encroaching on ours, I am left with no other choice. I, Commander Brynd Lathraea, of the Night Guard regiment and senior commander of the Imperial Armies, do hereby withdraw the military – what is left of us – from Imperial duty under your name. We do not recognize your lineage any longer. To build a new future, to recover sufficiently, and to form an alliance with alien races in order to fight a further war, we will serve the Empress Rika, who you once dethroned. This is not a politically motivated decision, but one of great urgency in order to defend the Boreal Archipelago."' Arta looked up and said, 'I can't see what the rest says, since the ink is blurred.'

'Is that why Urtica killed himself?' Caley wondered out loud. 'He's got nothing any more. No soldiers, no city, nothing.'

'What with the Cavesiders taking over much of Villjamur, he must have choked on how quickly things imploded.'

'Coward's way out, if you ask me,' someone muttered.

'I wouldn't be so sure that was all ...' Seemingly distracted, Shalev walked over to the window, allowing bright flashes to brighten her face momentarily.

Was that really lightning? Caley wondered.

'I have never seen such power,' Shalev breathed. Bolts of purple light shot upwards, and flared across the rooftops. 'This force is immense. What is that?'

The others gathered around the vast window and stared out at the scene. As the snow rattled against the glass, the city trembled. Now they'd stopped still, Caley could feel the ground vibrating beneath his feet.

'Is it a storm?' Arta offered.

'No,' Shalev said. 'No, I recognize that light. To the eye of a cultist, that is the energy of the ancients being used – as I would use it through relics.'

'Maybe a bunch of cultists then,' Caley said.

'No, little brother,' Shalev said. 'Not on such a scale. I've seen the clouds turn on Ysla with only a fraction of the power of this being used.'

They watched in horror as distant buildings collapsed and bridges buckled.

'Our brothers and sisters are out there,' Arta gasped. Caley turned to Shalev. While the anarchists were in control and there was something of a plan, he could go with the flow, happy to help in whatever way he could manage. All of a sudden came the realization that there were people under those falling buildings – his fellow Cavesiders.

'We've got to do something,' Caley pleaded, and Shalev looked down at him, surprised at his sudden raw emotion.

She placed a hand on his shoulder. 'I will see what I can do.'

*

Lan carried Fulcrom over her shoulder, from the depths of Balmacara and back up the way they came, until her body throbbed with so much pain that Tane had to take over. The four of them progressed through dark ornate halls, the light of dawn showing through tall, arched windows. Momentarily they paused outside one of the Jorsalir prayer rooms, where

Lan found a copper canister of holy water. As Vuldon and Tane stood guard, she mopped the blood from Fulcrom's face, and checked for any further serious injuries. Admittedly, once he was cleaned up a little, she didn't feel as bad. The stub of his tail was wrapped in cloth and that, too, would heal. He said nothing as she saw to his wounds – but his gaze was full of gratitude.

When they headed outside, Vuldon announced to the guards that an Inquisition officer had been injured in combat, that there was a situation developing. Unbelievably they headed inside looking as though they meant business with their swords drawn, their shields raised, and heads down.

They'll believe anything in such uncertain times.

The snow had abated, the wind had ceased, but sounds still travelled from afar: great rumblings, structures falling, screaming from the levels below.

'Where now?' Tane asked.

'First,' Fulcrom said, 'let me see if I can walk on my own.'

'It'll be quicker if we carry you,' Vuldon said.

'Let me try to walk,' Fulcrom said. Tane lowered him to his feet, and Lan came around to offer her support under one arm. 'My legs are aching like bastards,' Fulcrom said. 'I need to walk it off though, and to figure out my balance now I've no tail.'

The pain on his face eventually faded, as he either got used to it, or could control his reactions. The sky was the colour of wine, with flashes of lighter and darker purple denoting truly odd cloud formations.

Vuldon and Tane marched over to the viewing platform, and Lan then steered the hobbling Fulcrom towards them. The panorama revealed a city that on one side was still cluttered with glorious architecture, and on the other a void where bridges and tall buildings and slate rooftops should have been.

Half of Villjamur had collapsed. They were lost for words.

More and more stone toppled over amidst flashes of purple light.

'That's the mad cultist,' Vuldon said.

'We should have attempted to stop him,' Tane muttered.

'I doubt we'd have been much use,' Vuldon replied. 'We'd have been buried under there if we tried.'

'Look,' Lan said, pointing out the Astronomer's Glass Tower, which, almost out of sight, was still standing in the half of the city that had not been wrecked.

A column of white light extended upwards, into the clouds, turning them into a textured whirlpool, and creating vast and weird streaks that extended for miles above the city.

'Has the priest succeeded in whatever it was he was trying to do?' Vuldon muttered.

'Can we make our way there safely?' Lan asked aloud.

Tane peered directly down, then across, assessing the potential for a route. 'Well, there appears to be absolutely no fighting anywhere near us. Perhaps that chap who's ruined half of Villjamur has taken everyone with him.'

'That's a staggering death toll,' Vuldon declared. Even he seemed shocked by the violence.

'Ulryk,' Fulcrom said. In the light of the day, he looked much better. 'The priest is onto something we can barely understand. Given that this city is crippled, he's the only one with a future mapped out.'

THIRTY-SEVEN

Every minute brought more casualties and collapsed structures, until there seemed nothing left in their path that could possibly prevent them. Was Dartun yet satisfied?

Numb and broken, the remnants of the Order of the Equinox were marched in front of Dartun, through narrow streets, passing places that had not yet been wrecked by his savagery. Verain didn't care any more. She just wanted it to end.

Her legs ached, and she had no energy left, but somehow she found herself trudging ever upwards. Each of them slipped at least twice on the ice, falling face-first or flat on their backs. Images from the otherworld flashed into her mind randomly, though she didn't understand why, and she looked across at the members of her order not knowing who any of them were. Was such forgetfulness generated from her exhaustion? In the distance she could hear the movements of people, of skirmishes in the shadows, but she didn't have the energy to wonder what they were.

Like the undead creatures that Dartun had once bred with technology, she shambled without purpose.

Level after level, street by street, they eventually reached the platform before – *What was this?* – before Balmacara, a vast residence. Bodies littered the stone platform, their shadows cast long by the sun.

'Yes,' Dartun said. 'Yes, this will do nicely.'

'For what?' someone said. She didn't know who spoke, nor did she recognize the voice.

Dartun began to hunch and mutter something, not to himself, to someone else – but there was no one else but the members of the Equinox present. Suddenly he ran to one of the others and grabbed the man's throat: the cultist seemed too exhausted to struggle against Dartun's grip, pawing meekly at his wrist.

Dartun pressed his fingers into the man's neck, stilling him, and he peeled back the man's skin, ripping it from his head. Something weirdly ornate was in its place – a metallic object the shape of a head, with purple lighting webbing intricately along the surface. Dartun continued ripping the skin from the man's torso – clumps of flesh flopped uselessly to the ground, with a black liquid – not blood – pooling by his feet. Dartun did the same to all of them in turn, ripping them open one by one and discarding their skin and flesh in a thoroughly businesslike manner.

He arranged these metallic forms in a circle, like a primitive henge, and occasionally light flickered between them.

Finally, he came to Verain. She didn't cry, didn't scream, even though she knew what was coming.

'So is this all we were to you?' she breathed. 'Some fucked up containers for these . . . whatever they are?'

Dartun seemed to recognize something within her eyes then, a connection to his former self; but it was quickly gone, replaced by the cold, calm gaze he'd had since returning through the gates: 'You were once something, Verain, but we all have a greater purpose in life.'

'You sold your soul in that otherworld. I don't know what you did, but just finish it now.'

'I did love you,' Dartun said. 'I hope you realize. You would have been killed there anyway. I saved all of you – I gave each of you life, for just a little longer.'

Verain grunted her disapproval. 'Love – and what would you know about that?'

'I understand,' Dartun continued, 'that love quite often involves a little sacrifice.'

The last things she saw: his advancing form, his hands raised to her face, her head tipping back and blissful, blissful relief . . .

*

'What the fuck was that?' Vuldon demanded. The Knights paused at the foot of the Astronomer's Glass Tower, and stared back up towards Balmacara.

A thick column of purple light, as wide as the Imperial residence itself, extended up towards the sky and drove thunderously into the cloud-base. A vortex formed, spiralling slowly, whipping up debris and loose stone, whirling it upwards, crackling into the sky.

There came the sound of something ripping – a tearing through the fabric of the world. A form seemed to present itself just the other side of the lowest clouds – a dark bruise in the sky. The tip of it came into view.

'You are shitting me,' Vuldon gasped.

The darkness eclipsed the sky, bringing a shadow over the entirety of Villjamur.

A dark rock face, which stretched beyond the city limits, lowered itself slowly, and soon it came so close it clipped the top fortifications on the Imperial residence. Then it was clear this was something more: not so much a floating island, but a discernible city of sorts, with weirdly proportioned structures and baroque architecture.

*

Caley was the first one to break free from the column of light, his arms and legs windmilling as he careened down the streets of the city. He thumped into the angle of a wall and, stunned, he looked back to see if the others had made it –

445

they hadn't. Their bodies were floating clockwise, caught in the vortex suction of the light.

Caley was helpless. His brothers and sisters were destined to die, and all he could do was watch – and, yes, Shalev was in there too. He was all that was left from the mission to kill Urtica. He alone possessed the story.

Caley would tell no one of Shalev's breakdown and savagery in Balmacara. The Emperor was dead, that was all that mattered – and only he was present. He would tell all who listened how Shalev killed Urtica. He would make sure her name went down in legend.

Swallowing back emotion, he turned once again and charged through the streets.

A few people looked on idiotically and he screamed for them to get away. Many of them listened, a few were too numbed by the sight and he ploughed into them, knocking them sideways.

Soldiers paused from combat with Cavesiders as, in unison, the remaining populace craned their necks to watch the immense structure lower itself over Villjamur.

*

Lan scrambled up to the top of the Astronomer's Glass Tower, breathless as she crested the lip of the roof. She peered about and saw Ulryk hunched in the middle – *no, that isn't him*. This wasn't right. Ulryk wasn't wearing a dark-blue cloak with a hood, nor did he stoop as badly as this figure.

'Hello?' Lan offered, but the figure remained with its back to her. She approached and could see the books on the floor by the stranger's feet. Where was Ulryk then?

When she was just a few feet away, she paused – the figure reeked of some industrial odour. Its movements were minute and eccentric. The thing turned its head and she gasped. It reared up in front of her, several feet tall, with a face that was half bone and half metal, and two human eyes regarding her.

'Who are you?' Lan asked. 'Did Ulryk – did he summon you?'

The figure cocked its head as if remembering how to speak. 'I am ... Frater Mercury.' His voice was unnaturally soft and gentle, which surprised her. She was entranced by his gaze and stepped closer. Beneath his hood, the left side of his face was a silver plate, with tiny gemstones set inside, and the other half wasn't quite bare skull, but the skin was adhering so tightly it might well have been.

'Where's Ulryk?'

Frater Mercury grimaced at her words and indicated the books on the floor.

'I don't understand,' Lan replied. Then, 'He spoke of you like you were a god – are you one?'

'There is no god,' Frater Mercury replied. 'There is only what I constructed.' The immense floating structure in the sky lowered itself, Frater Mercury held up his hand. 'We must flee before this –' he said a word she didn't understand '– fills the city with abominations.'

'I was told to take Ulryk down, where a group of us are evacuating the city.'

'I need time to prepare. This was not meant to happen with such speed.' His weird hybrid face fiercely regarded the presence in the sky. Spires crumbled and objects – creatures – flapped and arced down in ragged patterns of slow flight.

'OK, we'll get you out.' If this was some saviour of the world, Lan wasn't terribly impressed. She bent down to collect Ulryk's books and slipped them in the discarded satchel. 'Can you climb down?'

Frater Mercury gave something that was close to a laugh. He stepped towards her, touched her shoulder, and—

—they appeared on the ground by the base of the tower.

'Fuck did you come from?' Vuldon said. Fulcrom slowly turned, a look of astonishment on his face, and Lan moved to his side. She explained who the newcomer was, and that

447

Ulryk had vanished. Tane padded around sniffing at Frater Mercury, while Vuldon stepped closer to him. No one quite knew what to make of the figure. Even Lan expected something more impressive, after all, she had gone to all that trouble to help Ulryk get *The Book of Transformations* to summon this supposed saviour.

Nearby houses collapsed. Screaming increased tenfold. Columns of light began drifting down from the sky structure, bringing with them more of the malformed creatures.

'We should go,' Frater Mercury declared.

'No,' Vuldon said.

'Come *on*,' Tane stressed. 'We need to clear out of here before the city is destroyed.'

'I have been made to help people survive,' Vuldon replied calmly. 'While there are people that need helping, I just can't go anywhere.'

'He's right,' Lan replied, and Fulcrom gave her a look of despair. 'What? He is. I know we said we'd escape, but how could you honestly go with all of this on your conscience?'

'This is rubbish,' Tane declared.

'And I'd just hold you up,' Fulcrom said.

'Tell you what – Fulcrom, you get this friend of Ulryk's out of the city.'

'OK,' the rumel said. 'Ulryk thought he had powers that would help . . . so I guess we'll see if that holds true. But, Lan, are you sure this is right?'

Lan nodded. It was difficult to explain to anyone, how being a Knight had given her a purpose in life she had never felt before.

'There's a hamlet half a mile towards the coast,' Vuldon said. 'Villreet. We'll meet up there when we make it out.' He gave precise directions to the others, but Fulcrom knew the route well.

Lan ran up to Fulcrom and she kissed his lips softly, before their foreheads touched and she closed her eyes. Eventually she pulled away and handed him the satchel with Ulryk's books.

Lan watched Fulcrom leave with Frater Mercury, who marched with an awkward, mechanical gait. Tane lingered there for a moment, then he said, 'They'll need looking after too', and went after them.

'Selfish fuckwit,' Vuldon said, but Lan was glad he was by their side.

*

Vuldon and Lan saved lives at random. There was no strategy, no plan of action other than to help with a mass evacuation. There were tunnels at hand, and well-known routes, and Vuldon and Lan tried to steer as many citizens out of the city before these passageways all collapsed.

People were running in all directions. Dust clouds from wrecked buildings drifted downwind, adding to the confusion. Orders were barked out, and occasionally soldiers attempted to establish some kind of order. People were aghast as they watched bridges fall from the sky. Debris clattered and caught the wind.

Someone had the ingenuity to be ringing bells by the entrance to escape tunnels, guiding citizens through the dust.

'Where are the children?' Lan asked. 'I've only seen adults up here.'

'They're hopefully already down below,' Vuldon said. 'If my plan worked and the priest was right.'

*

Caley suddenly wanted to be a kid again. He wanted to be near his family, listening to stories or being cuddled by his aunt or whatever – anything other than being out here, in this chaos. The anarchist networks were probably shattered – or, at least, he couldn't find anyone he knew.

He stopped still, as the panic flourished, and the thing in the sky started dismantling Villjamur. He came across one of the old information boards, where an old copy of MythMaker was still nailed up, and he looked at the comforting pictures, never quite knowing the full story. Suddenly another kid ran up to him, a very young blonde-haired girl. 'Hey, that's not the latest – other kids are saying there's more nailed to the tavern round the corner, and it's something everyone has to see urgently, but I'm ... too scared to go there on my own. My folks ... I don't know where they are.'

Caley was about to make a comment about how posh she sounded, when something exploded nearby. It was shortly followed by the presence of a hideous-looking half-beast, half-human form, with two horns. People began screaming as it lashed out at them.

'I'll go with you,' Caley said. *Sister*. He took the girl's hand and steered her along the street. They rounded the corner and at the end of an abandoned plaza was the tavern, and the door to the building did indeed seem to hold a nailed piece of parchment.

With the wind gusting behind, Caley and the girl focused on the flapping instalment of MythMaker.

'Can you read?' Caley asked.

The girl nodded and began reciting the story. Just then, she began to go into some weird trance. She breathed one word over and over again – 'Underground'. Caley looked at the pictures and saw some weird symbols sketched all over them.

The girl tugged his sleeve with remarkable force, ushering him back through the streets as if she knew the way on instinct – all the more strange considering she'd previously been afraid to cross the street on her own. There was an old stairwell by the corner of a butcher's shop, and she kept on muttering, 'Underground, underground ...'

They descended into the darkness, where Caley could hear voices – not one or two, but hundreds, a bizarre unison he hadn't heard since one of Shalev's early gatherings.

'Where is this place?' Caley asked her, but the girl ignored him, all the time muttering the same word as the city rumbled overhead. Caley slid his way through some of the patches where water had frozen, and used his hands against the wall to guide himself. It was only in this relative calm that he realized how tired he was – he had been up all night, and through the dawn. Presently he came across a flow of children of all ages, holding torches. They were in one of the old escape tunnels, a vast arched route that reeked of sewage. A few adults were shouting things to control the kids, but no one seemed to pay much attention to them.

And the children were all individually whispering the word: 'Underground . . .'

Caley released the girl's hand and moved through the throng until he came across an adult. 'Hey, mister, what the fuck is going on?'

'Mind your language, runt,' the man replied, pushing back his hood to reveal a bald head. 'Anyway, I've no idea. Took my youngest to read one of them Mythica things—'

'MythMaker,' Caley corrected.

'That's right. And he just started going all strange and was insistent we followed him outside. I didn't want to come, what with all the fighting, but he started screaming, so we came with him, and he brings us down here – and just look at all this!' He gestured around to the tunnel, and the children who were all marching one way.

*

'What do you mean?' Lan demanded. 'Did you have a plan?'

'MythMaker,' Vuldon replied.

'What about it?'

'It was my creation. I made it. Then the priest showed me a way of controlling people's minds with certain symbols. I knew some kind of shit was kicking off – though I'd no idea it would be this bad – and wanted all the children to get somewhere safe, underground. So I asked Ulryk on how best to do that.'

Lan didn't know quite how to respond. 'And did it work?'

'Can you see many children?' Vuldon replied.

They continued through the streets, steering people away. Where buildings had collapsed, Vuldon and Lan inspected the wreckage for any survivors. Where possible, they lifted people out. And strange creatures were walking about the city now, things she could barely comprehend, with two, three, five, nine legs, or sets of eyes, or wings. They had been sent down from the dark structure up above, which now hovered over Villjamur.

The creatures began attacking civilians – until Vuldon and Lan stepped in.

Vuldon picked up some discarded military swords, threw one across to Lan. By the time she caught it, Vuldon was hacking into some of the beasts using nothing but raw strength and brutality. Lan joined him, using her powers to step through air as her advantage. She chopped at the creatures in their purple columns of light before they had a chance to reach the ground. Blood splattered over a wide area, while citizens ran for cover.

In the following hour, Lan and Vuldon moved their way down-city, from the third to the second level, towards the outer walls, slashing down incomprehensibly structured creatures, or guiding people to safety. In the distance, the higher levels of Villjamur were no more. The enormous sets of city gates were open; it looked as though they had been blown apart by some astounding force and, from where they were stood, she watched a tide of humans and rumels pour out towards the refugee camps, into the snow, some travelling on horseback but many on foot.

'Vuldon,' Lan said, in a sudden pause in combat, 'what happens when we get out of the city? We're going to have to steer everyone to safety again. There'll be tens of thousands of people out there.'

Vuldon shrugged. 'Worry about that when we get out.'

'We should join them now,' Lan said. 'Look.'

More and more creatures were descending slowly upon the city, floating down to the streets where they would create carnage. Not even the exotic hybrids she had known in the circus could match these monsters for sheer macabre form. And there were more: it looked like rumels were among their ranks, red-skins, garbed in some alien military attire, and brandishing swords.

'There's hardly anyone left here to help,' she said. 'We should go.'

For a moment, Vuldon didn't do anything, and she prodded him again: 'I feel your need to help people as much as anyone, Vuldon. But seriously, there's nothing left of this city. And the people outside will need our help.'

Sunlight streamed across the tide of people, and she moved towards them, 'Come on, Vuldon.'

The huge Knight eventually turned to follow her, but then he shot to one side – a small family was backed up against a wall by a former jewellery shop, a woman and three children, while a bruise-coloured attacker with three legs and several arms reared above them. Bearing hideous, vicious rows of teeth, it must have been twice the height of a man. The woman brought her children closer to her, closed her eyes, obviously expecting that death was only seconds away. But Vuldon managed to get there in time: he shouldered the thing's legs, rolling under it and bringing it down with a colossal groan.

Lan ran towards the family, and pleaded with them to follow her. As she steered away from the conflict, she observed another beast emerging from a side street, running towards where Vuldon was struggling with the other one, rage set into its abnormal face, its maw wide.

The two creatures set upon Vuldon. The Knight lashed out but the creatures were quick. She couldn't see much of the combat because of the blur of their thick legs, but Vuldon was now on the ground, face down, his blade to one side.

She gasped and stood still, the family moving on without her. One of the creatures reared up and then stomped on Vuldon: blood pooled beneath him. His form was battered. She moved to help him but stopped as more creatures stumbled to seize this moment: things with three, four, five legs and a thick and shimmering hide. They set upon him with their gaping mouths, rows of teeth picking at him and discarding chunks of flesh to one side. Lan felt sick, wanted to look away, but couldn't. She backed off, knowing that she could not hope to help Vuldon.

In the following silence, she heard a foreign language – two red-skin rumel soldiers were giving orders to the beasts.

Tears in her eyes, she ran after the family, and when she caught up with them it took her a while to realize that it was the mother who was now helping her. She placed her arm around Lan and steered her into a vast flow of people, all the while whispering words of encouragement.

*

They entered a wide street, the main thoroughfare that led out of the city. Between buildings three or four floors high, hundreds of people from all walks of life were marching with bundles of possessions in their arms, on their backs, or in little handcarts. The noise was intense, the mood morose. Behind them, the destruction of Villjamur was clear to see.

Not one bridge was still standing. At their ruined edges, figures were waving down for help. Some – incredibly – were jumping to escape the horrors behind them. People screamed intermittently. Bass groans occasionally marked the collapse of a distant structure. Dust clouds from fallen architecture were coughed out as if the city was on fire. And all the while, the presence in the sky continued to emit shafts of light that delivered savage creatures down to the higher levels.

Villjamur was no more.

*

But from the chaos, came order. Surprisingly, it was people she had seen fighting for the anarchists who were now helping out their former enemies. They were steering people, guiding and directing. Groups had been organized to remove rubble from the main avenue out of the city, and from around the gates of the city. The elderly were helped onto horseback, two per animal, then guided through the throng. Soldiers, too, had joined in with the anarchists, suddenly putting aside their official orders because of the new priorities.

A fight broke out between Shelby Corporation soldiers and the regular military. All she could glean from the situation was that the Shelby soldiers refused to help out with the evacuation since it was not in their remit, and they hadn't the training to cope. They skulked out through the gates, protecting no one.

Lan passed them. She moved through the towering metal gates, burned and melted back around the edges, through enormous city walls, and she could smell the tang of the open countryside, the mud and the rank odours from the refugee camps. People were fleeing in one direction for the most part, along the sanctuary road, though smaller groups peeled off across the snow-covered tundra. And children – so many children were here.

Lan felt as though a part of her had vanished, that she no longer possessed the ability to aid these people. Lan turned towards the direction of Villreet, and prayed that Fulcrom was already there: he was her only hope for salvaging something from this wreckage.

Thirty-Eight

A hamlet with a population of about a hundred suddenly found itself swelling in numbers – thousands were now travelling through on its narrow mud road, on foot or horseback or bundled up in blankets in the carts.

Sleet fell strangely by the coast. The warmer onshore breeze forced it horizontally, and it was loaded with a salty tang, drenching the citizens who, wrapped in wax cloaks, shawls or furs, tromped the already muddy road into a quagmire. A village of two streets, or what approximated to streets, had been silently besieged. Locals peered out of their doors, either outraged or confused. Seagulls screamed along the beach and, in the distance, the sea fizzed its way onto the sands.

Late afternoon, and the sun suddenly revealed itself, creating rainbows – in one direction, that was. In the other lay the crippled ruins of Villjamur, and the landmass above it, which Fulcrom still couldn't believe could actually hang there – in the sky – without any columns or chains holding it up. Every time he saw a piece of the city fall, and a dust plume rise, he prayed – though he was not a religious man – that Lan and Vuldon would be all right.

'What's the plan now?' Tane asked.

A good question, that, Fulcrom thought.

Someone had recognized him as an investigator, and even

though he claimed he no longer worked for the Inquisition, he found that word instantly spread to dozens of people, and they looked to him for leadership.

The cloaked figure to one side, Frater Mercury, was hidden from view. Fulcrom didn't want any suspicion drawn to the figure. He needed to interview the man – if that was indeed possible – to find out what his purpose was. But not yet – not until he had found Lan.

He stood by the entrance to the village on an upturned crate, and scanned the masses for Vuldon: he would tower above these people by a good foot, but Fulcrom saw only the dreary faces of those who had lost their homes or loved ones.

And they came in vast numbers, crying or shivering or simply expressionless.

He stood there for a good hour, his body aching from the bruises. He was aware of a wide open wound on his thigh, conscious that it could become infected, but there were no medical supplies here, no cultists. Frater Mercury, possibly upon seeing the pain in Fulcrom's expression, moved nearer, his weird half-face showing beneath his hood. Those eyes seemed ageless. He hobbled towards Fulcrom's leg, and some connection transmitted between their minds, something Fulcrom was barely aware of. Frater Mercury slowly leant down and with a whip of his finger split the material above Fulcrom's thigh, exposing the crippled flesh to the air. Within a minute, the newcomer's fingers were at work within his flesh, and they moved at lightning speed. Using no materials other than the thick rumel skin, Frater Mercury patched up Fulcrom's thigh – and then rested a hot palm to the surface, cauterizing the wound, but Fulcrom felt no pain. After the act, the hand withdrew, leaving the flesh as good as new.

'That's a miracle,' Fulcrom said, his breath clouding the air.

Without saying a word, Frater Mercury backed off and resumed his motionless stance.

'Tane,' Fulcrom said, 'would you head out there to see if you can spot Lan?'

'Indeed,' he replied, and went into the throng.

'There's no need!' shouted a voice. Tane turned back to see Lan file in alongside him.

Fulcrom stepped down from his crate. He overcompensated, expecting some signs of strain in his leg, and immediately slipped in the mud, falling to one knee when that didn't happen. Lan came over to him with a wry smile. 'It's a bit early for a proposal don't you think?'

She lifted him up and pulled herself in to embrace him. Fulcrom's heart thumped. He didn't want to let her go – not any more. Her cheeks were cold, and she wasn't wearing any outer layers – just her stained Knights uniform. Tane had found a shawl and placed it on Lan's shoulders, and Fulcrom nodded his thanks to him. They must have been there for a good minute before anyone spoke.

'Where's Vuldon?' Tane asked.

Lan bowed her head and didn't reply.

'Is he still there?' Tane pressed.

'Later,' Fulcrom cautioned, and held up his hand.

They all turned to regard the explosion in the distance, too late to see whatever blast caused the remains of Villjamur to turn to fire. Clouds had recently drifted away from the city, exposing the landmass above in its full glory.

It was something quite macabre, a ragged floating island of black spires, around which creatures were fluttering – he imagined them to be immense.

'The gods help us. That floating fortification – it's moved, I swear. It's simply so large and moving so slowly, I haven't noticed until now, but its position has moved.'

Frater Mercury began pulling Fulcrom's sleeve, and he untangled himself from Lan.

Gods can't help. Maybe I can. We need to talk. The words seemed planted in his head. Fulcrom nodded. 'Come on.'

They walked to one of the nearest houses, a one-storey wooden shack painted bright green. There was a measly excuse for a front garden, full of dead or decaying flowers, and a small porch. Fulcrom marched them all up the steps and banged on the door.

There was no answer, so Lan moved in and kicked it open. A wiry looking fisherman stood up from his table and issued expletives.

'Villjamur Inquisition,' Fulcrom announced, and gestured for him to get back. The man meekly stood aside and they commandeered the table. Frater Mercury followed them in.

The room was basic: a round table, a few wooden chairs, landscape paintings, an old iron-framed mirror and a rust-encrusted stove.

Sitting down carefully, Lan looked at them, meeting Tane's searching gaze with a sad frown, 'Vuldon's dead.'

'Impossible,' Fulcrom gasped.

Lan nodded. 'He died saving a family. We were on our way out. I couldn't do anything.' Her gaze fell to the table.

Fulcrom placed a hand on her arm. 'It's OK, we can talk about it later.'

Tane remained silent and aghast.

'Death is not always the end,' Frater Mercury spoke suddenly. His accent was strained, his words pronounced slowly and clearly as if reading the words from some distant tapestry. 'His bodily pieces. Bring them. I repair.'

'Who and what are you?' Fulcrom asked. 'Why did the priest bring you here, and where is he?'

'Priest?'

'Ulryk,' Fulcrom said.

There was the flicker of expression on Frater Mercury's face. 'You have no . . .' *idea who I am*, the voice continued in

Fulcrom's head. Could Lan hear too? Her expression indicated this was the case.

Villjamur, my word she has grown. She was a village like this when I left. Ulryk has brought me back to this realm safely. He has been consigned to the book – a momentary cost. You must take me away from this place. The Policharos will move.

'The what?'

The Policharos in the sky. It will move. It will come for these people. It will eradicate them, and you. But not me, no – I had hoped to re-enter this Archipelago at a more suitable location. Of all the Wayfarer Towers, the priest chose the one in Villjamur where, it seems, plans were already afoot to invade.

'Pretty ungrateful towards a man who summoned you.'

I haven't the patience! The mirror on the wall shattered, everyone looked at each other, afraid. *Take me to your elders.*

'We have no elders. If you mean superiors, there are none – the city was destroyed. For all I know, the Emperor and the Council with it.'

There are movements in the east. Take me there.

'We know little about that,' Lan said. 'There was a war near Villiren, that's what was said in *People's Observer* – and where most of the military have been sent.'

Yes. Your people were successful. And have met others who can help – people who worship me. They seek an alliance. Your former ruler is alive.

'Urtica?'

No, the woman.

'Rika . . .' Fulcrom said. 'This changes everything.'

Yes. We all must move now.

'Look,' Fulcrom replied, 'I'm sure in your world you're rather important. But there are a few thousand people on the open road, many of whom are likely to die tonight. If we go east, then they're coming too. We can't leave them here, not at the mercy of that thing in the sky. I'm sure that tens of thousands of lives might not mean a lot to you, but they've nothing else.'

Frater Mercury looked repeatedly, and rapidly, from Lan to Fulcrom, Fulcrom to Lan.

If I must...

*

They lined up under a darkening sky on the porch to the hut. Fulcrom's gaze fixed on Frater Mercury's weird movements as he zigzagged through the crowd in desperate lurches, until he found the centre.

'What's he going to do?' Lan asked, holding Fulcrom's arm tightly.

'I have absolutely no idea,' Fulcrom replied.

Frater Mercury began wailing in some bizarre tones, until the ground began to shake. Fulcrom gripped the railing of the porch with one hand, and Tane stepped down to get a little closer.

There were terrified screams from the people huddled in the village centre as the muddied road on which they had travelled started to rise. A few jumped off hysterically, while others held on to each other. A segment of the very earth began to rise in the centre. Then came the sound of snapping planks: two of the wooden houses began to unbuckle themselves and collapse inwardly in a swirl of purple light, their structures disassembling, tumbling haphazardly, and then reassembling as circular constructs placed beneath the raised wedge of earth.

'Wheels,' Fulcrom gasped. 'He's making wheels to move that segment of earth.'

They watched in awe as an immense, basic carriage was formed from the elements: it was at least fifty feet wide, this mountain of mud and grass, and carried the better part of a hundred people – though it could easily carry more.

Fulcrom could see the obviousness of this construct: huge

numbers of people could be transported from the city's limits, away from the – *What did he call it?* – the Policharos. Well, they could if this ungainly chariot could be moved.

Another bank of earth rose ten feet up. Wooden wheels were formed once again beneath, and then another, until four of them – the entire length of the street through this village – lined up, one behind the other.

'How are they going to move?' Lan asked.

A few moments later, her answer came. In the brouhaha, Fulcrom had lost sight of Frater Mercury, but his vision was drawn to a group of horses – whose riders were pulled off and into the mud with a thud. The animals – four in all – were guided nearer the carriages, and stood alongside a wheel, their heights being roughly equal.

Then a hideous miracle: the beasts, in a haze of purple light, began to shudder and contort, growing in size – monstrously so. Bulbous and with abnormal musculature, the four horses – one black and three greys – loomed above what was left of the village.

It didn't take a genius to work out what would happen next.

Fulcrom leaned down to Tane: 'Get those people out of the way.'

Tane nodded and ran into action, bundling men, women and children away from the huge hooves, which kicked and stomped aggressively. Screams followed, as a handful of the unfortunate were pressed deep into the mud. People wanted to both leave and stay – they saw the sense of these earthly carriages, but were in fear of their lives. There was a magic at work now that they didn't comprehend – and neither did Fulcrom. He seldom thought of the word magic, especially after having worked with cultists, but what he had witnessed here was so . . . inexplicable, so unnatural, that there was no other term suitable.

Frater Mercury lunged into view and spoke into Fulcrom's

462

head. *Here is our transportation. I estimate we can take two thousand.*

'It's not enough,' Fulcrom said. Lan looked at him. 'We need to take everyone,' he continued, 'or there's no point.'

It seemed no effort to Frater Mercury, who tromped off into the masses once again, and then a boy came and stood before Fulcrom, a scruffy kid who wasn't young, but not quite a man either.

'Can I help you?' Fulcrom asked.

The boy looked wearily to Lan. 'Is she gonna arrest me if I say I'm an anarchist?'

Fulcrom shrugged. 'Why don't you ask her?'

'Are you?' the kid said.

'I'm busy,' Lan smiled. 'What do you want?'

'Name's Caley,' the boy replied. 'You both look like you're the authority here.'

Fulcrom contemplated the words, but didn't disagree with the sentiment. No one else had come up with any solutions.

'I came from Balmacara tonight,' the boy said. 'I was with Shalev. I was with her when she stabbed the Emperor, too. I just needed to tell someone important.'

A crowd had gathered behind him, curious as to his words. The boy turned and repeated the statements, describing the evening's actions of the anarchists, and a murmur rippled through the crowd.

What was the priority? Fulcrom wondered. Getting these people to safety.

'You want to make yourself useful, Caley, or are you enjoying the power of a little fame?'

Caley turned and spat on the floor. 'I don't enjoy *power*.'

'Good. Then if you know of any of your cronies in the anarchists, round them up. Any military personnel, point them to me. You've good networks: get them doing something beneficial, and spread word that we are all refugees now. Villjamur is no more and we are to evacuate the area.

What's more, that object in ing to eradicate us if we do not flee. We can't return.'

'You expect us all to walk across the fucking ice?' the kid asked.

'No,' Fulcrom replied, regarding the crowds. 'No, that would be suicide. Here's what's going to happen.'

*

Ten horses, as tall as city spires, hauled gargantuan platforms across the tundra and through the night. When each hoof connected to the ground, it created a bass groan that shook everyone on board, which meant they weren't going to get much in the way of sleep tonight, but that was a small price to pay to utilize this most absurd form of transportation.

Fulcrom and Lan huddled together at the front of one such contraption, a wax blanket draped across them both. They shivered, and were holding each other for warmth as much as comfort. The wind pummelled their faces, but at least there was no snow tonight. Open skies and starlight brought a deadly chill. Frater Mercury was perched with arms folded atop of their immense horse, which led the others through the wilderness. Tane lingered nearby, turning back to stare at the city with sharp eyes.

Many miles behind, Villjamur was burning.

They travelled for hours, until a dim-lit haze indicated a new day. Forests stood dark and majestic across the hillside, while large tracts of agricultural land, divided by stone walls, boxed up the landscape.

Lan woke up, and he kissed her forehead.

'I was hoping to leave the city in milder circumstances,' he whispered to her.

'We're together,' she replied, groggily. 'We're both safe. That's enough.'

'But for how long?' Fulcrom wondered. 'How did we find ourselves in the centre of all this?'

'Because we cared,' Lan offered. 'Anyone who gives a shit

464

about people will find themselves in the thick of it. People who don't just sit back and complain while the world messes with them.'

'You're a harsh girl tonight,' he joked.

Lan didn't reply, merely curled up a little more. He put his arm around her and, as he contemplated their future, his mind desired facts to analyse once again. He wanted to ask about Vuldon, too, about what she had seen at the end. He wondered what happened to Ulryk on the Astronomer's Glass Tower. There were so many questions that needed answering.

THIRTY-NINE

The Book of Transformations

If you read between the lines you will find me. I am here, forming words — I have been transformed, by the wonders of powers I can only begin to fathom, and imprisoned within my own book.

Frater Mercury and I have exchanged places and I can communicate only in script, though I know of no one who will open me up to heed these words.

I can see it all now — every answer I sought is here before me, in the realm into which Frater Mercury was exiled. Though it has broken into ours.

Worlds will collide violently. Already they pour into the other realm, both sides of this apparently eternal war. They bring this conflict to the Boreal Archipelago. I can glean only that it is going to be an immense conflict. There are armies of creatures which I have never before seen, not even in any old texts. They are abhorrent. I can see them now, pouring into the Boreal Archipelago, and their numbers are staggering.

I wish I could do something to help. I will continue my reports here, nonetheless. If these words can act as a warning, I can say only this: prepare yourselves for the battle to come.